DEATH BY
JURY

Also by John Lutz

DEATH BY
JURY

JOHN LUTZ

ST. MARTIN'S PRESS
NEW YORK

Production Editor: David Stanford Burr

Library of Congress Cataloging-in-Publication Data

Lutz, John.
        Death by jury : an Alo Nudger mystery / John Lutz.
                p.   cm.
        "A Thomas Dunne Book."
        ISBN 0-312-13613-7
        1. Nudger, Alo (Fictitious character)—Fiction.   2.Private
investigators—Missouri—Saint Louis—Fiction.   3. Saint Louis
(Mo.)—Fiction.   I. Title.
PS3562.U854D43   1995
813'.54—dc20   95-1163
                                                                CIP

First Edition: September 1995

10 9 8 7 6 5 4 3 2 1

For Lucas

The law is like Silly Putty.
                    —Professor Francis M. Nevins,
                    1988, over a glass of wine

DEATH BY
JURY

If attorney Gideon Schiller hadn't referred Lawrence Fleck to Nudger, Nudger would have thrown Fleck out of the office. He was that objectionable.

"You might think you know the ropes but you're an innocent," Fleck was saying in his rapid-fire nasal tone. He seemed to bark words out through his nose. "People won't talk to you, Nudger, they talk to me. Why? 'Cause I know how to ask. Knowing how to ask is everything. You get my meaning?"

"Sure," Nudger said. He leaned back in his *eeee*king swivel chair and studied Fleck. The pugnacious attorney was little more than five feet tall and had the face of a bulldog beneath an obvious black wig that contrasted with his gray eyebrows. His suit was brown with a faint dark check and his shoes were shiny brown wing tips that looked immense on such a diminutive man. He gave off a nauseating scent of some sort of cologne or deodorant that was no doubt supposed to smell like musk. A little musk went a long way, and Fleck must have used it by the gallon. He moved his arms a lot as he talked, his hands clenched into tight little fists that punched the air for emphasis. Nudger wished he'd quit building himself up and get to the point.

"I seen plenty of poor sad people try and thread their way through the law on their own, can't make headway. They ask but they don't get answers. I get answers. Know why?"

"Because you know how to ask?"

"No! Because I'm me! You go to this office or that office and they give you the runaround, know how to brush off your average

John Q. Citizen. Takes somebody knows the ropes, don't you think?"

"Yes."

"Wrong! Takes somebody knows the right ropes. You pull the wrong ropes, all you're doing is wearing out your arm. Maybe even yank something heavy down on top of you. Right?"

Twice burned, Nudger chose not to answer.

Fleck didn't notice. He paced back and forth in his clumpy shoes and continued to bark at Nudger. "Sometimes it's only one rope, but you gotta be able to recognize it. I can do that. Know how much I charge an hour?"

Nudger shook his head.

"Hundred and fifty an hour for a consultation. I get it, too. You know why? Because I'm goddamn worth it. You wanna hire a cheap lawyer?"

Nudger shook his head again.

"Do that you'll just lose time. You got a dollar waiting on a dime. He'll waste your time while he's wasting your money."

"Know what I charge by the hour for a consultation?" Nudger asked.

Fleck stopped pacing and stared at him. "No."

"It's not a hundred and fifty," Nudger said, "but it's something. And I charge a hundred a day plus expenses."

"Hell, that's cheap!" Fleck said, taking the high ground again. "But Gideon says you're good. Says you probably need the work, too. That right?"

"Right enough. Point is, Mr. Fleck—"

"Call me Lawrence."

"Point is, Lawrence, I need to know why you want to hire me."

Fleck cocked his head to the side and advanced on Nudger. Beyond him, Nudger could see pigeons strutting on the brick windowsill, their heads cocked and their chests puffed out just like Fleck's. Nudger didn't like pigeons, and so far he didn't like Fleck.

Fleck placed both hands on the desk and stared hard at Nudger.

2

This was going to be confidential, important stuff, all right.

"I'm defending an accused killer," Fleck said, in a somewhat lower voice than he'd been using to harangue Nudger.

Nudger wondered when the defendant would be executed. He waited, gaze locked with Fleck's tiny and intense brown eyes. There was a green fleck in the right eye. Odd.

"You hear about the Dupont murder?" Fleck asked.

Nudger had. If he remembered correctly what he'd read in the paper and seen on TV news, a local banker named Roger Dupont had been charged with murdering his wife. It had only been about a month ago; it was unusual for a case to reach court so quickly. Usually defense lawyers delayed trials as long as possible, hoping memories would fade or key witnesses would die or go blind. But then, Dupont apparently had Lawrence Fleck as his attorney.

"I'm defending the husband," Fleck said, without waiting for Nudger's reply.

"How's it look?" Nudger asked.

Fleck snorted, paced away from the desk. Paced back. "He's got a shitpot full of circumstantial evidence against him. One chance he's got is me as his lawyer, but the dumbfuck doesn't seem to know it."

Circumstantial evidence, Nudger thought. He knew plenty of cases where it had been enough.

"You want me to investigate and try to find the real killer before your guy's convicted?" he asked, thinking it sounded like something from a crime novel.

"Hell no!" Fleck barked. "You're hearing me but you're not listening! You understand?"

Nudger nodded.

Fleck threw a nifty right cross at the air. "This Dupont claims he's innocent."

"Maybe he is," Nudger said.

"Damn it! Try and listen to me! It doesn't make any difference if he's innocent, the way the legal system works. You hear that,

3

Nudger?'' He leaned over the desk, so close that Nudger felt spittle spray his arm as Fleck spoke, driving each word into the skull of the recalcitrant Nudger like a nail. "It-doesn't-make-any-difference!" He stood back and crossed his arms. "You got that Nudger? You finally got it?"

"Got it for all time."

"Poor naive guy like you and all the rest of 'em, they see movies and old *Perry Mason* reruns and they think the law's on their side, but it's not. What's on their side, what can save their asses, is a good lawyer. Know who that is, Nudger?"

Nudger didn't want to say.

"Me!" Fleck said. "Me-me-me! But I don't know if I can save Roger Dupont."

Nudger was surprised. He figured the Nuremberg trials would have gone the other way if the Third Reich had coughed up Fleck's hundred and fifty an hour. "Why can't you save him?" he asked. "You said the evidence is circumstantial."

"You were hearing but you weren't—"

Nudger raised a hand palm out, as if to deflect the machine-gun barrage of clipped words. "I need to know why you came here, Lawrence."

Fleck smiled and met the question indirectly. Nudger would simply have to wait for him to get to the point. "Call me Larry, why doncha? This Dupont told me right away he was innocent. You think I believe him?"

"I don't know," Nudger said, squirming in his squealing swivel chair. *Eeek! Eeek!*

"Doesn't matter," Fleck said. "Know why?"

Nudger was too weary to answer. Besides, he'd caught on that it wasn't necessary.

"Because I'm his attorney," Fleck said. "Innocent or guilty, he's got a right to the best legal representation he can afford. Know who that is?"

The breeze from the air conditioner was cold on his back, but

Nudger was sweating heavily. He wanted to kill Fleck.

"I'm the man," Fleck said. "Dupont's champion, just like the law provides. But here's the problem, Nudger, case you're interested. The evidence—circumstantial though it might be—is so strong against Dupont that even I might not be able to get him acquitted."

Well! Nudger thought.

Fleck stroked his pudgy cheek and looked thoughtful. A courtroom gesture? "What bothers me is this Dupont doesn't seem afraid. No, lemme correct that: He's definitely not afraid. I've seen hundreds of defendants and I can tell. Once the trial starts, my defendants are always afraid. I tell this Dupont we better plea-bargain. I can probably get him some time in exchange for a guilty plea. Save him from death by lethal injection. Know what he tells me?"

"What?" Nudger asked, before he could stop himself.

"He says he's innocent and he's got nothing to worry about. That he's got faith in the legal system and he knows he'll walk out of the courtroom a free man." Fleck shook his head as if to fling from it some impure thought. "Faith in the legal system, he says! You got faith in the legal system, Nudger?"

"Limited."

"Hmph! Only sensible thing I've heard you say. I ask this Dupont, what about all this evidence piled up like a mountain against him? He says it doesn't mean anything because he didn't kill his wife, and that's that. I ask, can he explain. That's that, is all he says. He can't explain and he says he doesn't have to, he believes in reasonable doubt. I tell him plenty of people been executed despite what they think's reasonable doubt. My last client, for instance, got a one-in-a-million bad break nobody could have done anything about even if they were Clarence Darrow or that Mason guy on TV or even Matlock. Know what Dupont does when I tell him that, Nudger? He just smiles."

"Maybe he's got a martyr complex and wants to be executed," Nudger said.

Fleck stroked his cheek again, exactly the same mannerism he'd used minutes earlier, and for the same number of strokes. Three. "Maybe. I seen that plenty of times. But this time I'm not so sure. The poor dumb naive guy's probably gonna wind up getting his final vaccination if he doesn't plea-bargain. He just doesn't seem to realize it."

"What can I do about that?" Nudger asked.

"I want you to look into the case."

"The police already did. That's why Dupont's going to trial."

Fleck made a backhand gesture, like a disdainful slap. "Gideon Schiller said you had a different approach, Nudger, that you some-times got the job done when nobody else could. Said you were stubborn even if you were . . . Well, he said you were the man for this job."

"Suppose I find hard evidence that Dupont's guilty?"

"Jesus, Nudger! Weren't you listening again? That'd be good news! The poor dumb schmuck would listen to me then and plea-bargain. He does that, I can save him from the big needle. I mean, how's it gonna look, me losing two clients in a row to the Grim Reaper?"

"I hadn't thought of that," Nudger said, staring unbelievingly at Fleck.

But Fleck recovered nicely. "I mean, my conscience wouldn't let me rest, even though God Himself couldn't get either of these guys off. If Dupont really is innocent and this trial goes the way it proba-bly will if he don't change his tune, how'm I gonna sleep nights, Nudger?"

Like a baby, Nudger thought. He said, "I might find proof that he's innocent, then everybody could sleep better."

"Maybe. Just maybe, Nudger, you could come through with the goods no matter what they say about you. Listen! I know I should simply do my job in a dispassionate manner and try and save this unfortunate trusting man-child from certain execution, but there's something obscure about this case that's disturbing my peace of mind, and I want to know what it is." He dragged a large, square checkbook from an inside pocket, the kind usually kept in desk drawers. "And I'm willing to pay."

Roger Dupont was the one who'd pay, one way or the other, Nudger thought. But if Nudger found out the truth about the murder, it might be the best money Dupont ever spent.

"One thing," he said to Fleck. "I go wherever the truth leads me."

"Think I don't know that?" Fleck asked. "I'm a lawyer. You haven't been listening again! What I'm hiring you for is the truth, then maybe I'll use it in court."

Nudger tried not to breath in the musk fumes while he stared out the window at the patch of blue sky visible between the buildings across Manchester. The musk, mingled with the sugary scent from the doughnut shop downstairs, was causing his nervous stomach to twitch against his belt buckle.

Fleck was tapping the big blue vinyl checkbook on the edge of the desk, as if Nudger were Pavlov's dog and would hear the sound and automatically reach for a contract and pen. Insulting little bastard.

But at least he'd finally gotten to the point.

Nudger opened a drawer and reached for a contract and pen.

CHAPTER TWO

Roger Dupont's trial was scheduled to begin in three days. That meant Nudger didn't have much time. The way it looked right now, neither did Roger Dupont.

Nudger parked his old Ford Granada in the parking lot behind the Third District police station at Tucker and Lynch. Most of the cars on the blacktop lot were marked cruisers. Three unmarked Chevy Caprices were lined along the fence in back, where the ranking officers parked. Nudger knew one of the Caprices belonged to Lieutenant Jack Hammersmith, his partner in a two-man patrol car when Nudger was on the force long ago. That was before his nervous stomach and a new police chief's policy landed him in the unemployment line, then in his present occupation, which at times was not unlike the unemployment line.

It was a typical St. Louis July day, and the heat-softened blacktop stuck to the soles of Nudger's shoes and made faint sucking sounds as he walked across the lot to the rear of the angular brick building. He pushed through tinted glass doors, nodded hello to a uniformed cop he knew, then walked down the hall to the booking area.

A skinny Black kid with wild hair and wilder eyes was standing cuffed before the booking desk while one arresting officer held him and another emptied his pockets and laid their contents on the desk: a comb; a wallet containing nothing other than a driver's license, a library card, and a carefully folded newspaper photo of Richard Nixon; a key ring with two keys and a tiny plastic replica of Michelangelo's *Venus* as an ornament; a ticket stub from the Saint Louis Opera Theatre; and a .38 caliber bullet. Nudger wondered about the kid.

The desk sergeant, a large, florid man named Foley whom Nudger knew slightly, duly noted the pockets' contents and placed them in a yellow envelope, and the kid was led away.

"I don't know nothing about no animals," he said several times to the arresting officers who flanked him.

"What's the charge?" Nudger asked Foley, when suspect and cops had disappeared in the direction of the holdover cells.

"Grand theft, zoo," Foley said. "Stole a gnu."

Nudger thought about asking why but decided against it. Kids these days . . .

He did say, "Wait'll the gnus media get hold of that one," but

Foley didn't smile. "Hammersmith in his office?" he asked in a more serious tone.

Foley nodded. "He said you called. Said to tell you to go on back."

Nudger thanked him and walked around the booking desk and down the hall to Hammersmith's office.

The door was open so he didn't knock. Hammersmith was seated behind his desk, a sleekly obese man with smooth skin, parted and combed white hair that had receded so it appeared his face had suddenly jumped forward, and a cop's pale gray eyes impossible to read. His clean-shaven, fleshy jowls spilled over his collar like liquid in a balloon.

He was on the phone, and he glanced at Nudger and motioned with his head for him to sit in the chair angled to face the desk. It was a straight-backed oak chair that was very uncomfortable; Hammersmith didn't like visitors to his office to stay long and waste his time.

". . . some kind of antelope," he was saying into the phone, as Nudger sat down. He looked at Nudger and rolled his eyes.

Nudger sat quietly in the chair and listened to distant sirens that seemed to be getting closer, as if the police had called for help.

He was relieved when the piercing yodel of the sirens stopped about a block away.

"It might be worth considering," Hammersmith said, then hung up abruptly without saying good-bye. He loved to cut off the other party at the end of phone conversations; Nudger, who had been the recipient of such treatment many times, thought it was some sort of control complex. Hammersmith looked at Nudger and folded his pink, well-manicured hands on the desk.

"The gnu thing?" Nudger asked, motioning with his head toward the phone.

"What new thing?" Hammersmith asked, obviously puzzled.

"What you were talking about on the phone, I suppose," Nudger said.

"Nothing new about a restaurant trying to serve protected species to its special customers," Hammersmith said. "People will eat anything, buffalo, snake, eggplant. There was this gourmet club in West County about five years ago—"

"Never mind," Nudger interrupted. "I think we're talking about two different things."

"Could be, Nudge." Hammersmith stared down at the clutter of papers on his desk as if searching for something. "You called and asked for info on the Dupont homicide. The perp's about to come to trial."

"Before we get into that," Nudger said, "do you know a criminal lawyer named Lawrence Fleck?"

"Of course," Hammersmith said. "Irritating little twit. He could get Mother Teresa convicted if she was his client."

"He's Roger Dupont's attorney."

"Good. Dupont's a killer. He deserves Fleck. He deserves to be found guilty."

"You think he will be?"

"Gotta be," Hammersmith said. "The evidence is all against him." He slid a file folder out from beneath the papers on his desk and opened it, but he didn't look at it.

"What do you know about the case?" Nudger asked.

"Lots. I was part of the Major Case Squad that investigated it. Dupont's a Vice President at Merchant Federal Bank, where his abilities are highly valued. Belongs to the St. Louis Country Club, and spends a lot of time there. Terrific golfer and tennis player. Also good at bridge and chess. He and his wife, Karen, had been married four years, no kids. Lived out in University City on Devlon, nice house with a pool and a tennis court. Kept the pool clean and the grass mowed. Neighbors said he was pleasant and quiet. All what you'd expect to hear about a forty-year-old veep at a conservative bank."

"But . . ." Nudger prodded.

Hammersmith leaned back in his swivel chair. It didn't squeak the way Nudger's did. Odd. Hammersmith was much heavier than Nudger. "I've talked to Dupont, and under the good manners and the self-assurance, the guy's an asshole."

Nudger raised his eyebrows. Hammersmith was using the word in the special cop sense: An asshole had no decency and no feelings. An asshole was capable of anything.

"That's just instinct. I got nothing specific to back it up," Hammersmith went on. "Except for this. We talked to all these business associates, club members, and neighbors, and we didn't find anybody who was a friend of Dupont. I don't think the guy cares about people. He just plays games with them."

"You mean, golf and bridge?"

"Other games too."

"You're saying he had affairs?"

Hammersmith shrugged. "Nobody could give us anything specific. They just said he seemed like the type of guy who'd fool around. Unusual for a banker."

Nudger wasn't so sure about that. He'd known a banker once who was a member of a wife-swapping club. But that probably wasn't typical. There were loans and then there were loans.

"So who reported the murder?" he asked.

"The victim's sister, Joleen Witt. The wife, Karen, had been gone from home for over a week, just up and went. Roger Dupont's story was that she'd suddenly decided to leave him and seek a new life in Chicago. She told him that, packed and left. He said he was dumbfounded. Couldn't believe it. Well, after a while, neither could the sister. So the University City police sent a man over and got Dupont's story, asked him if Karen had left a note, contacted him since she'd left, blah, blah, blah. Dupont said no, no, no, and stuck to his simple story."

"He wouldn't be the first man surprised like that by his wife," Nudger said.

"Wouldn't be the first to kill his wife, either."

Impeccable logic, Nudger thought.

"Then things began to crop up," Hammersmith said. "A neighbor told the police she'd heard screams the night Karen was supposed to have left. Dupont said the screams came from the TV. Turns out Dupont took out a half-million-dollar life insurance policy on Karen six months ago. When that was pointed out to him, he said, in effect, so what? A few of Karen's clothes seemed to be missing, but not enough to fill the large suitcase Dupont said she took with her. We asked for an explanation. She was in a hurry, Dupont said."

"Doesn't sound too bad for Dupont so far," Nudger said.

"Partially burned panties, along with a half-melted pair of Karen's earrings, were found in the furnace."

"Oh-oh," Nudger said.

"Yeah. In St. Louis in the summer, Nudge. Dupont claimed to know nothing about the panties or earrings. He said Karen used the furnace for an incinerator sometimes and might have stuck them in there with some other stuff she wanted to get rid of."

"Unlikely."

"It gets more so. In the trunk of Dupont's car we found a shovel with clumps of earth on its blade."

"Dupont said?"

"That he always carried the shovel, and he'd used it when his car got stuck in the mud the week before."

"Barely possible," Nudger said.

"Embedded in the mud on the shovel was a human hair the lab tests confirm matched one of Karen's that we took from her comb."

"Hmm."

Hammersmith shrugged his fleshy shoulders. "It doesn't take a Sherlock Holmes to figure this one out, Nudge."

"Even Watson could do it," Nudger said.

"What we'd like is for Dupont to get up off the body in exchange for a deal with the prosecution."

Nudger blinked. He remembered what this macabre cop expression meant, and he was surprised. Guilty men usually played the one high card they held. "He won't tell you where he buried Karen's remains?"

Hammersmith slowly wagged his massive head. His jowls sloshed over his collar.

"Incredible," Nudger said. "Of course you've offered to reduce the charges in exchange for his cooperation. Second-degree? Voluntary manslaughter?"

"That's up to the prosecutor," Hammersmith replied. "We're not worried. Don't tell me you're one of those misinformed types who think you need a body to get a murder conviction."

"You don't need one," Nudger said, "but it sure makes it easier."

"Not in this case, with all the evidence. Dupont won't say where he buried his wife, and so far we haven't found her. It's simple as that. We might never find her, if he's got her corpse well hidden. But that little matter won't thwart justice. There are plenty of murder victims out there who've never been found or identified. That doesn't keep their killers from being arrested and convicted."

"Sometimes," Nudger said.

"Well, Roger Dupont is one of those times. This guy's as good as strapped to the gurney with the needle in his arm." Hammersmith paused, and gave Nudger a meaningful look. "Might be in his interest to plea-bargain."

Nudger smiled. "Come on, Jack. Level with me. The prosecutor's very worried about not having a body, isn't he? He'd love to make a deal with Dupont."

Hammersmith smiled back. "You're right, Nudge. But you didn't get it from me."

"Well, you didn't get this from me, but Fleck wants to plea-bargain. Dupont won't go along with him."

Hammersmith's eyes opened wide with surprise. "You're kidding! I thought the problem was Fleck's delusions of grandeur. This Dupont guy must be crazy. He could cop to a lesser, get out in

13

fifteen years maybe. Instead he's going to trial and risking a death sentence."

"Maybe he's innocent."

"Then why'd he confess?"

Nudger sat back in his chair so hard that the wood groaned. Just like Hammersmith to withhold that kind of information then spring it on him. Nudger merely glared at him.

Hammersmith smiled. "We picked him up at his home and booked him out in U. City. He acted remorseful, and he just kept saying over and over that he'd killed his wife. Wouldn't say anything else, in fact. Like he was in some kind of trance. Then, in the morning, he rescinded the confession on the grounds he'd been coerced."

"Fleck's advice, you think?"

"No, this was before he'd hired Fleck. He looked in the phone book later that morning and made his call. Came up with Fleck. Some catch."

Did you coerce him?"

"C'mon, Nudge, we don't do that anymore. Not to bankers, anyway. Question is, did somebody coerce a guy like Dupont to hire a loose bolt like Fleck?"

"It's a good question," Nudger admitted. "I don't have a good answer."

Hammersmith handed Nudger a folded sheet of typing paper. "These are the names and addresses of people you might want to talk to, even though you're wasting your time. Only reason I'm helping you here is that you're also wasting Fleck's money. This Dupont is on his way, Nudge, believe me."

Nudger tucked the folded paper into his shirt pocket. "You're probably right, but business is slow."

"Your business is always slow. You're curious about Dupont. Or else you need the money to pay Eileen some back alimony."

"I always need money to pay Eileen," Nudger said. "She's insatiable." Eileen was Nudger's former wife, who with her devious lawyer had stripped the cooperative and unsuspecting Nudger of almost everything he owned during divorce proceedings, then continued to pursue him for more. Nudger was the only childless man he knew who paid alimony. Child support he would have been proud to pay, but alimony was absurd. Especially considering that Eileen was at the apex of a sales pyramid in one of those home product scams. She had dozens of "agents" working for her and was richer than most people, and certainly richer than hand-to-mouth Nudger. Lately she'd been sleeping with her lawyer, Henry Mercato. Nudger sometimes lay in bed late at night and imagined that their pillow talk was about him, about how they could make him miserable or pry more money out of him. Eileen made no secret that she wanted him to continue to suffer. She was a vindictive and unscrupulous person and a terrific seller of home products and had found her soul mate in the despicable Mercato. They deserved each other, those two. They deserved—

"Nudge?"

"Sorry, Jack. My mind wandered."

"I'll bet I know where." Hammersmith made a show of closing the file folder, a signal that the conversation was ended and he had crime to fight. He touched a cellophane-wrapped cigar in his shirt pocket. "Do yourself a favor, Nudge, and ditch this case. You can't stay too far away from a guy like Roger Dupont. Fleck's money's like bait with a hook in it."

Nudger stood up. The office was cool enough, but his pants legs were sticking to the backs of his thighs. Polyester did that sometimes if you sat for a long time in a hard chair. What seemed like a long time, anyway.

"I think I'll look into things for a while, anyway," he said. He used his thumb and forefinger to pluck the material away from his thighs, then moved toward the door. "I'll be careful of the hook hiding in the money. Thanks for your help, Jack."

" 'S okay." Hammersmith was already occupied with something on his desk. "Someday you're gonna grow gills," he muttered to or about Nudger, without looking up.

Nudger swam away without answering.

CHAPTER THREE

Nudger parked the Granada at the curb near Fleck's office and stuffed a quarter into a meter. As he was walking away, the car's overheated engine turned over once on its own then made a feeble coughing sound and died. Nudger hoped for reincarnation when he came back and twisted the ignition key.

Clayton was the rich near-suburb where many of the best and most expensive lawyers had their offices. Fleck's office was just beyond the Clayton line, in University City where the neighborhood started to go downhill. It was on the ground floor of a converted four-family flat, across the hall from a door lettered DUST-GONE WONDER VAC, INC.

Nudger let himself in through the door with Fleck's name on it and found himself in a small anteroom with a few chairs, some prints of English fox-hunting scenes, and a small window with a round hole in it. The window framed a pretty blonde girl who had wispy bangs and a blue dress with a white collar and puffy sleeves and looked about twelve.

Nudger was the only one in the anteroom. He approached the window and the blonde girl looked up from some papers she was laboring over with a pencil and smiled.

"Mr. Nudger to see Lawrence Fleck," Nudger said, as if Fleck had several partners in the firm and there might be some confusion.

"Do you have an appointment?" the blonde girl asked.

"No. Why? Is he busy?"

"Mr. Fleck's occupied at the moment, in an important meeting. But if you'll sit down I'll tell him—"

A door near the little window opened and Fleck poked his head out, then stepped into the anteroom.

"Nudger," he said. "What do you want?"

"I thought you were in an important meeting."

"Naw. Girl's got instructions to say that to the poor innocent saps when they wander in here trying to get out of trouble." He glanced at the confused blonde and waved a hand in dismissal. "She's just a temp. Gonna be gone tomorrow." The temp looked as if she might be about to cry. Fleck didn't seem to notice. "So c'mon into my office, tell me what's your problem and I can help."

Nudger had to resist patting the back of the temp's hand as they walked past her.

"Hold all calls," Fleck barked at her, as he opened the office door for Nudger.

The office was small, but the desktop was vast as an airport and made of bleached pine. Nudger saw that it was actually a finished door laid over two double-drawer filing cabinets. Behind it was a high-backed chair thickly upholstered in black vinyl. Two smaller chairs, also black vinyl but with wooden arms, sat in front of the desk. The carpet was a putrid shade of pink. Floor-length drapes on the single window were green with a pink check. On the back edge of the desk, near the center, was a brass lamp with a green shade. Nudger suspected its base covered the hole in the desk top that was meant to accommodate a doorknob. Various framed diplomas were scattered about the walls. Nudger didn't recognize any of the institutions that had conferred them. In a corner sat a tall wooden easel with a large sketch pad on it. The exposed sheet of paper on the pad was covered with scrawled numbers and complex mathematical symbols. Arrows had been drawn with bright red marker to point to this or that. Nudger could make nothing of what he saw on the paper.

Fleck told Nudger to sit down in one of the small chairs, then strutted behind his makeshift desk and sat in the high-backed chair. It made him look even shorter than he was. His suit was gray with a muted check today, but he still had on the giant brown wing tip shoes. His impossibly black wig was slightly askew.

"What do all those numbers mean?" Nudger asked, pointing to the easel.

"Nothing," Fleck said, "and something. I use that as a confidence builder. The poor marks that come in here needing my services have gotta know right off that I can help them. They see all that mumbo jumbo math like I'm Einstein or something. Know what that means?"

Nudger sighed. "What?"

"Means that right away they know I'm the guy can get them outa whatever mess they're in. You know why?"

"Because you must be smarter than they are?" Nudger ventured.

"Hey! You're a good pupil, Nudger! That's right. Makes no sense coming for help to a guy knows less than you, does it now?"

"No," Nudger said. "Which brings me to why I came here. You hired me to help you, and you know more about Roger Dupont than I do."

"It's my job to know," Fleck said. The phone rang. Seven times. Fleck sat waiting for the temp to answer it, but it stopped ringing and nothing else happened. Apparently she hadn't picked up. Fleck glanced at the intercom on his desk. It remained silent. "Gotta get little Della Street out there on the ball," he said with a smile.

"I thought you said this was her last day."

"Hey, who knows about tomorrow? Do you know, Nudger?"

"No," Nudger had to admit.

"Nobody can tell about tomorrow. Some say they can, but it's a lie. Don't you think so?"

"Yes, a lie," Nudger said.

Fleck rotated his wrist and glanced at what was probably an imitation Rolex watch. "Well, get to it, Nudger. I got appointments. You understand about appointments, don't you?"

"Sure. What I want is to talk to Roger Dupont."

Fleck appeared startled. "Are you crazy? Are you, Nudger?"

"I don't think so. We can go to the County Jail—"

"County Jail? He's my client, Nudger. Know what that means? Do you?"

"Listen, Fleck—"

"Larry! Call me Larry! Means he's not in jail. Means he's out on bail. Know why?"

"He's your client?"

"No! Because I'm his lawyer!"

Nudger tried to see the distinction but couldn't.

"He's out on bail because I know all the bondsmen in the city and county. Some other attorney asks the judge to let his client post bail, the judge says take a walk. The judges don't talk to me that way, know I don't stand for it. I ask that bail be set for my client, judge allows bail, says to the prosecutor, 'Hey, screw you!' Not in so many words, you understand."

"Of course not," Nudger said.

"My clients don't do jail time they don't have to, and usually they don't have to, 'cause I'm their lawyer. You listening?"

"Sure. But I still want to talk to Dupont."

"Damn it! You're listening but you're not hearing! You understand the difference?"

Nudger thought it had been the other way around last time, but he only nodded.

"You're working for me, not Dupont. He don't even know I hired you."

"He'll have to know eventually, if I go around asking questions."

"Eventually, sure. Earth's gonna get hit by a comet eventually.

19

Didn't we just agree about not knowing about tomorrow, Nudger?"

"We did," Nudger admitted.

"Dupont finds out, then we let him assume you're working trying to clear him."

"I am," Nudger said, "if he's telling the truth and he's actually innocent like he claims."

"Truth?" Fleck said, raising his gray eyebrows almost into his black wig. "I don't worry about truth! I worry about what can be proved or disproved. Then you know what?"

"What?"

"The truth will follow. Some kind of truth, anyway. You listening?"

"And hearing," Nudger said.

Fleck glared at him as if he were hopelessly slow. "I hope so, Nudger."

"Who posted bond for Dupont?"

"Sister out in Ladue. Put up her fancy-shmancy house. She loses the house if Dupont decides to run. But he won't run. Know why?"

"He's got you as his lawyer."

"You guessed it, Nudger!"

"What's the sister's name?"

"Effie Prang."

Nudger got out his little notepad and wrote that down. "Address?"

Fleck consulted a long yellow legal pad on his desk and gave Nudger an address in an area expensive even for Ladue.

Nudger replaced the notepad in his pocket. Fleck's phone rang again. This time the temp picked up on the second ring. "Your wife on line one, Mr. Fleck," she said over the intercom.

Fleck raised his eyebrows again, picked up the receiver, and cupped his hand over the mouthpiece. "My wife!" he whispered to Nudger. "Jesus!" He cleared his throat. "Honey," he said. "Yes, sure, no. Tell him he has to wait! I don't give a damn . . ."

Nudger stopped listening and leaned back in his chair, letting his gaze roam over Fleck's framed certificates. He wondered where Audie Murphy University was located, before switching his gaze to the adjoining wall.

Fleck abruptly hung up the phone. "The little woman," he explained.

"That one," Nudger said, pointing.

"Huh?"

"That one." He continued pointing at one of the framed diplomas. "It's from a college of veterinary medicine."

"Oh, Yeah." Fleck waved a hand. "I was that for a while. Now listen, Nudger. It's okay if you talk to anyone else involved in this case, but we better leave Dupont for last. You hearing me?"

"I'm listening," Nudger said.

"Same thing."

"A veter—"

"Now, how have you been earning your money so far?"

"I talked to a police contact about the Dupont case. He says your client's guilty and is probably going to be found guilty and die."

"He didn't call him my client, did he?"

Hammersmith had, but Nudger decided to go along with Fleck. Save energy that way. "Not exactly."

"There you are. And like I told you, it doesn't matter! Guilty, innocent, so what? We're talking about the law here, Nudger. Our justice system! Understand me?"

"I think so. But—"

"I don't care if Dupont killed his wife. My job's to get him the best deal possible in court. Poor dumb sheep won't listen to me and plea bargain, though. Won't listen to *me*, can you believe it?"

"He might be listening but not hearing," Nudger said.

"And it might get him death by lethal injection. A lesson in that, don't you think?"

"A hard one," Nudger said. He stood up to leave.

"You want the names and addresses of some of the other people involved?" Fleck asked. He flipped a page on the yellow legal pad and shoved it across the desk so Nudger could read it.

It took Nudger a while; Fleck's handwriting was frantic, the letters detached so that they stood alone or in groups of two or three and appeared vaguely Oriental. All of the names on Fleck's list were on the list Hammersmith had given Nudger.

Nudger moved away from the desk.

"Hey, you're not going to copy them down?" Fleck asked.

"Already got them."

Fleck stared at Nudger, then grinned. "Well, you're sharper than you appear."

"Because you were looking but not seeing," Nudger said, and went out the door.

On the way out of the anteroom, he paused and asked the temp what her name was.

She looked at him suspiciously, as if he'd just driven up and offered her candy. "Why?"

"I'm in business, and you seem efficient. If you don't object, I might ask for you next time I need a temp."

She smiled beautifully; it was probably the only positive thing she'd heard all day.

"I'm with American Office Commandos," she said. "Just ask for Wanda."

Nudger saluted smartly and assured her he would.

And he might.

Business was slow now, but who could tell about tomorrow?

CHAPTER FOUR

When Nudger had trudged up the narrow stairwell to his office door, he found a note lying on the floor. He saw the tab of cellophane tape on the top of the note and knew what had happened. The heat in the stairwell had liquefied the adhesive on the tape and it wouldn't stick to the door. The tape had given way and the note had fluttered to the floor. Nudger had found many such notes outside his office door.

He stooped and picked up the note, recognizing as he did so the large, scrawled writing, the grease stains in the margins. It was a message from Danny Evers, who owned and managed the doughnut shop beneath Nudger's office, and who served as Nudger's ersatz secretary.

The note said Danny wanted to see him about something important. Which meant Nudger had to trek back downstairs, outside into the afternoon heat, and make a sharp U-turn in through the door of Danny's Donuts. That irritated Nudger. Danny must have seen him drive up and park on the other side of Manchester by the broken meter. Probably saw him cross the street, since Nudger had almost been struck by a bus and the squeal of brakes had attracted attention. Surely had heard him making his way up the creaking stairs to the office and could have yelled up for him to come back down before he'd climbed all twenty-two worn and sagging wooden steps. It wasn't as if Danny had customers to distract him. His business was booming about like Nudger's.

Still irritated, Nudger went back downstairs and pushed open the doughnut shop door.

Danny was alone in the place, absently wiping down the stainless steel counter with the gray towel he kept tucked in his belt. His long, lined face with its sagging features and basset-hound eyes looked more forlorn than usual, and some of Nudger's anger left him. Some, but not all.

It was as warm in the doughnut shop as it was outside. The Dunker Delites, Danny's specialty, were probably continuing to bake right there in the glass display case, where they lay inert on greasy waxed paper. The scent of grease and baked sugar was almost overwhelming, making Nudger's stomach growl in protest.

Danny brightened noticeably when Nudger entered, and he gave the gray towel a flick so crumbs flew back onto the counter, then tucked it in his belt. "You get my note, Nudge?"

"Yes," Nudger said. "Why didn't you just—"

"Want some coffee?"

"No." Nudger looked at the immense and complex steel urn with its miles of tubes, hoses, and what appeared to be catalytic converters.

Sensitive Danny had picked up on Nudger's irritation. His somber brown eyes seemed to sadden and maybe even began to well with tears. Made Nudger feel smaller than a Dunker Delite.

"Your note said it was important," he reminded Danny, sliding up onto one of the red vinyl stools at the counter.

Danny nodded, then turned to the urn, rotated a few valves, and shoved a porcelain spigot lever to one side. There was a great deal of hissing and gurgling, some brief whistling as, very slowly, sludgelike coffee filled the foam cup that had already been in place in anticipation of the next customer.

Danny turned off the spigot then placed the steaming cup in front of Nudger on the counter. "Just in case," he said, smiling wearily. "You had lunch, Nudge?"

"About half an hour ago," Nudger lied. He did not want to fend off a free Dunker Delite. "What's important, Danny?"

"It's Ray, Nudge. I'm afraid he's got problems."

Ray was Danny's shiftless cousin who lived a few blocks west on Manchester in the St. James apartments. He feigned a bad back and collected every form of welfare possible, working only occasionally to build up his unemployment so he could again draw down his benefits. Ray was spineless and a liar and a blatant user of people and a Cubs fan. There was nothing about him that Nudger liked.

Danny, with the instincts and perceptions of a child, knew what Nudger was thinking.

"Now, I know you don't much like Ray," he said, "but he does need help, and he is family."

"He is not of the family of man," Nudger said.

Danny appeared hurt. "That would upset my Aunt Madge."

"Ray's mother?"

"Late mother, Nudge. My mother's sister. And I promised her I'd kinda keep an eye on Ray and see he doesn't get into really deep trouble." He said this as if the family accepted minor trouble as Ray's birthright.

"His trouble is deep this time?" Nudger asked.

"My Aunt Madge would think so, if she was alive."

Without thinking, Nudger lifted the foam cup and sipped. It took all his willpower not to make a face and insult Danny, who was particularly sensitive about his coffee and his pastry.

"Ray's got woman trouble," Danny said, in a tone of voice that suggested Ray had been informed of some terminal disease.

"Let me guess," Nudger said. "He's interested in a woman who's not interested in him. Is it rape? If it is, I don't think I can help him."

"No, no, Nudge. His problem's that a woman's interested in him, and he wants to be left alone."

Nudger was astounded. A woman who would allow herself to become romantically involved with Ray had to have the instincts of a lemming.

"Ever heard of Shag's?" Danny asked.

"The hamburger place?"

Danny nodded. Shag's was a small drive-through with a few booths inside that fancied itself, and advertised itself, as a burgeoning McDonald's. It was about half a mile outside the Maplewood city limits on Manchester, notable for its round architecture and brown roof that resembled the top of a bun.

"There's this woman, Heidran Kreb, that works behind the counter at Shag's and she's developed a crush on Ray."

Nudger almost took another sip of coffee. "Heidran Kreb? A crush? On Ray?" He could not bend his mind around it.

"That's the situation, Nudge. Ray went in there a few times for supper, got to know her a little. Well, he's been on unemployment a while, and when you collect that you gotta show them you've applied for at least three jobs a week. Ray turned in an application at Shag's, not dreaming they'd want to hire him. He didn't figure on Heidran using her influence with the manager."

"So what's the problem?" Nudger asked. "Why doesn't Ray take the job?"

"It pays less than his unemployment, he says. It'd be a losing proposition for him, what with gas money and all."

"Gas money? He could walk to Shag's from his apartment in ten minutes."

"You know Ray. He's got this bad back. Bad knee, too."

"He never mentioned a bad knee before."

"He don't like to burden other people with his troubles, Nudge."

Nudger was getting irritated again. Ray traded on his troubles as if they were coin of the realm.

"Sure you don't want a Dunker Delite?" Danny asked.

Nudger's stomach moved six inches this way and that. He used the back of his hand to wipe sweat from his forehead. "No, thanks. Please."

Danny looked at him curiously.

"So what can I do to help Ray avoid work?" he asked.

"I don't know, exactly. But he's got some ideas. He wants to talk to you. Will you go see him? Will you do that for me, Nudge?"

"And for Aunt Madge," Nudger said helplessly. "When can I find Ray at home and not at the track or some Maplewood bar?"

"He said to just call before you want to come over. He's laid up right now with his back and he'll be home most anytime."

"Hmph."

"Wearing some kinda brace," Danny said, hoping to gain credibility.

Nudger didn't dispute that. He knew Ray had all kinds of props.

While Nudger was here, he decided to get Danny's input on the Dupont case. Danny's uncomplicated way of looking at things sometimes provided otherwise overlooked insights. "You familiar with the Dupont murder?" he asked.

"Sure," Danny said. When he baked, he laid his fresh, hot doughnuts on pages of the *Post-Dispatch* that acted as grease blotters, so he was always up on the news. "Guy who killed his wife and buried her someplace. Don't he come to trial soon?"

"A few days," Nudger said.

"You professionally involved in the case?"

"Yeah. What do you think of it?"

"The guy's guilty, Nudge. He killed his wife."

"Why do you say that with no hesitation and such certainty?"

"Well, the evidence against him is no secret."

"But it's all circumstantial."

"So's the evidence that cigarettes cause cancer, but I quit smoking years ago."

Nudger didn't know how to counter that argument.

"Anyway," Danny said, "I seen Dupont on the TV news, telling the guy from Channel Five—you know, the one that wears the snappy sport jacket and has the expensive haircut—how innocent he is and pretending to worry about his wife. He was lying. I could tell that easy by looking at his mouth."

"His mouth?"

"Sure. Good liars can control the expression in their eyes, but when people lie, their lips always stiffen up. If you watch for it, you can see it."

Nudger thought about that. It might be true.

"You working for Dupont, Nudge?"

"His lawyer," Nudger said.

"You better be careful. He's a bad type."

"You know the lawyer?"

Danny looked confused. "No. I meant Dupont. He's dangerous. You can tell by his eyes. The way they're set in his head."

Nudger decided not to pursue that one. There might be something to the stiff-lip theory, but there were limits.

He got down off his stool.

"So can I tell Ray you'll be by to talk to him?"

"Yeah, go ahead."

"Thanks, Nudge. You on the way there now?"

"No," Nudger said, heading for the door, "I want to think about his problem. Right now I'm on my way to lunch."

"I thought you said you already ate lunch," Danny said in a voice that betrayed his bruised psyche.

"Hunch," Nudger said. "I'm on my way to follow a hunch. On the Dupont case."

"Remember what I said about that one." Danny plucked the towel from his belt, lifted Nudger's foam cup, and wiped under it. "You be real careful."

"You just don't want anything to happen to me before I help Ray," Nudger said.

Danny's face fell to belt level. "*Hey*, Nudge!"

Nudger grinned. "Kidding, Danny. Kidding."

Danny's sagging features folded into a smile.

Nudger went out into the summer heat and jogged quickly across the street to the Granada while there was a break in traffic.

He decided to drive down Manchester and have lunch at Shag's. A hamburger and a vanilla milk shake sounded just right, and he could eat inside where it was air-conditioned.

Danny was watching him out the doughnut shop's grease-spotted window, next to the sign advertising microwaved doughnuts at half price. PERFECT FOR DUNKING, the sign said in parenthesis.

Danny waved as the Granada pulled away from the curb, and Nudger waved back and then drove west on Manchester.

Admitting to himself that why he really wanted to eat at Shag's was so he could get a look at this Heidran Kreb.

CHAPTER FIVE

He remembered Heidran Kreb from the other times he'd been in Shag's. She was a large woman, about forty, broad through the shoulders and hips. Her features had begun to give way to fleshiness but were still strong. Her graying blonde hair was pulled back severely from her broad forehead and arranged in a tight bun at the nape of her neck. She wore no makeup, had thin lips, a narrow nose, and the cold blue eyes of a U-boat commander. An aging Valkyrie.

"Help you?" she asked.

Nudger ordered a Shagburger, fries, and a vanilla milk shake. He was one of four customers, and the only one at the serving counter. A teenage girl with acne and a drab brown Shag's uniform exactly like Heidran's, only several sizes smaller, was at the window servicing drive-through customers. She had on some sort of belt pack wired to bulky earphones with an antenna sprouting from them. She looked as if she might be ready to coordinate takeoffs and landings on an aircraft carrier flight deck instead of serving up burgers and fries. After receiving an order from the outside speaker, she would gyrate all over the place, calling out instructions to the cook, stuffing already wrapped burgers into brown Shag's bags, scooping fries into cardboard containers, asking if the customer out there wanted ketchup or mustard. Striving to please while her little antenna sproinged all around with her wild effort. She was like a mad little moon in irregular orbit around the stolid and efficient Heidran.

"Three-ninety," Heidran said, placing Nudger's order on a brown Shag's tray. Plastic envelopes of ketchup, paper ones of salt and pepper, and a brown paper napkin were neatly arranged at the base of the triangle formed by Nudger's burger, fries, and shake.

He handed her four singles. A clean, square hand without nail polish placed a dime in his hand. Heidran thanked him and turned away as if dismissing him from her mind entirely. Her attitude suggested that he simply was not important. Nudger thought that if he'd paid with a twenty-dollar bill, things might be different. Heidran didn't seem the type to make a career out of Shag's.

Nudger knew how Ray could spend his entire welfare check in one night, giving the impression that he had money to roll around in. He probably impressed Heidran by dressing up and ordering the Super Shag Huge Deal Meal that was printed in the center of the menu in large brown letters.

You're being unfair, he told himself, carrying his tray to one of the tiny brown plastic booths. She might be a perfectly lovely woman genuinely attracted to Ray and not at all to Ray's lies and illusory wealth.

Either way, Nudger thought, Ray deserved her, though she might not deserve him.

Still, Ray was Danny's cousin. Family.

By the time Nudger had finished eating and stood up to leave, the pimply girl was behind the counter and Heidran was wearing the belt pack and earphones and handling drive-through customers. Every move she made was coordinated and so efficient and smooth that the little aerial on the earphones didn't waver.

Nudger smiled a good-bye to the teenager behind the counter as he walked from Shag's and made his way belching to his car. He glanced up at the COUNTLESS SOLD sign and doubted that Shag's would ever overtake McDonald's.

Once inside the car, he got a roll of antacid tablets out of the glove compartment and popped two of the chalky white disks into his mouth even before starting the engine and air conditioner.

It was almost two o'clock when he drove north on the Inner Belt toward the address of Roger Dupont's loyal and well-heeled sister.

Effie Prang's house was low and seemed mostly made of glass and rough-hewn cedar beams joined at extreme angles. It was a few blocks off Ladue Road, on a large corner lot, and had a circular driveway.

Nudger parked by the front door and walked up onto the small porch shaded by a cluster of tall spruce trees. He pushed the doorbell button but heard no sound from inside the house. No one came to the door. He tried the bell again, waited a few minutes, and was about to leave when he heard the distinctive reverberating *plonggggg!* of a diving board, then a splash.

He walked along a stepping-stone path that led around the side of the house, and there was a swimming pool surrounded by a chain-link fence. A thin woman in a red one-piece bathing suit was pulling her dripping body up an aluminum ladder at the deep end of the pool. Her long brown hair was wet and in her eyes, which were almost closed, and the material of her suit clung to her rather good figure. She had a deep tan, with a jarringly pale line above the top of her suit.

She stood up straight and arched her back, shaking her head so that water flew from her wet hair in beautiful glistening arcs that caught the sun. Then she used both hands to tug up on the top of her suit so the paleness, and any sign of cleavage, disappeared.

As she smoothed her hair back, she opened her eyes all the way and saw Nudger. She held a cupped hand to her forehead like a prolonged salute, blocking the sun so she could be sure he wasn't an illusion.

"Effie Prang?" Nudger asked.

"Who are you?" she said, as if fearing a trick question. She had a heavy smoker's throaty voice.

"My name's Nudger. I'm doing some investigative work concerning your brother Roger Dupont."

"You police?"

"No, no. I'm on your side. Working for the court."

Almost the truth. Sort of.

She stood dripping, leaving a dark wet pattern on the pale concrete around her bare feet while she decided about him. Her toenails and fingernails were painted the same deep maroon.

"Okay," she said, "c'mon in through the gate." She pointed to a break in the fence and a chain-link gate ten feet from Nudger that he hadn't noticed.

He walked onto the concrete apron around the pool, feeling the heat radiating upward to warm his ankles.

Effie Prang sat down on the edge of a yellow-webbed, aluminum lounger. She kept her thighs pressed primly together. She was in her late thirties and had a sweet face with an extreme overbite that somehow added to her attractiveness. It was the kind of trusting face you'd expect to find on a woman who'd lay her wealth on the line for a brother accused of murder.

She said, "You're sweating, Mr? . . . "

"Nudger," Nudger reminded her.

"Want some lemonade?" She pointed to a round, white-enameled steel table where a tray with a pitcher and half a dozen upside-down tall glasses on it sat. They were in the shade of the yellow umbrella that sprouted from the center of the table. The pitcher was partly covered with a thin red cloth napkin. Nudger could see ice cubes floating in the hazy liquid.

He walked to the table and poured lemonade into one of the glasses. "One for you?" he asked, holding up an empty glass.

"No, thank you."

He placed the glass upside down again next to the four identical empty glasses. "Are you expecting company?" He waved a hand over the glasses.

"No," Effie Prang said, "but I never know when people are going to drop in."

"I guess the pool is a draw for the neighbors."

"The neighbors all have pools," she said.

"Ah." Nudger had forgotten he was in affluent Ladue. He sipped from the tall glass. "Good lemonade."

"It's from a can."

"Good anyway. You do anything to it?"

"Open it, pour it."

"Ah."

"Mr. Nutter—"

"Nudger."

"Mr. Nudger, what is it you want to ask me about Roger?"

"Why did you post bond for him?" Nudger, master interrogator, driving to the point.

Effie Prang appeared surprised. "He's my brother. My only sibling. Blood is everything in this world. It's all that keeps us from being alone."

"You must have friends." He smiled. "What about the people who drop by and drink lemonade."

"You're here drinking lemonade," she pointed out.

Nudger wondered vaguely if he'd been insulted.

"When it really matters, on the deepest level, you can't count on your friends," Effie Prang said. "You can't even count on your spouse."

Nudger wasn't sure about that. He'd discovered after the divorce that he could count on Eileen to make him miserable.

"We're all more alone than we think," Effie Prang continued, "and during trouble, or at the very end, we find it out. The illusions are all gone and we know."

Nudger had to admire her good cheer. "What about your parents?"

She picked up a folded towel and patted her bare, tan shoulders. "Both dead for years. Roger is my only family. He's all I have, and I'm all he has. Blood is the only thing you can trust without reservation."

"You think Roger is innocent, then."

"I know he is. We're close. Siblings can tell these things about each other."

"What about Karen?"

"She ran away to Chicago, just like Roger said. If you knew Karen, you wouldn't think the story so improbable. Among other things, she's impulsive."

"What other things?"

Effie Prang smiled at Nudger. Lots of white teeth. Nice. "You've come to the wrong place if you're trying to find out what Karen was like, Mr. Nubber. I didn't understand her. She came from a background so different from mine and my brother's.

"It's Nudger, actually. Do you think she married Roger for his money?"

Startled, she looked at him.

"Correct me if I'm wrong," said Nudger.

Effie hesitated for another moment, perhaps remembering the injunction not to speak ill of the dead. Or the gone-to-Chicago.

"All right. I never thought she was good for Roger."

"How long were they married?"

"Four years."

"Did you and your sister-in-law get along? I mean, were you civil to each other?"

"Of course. But Roger knew what I thought of Karen."

Nudger thought he'd play dumb, a talent that often came in useful. He shot a look at the house, at the glaze of sun on wide sliding glass doors. "Is Mr. Prang home?"

"There is no Mr. Prang. Not anymore. I've been divorced for six years."

"Then you live alone?"

"Then I live alone," she confirmed, with what might have been a note of sadness.

"Children?"

"No. Why do you ask?"

"You seem to believe in family, I thought . . . Well, you're right, it's none of my business. Is your former husband here in St. Louis?"

"No, he's far away. One night he turned to me and said his company was transferring him to the Abu Dhabi branch. I said I didn't know about moving overseas and he said that was all right, I wasn't coming. Then he went to his room to pack. He left me sitting astounded in front of the television. I remember *Jeopardy* was on."

"Not so unlike the way Karen left Roger," Nudger said.

"Exactly. And we're both better off without either of them in our lives." A large glass ashtray sat on the concrete next to her chair, and an unopened pack of Virginia Slims. She lifted the pack of cigarettes, realized what she was doing, and dropped it quickly into the ashtray. "I'm trying to quit," she explained. "There are fewer and fewer places where a smoker can indulge. They tell us what a terrible addiction smoking is, then expect us not to smoke except when and where they say it's okay. It's difficult."

"A compulsion," Nudger agreed. He could hear water lapping gently in the pool behind him, stirred by the action of the filter. "Maybe there are people who simply can't quit."

She started to answer, then stopped with her lips slightly parted. A low, grating sound made her look beyond Nudger.

He turned to see one of the sliding doors open. A tall man wearing a blue terry cloth robe stepped from the house onto the patio. He had straight, neatly parted graying brown hair, and a lean, patrician face with a ledge of graying eyebrow. For a second he screwed up his features in a squint to protect against the brilliant sun, then he drew a pair of glasses with darkly tinted round lenses from his shirt pocket and put them on. He walked toward where Effie Prang and Nudger were at poolside. When he got closer, Nudger saw that he had a slight overbite.

"Mr. Nudger," Effie Prang said, finally getting his name right, "this is my brother Roger."

CHAPTER SIX

Dupont shook Nudger's hand then poured himself a glass of lemonade. He sipped, swallowed with his head tilted far back, then actually smiled and emitted an "Ahhh!" the way actors did in TV commercials. Holding the glass at belt level, he turned and faced Nudger. His eyes were invisible behind the dark glasses; the lenses themselves reminded Nudger of the eyes of insects.

"So you're investigating in my behalf," Dupont said, after Effie had filled him in.

Nudger knew right away Dupont wasn't going to allow any vagueness as to his role, the way his sister had. Hiding behind his own glass of lemonade, he took a long swallow then nodded.

Dupont smiled again. "But if I understand correctly, you're not police?"

"The court," Effie said. "He's working for the court."

Dupont shook his head in puzzlement. "I'm afraid I still don't understand. Who exactly did hire you, Mr. Nudger?"

"Your lawyer," Nudger said, "Lawrence Fleck." Fleck wasn't going to like Nudger's involvement becoming evident so early in the game, but there was little choice. "It's standard procedure in many cases," Nudger went on quickly, smoothing and hastening. "Mr. Fleck doesn't like leaving stones unturned if whatever's under them might help a client."

"I turned over all the stones Mr. Fleck needs to look beneath," Dupont said with an edge of anger. Then, more reasonably: "It isn't that I don't appreciate his concern, but your services simply aren't necessary."

Nudger couldn't understand this. He wished he could see Dupont's eyes. "Mr. Dupont, you do comprehend, don't you, that in a few days you're going to go on trial for your life?"

"Of course. And while I realize that the situation isn't without some risk, I'm confident I'll be acquitted."

" 'Some risk' might mean that you die by lethal injection. In your position, you should want every avenue explored if it might lead somewhere that assures your innocence."

Dupont's smile was confident. Nudger could see two small images of himself in the dark glasses. Did the prey of spiders see such images? Had Karen Dupont? "I'm already assured of my innocence, Mr. Nudger."

What was this, word games? "I expressed myself a little incorrectly," Nudger said. "What you need is for a jury to be as assured as you are, or at least to have enough reasonable doubt to make you a free man. Contrary to what a lot of people believe, innocent people are executed from time to time."

"But not often," Dupont said. A bead of perspiration ran from behind his ear down the side of his neck to disappear beneath the collar of his robe. The only sign of any discomfort. "I truly did not kill my wife, Mr. Nudger. I have faith in our legal system. I have competent counsel. That should be sufficient, so I'm relatively unworried."

Nudger said nothing, but he wasn't so sure about competent counsel.

Dupont began to untie his robe. "Come on, Effie, time for our swim."

Nudger was amazed. But Effie took the announcement in stride.

"Do we have to? I've already done my laps, Roger."

"Then you're all warmed up. Let's race." Dupont threw off his robe. He was in excellent shape. "Shall we make it the usual? Ten lengths?"

His sister remained seated. "I'm a little tired."

Nudger said, "Mr. Dupont, I do have a few more questions, if you don't mind. There are only three days until the trial begins."

Dupont put his hands on his lean hips and looked to heaven. What a couple of spoilsports he was stuck with. "All right. I'll race you to the far end and back. How about that, Effie?"

"But what about Mr. Nudger?"

"He can say go."

Trading his sunglasses for tinted goggles, Dupont walked to the edge of the pool. Effie rose and followed. Nudger stayed where he was, sipping lemonade. He thought Dupont was kidding, until the man turned and looked at him with annoyance.

"We're on our marks," he said, "so just say, 'get set' and 'go.' "

Nudger sighed and got up. Perhaps this was all being done for his benefit. Perhaps Dupont was laying the groundwork for an insanity plea.

"Get set."

Effie didn't move, but Dupont dropped into a crouch, his arms straight back.

"Go!"

Dupont made a flat lunging dive that any Olympic competitor would have been proud of. When he was still airborne, he was one-quarter of the way across Effie's backyard-sized pool. Then he splashed and began pulling with a strong crawl stroke. Four strokes and he was at the far end. He executed a neat flip turn and stroked back, passing Effie, who was about halfway through her first lap. He didn't slow up, though. He was going for the gold. He touched at Nudger's feet and turned around to see how far his sister was behind him. She was just making her turn at the far end. Dupont grinned. He stayed where he was, hanging on to the side and watching Effie's slow progress. When she came up beside him, he said, "Beat you."

Here was a guy who liked to rub it in. Nudger wondered what the Dupont siblings' childhoods had been like. Rather, he wondered how Effie had put up with it. At the moment, she only smiled tolerantly.

Dupont levered himself out of the pool and padded back to the table. Nudger followed, noticing that Dupont was breathing hard. He'd put his all into that race. He switched back to the sunglasses and put on his robe.

Nudger figured he'd better hurry and get his questions in before the next event. "Since you are innocent, Mr. Dupont—"

"Of course I am."

"I have to ask, why did you confess?"

Dupont said stiffly, "Judge MacMasters ruled that confession inadmissible in a pretrial hearing. So you can just forget about it."

"All the same I have to wonder why you made it. If you're innocent and feel you have nothing to fear—"

"When you're under arrest, surrounded by cops, and alone, you have something to fear. I panicked and did a foolish thing."

Nudger nodded. It was hard to imagine Dupont in a panic, but there was truth to what he said about being arrested. Nudger decided to move on.

"I'm assuming you still haven't heard from Karen."

"Of course not. If I had, there wouldn't be a trial."

Effie returned to the table, hitching up the top of her swimsuit. As she sat down, Nudger turned to her. "Have you heard from Karen or anyone who might have seen her in Chicago?"

Effie looked slightly surprised. "No. Believe me, Mr. Nudger, I'd be the last person Karen would contact."

"That's not true, Effie," Dupont said. "Karen is fond of you."

Nudger studied the bland face. The man truly didn't seem concerned about anything except preserving harmony between in-laws. Nudger decided to see if a blunt question would unsettle him.

"Why did your wife leave you, Mr. Dupont?"

Picking up a towel, Dupont began to dry his face. He did not take off his sunglasses, but dabbed around them. "I believe it was the house."

"Your home on Devlon, you mean? What was wrong with it?"

"Nothing."

"I'm afraid I don't—"

"Well, that was the problem. Karen was a devoted homemaker. She spent four years working on that house, and finally she had it perfect. I believe she was bored."

"Uh-huh. Were there problems between the two of you?"

"Well—obviously there were. But I wasn't aware of them. I still don't understand."

"When Karen left, what reasons did she give?"

"She didn't give any. She came into my bedroom in the morning and said she was going to Chicago and it would be useless if I tried to find her."

"You each had your own bedroom," Nudger said. He tried to remember the polite phrase. "Then you weren't having conjugal relations?"

Dupont looked at him, and he looked at his reflection in Dupont's glasses. If the man was annoyed at the slipup he'd made, he didn't show it.

"Of course we were. I snore, that's all."

"Were you still in bed when she told you she was leaving?"

"In bed and only half awake. Karen had acted impulsively before, so I didn't think it was beyond her to open my bedroom door, poke her head in, and tell me good-bye. It wouldn't have surprised me to get up an hour later and find her in the kitchen eating breakfast."

"Then what?" Nudger asked. "Did you get out of bed and try to stop her?"

"No, I was sure that would be useless, if she really did plan on

40

walking out of the house that morning. She gave me one of her dispassionate looks, then gently closed the door. I didn't hear her leave, but half an hour later, when I got up, she was gone.''

"How did she leave?"

"I told you, I never saw her go."

"I mean, did she have her own car? Was it still in the garage?"

"Yes and yes," Dupont said. "I noticed it around ten o'clock, when I was leaving for my regular round of golf. I assumed she'd called a cab, but the police say they checked all the cab companies and they found no record of a fare being picked up at my address."

"Any ideas?"

"Perhaps a friend picked her up."

Nudger thought about that. It was possible. Wouldn't it be interesting to find that friend. "Mr. Dupont, is there any reason to believe your wife might have been involved with another man?"

Dupont didn't seem to resent the question. "None at all," he said.

"That doesn't mean it isn't possible," Effie said.

"Maybe you know something that makes it seem even more possible," Nudger said.

She opened her mouth as if to laugh, then said in a sober voice, "Karen and I didn't have that much to do with each other. I know nothing about her social life."

"Hear any gossip about her?"

"If I had, I wouldn't repeat it. Gossip isn't of much use in court."

"We're not in court. If you heard something about Karen, I should investigate it." He stared directly at Dupont as he spoke.

Dupont was in a quandary. If he didn't kill his wife, he shouldn't mind Nudger probing around for more facts. To demand that Fleck take Nudger off the case would seem too much like the action of a guilty man. Nudger figured that guilty or innocent, Dupont wouldn't pressure Fleck to fire him. And leaving Nudger in place would seem an acceptable risk for a guilty Dupont; after all, the police had come up with enough evidence to send the prosecuting attorney into paroxysms of joy. How much more harm could Nudger do?

"There are people," Nudger said, "who mistakenly assume a murder conviction is impossible without the body of the victim."

"Oh, I was never one of them, Mr. Nudger. In fact, I had a year of law school before deciding on a banking career. I've long been aware that corpus delicti refers to the body of the crime and not of the victim. The prosecution need only establish that the crime has been committed. A corpse isn't necessary for that. Which is what makes this entire farce possible. I'm sure Karen is somewhere in Chicago, staying with a friend or simply existing on her own, perhaps even under a different name."

"Would she come forward if she knew you were being tried for her murder?"

"I would hope so," Dupont said.

"Don't be too sure of that," Effie said. "Karen's heart can be stone once she's turned on a person."

"How would you know that?" Nudger asked.

"Once she decided I resented her marriage to Roger, she turned on me. I doubt if she'd come forward to save me from being found guilty of murder."

"What about if you were going to be executed?" Nudger asked.

Effie stared at the pool water glittering in the sun and seemed to consider the question. "I'd like to think she'd come forward to save me, or to save anyone, out of common decency. But I'm not sure she would."

"Of course she would," Dupont said.

"Is that what you're counting on?" Nudger asked.

"If it came to that," Dupont said, "I think enough publicity, perhaps a call for her help, running in the Chicago papers, would probably bring my plight to her attention and she'd emerge and make it clear that she was still alive. But I'm certain it won't come to that. Any fair-minded jury will acquit me. And Effie and I have told you how impulsive Karen is; it's possible she might have a change of heart and appear back at home today. A whim, and then another whim . . . that's Karen." He seemed unconcerned that the wrong whim might result in his death.

Nudger thanked Effie Prang for the lemonade, then told Dupont he hoped he was right about the jury. He said good-bye. Nobody told him there was a pair of trunks in the house that would fit him and urged him to stay. He placed his empty glass on the table, bumping his head on the big yellow umbrella, then walked toward the gate.

Thinking Roger Dupont would have benefited from another year or so of law school. Wondering what, if anything, was Dupont's game. Understanding now why Fleck had hired an investigator.

Fleck's erratic but devious mind kept telling him it was possible he was being had, but couldn't figure out how.

Nudger's stomach was telling him the same thing.

CHAPTER SEVEN

I can't hear you, Nudger!" Fleck bellowed.

"Sorry, can't help it," Nudger replied, raising his voice. "I'm calling from my car."

"Don't you know enough to roll up your window before you use your car phone? Do I have to tell you everything?"

Nudger couldn't roll up his window, because the phone chord had to come through it. He was calling from one of those roadside pay phones that allowed you to make a call without getting out of your car, provided you parked just right and had really long arms.

If Fleck wanted to assume that he had a car phone, so be it.

"I've talked to Roger Dupont."

There was a pause. Nudger could imagine Fleck glancing around to make sure no one was in earshot as he hunched over the phone. "What did you make of him?"

"He's still placing a lot of faith in the legal system—"

"Innocent! Fool!"

Before Fleck could get started on how lucky Dupont was to have Fleck as his attorney, Nudger put in, "He also seems to be hoping that his wife will turn up. That she'll hear about his problems and come forward, or something."

Nudger paused, but Fleck made no comment, so he went on. "I was thinking—"

"Yeah?" Fleck barked. "What were you thinking, Nudger?"

Sensing that he was being drawn into another of the legal genius's traps, Nudger pressed on regardless. "I was wondering if we ought to take steps to contact Mrs. Dupont."

"Like what?"

"Advertise in the Chicago papers. Even on television. Or I could go up there myself—"

This was what Fleck had been waiting for. He pounced. "Terrific! Wonderful! You get a little vacation and I get the bill. Why should I pay your way to Chicago? 'Cause you're not getting anything done here?"

"Listen, Fleck—"

"No, you listen, fella. You're the one who's been hearing but not listening. Now, what am I paying you for?"

"To find out the truth."

"Exactly. Now why won't you do what I'm paying you to do?"

"But if I could find Mrs. Dupont—"

"And how are you going to go about that, Nudger? Go to the top of the Sears Building with a pair of binoculars and look around? Ride the El round and round the Loop and hope she gets on?"

Nudger sighed and looked out the window at the traffic streaming past on Clayton Road. It consisted mostly of the Mercedeses and Volvos of homebound Ladue-ites. Rush hour. Everybody was tired and in a hurry to get home. Including Nudger.

He tried again. "If we find Mrs. Dupont, that's the end of the case."

Fleck exploded. "Think I don't know that? Haven't thought of the possibility? Haven't got it covered? Think I need you to tell me about it?"

Nudger decided not to answer any of these questions. The sun was beating down on him through the windshield. The phone felt slippery in his sweaty grasp. He was getting dizzy from the exhaust fumes of passing traffic. By now, he hoped, he had fallen into all of Fleck's traps. Maybe then they could move on to the part of the conversation where they exchanged information.

He asked, "Do you already have someone looking for Mrs. Dupont?"

"You bet."

"You've hired a Chicago investigator—"

"Wrong! Think I'm a fool, Nudger? That I'd pay my own investigator when someone else is doing it for free?"

"Doing it for free?"

"Somebody I know will find Mrs. Dupont, if she's there to be found. Somebody with the best motive in the world for finding her. You with me, Nudger? You know what the best motive in the world is?"

"Money," Nudger said. He'd sworn he wouldn't be drawn into one of these Q&A sessions with Fleck, but he was tiring fast.

"Right! Brilliant! And do you know—"

Nudger cut him off. He'd remembered now what Hammersmith had told him that morning. One of the damning pieces of evidence against Dupont was that he had taken out a big policy on Karen's life. "There's an insurance investigator looking for her, right?"

Disappointed, Fleck fell silent. Nudger reached in his shirt pocket for his notebook. The cover and the first few pages were soaked through with sweat. He flipped to a dry page and took out his pen. "Who is this investigator?

"Walter Blaumveldt, at General Mutual downtown. But I don't see why you have to bother talking to him. Don't see why you have to worry about Karen Dupont at all. You know what cheap suspicious bastards these insurance companies are. Or maybe you don't know, poor sad innocent that you are. I could tell you stories of people who suffered the most terrible injuries, who had the most one-hundred-percent valid claims, and they wouldn't have gotten a dime out of these insurance companies. Not a dime! If it hadn't been for Lawrence—"

"You're fading, Lawrence," Nudger said. "I must be leaving the cell."

"What?"

"Or maybe it's a dead spot." Nudger began to move the phone away from his mouth. "These darn car phones. You never—"

He hung up the phone. Thought, Whew!

"So," Claudia Bettencourt said, "you think that one way or another, the wife is going to turn up?"

Nudger shook his head. "No. I think he killed her."

She'd listened to him quietly while he told her about Roger Dupont. They were seated at opposite ends of the sofa in the living room of her South St. Louis apartment on Wilmington. Two glasses of the cheap red wine Nudger had brought sat untouched before them on the coffee table.

"It sounds as if Dupont's lawyer shares your opinion," Claudia said. She was a lean, dark-haired woman with a slender face, dark brown eyes, and a straight nose that was too long and somehow lent her a noble appearance. Not at all a flashy woman, but the longer men looked at her the more attractive she became. It had happened with Nudger, and he'd seen it happen with other men.

Claudia's understated sensuousness hinted at heat below the surface.

Now Nudger did lean forward and take a sip of his wine. He knew nothing about wine, but he liked this brand. It had a cap that was easier to take off than a cork, and it had a nice bite to it. "Anyone looking at the evidence would have to conclude Dupont's guilty. A jury is almost sure to see it that way."

"He wouldn't be the first person to put too much faith in the justice system," Claudia said.

Nudger glanced out the window. They were on the second floor and the view was of sun-dappled sycamore leaves. It still looked hot outside, but the huge, noisy air conditioner mounted in the dining room window was keeping summer at bay. From the kitchen wafted the scent of spaghetti sauce simmering on the stove. It smelled great but contained garlic. Nudger had plans for himself and Claudia; he regarded the garlic as a discouraging sign.

"I remember about a year ago when you decided to plead innocent to a traffic ticket," Claudia said.

His stomach kicked with irritation. Why did she have to bring that up? "I wasn't speeding," he told her. "The cop's radar gun was defective. I know, because the Granada won't go as fast as that gun had it registered."

Claudia looked at her wine but didn't touch it. She'd once mentioned she liked to give wine time to breathe. "You're saying you were innocent."

"Of course," Nudger said. "Because I *was* innocent."

He still sounded defensive.

"But you had to pay the fine. I remember how astounded you were. You'd put faith in your innocence, but you paid."

She was right about that. But Nudger had been more naive a year ago. Because he was innocent he'd assumed the judge would somehow be able to see into his mind, to know the police were mistaken in this instance. Why, the judge only had to turn in his chair and look out the window at the old Granada parked nearby to know it wouldn't go as fast as the speeding ticket said it had been going.

But the judge hadn't turned and looked outside. He'd listened to the officer who'd written the ticket, listened to Nudger, and told Nudger to pay. Nudger had started to protest, but the court clerk was already calling the name of the next defendant, who turned out to be a woman who'd been ticketed for speeding on the same street and on the same date as Nudger, and who stood behind him in line to pay her fine.

"Maybe Dupont really is innocent and has the same bright faith that blinded you a year ago," Claudia suggested.

"You're overlooking the evidence against him."

"It was your word against a traffic cop with a radar gun," Claudia said, "and you thought you'd walk."

"I did walk," Nudger reminded her, "after paying my fine. But Dupont is taking more of a chance. He might have to walk to a little room where the state will kill him."

Claudia picked up her wineglass, rotated it by its stem, then sipped. Grimaced. "Maybe he has more faith than you had," she said. "Maybe the evidence isn't as damaging as it seems. You know how a house of cards can come down all at once."

"This is a house of cast concrete," Nudger said.

She stood up and smoothed her jeans down over her thighs. She was one of those thin women who appear much taller than they are. "The spaghetti ought to be about done." She walked into the kitchen. He loved to watch her walk, the subtle undulation that fired his desire.

It bothered him that she felt Dupont might be innocent. He knew her and knew she was reasonably sure of it. Claudia and Effie were the only ones who shared that feeling. Not even Dupont's lawyer shared it.

"Are you going somewhere after dinner?" Claudia called from the kitchen.

Nudger raised his voice so she could hear him over the air conditioner. "That depends. Danny's cousin Ray's got some kind of problem with a woman who works at Shag's. I might drive by to talk to him. Or I might not."

"What's it depend on?" Claudia asked.

Playing coy, she was. Nudger smiled. "Oh, this and that." Keeping her on a string.

You want a salad with your spaghetti?"

"Sure," Nudger said. "What kind of dressing?"

"Dressing's already on it. Blue cheese with garlic."

"Oh."

"Garlic bread?" she asked.

"Why not?" Nudger said despondently.

"Come in here so you can help me," she said. "Bring your glass."

Nudger went.

CHAPTER EIGHT

Nudger had phoned from Claudia's, so Ray should have been expecting him. He knocked on Ray's apartment door a little after nine. It was still brutally hot, and only a few of the tenants of St. James apartments were out on the grounds. No one was at the pool, which Nudger could barely see from where he stood, because it was drained and under repair. The only sounds were the steady, shrill ratcheting of crickets and the faint voice of a baseball announcer from inside Ray's apartment.

It took Ray a while, but finally he opened the door. He looked as if he'd just awakened, only that couldn't be, because he was holding an opened can of beer.

Since Nudger had last seen him, Ray seemed to have lost a lot of weight except for around his midsection, giving him the look of one of those pear-shaped inflatable punching bags for kids that always spring back upright after being knocked down. But portly though his midsection had become, his face was almost gaunt and wore its perpetual expression of equal mixtures of self-pity and indignation. His yellowed, protruding teeth looked as if they'd moved and were even more crooked. Behind him Nudger could see a Cubs game on TV. There was nothing about Ray that Nudger liked.

"Hey, Nudge!" Ray said with overfamiliarity and feigned brightness. "C'mon in and sit yourself down."

Nudger did. The apartment was maybe two degrees cooler than outside. Before moving the sports page of a crinkled newspaper to make room and sitting down on the sofa, he saw into the bedroom. Ray's bed had been stripped of its sheet; suggesting that it was his biannual wash day.

He didn't offer Nudger a beer, and Nudger didn't ask for one. On TV the Cubs' genial and optimistic announcer Steve Stone was explaining how next year had to be better for the hapless ball club. But the Cubs were winning this game against the Giants, six to one.

Ray saw Nudger staring with distaste at the shot of the scoreboard on TV and visibly suppressed a grin.

"Danny tells me you've got a problem," Nudger said, fighting down his irritation.

"You bet I do," Ray said, slumping down in a stained brown vinyl recliner. He worked a wooden lever and tilted back slightly as a footrest sprang out to support his stockinged feet. "Her name's Heidran and she works over at Shag's."

"What's she done to you?" Nudger asked. He thought he'd let Ray tell him and see if the story would differ from the one told to Danny.

"She offered me a job," Ray said in an incredulous voice.

"Why would she do such a thing?"

"Because I gave her an application. Then she double-crossed me and said she'd hire me."

Nudger settled back on the sofa, trying to ignore the odor of Ray's feet and the smell of stale sweat that permeated the apartment. "Better do some more explaining, Ray."

"Sure, Nudge. You know I injured my back while I was working on a trucking company's loading dock, don't you?"

"Yes," Nudger said, "Danny told me." He knew the loading dock job was part of Ray's pattern of seeking out employment only when his unemployment benefits were about to expire. When sufficient time had passed and his new employer had paid in enough unemployment tax for Ray to be eligible to collect again, Ray would find a way to leave the job and go back on the dole.

"Well, I couldn't do the work there," he said, "what with my back and all, so they let me go and I went back on unemployment. The thing is, to continue collecting unemployment checks, I gotta show I've applied for work at a minimum of three places a week."

"So you turn in applications where you know you won't be hired," Nudger said.

Ray's scraggly eyebrows rose and his face screwed up in a way meant to convey pain. "It ain't like I got a choice, Nudge. What with my back and all. I applied last week at the railroad, but when I told them about my back they turned me down. Same way at a cement plant. Now, I been eating at Shag's off and on, and I knew this Heidran had a crush on me." He smiled and ran his tongue across his jagged teeth. "You know how it is sometimes when a woman finds you irresistible."

Nudger didn't, but he nodded.

"I figured if I explained my back problem to Heidran and gave her an application, she'd turn me down and I could list Shag's, the railroad, and the cement plant as my three places where I honestly applied for work. But she surprised me. She said she thinks I should learn to stand on my own two feet instead of the government's. When I reminded her about my back, she said the heaviest thing at

Shag's was their Three-eighths Pounder burger."

"So what's the problem?" Nudger asked. He watched the Cubs lead-off man hit a home run. "Why don't you just apply someplace else for your third attempt and not mention Shag's to the folks at Unemployment?"

"That's what I thought I'd do originally. But this Heidran won't let it go that easy. She says that I'm hired, and if I don't come to work at Shag's she'll notify the state employment office and my benefits will be cut off. She says it's for my own good and I'll thank her later. She actually told me that, Nudge, and you shoulda seen how she was looking at me! Like I was a Three-eighths Pounder and was just what she needed."

"She could be right," Nudger said. "About what she told you, I mean."

Ray's eyebrows rose almost to his receding hairline and he looked his most pathetic. "Hey, Nudge!"

"Sorry," Nudger said. Incredibly, the next Cubs batter hit a home run on the first pitch. Nudger needed to get out of there.

"So what do you want from me?" he asked, goading Ray to get to the point.

Ray leaned forward and his red-rimmed eyes became earnest. "Just talk to the woman, Nudge. Explain to her how serious my back injury is. Hell, I even gotta wear a special brace." He raised his dirty T-shirt to reveal a bulky gray wrapping around his midsection. It looked a lot like a bed sheet. "Tell her it might permanently injure me if I gotta do a lot of stooping and bending or scooping fries. Hey, tell her you're from workmen's compensation and maybe she'll listen to you."

"That I won't do," Nudger snapped.

Ray looked offended. "So okay, forget the workman's compensation thing."

"Why don't you consider going to work at Shag's?" Nudger asked, knowing the hopelessness of the suggestion even as he broached it. It simply wasn't time yet for Ray to work.

52

Ray merely stared at him.

Nudger stood up and turned to face away from the TV before another Cub hit a home run.

"This is damned serious," Ray said, writhing in his recliner so he could place a hand on the small of his back. He grimaced.

"How serious, Ray?"

"I mean, I know I cried wolf before—I admit that! But if I'm forced to twist and bend like a twenty-year-old kid, I might have to claim permanent disability. There isn't much money these days when people don't wanna pay taxes. I got nobody but Danny to take care of me if that happens. If you won't do this for me, Nudge, do it for Danny. Please! Talk to the woman. She won't listen to me because she finds me attractive, but she might listen to you."

Nudger sighed.

"I'll talk to her," he said, "but I don't know if it will do any good."

"Just give it a shot, is all I ask."

What Nudger felt like shooting was Ray. He started for the door, and Ray struggled to fight his way up out of the recliner.

"Don't get up," Nudger said. "The back, the back . . . I'll let myself out."

"Thanks, Nudge. I won't forget this."

Not until you're off the hook, Nudger thought, opening the door and feeling the somewhat greater heat outside move in and surround him.

"Hey, Nudge," Ray said behind him, "I meant to ask you, you been eating garlic?"

Nudger didn't answer as he went out and closed the door.

Getting angrier by the second, he flung himself into the Granada with such violence that he wrenched his back.

The engine started on the fourth try and was running raggedly as he pulled out onto Manchester, tuning in the Cardinals ball game on the car's static-plagued radio.

They were losing, too.

When he drove up Manchester to his office to check his messages and write checks for some overdue bills, he opened the door and saw that all of the desk and file cabinet drawers were hanging open and the floor was littered with papers.

He found it impossible to be surprised.

CHAPTER NINE

Nudger didn't have to look in the phone book for Walter Blaumveldt, the insurance investigator Fleck was counting on to find Karen Dupont. The General Mutual Insurance Company was located in the General Mutual Building, a glass-and-steel skyscraper that had been a prominent feature of the downtown skyline for many years.

While the receptionist paged Blaumveldt, he stood at the glass wall looking down. The building was across the street from Busch Stadium, and he was high enough to see a broad green wedge of the field, including the mound and first base. Too bad there wasn't a game going on, because Blaumveldt was taking a long time.

"Mr. Nudger?"

He turned. Walter Blaumveldt was a tall, thin man in his fifties, and everything about him seemed to hang down. A hank of gray hair flopped across his brow. His eyelids drooped over chilly brown eyes. His lips had a saturnine southward curl. His cheeks looked slack, as if the muscles other people used for smiling had atrophied in him. He was wearing a dark blue suit that looked too big for him; the coat hung in folds from his broad sloping shoulders. He kept his arms at his sides. He wasn't committing himself to a handshake yet.

Pleased to meet you would be too effusive for this character, so Nudger said, "Thank's for seeing me."

Even that might have been too much, because Blaumveldt showed no signs of leading Nudger to his office. He said, "You work for Lawrence Fleck."

"That's right."

"Are you his regular investigator? You see, we know Fleck well at this company. He's represented a number of plaintiffs against us. He was zealous. His clients' injuries were imaginary."

"I'm not his regular investigator. I was hired for this one case. Anyway Fleck isn't against you this time. He'd be delighted if you found Karen Dupont."

Blaumveldt thought this over. "All right," he said. He turned his back and walked away. Nudger presumed he was to follow.

They walked down the corridor and into his cubicle, which was one cell in a honeycomb created by chest-high dividers. A babble of phone conversations drifted in from other cubicles, along with the clickety-click, hum, and shuffle of office machinery. A green plant stood in the corner, and the furniture was white, with red chair cushions. The place seemed far too noisy and bright for Walter Blaumveldt. Nudger could more easily imagine him working alone in some dim, dusty, bare office—actually, an office pretty much like Nudger's.

That reminded him. Some time today he'd have to go to his office and clean up. Last night he'd simply closed the door on the mess his intruder had left behind and gone home.

They took seats on either side of the desk. "What does Fleck want you to do, exactly?" Blaumveldt asked.

"Find out the truth."

Blaumveldt sighed. "If you're not supposed to tell me, just say so."

"No, really, that's it. I'm going around talking to the people involved, trying to get a feel for the situation, figure out what really happened."

The corners of Blaumveldt's mouth turned even more sharply downward. "And Fleck's actually paying you for this?"

Ignoring the sarcasm, Nudger said, "I wonder if you could tell me what you've found out about Karen so far. I want to know what she was like."

"Is like." Blaumveldt said. "I expect you'll get a chance to meet her before this is over."

"You think she's alive, then. Why?"

"Not because I went around getting a feel for the people involved," Blaumveldt said with a sneer. Such a charmer the guy was. "The whole insurance business is based on trusting the percentages. You look at what's usually happened in the past, and you can be pretty sure it's what's happening in the present."

"Meaning—?"

"Meaning when a beneficiary comes to us, tells us our insured is dead, but there is no body, we think we're looking at a case of insurance fraud."

"Has Dupont filed a claim?"

"No. But he will."

Nudger considered, frowning. "But when the insured disappears, doesn't the beneficiary have to wait seven years before he can collect on the policy? And won't Roger Dupont be barred from collecting on his wife's policy, if he's convicted of murdering her? It'll be even tougher for him to collect if he's been executed."

Blaumveldt sat back and laced his fingers together over his midsection. "All I said was, they're trying to defraud us. Not that they made a good plan, or that it's working for them. Karen's alive, and Dupont's playing games."

Nudger nodded. "I think so, too. That Dupont's playing games, I mean."

Blaumveldt looked more interested now. "Why?"

"For one thing, my office was searched last night. After I'd talked to Dupont, and he'd said he wasn't crazy about having me on the case."

"You take this to the cops?"

"No."

"Why not?"

"Nothing was taken. I mean, there was nothing for Dupont to find. And I can't even be sure it was Dupont."

"Who else could it have been?"

Nudger hated to be on the receiving end of an interrogation. Especially with a cold fish like Blaumveldt on the other end. But now he'd started this subject he might as well finish it.

"Well, frankly, it's possible that my ex-wife and her lawyer hired a thug to toss the place."

To his surprise Blaumveldt's expression had changed. He looked interested and sympathetic. "You fell behind a little on your child support, right? And this jerk of a lawyer treats you like a deadbeat. How many kids you got? What ages?"

"None. She was awarded alimony."

"Man, that's rough. Me, I've been paying support for twelve years. Two daughters." There was a picture standing on his desk. He turned it to face Nudger. The photo had been snapped on a beach. Two tall, lovely, laughing teenagers stood on either side of their father, their arms around his shoulders. Blaumveldt had on a garish Hawaiian shirt and a lei. He seemed to be trying to smile. Nudger could discern a faint pucker in his left cheek, though it hadn't been enough to lift the corner of his mouth. "They're in college now. I don't know why General Mutual even gives me a paycheck. They might as well send it straight to Stephens College."

Nudger complimented him on his daughters. Blaumveldt took another crack at smiling, maybe his first since Hawaii. The atmosphere was improving: Nudger could hope for a good working relationship.

"You making any progress tracking Karen down?" he asked.

"I've found out a few interesting things checking out Dupont's statement to the cops. And I'm flying up to Chicago tonight. Sooner or later I'll find her."

"You sound pretty determined."

Blaumveldt nodded. "A lot of people tolerate insurance fraud. They say what the hell, it's just some big impersonal company that's getting ripped off. Don't you believe that. It's you and me who are getting ripped off. Honest working stiffs who pay our alimony and child support, pay our insurance premiums. People like Karen and Roger think they can break the rules the rest of us have to keep. Well, I'm going to prove them wrong."

Blaumveldt had worked himself into what was, for him, a passion. His eyes were wide open, there was color in his cheeks, and he even bestirred himself to push the lock of lank hair up off his forehead.

Nudger figured Fleck was right: If Karen Dupont was alive, Blaumveldt was going to find her.

According to Fleck, Karen Dupont's sister, Joleen Witt, worked the night shift as an assembler of stereo speakers at a small manufacturing company out in West Port. Nudger didn't like to phone ahead and give people a chance to concoct a stew of lies before talking to him; his hope was that Joleen was one of those night shift workers who stayed awake after work and went to bed in the afternoon.

Her address on Indian Lane turned out to be in a trailer park off Highway 44 west of the city. The park was called Cherokee Estates and had an air of permanence about it that Nudger, who had once lived in a trailer, didn't associate with them. Most of the trailers— or mobile homes, as they were more popularly referred to by the people who sold and lived in them—looked fairly new and had lattice-work around their bases that concealed wheels and axles. They had small porches and awnings added on, and the grounds around them were green and mowed and dotted with established trees and shrubs. At a glance, the trailers looked like houses.

Nudger parked the Granada across the street from Joleen's address, which was displayed on an upright rock that looked disturbingly like a tombstone on the well-tended lawn. The trailer was white with blue trim, fake blue shutters, and a blue awning over the door. In the gravel driveway next to it sat an old Pontiac convertible that had a new black canvas top but whose paint was a patchwork of pink body putty and dull gray primer. With a fresh coat of paint it would be a good-looking old car, and Nudger found himself staring at it and thinking how much more dash it already had compared to his rusty red Granada sedan wherein he now sat breaking out in beads of sweat.

Though there was no sign of imminent rain to break the summer heat, the temperature hadn't yet hit the mid-eighties, so he immediately felt cooler when he climbed out of the car and stood up. There was also a pleasant breeze pressing out of the west that would probably turn the area into a convection oven sometime around noon. As he crossed the street, the light glinting off the trailers hurt his eyes, and he could hear the sputtering and hissing of several lawn sprinklers laboring to soak the ground before the sun rose high.

A colorful flower bed was growing around the white latticework of Joleen's trailer, lots of geraniums, marigolds, and lowlying varicolored pansies in what looked like fresh dark brown mulch. Nudger stood in the shade of the blue awning and had drawn back his hand to knock on the white aluminum door when a woman wearing Levi's and a faded pink T-shirt with KILL 'EM ALL AND LET GOD SORT 'EM OUT lettered across the chest walked around the corner of the trailer. She was wearing brown cloth work gloves and carrying a small spade with dirt clumped on its blade.

She was tall, with thin legs and generous breasts, and had a wide face with the kind of large, hooked nose that prompted some women to have plastic surgery. Her red hair was piled high in a wild tangle on her head except where a strand of it curled down and was plastered to her perspiring forehead. She was attractive, but there was something wary and injured in her widely spaced green eyes that for some reason reminded Nudger of Ray.

Saying nothing, she stood about ten feet from Nudger and stared at him. Something in the way she held the spade suggested she was ready to use it as a weapon if necessary.

"I'm looking for Joleen Witt," Nudger said.

"She's found you," the woman said, still unmoving.

"I'm an investigator looking into the Karen Dupont murder," Nudger said. Let her conclude he was assuming Karen was murdered, if not by Dupont, by someone else. Which was possible.

"I thought the investigation was concluded. Time now for the trial, conviction, and execution."

"The trial doesn't begin until tomorrow afternoon," Nudger said. "Dupont isn't convicted yet." He formed what he hoped was a grim smile. "The more evidence the better."

Joleen lowered the spade to her side and her expression softened. "Why don't you sit down," she suggested.

She wasn't inviting him inside out of the heat, but Nudger considered her invitation progress. He sat down on the hard, meshed-steel step of the trailer, still in the shade of the awning. Joleen seemed to prefer standing in the sun. She was well tanned and hardy looking.

"You don't think there's any chance your sister is alive?" he said.

Her lips compressed. She shook her head once. "I have no hope. Even before the police found—the things in the furnace, I knew Karen was dead. If she were alive she would have contacted me."

"I understand it was you who brought the police into the case."

"I was suspicious from the beginning," she said.

"Why?"

She gave him a surprised look. "Does Roger's story sound plausible? That Karen just suddenly upped and went off to Chicago and never contacted anyone?"

"Doesn't seem plausible to me," Nudger said.

Joleen squatted down, chunked the spade into the ground and rested her elbows on her knees. She rotated on the balls of her feet until the crotch of the stretched Levi's was exactly in Nudger's line of sight.

Nudger wondered.

"How did you feel about Roger before this happened?" he asked.

"Hated him," Joleen said flatly. She reached down and plucked a blade of grass, then looked it over and stuck one end of it in her mouth, rested her elbow back on her knee. Nudger got the impression she gardened a lot and could stay squatted down like that for a long time.

"Why?" Nudger asked.

"I had a bad feeling about him from the start. I told Karen not to marry him. But she did. And right away it became clear to me she'd made a big mistake. The week after they returned from their honeymoon, he made a pass at me."

"You're sure?"

She rotated around on the balls of her feet again. "We'd just finished a set of tennis at Effie's place in Ladue, and Effie and Karen had gone in to make some drinks. Roger put his hand on me where it didn't belong. His exact words were 'Do you want to play?' He didn't mean more tennis."

The meshed steel step was beginning to dig painfully into Nudger's buttocks. He couldn't sit there much longer, but he didn't want to change the setting or flow of conversation, so he stayed put. "What was your reaction?" he asked.

"I hit him in the knee with my racket. Neither of us spoke of the incident again, but he knew how I felt about him."

"If he didn't love Karen, why do you think he married her?" he asked.

"Roger wanted someone to make a home for him. We're simple, unpretentious people, Mr. Nudger. Not like the Duponts of Ladue. Karen cared about keeping house and cooking. That's what

Roger wanted in a wife. He said one MBA in the family was enough.''

"But did he love her?"

"Roger's too shallow to love anyone. Everything's a game to him. He'd won Karen—married her—so he lost interest. He looked around for other women to win."

"He had affairs."

"I'm sure, but I can't prove it."

"Had Karen ever behaved rashly before? Some people have described her as impulsive. They've said it's in character for her to have suddenly run off to Chicago."

Joleen spat out the blade of grass. "I can guess at least one of the people who'd say such a thing. That sister of Roger's, Effie Prang."

"You don't like Mrs. Prang?"

"She's a snob and a drone," replied Joleen succinctly. "She thinks she's better than people like me, who work for a living. And all because she married a rich man and then drove him off to Abu Dhabi. And then hired a good lawyer."

How do you mean, a good lawyer?''

"The divorce settlement left her fixed for life."

"You don't think a woman ought to take money off her ex-husband?" Nudger asked.

"Not money she had nothing to do with earning. Not if there aren't any children involved. Let her get a job. Earn her own money like I do."

Nudger nodded, deeply impressed. Joleen was a wise woman, with a strong sense of justice.

"But you still didn't answer my question," he said. "Did Karen have a history of behaving rashly? Would you describe her as impulsive?"

Inside the trailer, a phone began to ring. Joleen stood up and moved toward the door, and Nudger got up from the step so she could pass. He could feel his underwear sticking to his buttocks from sitting on the mesh steel step. His rear end must look like a waffle.

Joleen brushed past him swiftly, not at all stiff from squatting so long in the same position.

"The answer is no," she said, before slamming the door. "No, no, no!"

Nudger wasn't convinced. There was a lot of sisterly loyalty operating here.

He waited a few minutes for Joleen, staring at the red-handled spade she'd left sticking in the ground, but she didn't come back outside.

Taking one of his business cards from his wallet, he scrawled a note on the back, asking Joleen to contact him if she thought of anything else she wanted to tell him. He tucked the card between door and frame, near the knob.

Then he crossed the street to the Granada and drove away.

CHAPTER TEN

Nudger had a Three-eighths Pounder, fries, and another vanilla milk shake at Shag's, then sat sipping a glass of water while he waited for the lunchtime crowd to drift back out into the afternoon heat. As people left and collective body heat diminished, it became comfortably cool in Shag's. Were it not for the thick and nauseating smell of fried grease and onions, the atmosphere would have been quite pleasant.

By one-thirty the place was empty except for Nudger, the teenage girl he'd seen behind the serving counter yesterday, and Heidran. The girl, whose name tag said she was Dorothy, bustled around for a while wiping down the brown plastic tables, then went outside.

She appeared outside the window a few minutes later dragging a hose and a bucket full of plastic bottles, then squirted the greasy pane where Nudger was seated, smiled in at him, and began making irritating sounds on the glass with a squeegee.

Nudger smiled back, then got up and walked over to where Heidran was counting those little plastic jugs of—he looked closely at the lettering on one of the peel-off lids—coffee whitener.

"Mizz Kreb," he said, "my name is Nudger."

She glanced up at him. "You made me lose count." Her brown Shag's uniform with the yellow collar fit her large, squarish body with military crispness. Her submarine commander's blue eyes were cold; she might have been telling him he'd made her miss an Allied ship with a torpedo.

"Sorry," he said. "I want to talk to you about Ray."

Now she seemed to give him total attention. Her eye's narrowed. For the first time, Nudger felt the full force of her personality and will. He had an inkling of what was scaring Ray. *Eeeeep!* screamed the squeegee.

"Who are you?" she demanded. "Are you a friend of Ray's?"

"Yes," Nudger said. But the single word turned his stomach, so he amended, "More a friend of his cousin, really. Danny Evers. He owns the doughnut shop down the street."

Heidran Kreb gave one bob of her formidable chin, granting him permission to speak.

"I understand you want to hire Ray to work here at Shag's."

"That's right." Almost absently, she began counting coffee-whitener containers again, sliding those she'd tallied into neat rows on the countertop as if working an abacus. "He put in an application, and Shag's has decided he's qualified."

"You mean you've decided."

"Same thing. I do the hiring at this unit."

"The problem is," Nudger said, "you wouldn't be doing Ray a favor by hiring him."

Heidran interrupted her counting to aim her cold gaze at him again. "You should know I've already heard the story about the injured back."

"You don't believe it?"

"Not entirely. I phoned Ray's previous employer at the trucking company. He doesn't believe it at all, but he said that contesting Ray's unemployment claim would be futile. In a roundabout way, so he couldn't get into any legal trouble, he strongly advised me not to hire Ray."

"Then why hire him?" Nudger knew the answer; he wanted to see how Heidran reacted to the question.

Her eyes softened. Slightly, but they softened. "I know Ray's a slacker, Mr. Nudger, but I see something else in him. I think that if he were given some motivation, made to do work and be proud of it, he'd soon straighten up and become a man."

Nudger swallowed. He was amazed to find himself genuinely touched.

Eeeeep! Dorothy smiled in at him again through glass so clean as to be invisible. She was a perky kid with an infectious smile. And obviously a hard worker. Nudger wondered if she'd been a shiftless teen drifting toward a troubled, slothful adulthood until being dramatically rescued by Heidran and Shag's.

Heidran said, "Bad back or not, there's nothing around here heavier than a hamburger."

"Those Three-eighths Pounders add up over the course of a day," Nudger said. Heidran didn't smile. He wondered if she would when Ray made the same observation with deadly seriousness. She really was underestimating Ray's dedication to worthlessness. "Ray's idea of a hard day," he told her, "is watching a Cubs game from his recliner without beer."

"That's *your* Ray," she said. "That's not the Ray I see."

"You're threatening to interrupt his unemployment benefits,"

Nudger said. "To Ray, that's like denouncing his religion and persecuting him. He'll hate you for it."

"At first, maybe. But time will pass, then he'll thank me for providing him with useful and profitable work. For giving him back his dignity."

"Ray perceives a certain dignity in avoiding toil," Nudger said. "I know him. I know the pride he takes in sidestepping responsibility."

"He's better than that," Heidran said simply.

"No, he's just Ray. If you'll forgive me for saying so, I think you see him in a different and more flattering light because of a fondness you feel for him. But if you'd switch off that light, you'd know the truth. What you see is what you get, and it's just Ray."

Heidran blushed and tucked her chin in. A few seconds passed before she could look Nudger in the eye.

"Do yourself, and Ray, a favor," Nudger said. "See him as simply another customer hooked on Shagburgers."

Heidran turned slightly and looked outside where Dorothy was laboring with the squeegee. Oh, no! Nudger thought. It was true!

"See that girl?" Heidran said, beginning to justify his fears. "When she came to work here three months ago her grammar was so mangled the drive-through customers couldn't understand her. Every other word she said was 'like' and she chewed gum with her mouth open. Look at her now."

Eeeeep!

"She appears to be a good soldier," Nudger admitted.

"And in three months that's what Ray will be. I promise you."

"I wish I could convince you," Nudger said, "that you won't be able to keep that promise. It's a silk purse and sow's ear situation. Ray will always be Ray."

"He cannot like himself the way he is," Heidran said.

"You're wrong. He's quite happy with himself. It's true that few other people like him, but he wouldn't care even if he were sensitive enough to notice."

Heidran leaned back and stared at Nudger as if she might hurl a lightning bolt at him. "You're being cruel, Mr. Nudger."

"It's Ray's position that you're the one being cruel."

"The difference is, I'm being cruel to be kind. To help him."

"You're threatening him with a job and dignity, when what he really wants is beer and potato chips."

Heidran gazed out a crystalline window and seemed to think that over. Then in a controlled, chilling voice, she said, "Tell Ray that when he is called, he should be ready to report for work immediately."

"I'm only trying to save you heartache," Nudger said, still pressing. After all, he'd promised Danny.

"The world would profit from fewer do-gooders like you and more men like Ray."

"It's men like Ray who make work for the do-gooders," Nudger pointed out. "Your misguided notion that you can reform him is a case in point."

An unnatural calm and stillness gripped Heidran's body. Nudger knew he had gone too far.

"Mr. Nudger, don't make me come around from behind this counter."

He took that as a suggestion that he should leave. She was determined and sincere. It amazed him to have met someone who saw even Ray as a person of basic decency and worth, and it made him think about Effie's faith in her brother Roger. Probably he could never be a murderer in her eyes. Even after his almost inevitable conviction, she would cling to her faith in him.

He shook his head and backed away, making it clear to Heidran that he was heading for the door. "I tried my best," he said.

"And a puny attempt it was. But don't feel bad. Any attempt would have fallen far short of the mark."

"Ray doesn't deserve you," Nudger said, letting her put whatever interpretation she wanted on the remark. What did it matter? There was a sense of unreality pervading this place anyway. Heidran would reform Ray when Shag's sold more hamburgers than McDonald's.

He crossed the brown tile floor, pushed open the door, and went outside.

Squirting soap onto a window, Dorothy, the former offensive elocutionist and gum-chewer, smiled dazzlingly at him.

"Great day, isn't it?" she remarked in the hundred-degree heat.

Had the world gone mad? Everyone was as naively optimistic as Roger Dupont.

But Nudger agreed with her, then got into the broiler that was the Granada and drove down Manchester to his office.

Chewing an antacid tablet, he sat at his desk and checked his messages, absently looking around at the uncharacteristic neatness of the office since he'd cleaned up the mess made by the intruder.

Beep: "This is Wilma Berkshire, Mr. Nudger. No one has yet contacted us about paying ransom for the recovery of Alan—"

Nudger fast-forwarded. Alan was a cat that was missing from the wealthy Wilma Berkshire, who had convinced herself he'd been abducted. Now she was debating on hiring Nudger, since she couldn't get the police interested. She was waiting for a call from the kid(cat?)napers, but Nudger thought it would never come. Alan had probably run away and been run over by a car or was shacked-up happily with a female cat from the wrong side of the tracks.

Beep: "You miserable bastard, Nudger—"

Eileen. Fast-forward.

Beep: "Lawrence Fleck here, Nudger. Hey, remember me? I expect people to be in when I call. They usually are, if they know it's going to be me. Why haven't you called and given me a progress report? The trial starts tomorrow, and if any other attorney had the popgun ammunition Dupont's given me he'd be certain dead meat. His client too, by the way. Let me know what the hell's going on. You should know my number. If you don't, ask anyone in the legal profession. Don't make me call you again. I—"

Nudger pressed the erase button. Then he chomped another ant-acid tablet and used the end of the half-roll that was left to peck out Fleck's office number.

"Nudger!" Fleck barked when the call had been put through. "Where have you been? What have you been doing for my money?"

"I—"

"I hired you to keep me informed, not in the dark."

"What I've—"

"I thought you and I had the understanding that—"

Nudger hung up.

He waited.

Ten minutes later the phone rang. He lifted the receiver on the fourth ring.

"Dammit, Nudger! Once the president hung up on me and lived to regret being rash!"

Nudger was thrown. "The President of the United States?"

"I didn't say that. Now what have you found out?"

"I talked to Effie Prang and Joleen Witt. Effie's your friend, Joleen isn't."

"Any new evidence?"

"No, it doesn't work that way. I'll keep asking around and eventually a picture will form."

"Eventually there'll be another ice age. The picture I'm getting is your fee—my money—flying out the window."

"Your money or Roger Dupont's?"

"At this point that doesn't matter. What counts is getting the best deal for my client. Which is why I employed you, my friend. Another attorney would have told you to get lost a long time ago. Know why?"

"No."

"Another attorney would have decided the hell with that poor naive innocent Roger Dupont and let him go to his death. I see injustice and I fight it. You believe that?"

"Sure."

"Then you're a poor dumb innocent like Dupont. What I'm talking about here is odds. Know why I hired you?"

"To make the odds better." Even as he answered Nudger realized he'd been pulled into another rapid-fire question-and-answer riff by the annoying little lawyer.

"Yes! Bingo! You score! I hired you to improve the odds in favor of my client. Have you done that?"

"I don't know. I'm—"

"So what are you gonna do about it? God's sake, Nudger, what have you got to tell me I can use?"

"You hired me because something other than your client and your toupee is crooked here, and you can't figure out what it is. I can't make the case fall open like your cheap briefcase; I haven't been on it long enough. You want to hire someone else?"

"Hey! Calm yourself. Don't get your back up for no reason like you been insulted. It's hypersensitive jerks like you who make justice hard to come by. Another attorney would fire your ass in a Philadelphia second, but not me. Know why? I see something in you makes me think you're the kinda loony's gotta keep digging till he finds the bone. Like a psycho bloodhound or something. Now don't get overconfident 'cause I complimented you. Just tell me what strikes you so far. Not facts, necessarily, but impressions. Can you at least do that much?"

"Effie Prang thought her brother's marriage to Karen was a mistake."

Silence. Then: "What the hell does that mean? You think she might've been in on it with her brother! Hey, you think that's possible? A conspiracy?"

"I don't know," Nudger said. "I'm trying to find out."

"Well, keep trying. And hard. Remember, they can say what they want, but I got faith in you."

"Everybody seems to have faith in somebody," Nudger said. "You in me, Effie in Roger, Heidran in Ray. Amazing."

"Who're Hydrant and Ray?"

"Heidran. It's a German name."

"You think a German's mixed up in this case?"

"I'm not ruling any country out at this point," Nudger said.

"You gonna be in court tomorrow afternoon?"

"As long as you promise not to defend me. By the way, I found out something else kind of interesting."

"So why didn't you tell me? I pay you good money and call you up and you make small-minded small talk—"

"Joleen hates Roger."

"Who? His sister-in-law?"

"The same Joleen. The presumed victim's sister."

"Hmm. Plenty of hate going around in that family."

"Maybe too much for Karen."

"Meaning?"

"Roger might be telling the truth. She simply might have gotten fed up with the lot of them and struck out for Chicago. Which would mean she's still alive and your client is innocent."

"Santa Claus, Nudger! You must believe in Santa Claus, the bunny that brings eggs, the tooth fairy, guardian angels—"

"That last," Nudger said.

"Well, Roger's gonna need his guardian angel if I can't convince him to plea-bargain. And he's got one. Know who I mean?"

"Yes," Nudger said, "and he has an ego for a halo."

"Listen, Nudger—"

Nudger hung up again.

This time Fleck didn't call back.

Thank God, Nudger thought, and peeled back the silver foil on his roll of antacid tablets.

CHAPTER ELEVEN

After finishing his antacid tablet, Nudger left the office and descended the hot stairway to the street door, then entered Danny's Donuts.

It was plenty hot in there, but a solitary customer on the end stool at the counter was braving it out to finish his Dunker Delite. He was a raggedly dressed, possibly homeless man named George whom Nudger had occasionally seen roaming Manchester late at night and poking around in the trash receptacles. George had a toothless grin, a yellow-white beard, and fierce blue eyes. Nudger figured Danny had probably treated him to the Dunker Delite and coffee. George didn't look happy about it, but he chewed and swallowed dutifully. A handout was a handout was a Dunker Delite.

Danny was wiping his hands on the gray towel tucked in his belt. Nudger didn't see anything on his hands; he knew the gesture was mostly nervous habit. Danny was so often wiping flour or grease from his hands that he went through the motions unconsciously dozens of times a day. He was watching George eat, a beatific expression of satisfaction on his basset-hound features, and when Nudger entered he looked over and smiled.

"Hi, Nudge. You talk to Ray?"

"Sure did," Nudger said, sitting down several stools away from George at the counter. "Talked to Heidran, too." He glanced over at George, who appeared to be in his own world and totally without interest in their conversation.

Danny let the gray towel fall limply against the front of his thigh and walked over to stand near Nudger. "You work fast. That's why I hired you."

Nudger didn't remember being hired, but he let it go.

"What'd Ray say?" Danny asked.

"Said to do everything possible so he wouldn't have to go to work."

Danny nodded solemnly. "Yeah. Well, you know . . . his back and all. And going to work right now would mess up his unemployment benefits."

"I mentioned that to Heidran. She wasn't impressed. She says the heaviest thing he'll have to lift is a hamburger. She has a point."

"Well, sometimes with a bad back, Nudge, it ain't the weight, it's more the bending motion."

"Sometimes it isn't even a bad back," Nudger said. "We both know Ray would rather sit out the summer slurping beer and watching Cubs baseball on television."

Danny glanced over at George, who ignored him and chewed. Danny lowered his voice anyway. "Between you and me, Nudge, you might be right. I mean, neither of us is a doctor, so we can't tell about a sore back. But Ray has always been on the slothful side."

"The man probably has two toes on each foot," Nudger said.

George glanced over but said nothing.

"So what can you do if Heidran phones and tells him to come in to work."

"I think he'll have to go, Danny. If he doesn't show up, my feeling is that Heidran's next call will be to Unemployment, and that will be the end of Ray's benefits."

Danny looked as if he might be about to cry. "I just don't understand. What's wrong with her? Why would she do a thing like that to Ray, make him go to work?"

"She thinks she can make man of him."

"That's silly, Nudge."

"I know, but she doesn't think so."

"She blind?"

"In a sense."

"Whoa," Danny said. "I'm forgetting my manners. You had supper?"

"No, but I've got to run," Nudger said, suddenly alarmed at the prospect of a free Dunker Delite headed his way like a Scud missile. "Got to interview a witness."

"Oh, that Roger Dupont thing."

"Right." Nudger got down off his stool.

"Wait up! Take one to go!" Danny hurried over to the display counter and got out a Dunker Delite, which he handed to Nudger on its white napkin.

"Thanks, Danny." Nudger took the weighty object and held it down at his side. "I'll eat it while I drive." He turned to leave.

"Make a man of Ray, huh?" Danny said. He seemed bemused.

"So she says, though not in so many words."

"Who's she think she is, the Marines?"

"You talkin' about that Heidran works down at Shag's?" George asked abruptly.

Nudger and Danny stared at each other and nodded.

"She's the Marines," George said. He belched then began work again on his Dunker Delite, apparently determined to finish it so he wouldn't have to eat again for several days.

Nudger carried his Dunker Delite something like a football as he jogged across Manchester, dodging traffic like a broken-field runner, to where the Granada was parked by the faulty meter. The quarter-size slug was still jutting from the meter's coin slot, where it was stuck firmly, making it obvious to the police that the problem was mechanical and the city's and no blame could be attached to the driver of the car parked alongside.

Inside the Granada, Nudger got the engine and air conditioner started, then pulled away from the curb. After driving about a block, he tossed the Dunker Delite on the floor, telling himself not to forget to remove it before Danny might find it. The last time he'd left one on the floor and forgotten it, Danny had been walking toward the car to get in when Nudger saw the thing. Leaning across the seat, Nudger had been able to slide the Dunker Delite out onto the ground, but that was the best he could do. Fortunately, as Danny rounded the car to get in on the passenger side, a woman walking a dog passed, so the Dunker Delite didn't draw any undue attention.

He decided that since he was in the car and moving, he might as well do what he'd told Danny and drive over to University City and see if he could talk to Roger Dupont's neighbor. The woman who supposedly had heard screaming the night of Karen Dupont's disappearance.

Twenty minutes later, he parked in front of Dupont's house on Devlon. It was pretty much as Fleck had described, moderately expensive in an upper-middle-class neighborhood of professional people and faculty members from nearby Washington University. Nice, but several hundred thousand dollars below the value of Effie Prang's house in the more affluent suburb of Ladue.

Most of the houses on Devlon were about the same age, maybe sixty or seventy years old, brick with some stucco here and there, and tile roofs. Dupont's had lots of stucco and some exposed beams to make it seem English Tudor. There was a two-car garage attached that looked newer than the rest of the house.

Nudger wanted to talk to the neighbor, a Miss Alicia Van Moke, without Dupont seeing him if he happened to be home. So he parked a hundred yards beyond both houses, then strolled back along the tree-shaded sidewalk.

The Van Moke house was separated from Dupont's by about twenty feet of yard overgrown with ivy. Some of the ivy was crawling up the brick sides of both houses. Nudger quickly made his way along a curved, stepping-stone walk to a concrete front porch with an arched, tiled roof. As he'd walked, he'd gotten a glimpse of the small pool and tennis court in Dupont's backyard. They weren't in a league with Effie Prang's; the pool was round and reminded Nudger of a fish pond with a diving board, and the tennis court had weeds growing up through cracks in its blacktop surface. Still, court and pool were good for working up a sweat then cooling down.

Nudger pressed the doorbell button and Westminster chimes sounded inside the Van Moke house.

A moment later a tall, thin woman with straight gray hair and dramatic features with high cheekbones opened the door and stared out at him. She was in her mid-fifties but dressed and carried herself as she might have thirty years ago. She wore a long gray dress that was loose-fitting and almost shapeless, large silver bangle bracelets on each arm, black leather sandals. She smelled fresh and clean, not like perfumed soap but like exotic spices Nudger couldn't identify.

He introduced himself and explained that he was investigating the Karen Dupont disappearance.

Alicia Van Moke started to say something, then caught herself and smiled. "Won't you come in, please?" she said, instead of what she'd originally begun saying.

Nudger followed her into a foyer, then through a room furnished in dark woods and Oriental print drapes and carpet. There was a lovely Steinway upright piano in one corner with dog-eared sheet music opened on it beneath a brass lamp. Nudger got the impression the piano was played frequently.

When they'd reached a large room, more brightly furnished in lighter woods and pale blue throw rugs, Alicia Van Moke asked Nudger if he wanted something to drink. He told her ice water would be fine, then stood in the center of the room and looked around. There were two large ceiling fans slowly rotating, rows of windows with white mini-blinds raised high so the view outside was visible beyond potted plants hanging from the low eaves on the outside of the house. A glass-fronted set of shelves held books haphazardly placed at angles against each other. At least two of them were books of poems by Alicia Van Moke.

Nudger looked back outside. What had really caught his attention were the obvious signs of recent digging in the Dupont yard next door.

Alicia Van Moke returned and handed Nudger a large, stemmed goblet of water with cracked ice in it. An ornate *AVM* was engraved on the side of the glass.

"I understand you're a poet," Nudger said.

She smiled slightly as if pleased by his knowing. He decided not to tell her he'd deduced that by looking at her bookshelves.

"Of some small reputation," she said, still smiling. She really must have been beautiful when she was younger, but in a more conventional sense. Her beauty was different now and perhaps more impressive. She'd held its essence and doubtless would until she died—it was in her direct gray eyes and effortlessly erect bearing, in her character.

He realized she knew he was admiring her. He looked away and sipped ice water.

"Do you know if Roger Dupont is home now?" he asked.

"He isn't. He's been out on bail, but since the trial starts tomorrow, he's been incarcerated again. Is it the usual thing for an accused killer to be roaming around on bail while awaiting trial?"

"Not the usual," Nudger said, "but it happens."

"Among upper-class White folks like Roger," she said with a trace of bitterness. "Bankers and such."

"Generally they're the ones," Nudger said. "Were you afraid? I mean, with an accused murderer next door?"

"No," she said. That was all, simply no.

"Do you think he killed his wife?"

"I'm not sure. I understand there's a great deal of evidence against him. The trout in the milk."

"Pardon?"

"Circumstantial evidence. Someone once said it could be strong but wrong, such as when one finds a trout in the milk. The milk is assumed to be water, but it's still milk."

"I see," Nudger said. He thought he did.

"I really can't tell you much," Alicia Van Moke said. "The Duponts and I have been neighbors for quite a while, but we really didn't know each other well. We got along, exchanged pleasantries, but that's all. I travel a great deal, and when I am home, I usually stay in the house."

"You live alone, then."

"No. I have my books and my work."

And no time for people like the Duponts, Nudger thought.

"The only times I saw much of Roger were when he was out on his tennis court. He's a very noisy player. Always urging himself on, taunting his opponent, telling the ball to drop in. He'd only be quiet when he was losing." She gave her placid smile. "I treasured those times. I'd get some peace."

"Did he lose often?"

"No."

"He was very good then."

"Not really. If somebody beat him, he wouldn't invite that person over again."

Nudger took another sip of water. He had the feeling that Alicia Van Moke was assessing him, playing out line to see how he swam. Or rope to see something else altogether. "You said you didn't know the Duponts," he told her, "but did you know *about* them?"

She smiled again, as if he'd done something right. "They argued a lot. They were loud. I don't think he physically abused her, but they quarreled."

"About what?"

"Things that didn't matter."

"Someone told me Karen Dupont was impulsive."

"Was it meant as a compliment?"

"I'm sorry?"

"Did the person who said this think that impulsiveness was a good or bad thing?"

You had to think hard, talking to a poet. Nudger considered Effie Prang and said, "This person feels that impulsiveness is bad."

"Ah. Our impressions probably won't jibe, then. I think impulsiveness is a very good thing"—she shot him another disturbing look—"and I would never have called Karen impulsive. Quite the opposite."

"How so?"

"She was such a dedicated little hausfrau. Everytime I looked out the window I'd see her slaving over her house and grounds. She wanted it all to be perfect. That's so hard, and such a waste of effort, with a seventy-year-old house. Perfection is for the new. The old should wear their imperfections proudly, don't you think?"

She gave him another direct look. Nudger was feeling out of his depth here. "Do you think there's any chance that Roger's story's true? That Karen left him and went to Chicago?"

"I can't see Karen leaving her house. I think she would have done the old-fashioned thing: stayed in the house and ordered him out."

"I don't think Roger was the type to go quietly."

"Well," said Alicia Van Moke, "there you are."

She stood hip-shot in her long, loose gray dress, shapeless except for the tantalizing hint of her shape beneath. It seemed a deliberately seductive pose. When he didn't say anything, she said, "There really isn't much I can tell you. No more than I told the police."

So she wasn't assuming he was from a law enforcement agency. "You told them you heard Karen scream at around eleven o'clock," Nudger said.

"Three minutes after. I was in bed, reading, and I looked over at the clock."

"What kind of scream was it?"

"She screamed, 'No! Stop! Stop! No!' and then was silent. Those words, in that precise order." Again the wise smile that suggested images of wildflowers beneath wide skies, calm as a prairie with its secret knowledge and perhaps secret desires. "I thought it was simply another of their arguments. It's a shame they couldn't maintain the tender and fulfilling intimacy that so enriches the lives of men and women who are in love or at least in lust with each other."

"I'd like to read some of your poetry," Nudger said nervously.

"It's in most libraries."

So, she was a pro. No free books.

She turned to stare out the window toward the Duponts' back-yard, and so did he.

"It looks as if the police have been doing a lot of digging," he said.

She nodded, still with her back to him. "Yes. Searching for Karen. I tried to get them to search over here on this side of the fence." She twisted her long body gracefully to gaze over her shoulder at him. "I need my soil turned, Mr. Nudger. Need it badly."

Puzzled, he thought he'd better get out of there. Poets! Ignoring the weakness in his knees, he thanked her for the water and her time.

She saw him to the door, walking so close to him that the long gray dress flowed and rustled against his leg.

"The police aren't as thorough as they think," she said. "They didn't find the door key the Duponts kept in the artificial rock near their front porch."

"Artificial rock?"

"Yes. One of those cheap mail-order gimmicks they sell to make people think they're clever. Well, it was clever enough that the police, as far as I know, never noticed it. The rock hasn't been moved."

Nudger didn't think that was such an indictment of the police. After all, they were searching for something considerably larger than a key. Still, a phony rock, probably with a seam in it. Or maybe it was more realistic than he thought. "Were you watching to see if the police found the fake rock?" he asked.

She smiled. "I take my amusement where I can, Mr. Nudger."

Nudger swallowed.

"If I think of anything else, I'll call you," she said, when he was standing out on the porch in the evening heat.

Not knowing what else to say, he thanked her again.

Driving away, he wondered if Alicia Van Moke really had been coming on to him, or if he'd been imagining it. He did that sometimes, he had to admit.

Her scent was still with him even in the car, erotic—no, exotic—spices. She'd seemed to send signals he could almost feel, yet she hadn't actually invited him to stay.

But the woman wrote poetry, so she wouldn't say anything directly. It wouldn't be in her nature. He couldn't imagine Alicia Van Moke saying, "Hey, big boy, wanna party?" Not even when she was younger.

But he knew how different reality could be from imagination. The gap between the two was one of the things that kept him working more or less steadily. The private Alicia Van Moke might be quite different from the public one.

As he turned onto Midland Avenue, he wondered if her next-door neighbor, the alleged murderer and womanizer Roger Dupont, read poetry.

CHAPTER TWELVE

Nudger went to his office and phoned Terry Donnelly over at the Maplewood Library and asked him if he'd check under "Authors" for Alicia Van Moke.

"I don't have to, Nudge," Terry told him. "She's a well-known local poet, and we have all her books."

"All? How many is that?"

"I don't know exactly. Maybe half a dozen. She's won several national competitions, and her work's been published mostly by university presses, collections of her poems from literary magazines. But that puts her into the major league of poets. In our society, even the best poets work cheap.''

"Like private investigators," Nudger said.

Terry said nothing. Apparently he didn't think Alicia Van Moke was to poetry what Nudger was to investigation.

Nudger thanked him and asked him to hold a few Alicia Van Moke collections for him, just in case the library experienced a run on her books. Terry assured him her work would be there waiting for him to pick it up, then reminded him that his library card had been expired for the past two months. Always something.

After hanging up on the library, Nudger phoned Claudia and invited her to dinner at Shoney's on Manchester, where they often met and enjoyed the salad bar, which happened to be the most economical choice on the menu. She declined, telling him she had summer-school papers to grade, but she would meet him in an hour at Ted Drewes frozen custard stand on Chippewa, where they also often met and enjoyed Chocolate Chip Concretes while sitting in his car listening to Cardinals' ball games.

Nudger used the extra time to pick up the Alicia Van Moke books at the library and renew his card. He placed the books in a clean area of the Granada's trunk, then drove east on Manchester and cut over Southwest Avenue to McCausland to wind his way to Chippewa where he was to meet Claudia.

Ted Drewes was a mob scene, as it was every hot summer night when there weren't thunderstorms and tornado warnings. The little white clapboard stand with the carved wooden icicles lining its peaked roof was surrounded by at least a hundred people. A uniformed cop was keeping an eye on things and directing traffic as Nudger steered the Granada into the lot and found a parking space facing Chippewa.

He didn't see Claudia's little blue Chevette anywhere, so he cranked down all the Granada's windows to let the breeze through, then walked back and got one of Alicia Van Moke's books out of the trunk.

Ignoring the turmoil of frozen custard eaters around him, he settled back to sample *Breezes of Youth*. The book was small and had a pale blue cover with an illustration of a young girl with flowing hair sitting under a shade tree. It had been published in 1987 and the dedication was to someone named Oscar Bennedict. As Nudger leafed through it, a poem titled "Fashion and Passion" caught his eye:

> Thirty-four A's and shoes size nines
> Four-inch heels and daring necklines
> Gaunt women with bereaved eyes
> Strutting, hungry for sex and lies
> A jutting hip
> A tongue-wet lip
> Offers passion, stay a while
> A fashion always in style

Hey, Nudger thought, this was hot stuff. He couldn't help imagining Alicia Van Moke—

"Hi, Nudge." Claudia was leaning close to the open car window and smiling. "What are you reading? Not another of those John Grisham novels, I hope."

"Poetry," Nudger said, hurriedly closing the book.

"Good." She narrowed her dark eyes at him. "Why?"

"Part of a case I'm working on. I could use your judgment on this. Let's get our Concretes and you can have a look and see if you think this poet is any good."

Claudia was silent as Nudger got out of the car and they stood in the nearest of half a dozen lines, waiting their turn so one of the horde of teenagers with yellow TED DREWES T-shirts could convey his order so the yellow-shirted workers in the background could speed around and fill it. Nudger wondered where Ted Drewes found such ambitious and hard-working teens. Flitting about and serving up custard concoctions inside the little white structure, they reminded him of worker bees inside a hive. Making money instead of honey. Oh-oh, already reading Alicia Van Moke had affected him.

Claudia was wearing a sleeveless white blouse, dark blue shorts, and black leather sandals. She was drawing quite a few stares from admiring males. Nudger didn't mind. Anyway, the men soon were concentrating again on whatever they intended to order at the serving window; the more immediate need of frozen custard was becoming increasingly accessible.

He and Claudia each got their usual medium-size Chocolate Chip Concrete, then dodged a stretch limo—not an unusual sight at the perpetually trendy custard stand—and returned to the Granada.

Nudger switched on the radio and tuned to the Cardinals ball game, which turned out to be a scoreless pitchers' duel with the Cincinnati Reds.

At the moment, Claudia wasn't interested in baseball. She spooned in a few bites of her Concrete so it wouldn't overflow the paper cup's rim and drop onto her shorts or bare legs, then stuck the plastic spoon in the thick concoction like a flag and picked up *Breezes of Youth*.

"Oh," she said, "this is by Alicia Van Moke."

Nudger wondered if he was the only one who'd not previously heard of this woman.

"She any good?" he asked.

"I don't have to read any of the poems to tell you she is. I've read her work before, even assigned some to my sophomore English class. She's one of the best in the country. Certainly in the midwest. What's her poetry have to do with the Dupont case?"

"She lives next door to the Duponts in University City."

"No kidding?" Claudia was obviously fascinated. A glob of Concrete dropped from her tilted cup onto her leg. She absently reached for one of the paper napkins they'd brought from the serving counter and wiped her thigh clean before Nudger could gallantly offer to lick the frozen custard away.

Alicia Van Moke again, affecting his thought processes. Some poet.

But then, Nudger was at times a romantic. He thought so, anyway.

Claudia asked him to explain, and they slowly ate their Concretes while he brought her up to date on the Dupont case, ending with his visit with Alicia Van Moke. He left out the part about him thinking the famous poet was coming on to him. Why complicate the tale?

"Fascinating," Claudia said, dabbing at her lips with the napkin she'd used on her thigh.

"She remembered exactly what Karen Dupont screamed the night Roger says she left him of her own volition."

"When a witness like that quotes someone verbatim, it carries weight in court," Claudia said.

"I'm sure the prosecution will have her say it in court." Nudger scooped the last spoonful of his Concrete with the usual regret and guilt. Regret that there was no more of the addictive stuff, and guilt that he'd surrendered to desire and ingested the calories.

But Concretes always calmed his jittery stomach. Their ingredients were kept secret, so maybe they contained an antacid.

Claudia handed him her empty cup and the wadded napkin to throw away. He fit her cup in his own, then got out of the car and dropped them in one of the orange-lidded trash receptacles placed around the parking lot. Traffic was backed up on Chippewa now, waiting to turn into the lot, and another cop was on duty. Yuppies from West County, as well as local South St. Louisans, would crowd around the custard stand until it closed in the fall and was later converted to a busy Christmas tree lot. The place must be a gold mine, Nudger thought. Why couldn't he come up with an idea for a business like this? Something he was more suited for and was easier on his nervous stomach. Something more profitable. Why wasn't Danny's Donuts overrun by customers like this?

But he knew why.

When he got back in the car, the Cincinnati pitcher struck Ozzie Smith in the back with a fastball. The crowd became incensed. The announcer Mike Shannon, himself incensed, said that Smith, apparently also incensed, was charging the mound. Nudger held his breath. Smith, while a great ballplayer, was not a big man, and the Cincinnati pitcher was huge.

Fortunately, the Cincinnati catcher put a bear hug on Smith as players from both benches charged onto the field and fought in the usual baseball manner, wherein there were few injuries to valuable skilled bodies.

The crowd and the announcer loved it.

Claudia said, "Why can't they just play baseball?"

"That is baseball," Nudger said.

"That's baseball and testosterone," she corrected. "The evil hormone."

Nudger thought of mentioning how dull women's softball was but thought better of it. This was a time for political correctness rather than honesty. And there existed, at least in Nudger's mind, the possibility that he'd return with Claudia to her apartment. How right she was about testosterone.

"Do you think Alicia Van Moke was having an affair with Roger Dupont?" Claudia asked.

Nudger was surprised. "Why on earth would you suggest such a thing?"

"I remember one of her poems, 'Fashion and Passion.' "

"Hmm," Nudger said. "I'll have to read it."

No sooner had the announcer said the field was cleared and play was resumed when the Cincinnati pitcher hit the next batter in the arm. The umpire ejected the pitcher. All hell broke loose at the ballpark. The announcer was screaming.

"Throw the Cincinnati manager out!" Nudger shouted, upset by this turn of events and gross injustice. Other men, and a few women, in other cars with radios tuned to the ball game were shouting.

"So stupid," Claudia said. "They should be playing baseball."

"Have you ever seen a women's softball game?" Nudger asked.

In bed alone in his apartment that night, he watched the ten o'clock news on TV. Somber anchorman Julius Hunter mentioned that Roger Dupont was going to trial tomorrow, and there was a taped update on the case. Alicia Van Moke was shown quoting Karen Dupont the night of her alleged murder. "No! Stop! Stop! No!" Exactly as she'd described Karen's screams to Nudger.

Nudger fell asleep wondering how Lawrence Fleck was going to dance around that one.

CHAPTER THIRTEEN

The St. Louis County Courthouse was an imposing old building that stood atop a hill in downtown Clayton. Trials were no longer held in it, though. Roger Dupont's fate would be decided in the Courts Building, on Central Avenue behind the Old Courthouse. It was a tall, boxy structure that looked just like the office buildings around it, except for the line of police cars parked in front of it, and the prison vans waiting at the rear entrance.

The courtroom in which *State of Missouri v. Dupont* was being heard was deceptively bright and cheerful, with cream-colored walls and a lot of polished wood. The spectator area was crowded.

As he entered and sat down toward the back, Nudger saw several people he recognized as being from the news media. This case was interesting to the public and good for readers and ratings. One of the TV newscasts had even run a poll to see if the viewing public thought Dupont was guilty. By a wide margin, they'd convicted him. A new poll was considered to see if he should be executed. Nudger wondered if the courts could be eliminated and the whole thing done by television polls.

Roger Dupont, wearing a plain gray suit and a white shirt with a blue-and-red paisley tie, sat next to Lawrence Fleck at a table on the right of the bench. Fleck was wearing a not-so-muted brown plaid suit with a red shirt and red-and-green tie and looked more prepared to sell the jury a used car than to convince them of a defendant's innocence. The prosecutor was Seymour Wister, a shark of a lawyer Nudger had seen in action during a previous murder trial, when he'd so persuaded the jury of the defendant's guilt that they disobeyed the judge's instructions and recommended two death sentences to run concurrently. The prosecutorial team were all dressed like attorneys, which made Fleck look like an underdog.

The judge was Robert MacMasters, a dignified, handsome, no-nonsense type of man, and not the sort to doze on the bench. He had sharp and intelligent blue eyes that were about all he needed to maintain order in his court.

Wister, a tall, painfully thin man with a hatchet face and bushy gray eyebrows, came out from behind the prosecutor's table and surveyed the jury with keen gray eyes. He had thick, graying hair, razor-cut but left long in back to lend him a biblical appearance.

Jury selection had honed the group down to five men and seven women, some of whom had claimed they'd never heard of the Dupont case and so could be impartial, some of whom admitted knowing something of the case while maintaining they could achieve impartiality. They looked like a cross-section of folks you might meet at a PTA meeting where money for the school play was being discussed. Death, like life, could be a crap shoot.

"The prosecution will prove that Roger Dupont—" Wister pointed directly at Dupont, who smiled slightly—"murdered his wife Karen and disposed of her body in a place as yet unknown.

The witnesses will attest to this fact, the evidence is overwhelming . . .''

Nudger tuned him out while he continued stating his case for another ten minutes, playing to the press as well as the jury, saying the same thing in different ways, drilling it into the minds of the jurors through repetition: Dupont was a killer.

When Wister finally sat down and it was Fleck's turn, Fleck strutted out to face the jury and said, "Everything you've just heard about my client is untrue. Not lies, necessarily, but untrue. You know the difference? Of course not. Well, I'm here to show you the difference, and it's going to make the difference. You understand? Well, you will understand. My client is innocent."

He returned to the table, sat down beside Dupont, and became interested in some papers in one of his opened brown cardboard accordion folders.

Dupont stared at him. MacMasters stared at him. Wister and his team stared straight ahead and looked smug.

MacMasters shook his head slightly, then instructed the prosecution to begin presenting its case.

It didn't go well for Dupont. The prosecution called the lead investigating officer to the stand. He was Detective Sal Vincenzo, and he was about fifty years old with a face like a topographical map of his hard years as a cop. An experienced witness, his answers to Wister's questions were concise and delivered in a terse, clipped voice. He testified that the police had gone to see Dupont after Joleen Witt reported her sister missing. Roger's dubious story of Karen's disappearance, his evasiveness, and initial unwillingness to let them search the house for clues, made them even more suspicious. Then they'd found the muddy shovel in his car's trunk, strands of hair on the shovel that matched a sample from Karen's comb, the singed panties, the partially melted earring in the furnace, and the bloodstain on the defendant's garage floor.

That bloodstain was something Nudger hadn't known about.

On and on went the litany of evidence pointing to the extreme likelihood that Dupont had murdered his wife. By the time he was finished with Vincenzo's testimony, Wister was absolutely gloating.

When Wister had settled back down at the prosecutors' table, Fleck stood up and strode forward with an indignant expression on his florid pug face. Vincenzo was still on the stand, placidly waiting to be cross-examined.

"The shovel you found in the car," Fleck said, "did it or did it not contain traces of blood?"

"It did not," Vincenzo said.

"Was the plastic drop cloth in the car's trunk tested for signs that it had come in contact with a body?"

"It was."

"And were the results positive?"

"Negative."

"Is that a no?"

"Yes. Negative."

"Yes, it was a no?"

"No, it was a yes. I mean, to your second question. The drop cloth tested—"

"Will the prosecution stipulate that the plastic drop cloth found in the defendant's car tested negative?" Judge MacMasters interrupted impatiently.

"Inconclusive, your honor," Wister said.

"Well, make up your mind."

"I mean, the tests were inconclusive. The prosecution maintains that though no signs of the victim's body remained on the plastic, it could still have been used to transport the body. The drop cloth could have been washed and then replaced in the trunk."

"Is that the testimony of the witness?" MacMasters asked.

Vincenzo, no fool, repeated Wister almost word for word.

"Was the tiny stain of blood found on Mr. Dupont's garage floor a match with the supposed victim's blood?'' Fleck asked, forging ahead.

"It was the same type."

"I didn't ask you that," Fleck snapped.

Vincenzo didn't look the slightest bit annoyed. "The types matched," he tried.

"What about DNA analysis?"

"Comparisons were made with DNA samples taken from hair follicles from hair in the victim's comb, and from hairs imbedded in mud found on the shovel in the trunk of the defendant's car."

"What were the results?"

"We were told not to rule out that the blood could be that of Karen Dupont."

"Yes, but were the tests not inconclusive as to a precise DNA match?"

"Yes."

"You are saying they were conclusive?"

Vincenzo looked thoughtful. "No."

"Then they were inconclusive."

"Yes. They weren't conclusive."

"Then is it not true that they did not match?"

"No, it is not not true—I mean, yes, they did not match conclusively as to DNA analysis. But the sample was small and there was a strong likelihood of a match, and considering that the blood type was the same as Karen Dupont's, we determined that it was probably her blood."

"What type was the blood?"

"Type O."

Fleck smiled. "I happen to know that Judge MacMaster's blood is type O. Have you questioned him about Karen Dupont's disappearance? Have your officers searched his home and dug up his yard? Are you, by God, insinuating that Judge MacMasters had something to do with this alleged murder?"

People around Nudger gasped. Now Vincenzo raised his eyebrows in surprise and a kind of awe mixed with revulsion. He stared at Fleck as if he would like to stamp him out before he had a chance to multiply. Nudger knew the feeling.

"Objection!" Wister was on his feet, a forefinger raised to point to the ceiling.

There were a few snickers, and a murmuring ran through the courtroom.

MacMasters appeared pained and held out both hands as a signal for everyone to settle down. He looked at Fleck as if he were particularly unpleasant roadkill.

"We'll recess for a few minutes while counsel from both sides joins me in my chambers." He stood up with slow dignity, as if his back ached, and disappeared through a door set in the wood paneling.

Fleck and Wister followed him. Fleck made a big deal about letting Wister enter first.

Nudger looked over at Dupont. He was sitting motionless, staring at a painting of Thomas Jefferson on the wall behind the magistrates' bench. He might have been smiling, or maybe it was simply the way his face looked in repose.

The hard bench seat was getting uncomfortable, and sitting hunched over and listening intently was making Nudger's stomach twitch and threatening to give him heartburn.

He thought he might as well leave. He could pretty much tell the way the trial was headed even at this early date. Dupont was going to be convicted and both he and his lawyer would be executed.

He stood up, squeezed past the knees of the heavyset woman who'd been sitting next to him, and left the courtroom.

Out in the hall, he tucked in the back of his shirt, making sure not to get the material beneath the elastic band of his underwear, then made for the elevator.

As he stood waiting to descend, he wondered about that bloodstain on the garage floor. Fleck seemed to have known about it, even to the point of having foraged about for the presiding judge's medical records so he could play Perry Mason in court, but he hadn't mentioned the blood to Nudger. Nudger would have to ask him about it.

It seemed pertinent, as Seymour Wister would say and Fleck would contest.

CHAPTER FOURTEEN

Nudger drove from the courthouse in Clayton to downtown St. Louis and parked at a meter opposite Merchant Federal Bank on Locust Street, where Roger Dupont was a Vice President. The sun had climbed high and even tall buildings cast too little shade to provide relief. It was that time of year in St. Louis where the relentless heat that subsided only slightly at night killed the old folks cooped up in their brick flats and apartments, especially those in the rougher neighborhoods where to leave a window open was to invite an intruder. Charitable organizations provided them with free fans, but when there was only heated air to move, the fans did little to ease their suffering.

Nudger got out of the car and stood in the heat, then crossed the street when the light at the corner turned red and the flow of traffic temporarily ceased.

It was cool inside Merchant Federal, made to seem cooler by the high-ceilinged vastness and all the cold black-veined gray marble, and maybe all that cold cash. Where there wasn't marble there was dark, heavily grained walnut.

Nudger walked over to one of several long walnut tables. On it were pens attached with cords to black plastic holders, next to wooden racks stuffed with deposit and withdrawal slips and interest rate information. He stood and doodled for a while on the back of a deposit slip while he studied the tellers behind the old-fashioned brass-barred cages, the gray-haired, helpful woman behind the information desk, the conservatively dressed men and women seated at desks. To his right was the loan department with separate frosted glass cubicles making up small offices. At the opposite end of the long lobby was a small area defined by a low wooden rail, where a man and a woman sat at desks facing each other and sold mutual funds to those savers unhappy with interest rates on their savings. These were uncertain times, for savers and for bank vice presidents accused of murder.

He looked down at what he'd absently doodled on the deposit slip, just in case his unconscious mind knew something his conscious mind didn't. A number of crude, identical fish, and some simple five-pointed stars. What did they mean?

He stared for a while then decided they probably meant that his meager artistic talent was confined to drawing fish and stars.

After crumpling the deposit slip and dropping it into one of the green metal trash receptacles under the table, he walked back outside and returned to the parked Granada.

Pigeons had fouled its windshield. Nudger tried the windshield squirts but they were out of water and the wipers made more of a mess. He sat in the hot Granada, slightly sick to his stomach, and kept his eyes trained to the side, on Merchant Federal. It was almost noon, and some of the employees would surely be leaving soon to go to lunch.

A fluttering in the corner of his eye caught his attention. Through the smeared windshield he saw that a gray and white pigeon had flapped to a landing on the car's hood. Actually on the hood, where it strutted about with its feathered chest puffed out, too proud to notice the heated metal that should be making it uncomfortable.

Nudger refused to pay attention to it.

* * *

At four minutes past noon, two of the tellers, a man and a woman Nudger had made note of inside the bank, walked out onto the sidewalk and headed east together. He thought about getting out of the car and following them, when one of the women he'd seen behind a new-accounts desk emerged from the bank. She walked west along Locust.

He climbed out of the car, hurriedly stuffed another quarter into the meter, and followed her.

Near Sixteenth Street she entered a small restaurant. Nudger stood across the street for a while and was about to go in after her, but she came out carrying a waxed cup with a straw stuck in it. In her other hand was a lidded white foam container she was being careful to hold perfectly level.

He followed her several blocks south, until she got to the Serra Sculpture, a piece of artwork that to Nudger looked like a rusty iron temporary wall surrounding a construction site in the middle of a grassy lot. None of the walls met at the corners. That was how Serra saw the world, Nudger guessed. He might have a point there.

The woman sat down on the grass near where two of the walls did not meet, crossed her legs beneath her, and set the cup down on the grass. Then she opened the foam container. She began eating her carryout lunch—some sort of pasta—with a white plastic fork.

Nudger strolled over and smiled down at her. She was a pale blonde woman in her forties with a blotchy complexion and strangely oblong hazel eyes. She wore no makeup. The slight breeze plastered her thin dress to her skinny frame. It was a white dress with a blue flower print on it and a crinkly kind of white panel over her meager breasts that came high up on her neck. From his extreme angle, Nudger glimpsed what might have been burn scars beneath the edge of the panel's delicate material.

"Millie Cookson?" he asked, remembering her name from her brass desk plaque.

She chewed pasta and gazed up at him with her oblong eyes,

then nodded. He got the impression she would have walked away from him if she hadn't been sitting there cross-legged on the grass with her lunch spread out before her.

"My name's Nudger," he said, squatting down next to her. Gee, that hurt his knees. He scrunched around on his heels until he found a more comfortable position, but his knees still ached. "I'm investigating the death of Roger Dupont's wife."

"You police?" she asked, in a way that suggested distrust.

"No. Quite the contrary. I'm private."

She took a sip of what looked like iced tea from her paper cup and blatantly looked him up and down. "Who or what are you working for?"

"Truth, justice, and the contrarian way."

She placed her cup back on the grass. "Sounds right."

"Have the police questioned you?" he asked.

"Only briefly. They talked to just about everyone at the bank."

"Do you know Roger Dupont well?"

"No."

"Do you think he's guilty?"

"I'm not sure. What do you think?"

"Innocent," Nudger said. Maybe he could provoke her into saying something meaningful.

"I don't think he's innocent," she said slowly. "I think he might have done it."

"Did you tell the police that?"

"No. But then they didn't ask my opinion. I was thinking of something I saw about two months ago, but it might not have anything to do with anything."

Nudger waited, staring at the Serra Sculpture, wondering if it really was a monstrosity or if it was artistically beyond a guy who drew fish and stars. He remained silent, knowing when not to push.

"I was eating lunch here," Millie said, "near where I am now, when I saw him with a woman."

"Hmm. Could it have been his wife, come downtown to meet him for lunch?"

"Maybe. I don't know what she looked—looks like."

"Pretty, medium-length dark hair."

"That's what this woman looked like."

"So maybe he was just having lunch with his wife."

"Maybe. But they were on the grass inside the walls of the sculpture, lying on something like a beach towel."

"It's not unusual for people to go inside the walls," Nudger pointed out. "I read somewhere that's the idea of the sculpture; you go inside and look out through the spaces where the walls don't meet at the corners. Or what would ordinarily be the corners. Do you like this thing?"

"I never gave it much thought. But that's how I happened to see them, when I glanced in through that space right over there." She motioned with her hand not holding the fork. "They were side by side, and Dupont wasn't acting toward her anything like my ex-husband used to act toward me. Are you married, Mr. ? . . .

"Nudger. No. I'm divorced."

"Aren't we all?" Millie said with an air of despondence.

"How was Dupont treating the woman?" Nudger asked. "What exactly was he doing that your husband never did?"

"Oh, you know. Kissing her every now and then like he really meant it. They had some stuff on the towel that looked like it was carryout food, but they weren't paying much attention to it. They were hungry for each other." She poked at her pasta with the plastic fork. "If I sound envious, I guess I am."

"Envious because the woman was with Dupont."

Millie appeared horrified. "God, no! Dupont doesn't appeal to me at all. And besides, he's married. Or was. Is. Who knows for sure?"

"Not me," Nudger said. "But right now it looks like he'll be convicted."

"Even though you said he was innocent?"

"Everyone who gets near his lawyer in court might be found guilty," Nudger said.

Millie stared at him curiously but didn't ask him to explain.

"Would you recognize the dark-haired woman if you saw her again?" Nudger asked.

"Oh, I doubt it. But it's possible. Her hair wasn't just dark brown; it was so black it shone almost blue. 'Raven,' they call it on the hair-coloring bottles. Do you know what I mean?"

"I know."

"Almost as soon as I saw them, I scooted over a few feet. I didn't want them seeing me."

"Do you think they did?"

"No. I'm pretty sure Dupont had no idea I was here. Still doesn't know."

"Then you left before they did."

"I started to. I stood up and crossed the street, and when I glanced back, I saw Dupont and the woman had left a few seconds after I did and were standing at the curb by a little white convertible. He kissed her on the cheek, and she got in the car and drove away. I hurried back to the bank and beat Dupont there. He didn't seem at all suspicious that I or anyone else he knew had seen him and the woman on the beach towel inside the walls of the sculpture. For all he knows, I brown-bagged it at my desk."

"Did you tell the police any of this?" Nudger asked.

"No. They didn't ask, and I didn't want to get involved. I used to be a recreational drug user, and I have a rational fear of the police."

"Then why are you telling me about it now?"

"Because you're not the police, and I think somebody should be told. And I still don't want to get involved."

"Meaning you'll deny this conversation if you're asked about it."

She smiled only with her oddly shaped eyes.

"Let's just say I won't remember it," she said. "Or remember seeing Dupont and the woman here." She forked a generous bite of pasta into her mouth, chewed, then said, "What you do with the information is your business."

He thought of asking her if she intended perjuring herself if she were called as a witness for the defense, then decided not to alarm her. Or maybe she wouldn't be alarmed. Maybe she'd just smile and lie. There was something in her smile that suggested she could do that, and he might look like the one who was lying.

"Did you get a better look at the woman's face when she drove away?" he asked.

"No. She made a U-turn and went in the other direction."

Nudger could squat no longer. He stood up slowly, actually hearing his left knee grind.

Millie Cookson winced at the sound. "I do remember her car's license plate, though, because it was one of those vanity plates. It said M-E-E-E-E."

Nudger smiled, thanked her, and hobbled in a little circle to try to get his legs working.

"It takes a selfish woman to have a vanity plate like that," Millie said.

"Obviously she could spare some love for Roger."

"Probably thought he was rich. Women see the suit and tie and think bankers make more money than they really do, just because they handle all that cash."

"Is Dupont popular with his colleagues?" Nudger asked.

"I wouldn't say Mr. Dupont is the best-loved vice president at the bank, even if he might be the most loved."

Nudger met her eyes, held her gaze. "Would you describe him as a womanizer?"

"I would. And I'd know."

She looked away, toward the hulking rust-colored creation that might be art, her pale face a bitter mask.

"I understand," Nudger told her, limping toward the sidewalk. Thinking, MEEEE.

Thinking Eileen should have that license plate on her car.

CHAPTER FIFTEEN

Nudger drove to his office and cursed as he saw that another car had claimed the space with the broken meter. He found a different parking space, half a block away, pumped a quarter into the meter, then walked back to his office. The sun was hot and heavy on his shoulders and felt almost like the weight of a backpack.

He had his window air conditioner on a timer he'd bought at the Kmart down the street. It was supposed to click on at eight-thirty every morning except for weekends, when Nudger didn't want to waste the electricity. He smiled with satisfaction as he heard the soft, gurgling hum of its efforts and glanced up and saw a drop of condensation, bright as a diamond in the sunlight, plummet from it to join a small puddle on the sidewalk.

But he wasn't in his reasonably cool office; he was down here on the hard, heated plane of the sidewalk, and he was hot and thirsty. He decided to drop into Danny's Donuts and get a diet Coke to take upstairs.

The doughnut shop was hot, but cooler than outside, and a few customers were still hanging around from lunchtime, when Danny did 90 percent of his sparse business. A very tall woman who worked in one of the office buildings across Manchester was seated at the counter absently munching a Dunker Delite. A sweaty-looking guy in a white shirt and bright green tie, a salesman from one of the used car lots down the street, was at the other end of the counter, sipping coffee and sneaking looks at the woman with an expression suggesting he was estimating mileage. Danny was behind the display counter, using his fingers to pluck a variety of goodies for a teenage boy and dropping them into a grease-spotted white box.

"That's a dozen," he said, then noticed Nudger and nodded hello to him.

"I only counted eleven," the boy said.

Danny held the box out, lid raised, and he and the kid examined the contents.

"Thirteen," Danny said, somewhat surprised. He lifted out a Dunker Delite and replaced it in the display case.

The kid looked about to cry as he paid for his dozen doughnuts and stalked out.

Nudger figured there had to be a moral there but couldn't come up with it.

Danny watched the kid leave, then a concerned look dragged at his already droopy features and he motioned for Nudger to come to the center of the counter where the remaining two customers might not be able to overhear what he had to say.

Nudger went over and sat on a stool. "Need a diet Coke," he said, plucking at the material of his sweat-soaked shirt to demonstrate how hot he was.

"Machine's broke down, Nudge," Danny said. "Ice water okay?"

"Sure."

In less than a minute Danny had a plastic foam cup of water with a few oval ice cubes floating in it on the counter in front of Nudger.

Nudger sipped. Wonderful! Now that his throat was open, he felt more like coping with whatever Danny had to say.

"It's Ray," Danny said, leaning in close with his elbow on the counter. His tone of voice suggested that Ray had suffered some sort of grave mishap.

"Ray?" Nudger said, peering into the sad brown eyes before him.

"He's been notified to report for work," Danny said solemnly, as if Ray had just been drafted into the Marines prior to Iwo Jima.

"Shag's?"

Danny nodded. "That Hydrant woman's gonna be the death of Ray."

"Heidran," Nudger said. "Her name's Heidran. It's German."

"It's Nazi," Danny said.

"When is Ray supposed to report?"

"Tomorrow morning. He's awful disappointed in you, Nudge."

"I talked to Heidran," Nudger said. "She was immovable."

"So was the Maginot Line."

Nudger sat back and stared at Danny. Was he a closet World War Two historian?

"I was watching *Victory at Sea* last night," Danny explained.

"The Maginot Line wasn't at sea."

"It was one of them other World War Two programs, then. Anyway, Ray figures you shoulda found a way around Hydrant. It's the kind of work you do, and Ray says he thought you were good at it. He says now he thinks he's misjudged you."

"Well," Nudger said, fighting back his irritation, "he can think that while he's mustarding up the buns."

"He'd like for you to try talking to Hy—the German woman one more time, see if you can come up with a way to make her change her mind."

"Her mind is on Ray," Nudger said, "and she's not about to change it."

"But you could try. Ray says he'd like to give you one more chance to make good on your promise."

"I never promised Ray anything," Nudger said, feeling his stomach turn on itself. Conversation about Ray could do that. "I'm not talking to Heidran Kreb again. You can tell Ray that for me."

"If you won't talk to the German woman," Danny said, "Ray would like you to call him."

"I feel like calling him a number of things," Nudger said.

"He'll be home the rest of the day and all evening, he said to tell you. Resting up and getting his back in as good a shape as possible."

"Hey!" the tall woman at the end of the counter said.

Nudger and Danny stopped talking and turned. Their voices had risen to conversational volume and both the man and woman at the counter were staring at them, or perhaps past them at each other. Nudger thought the woman might have been addressing the man, who was now openly leering at her.

"I'd like another of those Dunker Delites," the woman said to Danny. "They're delicious."

Nudger looked at her in disbelief as Danny got the Dunker Delite he'd taken from the teenager's overfilled box and laid it on a white napkin before the woman.

"Refill on the coffee?" Danny asked her.

"You bet."

He topped off the woman's cup then returned to where Nudger was seated. His elbow back on the counter, he leaned toward Nudger and kept his voice to a whisper. "Just give Ray a call, okay? For me, okay?"

Nudger finished his ice water. "For you," he said. "Not for Ray."

The creases in Danny's face worked their way generally upward into a smile. "Thanks again, Nudge."

Nudger said nothing as he slid off his stool, taking in the woman at the counter as the stool swiveled. Tall, skinny, receding chin, stringy hair that looked as if it needed washing. Great digestive tract, though, Nudger had to concede. But he doubted if that was what interested the car salesman at the other end of the counter.

After climbing the creaking wooden steps in the hot stairwell, he let himself into his office and sat at the desk where the breeze from the air conditioner blew directly on his back and arm. He felt the cold penetrate his damp shirt, watched the air flow ruffle the hair on his forearm.

The only message on his machine was from Eileen. Something about puncturing Nudger's lungs. He barely listened before pressing the erase button and sitting back again to bask in the cool air.

After a few minutes, he reached out without moving his body, dragged the phone closer, and pecked out Fleck's office number on the keypad.

He was hoping Fleck wouldn't be there and he could just leave a message. Unfortunately, court was in recess.

"What is it, Nudger? Talk fast. I'm busy."

"Okay. What about this bloodstain?"

"What bloodstain?"

"The bloodstain on the garage floor, the one you didn't tell me about."

"Oh, that. That's Karen's blood."

Nudger could hardly believe his ears. "Then why were you arguing with that detective that he hadn't proved it was hers?"

" 'Cause he hadn't, that's why. Besides, it gave me a chance to demonstrate my mastery of scientific evidence. Gotta let the bastards know early on, they can't get away with anything when they find themselves up against Lawrence—"

"Why didn't you tell me about this bloodstain?"

"Scientific evidence, Nudger. Takes a specialist. Way beyond a poor dumb innocent like you. Anyway, it's not important. Roger explained. Apparently it happened the week before Karen disappeared. She was sorting the cans in the recycling bin and she cut her hand."

Nudger nodded to himself. This was actually a lot more credible than most of Roger's explanations.

"So you were in court," Fleck went on. "Saw me slaughter that cop."

"Um—yes," said Nudger hesitantly.

"How you think it's going?"

"Well, I think the prosecution is scoring some points."

"Of course they're scoring!" Fleck shouted. "It's their turn. I can't slaughter every one of their witnesses. Not even Lawrence Fleck can do that. But when my turn comes to put on my case, I'll turn the tables. I'll have 'em on the run like roaches when the lights come on. Believe me."

Nudger didn't. Fleck was straining to keep up his self-confidence. He couldn't quite keep the desperation out of his voice when he asked, "You come up with anything I can use?"

"Not yet. But I'm following up an interesting lead. I'll let you know if it pans out."

"Take your time, Nudger. No hurry at all," Fleck snarled, and slammed down the phone.

Nudger held on to his receiver. Might as well get both unpleasant calls out of the way. He broke the connection and tapped out Ray's number.

Ray didn't answer until the sixth ring.

"Nudge," he whined, when he'd found out who was calling, "you just gotta do something!"

"I tried, Ray. The woman is determined to plum your depths and find something worthwhile."

"But I was counting on you to convince her that's a waste of time."

"I tried, I tried." Nudger could hear a soap opera theme in the background.

"Will you talk with her again?"

"No, Ray. If I thought it would help, I'd give it a try. But it won't help. Probably it would only get her mad and she'd have you washing Shag's windows."

"God, Nudge, I don't—"

"Stop, Ray! Why won't you simply be a man and give this job a chance. You might learn to like it."

"That's not what this is all about!" Ray sounded exasperated almost to the breaking point. "I had my fiscal year all planned out. My unemployment was gonna run out in November and I was gonna apply for an extension. This Shag's thing not only messes up what I'm drawing now, it ruins any possibility of an extension."

"You'll have a job, Ray. You won't need an extension. You won't even need unemployment checks."

Ray made a noise something like a growl. "You just won't understand, will you?"

"Maybe not, Ray."

"I didn't think so. Which is why I got a suggestion, something you should maybe try with this Heidran."

"She's tough, Ray. Nothing will move her. She's a regular Maginot Line."

"Well, I ain't talking about football here. And keep in mind this is a last resort kinda thing."

Nudger listened with trepidation.

"A woman like that, Nudge, sorta on the hefty side and we gotta admit not the most attractive, usually she's got some kinda secret kinky sex life. If you could find out what sorta action she's been involved in . . . Maybe with electrical or rubber gadgets or other women or something. We could use it to persuade her—"

Nudger slammed the receiver down, hoping Heidran would hand Ray the bucket and squeegee first thing in the morning.

He gave the laboring air conditioner time to cool him down some more, then he lifted the receiver again and dialed Hammersmith at the Third District station.

CHAPTER SIXTEEN

Hammersmith was in his office and picked up the phone immediately, but he told Nudger he didn't have time to talk, he was on
his way to testify in court about a multiple homicide case involving
a teenage hit man.

"Crime-fighting is a thriving industry," Nudger said.

"It's the apprenticeship system," Hammersmith said impatiently. "Best get to the point, Nudge."

"I need you to get me the owner of a vanity license plate, Missouri M-E-E-E-E."

"This have to do with Roger Dupont?"

"It might, though it could be that even if it does, it isn't important. It turns out Roger's a bit of a skirt-chaser."

"We found that out right away, but it doesn't mean he had to
kill his wife. That's why we have divorce laws, Nudge."

"It's something I'd like to follow up on, though. Another
woman might be a motive."

"The guy had plenty of other women without having to marry
them. It's the nineties, Nudge. And Karen Dupont's big life insurance policy is motive enough for Roger."

"Still, will you indulge me and find out who owns the vanity
plate?"

"I'll indulge you because I'm in too big a hurry to object. I don't
want to keep a teenybopper killer waiting."

"How old is he?"

"Fifteen."

Nudger winced. "Is he being tried as an adult?"

"Yes, and why not? He killed three adults. He's impressionable
and easily led, and well paid. It's time he was taught a lesson."

"Death by lethal injection is a hard lesson."

"Tell it to Roger Dupont," Hammersmith said, and hung up. He sure was in one of his moods.

Nudger replaced the receiver, then spent a while doing paperwork, sending out past-due notices to former clients who hadn't paid him, sending out excuses to creditors he hadn't yet paid. It struck him that it was all a waste of effort; if only there were some way to have his creditors bill his former clients direct, there would be no need for middle man Nudger. Computers should be able to do that kind of thing. Life was supposed to be easier because of computers.

The electric bill was so old that Nudger glanced up to make sure the second hand on his electric clock was still moving. He wrote out a check for the full amount, an astronomical figure brought about by the almost constant running of the air conditioner. Every summer, he was shocked anew by his electric bills.

He worked another twenty minutes on his other bills, then sat back and stared at how tall the must-be-paid stack was when compared to the past-due pile. It was depressing.

There was so much woe in the office that he decided to return to court and see how Roger Dupont was progressing with his dilemma. Sad to say, it was always a bit buoying to observe someone with even more problems than oneself.

". . . never liked him from the beginning," Joleen Witt was saying on the witness stand as the elegant Seymour Wister conducted his examination.

Nudger slipped quietly into the courtroom and sat almost exactly where he'd been this morning. But the heavyset woman who'd sat next to him was gone. The crowded courtroom was cooler than his office, but not so cool that the collective heat and body odor of the jury and gallery weren't evident.

"Was there a particular reason why you disliked the defendant?" Wister asked.

"There were a lot of reasons," Joleen said. "For one thing, he abused Karen even before their marriage."

"Abused her how?"

"Verbally and physically. Karen would tell me about their arguments, the names he called her."

"Objection!" Fleck shouted from behind his stuffed cardboard accordion folder. "Hearsay."

Judge MacMasters sustained the objection, and Fleck gazed smugly at Wister. Pure hate showed for a second even through Wister's impassive, professional facade. Fleck was getting to him.

You mentioned other reasons why you disliked your brother-in-law. What were those reasons?"

"He was an Airedale."

"Pardon me?"

Nudger knew from long-ago conversations with his grandmother that 'Airedale' was a very old term for a husband who ran around on his wife, from when the breed was popular and had a reputation for canine roaming and romance. According to Nudger's grandmother, Nudger's grandfather had been an Airedale.

Joleen was as old-fashioned in appearance as in vocabulary. Her red hair was pulled back into a tight bun, and she was wearing a high-necked white blouse and a dark tailor-made suit that probably hadn't been out of her closet since the last time she went to a funeral or job interview. She was almost Wister's match in severity and rectitude.

"He was a womanizer," Joleen explained. It intrigued Nudger that she referred to Roger in the past tense, as if he were as dead as she thought Karen to be. Though he was sitting at the defense table twelve feet from her, she never looked at him. "I warned Karen he wasn't going to be faithful to her if she married him."

"Why did you tell her that?"

"Because it was true," Joleen said smugly.

"I mean, how did you know it was true?"

"It was just a feeling then, but the feeling was borne out quickly enough. The week after he and Karen returned from their honeymoon, he made sexual advances to me. I rebuffed him."

"How did you rebuff him?"

"I hit him with a tennis racquet."

A ripple of amusement passed through the spectators. Judge MacMasters didn't gavel, but he glared.

"Did you tell your sister about these sexual advances?"

"Of course. Karen and I were very close. And as her marriage became harder and harder for her to endure, we became even closer. She told me everything."

Fleck leaned forward, preparing to make another hearsay objection. Wister glanced over his shoulder at him.

"Ms. Witt, did you and your sister ever take any actions with regard to the marriage?"

The question seemed to surprise Joleen. "Actions?"

"Well, did you and your sister make any preparations to file for divorce?"

"Oh. No. But I'm sure Karen would have divorced Roger if she had lived."

"No further questions, your honor."

She'd recovered to finish strongly, but Joleen had been rattled by Wister's last question. Nudger was sure of it. More had been going on between the sisters than she wanted to talk about. But Nudger dismissed the speculations from his mind, because Fleck was rising to cross-examine.

The little attorney scratched his chin as if in deep thought as he stood up and walked forward.

"Have you ever been married?" he asked Joleen.

"No."

"Uh-huh. And do you not live alone?"

"I do live alone."

"Uh-huh. Would it be safe to say, in light of your previous testimony that we've just heard, that you dislike the defendant."

"Oh, it would be safe to say that."

"Isn't your sister Karen younger than you?"

"Yes" Joleen looked with pure contempt at Fleck.

"How much younger?"

"Six years."

"Would you describe your social life as active, Ms. Witt?"

"Objection," Wister said calmly. "The line of questioning is completely irrelevant."

"Sustained," MacMasters said, almost automatically.

"Let me rephrase the question," Fleck said. "Ms. Witt, are you seeing anyone?"

"Objection!" Wister said with a little more heat. "Now it sounds as if counsel is making overtures to the witness."

Laughter rippled through the courtroom. Even Roger Dupont appeared amused. Nudger thought Dupont should have been embarrassed, and afraid.

"Mr. Wister," MacMasters said wearily, "please make your objections with more decorum and propriety. The objection is, however, sustained." He gazed almost with horror at Fleck. "Where are you trying to go with your line of questioning, Mr. Fleck?"

"I'm merely trying to establish, your honor, that the witness is a lonely and jealous sibling with a suspicious nature and active imagination and is operating under the misconception that her sister's been murdered."

"Objection!"

"Sustained! I think it's time to recess until tomorrow morning. And I'll see both attorneys in my chambers."

As court was adjourned, Nudger knew that in his crude way Fleck had managed to impugn Joleen's testimony and impress the jury. And there might indeed be some truth to the picture of her that he'd painted. Nudger was beginning to understand that the little firebrand of a lawyer sometimes used his pugnaciousness and apparent ineptness as cover from which to ambush and make his point. Roger Dupont might have better and more knowledgeable representation than Nudger had first imagined.

But as Fleck's eyes met Nudger's they were puzzled and questioning.

And Nudger had no answers.

CHAPTER SEVENTEEN

The only message on Nudger's answering machine was from Hammersmith, telling Nudger to call him not at the Third District but at his home in Webster Groves. Hammersmith had lived in the leafy suburb for decades.

His son Zack answered the phone, and after much yelling and conversation in the background, Hammersmith came to the phone.

"Did I interrupt your dinner?" Nudger asked.

"Yeah," Hammersmith said, "but it's okay. We were having one of those family discussions that can lead to people being disinherited."

"You're lucky to have a family to gather around a table and discuss things," Nudger said, feeling a pang of loneliness. He couldn't imagine sitting down at a table with Eileen and not arguing over money. Even after the divorce they did that occasionally in attorneys' offices.

"Lucky, all right," Hammersmith said glumly. "My wife hit our garage door with our car and did a thousand dollars worth of damage, and when I got mad she accused me of sexual harassment because I implied she was a typical female driver. Implied, she said. Zack is determined to ask his high school algebra teacher to the prom. Our dog Bart died last night."

"I'm sorry," Nudger said, thinking being single maybe had its advantages after all. "About everything. Especially about Bart. He was a fine dog." In truth Bart had been an ill-tempered bassett hound that Nudger was reluctant to pet for fear of being bitten. Still, Hammersmith had been fond of the animal.

Hammersmith grunted. "One thing that has gone right today is I got the info you wanted on the M-E-E-E vanity plate. It belongs to a white '95 Mercedes convertible owned by a Vella Kling." Hammersmith gave Nudger Vella Kling's address on Osage Avenue in South St. Louis.

"That's not the kind of neighborhood where you'd expect to see a Mercedes parked," Nudger said.

"No doubt she's got a garage, Nudge, or she wouldn't still have the Mercedes."

Nudger finished making a note of the address on the envelope of his past-due rent notice. "Thanks, Jack."

"If you do stumble across anything pertinent," Hammersmith said, "clue me in immediately. The Karen Dupont murder is still technically an open homicide case."

"You'll know anything important almost as soon as I do," Nudger assured him.

"Humph. I understand you were in court today."

"How'd you know that?"

Hammersmith chuckled. "I got my little birds that tell me things. How's it looking for Roger Dupont?"

"Your little birds didn't tell you that?"

"They did, but they're biased in this case. They think Dupont should be found guilty then be executed."

"They wouldn't be biased if they told you that's the way he seems headed. Even his lawyer thinks he's guilty."

"Does Fleck have any idea why Dupont won't plea-bargain?"

"Not the slightest. Neither would you, if you sat in that courtroom for a while."

Nudger heard argumentive voices raised in the background. One of them cried, "Jack!" Hammersmith's wife Linda.

"I gotta go, Nudge," Hammersmith said.

"Okay, Jack. Thanks again. And don't worry, love always finds a way."

"It found a way to run into the garage door," Hammersmith said.

"I was thinking of Zack and his algebra teacher."

Grinning, Nudger tried to hang up before Hammersmith but failed.

Vella Kling's address turned out to belong to a brick four-family flat near Carondolet Park. It was in a neighborhood that had gradually declined over the past several years. While it wasn't a dangerous part of town yet, it was still not the place where one parked a Mercedes—or owned one—without expecting it to be vandalized or stolen. For spite if not for parts.

And Nudger didn't see the white convertible with the vanity plates as he parked the Granada on the opposite side of Osage from the flat-roofed brick building. There was an alley behind the building, and it had a long, four-car clapboard garage, as did most of the similar buildings on the block. Nudger had driven down the alley, stopped the car, and gotten out briefly to peer in through the garage's dirt-streaked windows set in the overhead doors. The garage wasn't divided into stalls. It was empty except for what appeared to be a very old Buick sedan parked at the west end.

The address Hammersmith had given Nudger indicated that Vella Kling lived in the unit on the second floor, east. Nudger sat in the Granada, perspired freely, and listened to the ball game until it was almost dark. Then he climbed out, stretched his cramped muscles, and crossed the street to enter the building.

A narrow, cracked concrete walk bisected a parched lawn that was brown where it wasn't bare earth. Near a dead yew on the right of the entrance lay a child's rusty tricycle worthless enough not to be stolen. A sparrow set down on the lawn and began pecking at barren earth that had to be baked as hard as the concrete walk, as if it actually expected to find a worm. Nudger thought the heat had probably driven the bird insane.

The building had no intercom. A glance at the vestibule mailboxes confirmed the location of Vella's unit. Nudger pressed the door buzzer button above her mailbox, then climbed the rubber-treaded wooden steps. Somebody was apparently cooking something containing cabbage in one of the units. Nudger had been in a lot of flats and apartment buildings, and someone always seemed to be cooking cabbage. Of course that was impossible; the smell of the stuff must permeate walls.

When he reached the closed door of Vella's unit he knocked three times, then waited at least three minutes. Nudger's three-minute rule.

After making sure the door was indeed locked, he removed his honed expired Visa card from his wallet and tried to use it to slip what looked like only a cheap door latch lock. There didn't seem to be a dead bolt to contend with, though he knew there might be a chainlock or something of that nature.

The old six-panel door fit too tightly to admit even the thin plastic of his card.

Okay, he thought. Okay. He leaned his shoulder against the door, drew back about a foot, then threw his weight against it.

The door gave without a lot of noise, leaving the wooden door-jamb splintered near the knob and above, where a brass chainlock dangled. One of the screws Nudger had ripped from the wood fell and rattled on the bare floor.

He was about to enter, when he heard the door across the hall open.

His stomach and his heart struggled to occupy the same space at the same time. Nudger quietly pulled the door closed and knocked on it.

"Help you?" a woman's voice said behind him.

He turned around as if he'd just realized he wasn't alone. A woman stood holding her door half open, gazing out at him. She was in her seventies and looked unhealthy. Her face was gaunt and her complexion was pale. Her blue eyes had about them the startled look of the very old and infirm who were suddenly wondering how they'd arrived near the end of life so abruptly. Nudger, still in his forties, already feared seeing that look someday in the mirror.

He gave the woman the old sweet smile. She seemed unmoved.

"I'm looking for Vella," he said, broadening the smile. "Vella Kling. She does live here, doesn't she?"

"Sure does," the woman said. Now she was smiling back.

He breathed easier. She was probably alone in the world, and lonely. Like Nudger. Only she was older and eager for someone to talk to, to listen to her. "She's not home, though. Left late this afternoon."

"Oh. I hadn't figured on that." Nudger made his voice drip with disappointment. "We were supposed to meet today. Unless I have the wrong day."

"Maybe you do," the woman said. "Time, days, can get away from people."

Years, Nudger thought sadly. "Do you know when she'll be back?"

"Not for about a month, is what she said. She left me her plants to water. I've got them in my dining room where they'll get plenty of light. A ficus and some vinca vines in hanging pots."

That one threw Nudger. "Oh, no," he said. "It's not possible she's going to be gone that long."

"That's what she told me. She went skiing someplace out west."

"Colorado, probably," Nudger said. "She likes several places out there. Did she tell you how to get in touch with her?"

"No. She said she'd be moving around, so it wouldn't do much good to leave a phone number. Anyway, there won't be much need to talk about the plants. I can take care of them well enough. Do you like plants?"

"Yes, I've got a lot of them at home." Nudger glanced at Vella's closed door and shook his head. "That woman goes skiing more often than anyone I know."

"First time I know of," the woman said.

"Really?" Nudger pretended to be astounded.

"She travels a lot because of her job buying for antique shops, but I never knew her to ski or do much of anything else athletic or requiring physical exertion. Except—"

"Except what?" Nudger asked. Some double entendre here?

"Nothing," the woman said, obviously feeling guilty for what she'd been thinking and almost said. "If she calls, do you want me to mention you were by?"

Nudger feigned deep concentration. "No, that's not necessary. Since I know she went skiing, I should be able to get in touch with her without any trouble. She's probably at one of the three resorts she always goes to."

"Do you ski?"

"Sometimes," Nudger lied. "That's where I met Vella."

"I thought you were more likely to be into antiques. I mean, you're average size and all, but you don't look particularly athletic."

He smiled again. She had no way of knowing he'd played Little League baseball as a youth. He might have made the high school team if he'd had an arm, if he'd been able to hit. "Thanks for your help, Mrs? . . . ."

"Finnegan. Iris Finnegan."

"Thanks-again-Finnegan," Nudger said musically, a little joke to avert suspicion of misdeed.

Iris Finnegan smiled wanly and closed her door.

Nudger made some noise as if he were descending the stairs, then crossed the landing as quietly as possible and entered Vella Kling's apartment.

CHAPTER EIGHTEEN

There were miniblinds on the windows that admitted only narrow bars of faint light from outside. The air in the apartment was warm, thick, and still. That and the almost total silence reassured Nudger that Iris Finnegan was right about Vella being away. He was alone.

The faint rushing sound of a car passing outside wafted into the apartment then faded. Something, probably the refrigerator, abruptly began a soft, steady hum that seemed only to emphasize the silence.

As Nudger made his way across a wooden floor, then thin carpet, to the outline of a bulky lamp on a table, he caught a whiff of what smelled like lemon-scented furniture polish. He groped beneath the large lampshade, found the switch, and turned on the lamp.

In the flood of light he saw that it was a squat, beige ceramic lamp with colorful small shells and rocks imbedded in its base. He looked around and saw that he was in Vella Kling's living room. It was sparsely but expensively furnished, with what had to be genuine brown leather matching chairs and a low-slung modern sofa. In front of the sofa was a long coffee table with a silk flower arrangement visible beneath its glass top. One wall was entirely shelves containing a sleek black stereo surrounded by a collection of small crystal animals, framed photographs of attractive people Nudger didn't recognize, and leather-bound books that looked as if they'd never been opened but contrasted nicely with the earth tone decor. On the wall opposite the sofa was a large-screen TV that Nudger knew Ray would love using to watch Cubs games. Well, maybe with enough hours at Shag's such a thing could come to pass.

The only jarring note in the room was a large, aluminum-framed poster of an inanely smiling Tom Cruise, mounted on the wall over the sofa.

Feeling the barely suppressed fear and delicious sense of secrecy he always experienced when he trespassed in people's homes, Nudger moved through a dining room furnished with matching modern oak table, chairs and hutch, into the kitchen. He saw white cabinets with porcelain handles, a tall white side-by-side refrigerator, combination stove and microwave, Cuisinart food processor . . . Vella was doing okay as a middlewoman in the antique business. He attempted to pluck a grape from a fruit bowl on the table, then realized the fruit was artificial and moved on.

The bedroom was outfitted with lacquered black chest and dresser, and a large round bed with a red quilted spread. There were two brass hooks screwed into the ceiling in front of the window, probably for the hanging potted plants now in the possession and care of Iris Finnegan across the hall. Nudger leaned over and pushed down with his hand on the bed, watching its water-filled mattress undulate. His imagination soared then returned to reality.

Wall shelves in the bedroom held a collection of Hummel figurines, except for the bottom shelf, where a stuffed bear with an exaggerated penis leaned its back against a stack of computer software manuals. On the wall nearest the bed was a large oil painting on velvet of a man and woman doing what looked to Nudger like a tango. On another wall was a print of a painting of a woeful, long-haired young woman in a white dress. It was signed by Whistler, and even Nudger knew it was of higher quality than the painting of the man dipping the woman in the tango against a background of blue velvet. Though that one *was* an original; he could even see the textured brush strokes and where the paint had glopped up.

The mirror-doored closet contained plenty of clothes. Some seemed cheap, and some boasted exclusive labels. There were several dresses anyone would regard as sexy, and a few conservative blazers with matching skirts. The jumble of shoeboxes on the closet shelf contained—shoes. In the dresser drawers, Nudger found folded T-shirts, sweat socks, panty hose, and silk lingerie. There was a jumble of those Wonderbras that were supposed to increase cleavage. Behind the Wonderbras was a small leather box that contained a sparkling collection of jewelry. Undoubtedly real and valuable. Vella should be more careful; if Nudger were a thief, he'd be making a nice haul.

He left the bedroom, wondering why there wasn't a mirror on the ceiling above the round bed, then went into a second, smaller bedroom that contained only a bookshelf, desk, and chair. The bookshelf held only worn paperback romance novels and some of those limited-edition collectors' plates propped in holders. There were buffalo on one plate, John Wayne on another, some flying geese in V-formation on a third. The desk, a small kneehole cherry wood affair, held the usual assortment of rubber bands, paperclips, and envelopes. Beneath a fancy glass paperweight was a stack of opened envelopes. Nudger examined them and found that they were all bills, many of them past due. There was also a letter from a bank informing Vella that she was two months behind on the payments for her Mercedes, on which she still owed over twenty thousand dollars.

Nudger replaced the envelopes and stood with his fists propped on his hips, disappointed. He'd found nothing in the apartment that in any way explained the relationship between Vella and Dupont, or even confirmed its existence.

He walked back into the living room, paused, and looked around. Like the rest of the apartment, it had about it the whiff of a professional decorator, but one whose taste and decor had been polluted by those of the occupant. He doubted that it was the decorator who'd chosen the Tom Cruise poster, the well-endowed stuffed bear, or the tango painting. Not to mention the round water bed and various other signs of a non-decorator personality.

Nudger shrugged. Who was he to judge decor, with his mismatched furniture, his ancient portable TV on its listing stand, and his baseball signed by Stan Musial displayed in his living room? If he'd been able to afford a decorator a year ago, his apartment might very well look something like this one. Except for those collector plates and that bear. And . . . No, he decided after all, nothing like this apartment.

He'd touched little after his first few minutes in the apartment, and had opened and closed drawers and worked wall switches with the back of his hand or his knuckles. After wiping his fingerprints from the lamp and doorknob, Nudger suddenly remembered the rubber grape he'd tried to pluck from its rubber vine. He returned to the kitchen and wiped the grape clean with a dishtowel.

Then he left the apartment quietly.

There was no sign of damage on the outside of the door. If Vella Kling really was off skiing as she'd told her neighbor, a month would pass before anyone would realize the apartment had been illegally entered.

He drove back to his own apartment on Sutton in Maplewood, thinking that while it was nothing like Vella Kling's, it was more like home. There was something to be said for eclectic decor, even if it was prompted by near-poverty. On the other hand, a Norman Rockwell print in the living room would do no harm. Or perhaps one of those paintings of dogs playing poker. He thought he remembered seeing some at Kmart. In nice frames, too.

As soon as he opened the door to the apartment, he smelled liquor. Bourbon, he thought.

While he was thinking that, a deep male voice said, "Don't turn on the light."

A huge, hulking form emerged from the shadows and came toward him. In the dim light Nudger could see that the man was close to six and a half feet tall and had long, apelike arms with huge hands. Shoulders like the slopes of mountains. A narrow waist with baggy pants.

"You leave Vella alone," the voice rumbled. "Stay away from her. You stay away from everything and everyone's got anything to do with her."

Nudger was paralyzed with a combination of fear and surprise. His stomach was pulsating and made a noise he'd heard before that sounded like *Rrrruuuuunnnn!* It already knew what his fear-numbed brain couldn't process.

But Nudger couldn't run. Wouldn't have had time, anyway.

The smell of bourbon grew stronger and the man seemed to grow even larger as he approached. One of the massive hands became a massive fist.

It struck Nudger's chest like a truck.

Massive pain.

CHAPTER NINETEEN

Someone or something was gently prodding his shoulder.

Sunlight lanced painfully beneath Nudger's eyelids, and he heard Claudia's voice say, "He can't fight, he doesn't like guns, so why is he in this line of work?"

"Why do I sell doughnuts?" Danny's voice. Nudger thought it was a pretty good question. "It's all we know, I guess." Ah, the answer.

Nudger heard himself groan.

Conversation ceased.

Memory flooded in. He moved his fingertips and felt carpet nap. He must be lying on his back on his living room floor, where his giant assailant of last night had left him. Vella's lover. Or so the big man had implied.

Nudger opened his eyes and the sunlight splashed into them like acid.

"Are you all right, Nudger?" Claudia asked in a concerned voice.

"Sure. I always hurl myself against a few hard objects then sleep on the floor. Is the place on fire, or is it morning?"

"Morning," Danny said. "Almost ten o'clock."

"Am I having a *soiree?*"

"Not unless that's some kind of fit that would leave you hurt and unconscious. What happened is, I wanted to talk to you about Ray, but you weren't in your office. So I phoned about nine o'clock and you didn't answer your phone. I hung the CLOSED sign in the shop window, drove over here, and saw your car. Your apartment door was unlocked, and I opened it a crack and saw you on the floor. Naturally, I came on in."

"And?"

"And tried to bring you around but couldn't."

"He phoned me then," Claudia said.

"Why aren't you in school?" Nudger asked.

"That's where I phoned her at, Nudge," Danny said. "I knew she was teaching summer classes out at Stowe School."

"I got Biff to take over my remedial English class and drove here right away," Claudia said.

Nudger groaned again. Biff was Biff Archway, girls soccer team coach and sex education teacher at Stowe High School. He was in love with Claudia, Nudger was sure. Sometimes Nudger suspected that Claudia loved Biff back. Nudger hated Biff.

He tried to sit up, and Claudia and Danny helped him so that he was leaning with his back against the wall, his numbed legs stretched out in front of him with only a slight bend at the knees. His chest felt as if it were caved in. He fumbled with the buttons on his shirt and looked down. A nasty multicolored bruise the size of a dinner plate was glowing there.

"Wow!" Danny said. "I thought it was only your head."

Nudger averted his eyes from the bruise where the big man had punched him. It was the only blow he remembered being struck. "My head? What about my head?"

"You've got scrapes and bruises on your face, Nudger," Claudia said. She touched his cheek gently with the tips of her fingers. "And your nose has been bleeding, but it stopped."

"Looks like you been in a hockey game," Danny observed. "What happened?"

"I got home last night and a shaved gorilla was waiting for me. He told me I should stay away from Vella. Then he slammed me in the chest to make his point, and that's all I can recall. He must have worked me over some more when I was unconscious."

"Vella who?" Claudia asked, an edge of suspicion in her voice.

"I was trying to find out about her," Nudger said. "Seems she and Roger Dupont had a thing going."

"Then why didn't the big man beat up Roger Dupont?"

Nudger shrugged. "Unavailable, I guess."

"This reminds me of *Farewell, My Lovely*," Claudia said.

"Huh?"

"It's a famous novel by Raymond Chandler. My English class did a report on it last year. A giant ex-con named Moose Malloy hires Marlowe to find his old love, Velma."

Nudger didn't ordinarily read detective novels and had never heard of Moose Malloy or Velma. He'd heard of Chandler, though. If Nudger wasn't mistaken, Chandler had also written that famous detective novel about the falcon. Or maybe he was the one who'd written about a detective known as The Falcon.

Nudger was a detective and had never felt like a falcon.

"I think I read a book by Chandler once," Nudger said. "There was this one great line, something like—'She had a body that could make a man kick a hole in the wall.' "

"I don't think you've got the quote exactly right," said Claudia.

"Probably not. I'm not at my best."

He tried to stand up. His head exploded. Felt like it, anyway.

Claudia helped to support him as he sagged against the wall. "I've gotta get to court," he said.

"No," she told him. "You're going to the Emergency Room at St. Mary's Hospital."

"No."

"Yes."

"Better listen to her, Nudge. That bruise looks bad. So does your face."

"I'll go to see Dr. Fell," Nudger said. Dr. Fell was a general practitioner with an office near Nudger's in Maplewood. Nudger's personal physician, when he needed one.

"Dr. Fell will tell you what you want to hear right up until the minute you die," Claudia said. She did not like Dr. Fell. She had never been able to tell Nudger why.

"No hospital," Nudger said. "Dr. Fell or nothing."

"Little to choose between them," Claudia said, "but come on. I'll drive you to Dr. Fell in my car. Danny's got to get back to the doughnut shop."

"She's right, Nudge," Danny said apologetically. "If I don't bake some fresh Dunker Delites before the lunch crowd comes in, I'll have to microwave some from yesterday."

Nudger looked at him in disbelief but said nothing. The term "fresh Dunker Delite" was an oxymoron. The missile-like confections seemed to pop out of the oven weighty and stale.

"About Ray . . ." Danny said.

"What about him?" The last person Nudger wanted to think about was Ray, who surely was a blight on every life that had intersected his own.

"He went into work this morning at Shag's. Got there right on time, too, he said. But he hurt his back and went home."

Nudger squinted at his wrist watch. "It's only ten o'clock. He didn't last very long."

"That German woman doesn't believe Ray's back's really hurt so bad he can't hoist a bun and beef patty, and she's threatened to fire him."

"Ray should appreciate that."

"No, no. You don't understand. Getting fired for deliberate nonperformance—which she might somehow be able to prove—doesn't fit into Ray's plans. If that happens, he'll be turned down when he applies to collect his unemployment checks."

Nudger almost smiled. He had to admire Heidran's guile. She had Ray where she wanted him now, by the wallet. She was something like Eileen only with character.

"Maybe he should go back to Shag's," Nudger said. "It might be smart if he begged forgiveness and offered to mop the floor."

"No, that's not in Ray's plans, either."

"Big surprise."

"He wants you to talk to the German woman so he don't have to go back there. He wants her to make it like he was never hired."

Nudger stood up straight and remained standing even though his headache flared and each breath hurt his bruised chest. He'd taken a punch to the heart powerful enough to knock out a heavyweight contender. Maybe Claudia was right about skipping court today and going easy on himself.

"Will you talk to the German woman, Nudge?"

"No," Nudger said. "Who does Ray think I am, Jimmy Carter? He should be the one to talk to her."

"Nudger," Claudia said. "It can't hurt for you to talk to this person."

He stared at her in anger and disbelief. She had betrayed him.

"It's something you might be able to do today that won't be a strain on you, and I can go with you."

"I have other ideas," Nudger said.

"He'll talk to the woman at Shag's," she assured Danny. "If he feels well enough."

Danny smiled like a grateful bloodhound. "Thanks a lot, Nudge." And he loped out the door, headed for his Dunker Delites.

Nudger tucked in his shirt and tried to rearrange his wrinkled clothes so they'd be passable. His shirt looked okay, but his pants were creased and twisted in some way that made him appear to be standing in a strong wind. Oh, well. He located his sunglasses and put them on. That should help his headache some.

Then he sighed in resignation. "Okay, let's go see Dr. Fell." He really didn't think it was a bad idea. He was definitely feeling punk.

"Don't we have to phone for an appointment?"

"No. You don't need an appointment to see Dr. Fell. He's a humanitarian."

"But you do have to pay for his services."

"Yes," Nudger said. "In cash, before he'll see you."

CHAPTER TWENTY

Dr. Fell's office was down the street from Nudger's, above a hardware store across from the Kmart that had closed when the new one several blocks east on Manchester had opened for business.

Nudger sat next to Claudia in a plastic chair in Dr. Fell's small waiting room. It was one of a row of plastic chairs, different colors but all attached together in some way. In the center of the room was a low wooden table on which sat a large glass ashtray and some old copies of *Reader's Digest* and *Practical Science*. There were no other patients waiting.

Claudia had obeyed a sign instructing patients to press a button, and the buzzer that alerted Dr. Fell had rasped in the inner office. Nothing to do now but wait.

In the waiting room.

Silence. Except for occasional sounds of traffic from outside on Manchester.

"It's been years since I've been in a doctor's waiting room where there was an ashtray," Claudia said in a hushed tone, as if they were in a church that might echo her words and disturb the devout.

Nudger absently touched his bruised chest with his forefinger and winced with pain. "Dr. Fell isn't a moralist."

"Smoking's not a moral issue, it's about health. And that's what a doctor's supposed to be about."

"Don't bother me with logic," Nudger said. "I'm hurt."

"You should be at St. Mary's. It's hot in here. This place should be air-conditioned. I'm surprised Dr. Fell doesn't have to treat all his patients for heat prostration."

Nudger agreed with her there. He was perspiring heavily, and he could feel body heat emanating from Claudia, who was sitting practically on top of him because of the closeness of the tiny, attached plastic chairs.

The door to the inner office opened and a small, bearded man with a limp emerged, followed by Dr. Fell. The bearded man's face was pale and his eyes had an odd yellow cast to them. In his hand was clutched a white prescription slip.

Dr. Fell was a lean, dark-haired man who seemed bent inward at the middle so that he always stood with a forward lean. He had very dark eyes, a very white smile, and was of some foreign extraction that Nudger had never placed. "Rub that on your chest," he said to the small, bearded man in his peculiar accent, "and you should feel better by tomorrow."

The bearded man nodded weakly and limped from the office.

Dr. Fell, who was always smiling, smiled wider. "Ah, Mr. Nudger. Please come in and tell me what is the problem."

Claudia helped Nudger stand up. "Should I go in with you?" she asked.

"Not necessary," Nudger said. "I'm in good hands."

Claudia rolled her eyes, then wiped perspiration from them with her knuckles and sat back down. She was resignedly picking up *Practical Science* as Nudger followed Dr. Fell into his office.

No sooner had Nudger paid the standard office-visit fee and removed his shirt than Dr. Fell spotted the problem.

"Ah, what have you been doing, Mr. Nudger?"

"It's what's been done to me, Dr. Fell."

"Your work. You are in a dangerous occupation, Mr. Nudger. Last night on *Barnaby Jones*—"

"Those are reruns," Nudger interrupted. "It's not like that any- more."

"But it was for you recently," Dr. Fell said, touching Nudger's colorfully damaged chest. "Did someone run into you with a car?"

"Something like that."

Dr. Fell moved his hands around Nudger's torso, not without some expertise. "Does this hurt, Mr. Nudger? This? This?"

"Yeow!"

Dr. Fell moved back and stood with his fingers touching his chin, studying Nudger. "You are putting on weight, Mr. Nudger."

"It's my age, I guess. I have a headache, too."

Dr. Fell stepped forward and used his fingertips to apply pres- sure to Nudger's temples, then he used an instrument with a bright light on it to peer into Nudger's eyes.

"There is no sign of concussion," he said. "The bruises and abrasions on your face are consistent with those of a man who's been in a fist fight. Yet your knuckles are unblemished."

"You should be the detective, Dr. Fell."

"And you should be in some other occupation, it appears." Dr. Fell turned to a table with bottles and instruments on it, then swabbed Nudger's face wounds with something that stung. "You are fortunate you don't require stitches, Mr. Nudger." He dropped his cotton swab into a wastebasket. "Does your chest hurt when you breathe?"

"Sometimes."

"You have a badly bruised sternum. What it needs is to be given a chance to heal. I will wrap it to give you some support and to protect it somewhat, and it shouldn't hurt so much when you breathe or when it is touched, but it needs time. You should go home and rest."

"I'd better not do that, Dr. Fell."

"Well, you had better rest, but I know you will not. I'm going to write you a prescription for pain pills and for a salve that will facilitate the healing of your massive chest bruise. You will be able to function, but please heed my advice and be careful. Infection could be a serious matter."

Dr. Fell wrapped Nudger's torso with a flesh-colored Ace elastic bandage, and Nudger stood up and put his shirt back on.

"Your clothes look as if you've slept in them," Dr. Fell said.

"I did."

"Ah, you must lead an exciting life. Like Jessica Fletcher in *Murder, She Wrote*."

Did the man do nothing in his spare time but watch television?

"Exciting," Nudger said, "but all those celebrities can be a trial."

Dr. Fell wrote out the prescriptions for Nudger and handed them to him, then he walked ahead of Nudger and held open the door to the waiting room.

"Rub that on your chest, Mr. Nudger," he said with a smile, as Nudger edged past him, "and you should feel better by tomorrow."

"Thanks, Dr. Fell. I feel better already."

Claudia said nothing as she went with Nudger downstairs and through the hardware store. She was sweating profusely and he could see that she was aggravated.

When they were out on the sidewalk, where it was even hotter, she said, "I don't understand what *Practical Science* is doing in that waiting room."

"Drive me back to my place," Nudger said, "so I can pick up my car."

"You're going back to your apartment and lie down," Claudia said.

"I can't. Life and death hang in the balance."

"Don't go all Laurence Olivier on me, Nudger. Where did you think you were going?"

"Down on Cherokee Street, then maybe out to St. Charles."

"You're not."

"I am."

She stared at him. "Why?"

"Those are the locations of a lot of antique shops. Collectors' paradise. I need to find out if any of the shops bought antiques from Vella Kling. If they did, the owners might be able to tell me something about her."

Claudia continued to stare at him.

"Want to go with me?" he asked.

"You are stupidly machismo and adhere to an antiquated and self-destructive male code that is someday going to get you killed and if it happens I won't care."

He knew she was certainly angry when she talked like that, without commas. They both knew he was no hero. "It's more that I'm curious," he said honestly. And it was his job, though he didn't tell her that. He was persistent in his work. If he wasn't persistent, what was he?

Simply scared. That was all.

"I could use your help," he said. "Coming with me?"

But he knew she was.

"We'll take my car," she said through clenched teeth. "Its air conditioner works better than yours."

He was sure she let him stand for longer than was necessary out in the heat before she leaned over and unlocked the passenger-side door.

Nudger scrunched himself down in the tiny car's miniature seat and buckled his safety belt. "Let's stop off first thing at a pharmacy and get my prescriptions filled," he suggested.

Figuring, there, that should mollify her.

"*Practical Science* . . ." she muttered unbelievingly, as she zoomed the little car away from the curb so abruptly it caused Nudger's aching cranium to bounce off the headrest.

CHAPTER TWENTY-ONE

After the first in the lineup of antique shops on Cherokee, Nudger and Claudia realized the dimensions of their job and decided to question shop owners or clerks separately. Claudia took the north side of the street, Nudger the south.

At one o'clock they met as planned on the corner of Cherokee and Iowa to compare notes.

They had no notes to compare. No one in any of the antique shops had heard of Vella Kling.

"I did see a beautiful nineteenth-century cuckoo clock," Claudia said. "I thought you might be interested in it."

Was she being snide? Nudger couldn't be sure so he said nothing.

"Maybe Vella Kling's supposed occupation is a front," she said.

"For what?" Nudger asked. He'd almost reached the same conclusion, but he wanted to hear what Claudia had to say.

"Who knows? She might make her money in some illegal way and need something to tell people if they ask about her occupation. Or maybe she fakes income to stay on the sunny side of the IRS."

Nudger began walking back toward where Claudia's car was parked on Cherokee, and Claudia fell in beside him. His chest felt better but his head was pounding. Perspiration was stinging the wounds on his face.

"Maybe the people in the shops are afraid of you," Claudia suggested, "considering you look like a goon who isn't too good at the protection racket."

"Not many antique shops pay protection money to goons," Nudger said, but he really didn't know that to be true.

"Let's get some White Castle hamburgers to go, then drive to your apartment," Claudia said. "We can eat lunch, then you can rest. It's what you need, remember? Dr. Fell said so."

"I need White Castle hamburgers?"

"You need rest."

"You said Dr. Fell was a quack," Nudger told her.

"I did not."

"Implied, then."

"Only implied. After lunch, I can rub some of that ointment he prescribed on your chest."

Now that was tempting. But Nudger said, "No. Let's stop someplace for lunch that isn't carryout. I want to make a phone call, then we can drive out to St. Charles and check out those antique shops."

"You are hopelessly stubborn."

"Dogged. In my business, it's called dogged."

"Not what I call it," she muttered. But Nudger ignored her.

They drove to a restaurant on Grand and ordered club sandwiches and iced tea. While they were waiting for the food, Nudger begged a quarter from Claudia, then went to the pay phone near the back of the restaurant and called Lawrence Fleck's office.

"Mr. Fleck's in court today," the temp said. He could tell by her voice it was the same one, the bewildered young blonde woman he'd seen during his visit to Fleck's office. What was her name?

"Court should have recessed for lunch by now," Nudger said. "Will you call his car phone or page him and have him call . . ." He squinted and read her the number from the phone he was on. His head was really pulsing with pain, and his stomach was threatening to join it and gang up on him.

"Mr. Fleck said I should just take messages today," the temp said. Her name suddenly came to him: Wanda.

"Tell him Nudger needs to talk with him. You remember me, don't you, Wanda?

"Sure, the guy who saluted when I said I worked for American Office Commandos." Wanda tittered.

Some people appreciated his sense of humor. He would have to tell Claudia. "It's important. Have Mr. Fleck call me and he'll thank you for it."

"Oh, I'm not so sure."

"He'll be furious if we don't talk. He might fire you."

"He hasn't hired me yet. Anyway, I'm not sure—"

"Not sure of what?"

"If I want him to."

"To what?"

"Hire me. I have other offers."

"Then what's to lose if you call and give him my message?" She hesitated. "C'mon, Wanda, help me out here.

"I'm just not sure. Mr. Fleck's in a really, really bad mood today. I think I better not."

"How much worse than usual can he be?"

"A lot worse. Sorry. Bye."

Trying to walk steadily under Claudia's baleful gaze, Nudger returned to the table. The waiter, a bearded, intense young man who looked like a terrorist, had brought their iced tea. Nudger added artificial sweetener, stirred and sipped. Wonderful! Exactly what he needed. Iced tea was one of the few good things about fiercely hot St. Louis summers.

"They say the caffeine in tea and coffee is bad for headaches," Claudia told him.

"That's not what my doctor says." Nudger sipped again. "Okay if we stop by the courthouse on the way home?"

"You need rest, remember?"

"I have to talk to Fleck before court resumes."

"That doesn't sound very restful."

"No worse for me than caffeine," Nudger lied.

Had he been on his own, Nudger would have had to park blocks away from the County Government Center and hike across town in the dizzying sun. But Claudia drove him right to the entrance to the Courts Building. She'd wait for him here. Not bad, Nudger thought, as he rode the escalator up. He ought to consider hiring a chauffeur, if he ever got rich in the detective business.

Seymour Wister, the prosecutor, was being interviewed by a TV crew just outside the door of the courtroom. The light mounted on the TV camera threw a brilliant glare on his severe, Old Testament prophet's face, and cast a looming black shadow on the wall behind him. He might have been facing the burning bush. He didn't look awed, though. He looked smug. The trial must still be going well for him. And badly for Fleck.

Nudger entered the courtroom. Some spectators had returned to their seats, but the jury box was empty. In fact, the whole front of the courtroom was empty except for Fleck, who was sitting hunched over in his chair at the defense table. As Nudger got closer, he saw that the lawyer was studying the meaningless diagram he kept in his office to impress clients. Doubtless he was hoping it would have the same effect on the spectators.

"Fleck?"

He turned. "Nudger! You got anything I can use?"

"I have a question."

"More questions I don't need. You're an investigator, right? So go investigate."

The presence of an audience made Fleck's tirades more difficult to bear. Nudger sat down next to him, hoping to get him to lower his voice. "I tried to call, but your secretary said you weren't to be disturbed."

"Well, excuse me, Nudger, but I happen to be a bit busy. Who's the one in court trying to save Dupont's ass? Not you!'' Fleck said, before Nudger had time to answer. ''I gotta have strength to think and act and outsmart the judge and jury and dumb-ass prosecuting attorney. Think that's easy, Nudger?''

''Not for—''

''Well, it's not.''

Nudger was getting more exasperated. ''I only want you to do something for me to find out if a small error's been committed.''

''Napoleon said there are no small errors.''

''Napoleon said that?''

''Lajoie. Napoleon Lajoie the old-time baseball player. Also said, 'Oh, those bases on balls.' ''

''No he didn't, that was—''

''So get to the point, Nudger! What is this so-called small error you want checked out?''

''I'm not sure it is an error. I want you to ask Roger Dupont if he knows a woman named Vella Kling.''

Silence for a few beats. ''Who is this woman, Nudger?''

''That's what I'm trying to find out. One of the employees at Dupont's bank thinks she saw him and Vella Kling necking downtown inside the Serra Sculpture shortly before Karen Dupont was— before she disappeared.''

''Inside that thing? The employee's gotta be kidding.''

''She isn't kidding,'' Nudger said, ''but she might have the wrong woman. I want to know Dupont's reaction when you ask him about Vella.''

''Whatever he says, I'll be able to tell if he's lying. Know how?''

Nudger inhaled to ask how.

''You wouldn't know if he lied to you, but you're not me. I've seen more lying than undertakers, Nudger. I don't even have to look at their eyes and I can tell. Know how? By the way their voices sound. Dumb innocent like you, you'd just listen to the words, listen but not hear. I do both. When people lie, they don't exhale as much when they speak. Makes their voices sound different. You believe that?''

''Sure.'' He wondered if it were true.

''Well, that's because you're a poor naive soul. It doesn't happen all the time. But there are other symptoms. I can spot them and you can't. Don't feel bad; most people can't. If you were a doctor, you'd see a pimple and tell the patient he had measles. Know why?''

''I don't care why,'' Nudger said. ''Will you ask Dupont about Vella Kling?''

''Ask him yourself,'' Fleck said. ''here he comes.''

Nudger looked around. During the conversation, preparations for court to resume had been going forward. The court reporter was in her seat. The jury members were trooping into their box. And the bailiffs were bringing the defendant through the door in the wall of the courtroom that led to the cells.

Roger Dupont looked as relaxed as he had the last time Nudger had seen him, poolside at his sister's.

Nudger rose: He was sitting in Dupont's seat. A cleft appeared in the prisoner's brow as he tried to remember who Nudger was.

Fleck didn't stand. ''This is Nudger, my investigator. He's got a question for you.''

''Nudger. Yes.'' Nodding to himself, Dupont stepped right up to Nudger. His eyes were on a level with Nudger's. ''What is it?''

How to put it to him? Nudger wondered, distracted by the scrutiny of those eyes, so close and so remote. He decided on the direct approach. ''Do you know a woman named Vella Kling?''

Dupont's eyes widened. His chin went up and his shoulders went back. He was like a man standing in ocean surf, trying to keep his head above water when a bigger than usual wave came along.

It was only a moment, then he recovered. ''Vella Kling?'' he asked, then shook his head. ''No. I've never heard of anyone by that name.''

Then, without asking who she was, or why Nudger had asked,

he hitched up the pants legs of his impeccable banker's suit and sat down. He turned away from Nudger, toward his attorney. "So, Lawrence, what do you expect from the rest of the day?"

His languid tone suggested that if the proceedings didn't pick up soon, he would ask to be taken back to his cell, where he could read a book. Fleck shot Nudger a baffled look before he replied.

"Uh—it'll be a tough session, Roger. The prosecutor's planning to rest his case this evening, so you can be sure he's saved his strongest witnesses for last."

Dupont patted Fleck's forearm reassuringly. "You'll get your chance to put on your case tomorrow, Lawrence. You'll pulverize 'em."

Fleck's mouth was hanging open.

Nudger glanced around. Everyone seemed to be in place, waiting for the judge to appear. He'd best be off.

But as he turned away, Fleck called out, "Nudger!"

The little lawyer scurried over to him. Grasping his arm, he whispered, "What do you think? Was he lying about the woman?"

Nudger nodded. "I think so. What do you think?"

"About what?"

"Was Dupont lying?"

"How should I know?"

"But you told me you could know if somebody was lying by listening to their voice. The way they held their breath slightly when they lied. Remember?"

"I said that?"

Nudger was incredulous. "About five minutes ago."

Fleck didn't say anything for a long time.

Then: "This Dupont guy is different, Nudger. I thought at first he was lying, then . . ."

"You don't know," Nudger said.

"Did I say that?"

"No, not exactly. Do you think he was lying?"

"Think? Now that's different, Nudger."

"Then what *do* you think?"

Another stretch of silence.

"Dammit, Nudger, I don't know what to think? Isn't that why I hired you?"

"Yes, but—"

"Then why are you asking me the questions you're supposed to be answering?"

"I have answered. I think he's lying."

Fleck nodded. He seemed disposed to take Nudger's word for it. "This Vella is his girlfriend, you say."

"Seems like."

"Nudger, you got to find her. Soon as possible."

"I'll try, but—"

"I need her bad."

"To testify? I doubt she can say anything to help your case."

"What case?" Fleck asked. For a moment, his despair was naked for Nudger to see. He got a grip with both hands on Nudger's arm. "I don't need her to testify. I need her to talk to Roger. If she's his girlfriend maybe she can talk sense into him."

"Sense?"

"The guy's got to let me make a deal, or he's going to get the needle for sure."

"Is there still time to make a deal?"

"It's running out. Find her, Nudger."

"All rise!" It was the call of the bailiff, as Judge MacMasters appeared in the doorway. Releasing Nudger, Fleck rushed back to the defense table.

"Feeling okay, Nudger?" Claudia asked.

Nudger settled himself painfully into the seat beside her. She had the car moving by the time he worked out a reply.

"Why don't you drive me back to my apartment so I can lie down," he said. "You can ask around at the antique shops in St. Charles without me, if you don't mind."

She smiled. "Finally you're being sensible, Nudger." The smile wavered and disappeared. "You sure you're going to be okay?"

"I only need rest, and some of that ointment rubbed on my chest. Like Dr. Fell prescribed."

She asked about his chest and his head during the drive to his apartment. He was brave about it and made light of his injuries.

It was only when she was rubbing the foul-smelling ointment on his chest and he tried to pull her close and kiss her that she seemed convinced there was nothing seriously wrong with him.

She went into the other room and returned with a tattered paperback copy of *Farewell, My Lovely*, by Raymond Chandler. "Here, see if you can find that quote for me."

" 'She had a figure that could make a guy kick a hole in the wall?' You're sure that's not it?"

"I'm sure. See if you can find it."

Just like an English teacher to give him work when he was home sick.

"But I'm not even sure it was in this book," she admitted.

Great! Leaving him to lie on the sofa, she went to the door and opened it.

"Rest, Nudger," she said, in a tone that carried a kind of command and threat. "Leave St. Charles to me."

"I intend to," Nudger said.

She gave him a rather stern and suspicious look, then closed the door behind her.

Nudger lay still, thinking the ointment on his chest must have some kind of hot pepper ingredient, which was possible, as Dr. Fell prescribed a lot of medicine from Mexico. It felt like a thousand tiny needles pricking his skin. Well, if it hurt, it must be good for him.

He counted to twenty, then he rose from the sofa and walked to the window.

He watched Claudia emerge from the building, stride to her car, and get in, sitting down on the tiny bucket seat and swiveling gracefully on her bottom with her legs pressed together before closing the car door, the way women did if they were wearing skirts. She really did have beautiful ankles.

As soon as she'd driven away and turned the corner, he went downstairs to where the Granada was parked.

Thinking: liar, liar, chest on fire, he drove to Roger Dupont's house.

CHAPTER TWENTY-TWO

Nudger didn't want Alicia Van Moke to notice his car, so he parked around the corner in the shade of a large sycamore tree then walked to the Dupont home on Devlon.

To the right of the front porch was a small rock garden, now a bit weedy from neglect. He stood looking at it with his arms crossed, studying individual rocks.

Alicia Van Moke had been right. The false rock was a cheap mail-order one with, on not-too-close inspection, a very obvious seam.

Nudger picked it up from where it lay next to a geranium, opened it like a clam shell, and removed a brass door key. The whole thing hadn't taken more than a few minutes, and he was reasonably sure he hadn't been seen. Or if he had, it might be assumed he had business at the house and had been given instructions as to where to find the door key. A cop, maybe, still on the case. By now, the neighbors were no doubt used to seeing the police come and go.

He replaced the rock, then stepped up on the porch and tried the key. Being kept outside had taken its toll on the key. It took some effort to force it into the lock, but after that it worked smoothly and he opened the door and stepped inside.

The harsh sunlight was softened and diffused by sheer white curtains between green drapes. It revealed an inviting living room. As he walked into it he could feel the depth and softness of the carpet even through the soles of his shoes. There were sofas with plump cushions, covered in a rich, subdued floral pattern, and easy chairs in dark green leather, with matching ottomans. Nudger felt like sitting down and putting his feet up.

It was strange that he, an intruder, should feel so welcome here. Several people had told him of Karen Dupont's skills as a homemaker. Now he could see what they'd meant. Until now Karen had been the blank spot at the heart of the case to him; he realized that he had only the vaguest idea of what she looked like. Now, in her house, he got the sort of feeling that he sometimes got when reading a person's letters, or studying her photograph. He felt that he was in touch with Karen Dupont.

Her care and taste were evident everywhere in this room, even though it was dusty and neglected. He remembered what Alicia Van Moke had said, that Karen would never willingly have left her house. Nudger agreed. He had never been more convinced of Dupont's guilt.

Padding around the room on the thick carpet, he noticed that the wallpaper, which was beige with subdued stripes of gold and pale green, had been applied so that all the stripes matched up, all the way around the room. He had vivid memories of paper-hanging from his married days, and he shook his head at the effort involved.

So it seemed all the more jarring when he noticed that one of Karen's window treatments was crooked.

He walked over to the right front window and pushed the draperies aside. There were gouges in the plaster: The brackets that held up the curtain rod had been pulled out of the wall, and clumsily replaced. The poor repair job had not been done by Karen, he was certain of that. He wondered who had pulled down the drapes.

On the opposite wall was what appeared to be a large wooden wardrobe. An entertainment center, Nudger figured. He opened its doors and found a TV, with a complicated-looking VCR and stereo. A row of cassettes with handwritten labels was on the shelf above the VCR. Most of them were of hit movies of a few years ago. Nudger saw The Firm, the remake of Cape Fear, and Single White Female. Hmm . . . Lawyers and psychotic killers. Then Nudger considered that almost all contemporary movies featured at least one lawyer or psychotic killer. Sometimes they were the same character. There were other movies, classics dating back into the thirties, many of them adventure films, Dupont's taste in movies meant little if anything. Next to the video cassettes was a stack of Consumer Information magazines. Figured. On a bottom shelf were stacks of many of the other magazines that informed people on how to squeeze a dime till Roosevelt bled, never mentioning that the magazines were available at libraries so money could be saved by not subscribing.

Keeping in mind that the police had searched the house, and Dupont had had time to rearrange things afterward, Nudger began a methodical examination of each room's contents, trying to leave everything as he'd found it.

The other rooms were as tastefully and comfortably furnished as the living room. Nudger found no other signs of destruction like the torn-down and replaced draperies in the living room. Nor did he find what he was really looking for: any clue that would connect Roger Dupont and Vella Kling.

Disappointed, but telling himself he'd had to conduct such a search, Nudger let himself out and locked the door behind him.

He'd just straightened up after returning the key and artificial rock to where he'd found them next to the geranium, when a voice said, "You made a small error, Mr. Nudger, when you parked your car around the corner. It happens to be visible from one of my upper floor windows."

He turned and faced Alicia Van Moke. Her gray hair was pulled back today, making her strong face all the more striking. Her blue eyes seemed larger, more penetrating. She was wearing a dark blue dress with a fine white pattern that looked like delicate vines.

"There are no small errors," Nudger said, recovering his composure nicely.

Alicia Van Moke smiled. "Napoleon Lajoie, Hall of Famer ballplayer, after a one to nothing loss."

"How did you know that?" Nudger asked.

"I'm a baseball fan. Most poets are. It's a very poetic game, you know."

"I do know," Nudger said.

"So, how do you view the Cardinals' chances this year?"

"They'll stay competitive," Nudger said. "The owners have changed the play-off system and seen to it that all but a few teams will be competitive most of the season. There's more money in it for them that way."

"The bastards!" Alicia Van Moke said with passion.

"Yes," Nudger said, a bit taken aback by her sudden fire, but agreeing with her. There were a few reasonable owners, but for the most part baseball team owners were corporate giants who saw their teams as integral parts of their business that needed to show wins only on the bottom line, or owners who simply wanted to gain power and wealth—even if it meant the destruction of the game.

"I hate artificial grass and the goddamned designated hitter," Alicia Van Moke said. She turned her head for a moment, and Nudger thought she might actually spit with contempt, but she didn't. "What were you looking for in the house?" she asked.

Nudger knew it would be pointless to lie to this woman. She'd known about Napoleon Lajoie. "I was trying to find proof of a connection between Roger Dupont and a woman named Vella Kling."

"A romantic connection?" she asked. There might have been something in her eyes . . . what he'd seen for an instant when she'd contemplated the traitorous greed of the baseball owners.

"I was told it was a romantic relationship," he said, still watching her.

Her eyes were calm now. Her sensuous lips not so compressed.

Or was he imagining things, looking for more evidence of Dupont's extramarital affairs?

"I never slept with Roger Dupont," she said calmly.

What was she, psychic? "Why tell me?" Nudger asked.

"If I were in your place, I'd be wondering. I'd ask."

"I wasn't going to ask," he said. "If you had slept with him, you might not tell me the truth anyway."

"Might not," she admitted.

He grinned. "My conversations with you always seem to lead nowhere."

"That's true of most conversations, when you stop to think about it, which most people don't do. Most people don't stop to think about very much at all. You're different, though, because of your occupation. Or are you in your occupation because you're different?"

"I don't know." Nudger had never stopped to think about it.

"Do you think I'm the sort of woman who casually sleeps with men then discards them, Mr. Nudger?"

"I doubt if you do anything casually, though it seems that you do everything that way."

She smiled broadly at him and nodded her head in admiration, making him feel like her star pupil who'd just scored an A on his oral exam. He wished she'd reach out and ruffle his hair.

Then she glanced at her house. "I have to go inside now, Mr. Nudger. Something might be overheating in my oven."

He thought she might invite him in for supper, but she didn't. He told her good-bye and watched her walk to her front door. He loved the way her dress flowed when she stepped out with her long legs.

He stared for a few seconds at her closed front door after she'd gone inside.

If he wasn't going to have dinner at Alicia Van Moke's house, he knew where he might as well eat.

CHAPTER TWENTY-THREE

Shag's was doing a brisk business. Conscientious little Dorothy was handling drive-through orders, wearing the black box strapped to her waist with wires leading up to the bulky headphones with the jiggling antenna. "You want diet or regular?" Nudger heard her shout into the slender wand microphone that arced around from the headset to within inches of her lips.

Heidran was taking and serving up food orders at the counter. Her expression was calm but her U boat–commander eyes were as gray and threatening as the North Atlantic on the Murmansk run.

She saw Nudger and nodded curtly to him, then continued waiting on a tired-looking woman with two preschool kids hanging on her. The woman and both kids had the same oval features and thin red hair. Nudger fell into line behind a big man wearing paint-spattered white overalls and wondered if Heidran had counted on Ray being there all day, and that was the reason she and Dorothy were barely keeping up with customers' demands. If Heidran didn't shed herself of Ray, it wouldn't be the last time he'd let her down. Nudger knew it the way he knew that darkness followed light, another sad inevitability.

The woman with the kids trudged wearily to a far table, balancing her brown tray full of burgers, fries, and drinks and pleading for her charges to quiet down. The big guy ordered four hamburgers and a shake. When it was Nudger's turn, he asked Heidran for a Three-eighths Pounder, fries, and a glass of water.

"If you're on a diet," she said, "we've got diet drinks."

"It's not so much for my weight as for my nervous stomach," Nudger explained. His stomach overheard mention of it and twitched. "Plain water helps sometimes."

Heidran nodded and got his order. She put crushed ice in his cup without asking.

As Nudger paid her, she said, "Ray was supposed to be in for work this morning."

"I know," Nudger said. "I understand his back's acting up again."

"I understand who's acting," Heidran said. There was muted thunder in her voice and in her look.

"He warned you he had a chronically sore back," Nudger pointed out.

Heidran frowned, then smiled unconvincingly, and looked beyond Nudger's right shoulder.

Three bearded guys in work clothes had entered Shag's and fallen in behind Nudger to be waited on.

"We can talk later," Heidran said.

Nudger got out of the way and carried his order on his brown tray to a booth as far away as possible from the weary woman with the two kids.

He ate slowly, then got a refill on his ice water and sat for another twenty minutes, staring out the window and listening to the customers coming and going. Watching cars thread their way along the drive-through lane and then turn onto Manchester with their carryout orders. Dorothy's queries and the static-filled replies from the drive-through customers were like background music.

Finally, at about six forty-five, business slowed to nothing other than sporadic drive-throughs, and Heidran walked out from behind the counter, crossed the brown floor, and stood over Nudger with her arms crossed. He could see an impressive bulge of bicep straining her brown uniform sleeves.

"Why do you care so much about what happens to Ray?" she asked.

"I told you, I'm acting on behalf of Ray's concerned cousin."

"He should keep his nose in his doughnuts."

"Probably. But in one way, he's like you. For some reason, he believes in Ray. Of course, it could be because they're related. Family's not blind, like love, but it can be nearsighted."

"You apparently can't see very well yourself. Not well enough to see that there is something good and even ambitious in Ray. I will admit that at times it's almost invisible, and one of those times is now. I'm mad enough at Ray to fire him when he reports here for work tomorrow."

"You think he'll be back?" Nudger asked.

"I hope so. And we both know I won't fire him. I only said I was mad enough to do that; didn't say I was going to. What I'll do is give him another chance. After getting to know Ray, I perceived that's his problem in life, nobody ever gave him a second chance."

Nudger knew better. Ray's problem was Ray. Nudger also knew it would be hopeless to tell that to Heidran. If Danny couldn't see how truly worthless Ray was, how could love-lamed Heidran possibly see it?

"What if Ray's back really is hurt?" Nudger asked, remembering his promise to Danny. "If you force him to come in here and make him choose between work or losing his livelihood, you might cause permanent injury—either physical or mental. We wouldn't want to break his spirit."

"This could be his livelihood," Heidran said, waving a big arm to encompass all of Shag's, "rather than his unemployment checks. It's his spirit I want to revitalize."

"It won't happen," Nudger said. "The truth is, he didn't come here to work today because his spirit is beyond revitalization, either by the love of a good woman or by antioxidants. I warned you he was useless. Why don't you simply give up on him? If you're at all fond of him, make it appear as if you never hired him. Why run the risk of messing up his unemployment benefits?"

Heidran uncrossed her arms. She would have looked slightly less foreboding if she hadn't clenched her rather large hands into fists. "Regardless of what you say, Ray is worth fighting for. I wouldn't be doing him a favor by helping him claim fraudulent unemployment benefits and reinforcing his dependence on a pattern of public support."

"Some people were born for public support. They're of a breed, and Ray is one of them. He might be among the most highly evolved."

Heidran stared disdainfully at Nudger, as if he were . . . well, Ray. "I don't know who you think you are, to pass that kind of judgment on a person."

"Not a person," Nudger said. "Ray. Look at him under a microscope, and you'll see little suckers all over him, like on an octopus."

He could see her chest heaving. He really thought for a moment he'd gone too far and she might strike him. But dammit, he'd promised to do what he could for Ray, to give her a true picture so this woman would stop badgering him. Why should she care if Ray was a welfare leech? But Nudger knew her motive. So much harm was routinely done under the banner of love.

"If he reports for work here tomorrow," Heidran said in a curiously tender voice, "he has another chance. You tell him that for me, Mr. Nudger."

"I'll tell him, but he'll interpret it as a threat."

"Maybe it is. You might also tell him I don't believe his back is really injured. I've known a lot of slackers, and most of them have had bad backs, or said they did. You'd think there was an epidemic."

Nudger finished his ice water and stood up. "You're a good woman, Heidran. You don't deserve Ray."

Her cold gaze drilled into Nudger. "If Ray chooses to continue his aimless, parasitic drift, I will have failed."

"It won't be you who'll fail," Nudger said, "it will be Ray."

"Not if I can help it."

She couldn't, but Nudger had no way of convincing her of that.

He went out into the lingering heat and climbed into the Granada. Since he drove past the St. James apartments on his way home, he thought he might as well stop by and see Ray in person instead of phoning.

* * *

No one answered when Nudger rang Ray's doorbell. Nudger had heard a snatch of a Cubs game broadcast on WGNU cable. The TV's volume had fallen silent after the ring of the doorbell.

Nudger knocked hard on the door. "It's Nudger, Ray!"

No answer.

"I've got great news for you!" Nudger lied.

There was a faint sound from inside the apartment, then the door opened.

Ray was wearing pajamas and still had some sort of bulky wrapping around his waist, ostensibly for his back. His pajama tops, which had gray and black vertical stripes like a football referee's uniform, bulged and made him appear misshapen. Nudger remembered that his own torso was wrapped; he didn't like having even that in common with Ray.

"I was afraid you might be Heidran," Ray said.

"I'll bet."

"What's this great news, Nudge?"

"There is none."

"What? Then why'd you—"

"You wouldn't have answered my knock if I hadn't lied to you, Ray."

Ray put on his hurt expression. "That's not true, Nudge. I was on my way to answer it."

"Like the check is in the mail."

"Huh? Listen, the real reason I didn't want to come to the door right away—"

"Never mind. I talked to Heidran a little while ago at Shag's. She said she doesn't believe you have a sore back. You have one more chance, she said. She expects you to report for work tomorrow."

Ray widened his eyes in indignation and disbelief. The whites showed all around the pupils. "There's no way I can even get out of bed tomorrow morning with this back. It's been like this before, so I know how much pain I'm gonna be in after laying in bed all those hours. It's always worse the morning after it gets hurt."

"I think she'll fire you if you don't show up," Nudger said.

Ray made a show of pacing nervously, trying to keep himself between Nudger and the Cubs game on the silent TV visible inside the apartment.

"They winning?" Nudger asked.

Ray stopped pacing. "Who?" Then he feigned sudden comprehension. "Oh, the Cubs, you mean. I don't even know the score. Damned television's been on for hours because I didn't wanna go through the pain of getting up and turning it off."

"Don't you have a remote?"

"Sure. I keep it on top of the television." He absently inserted his hand inside his pajama tops and scratched beneath whatever was wound around his midsection. "Nudge, you sure Heidran won't change her mind and just pretend I never even worked at that hellish place?"

"I'm sure, Ray. She wants to do you a favor and break your cycle of welfare dependence."

"Ohhhhh!" Ray hugged himself as if he were cold.

If it weren't for the fact that Ray was Danny's cousin, and Nudger had promised to try to intercede on Ray's behalf, Nudger would have run fast away from Ray and never thought about him again. Nudger knew he could still do that, and for a second or two considered it. He could almost see himself bolting toward his car, leaving Ray's puzzled, self-pitying face to become part of the past.

But Danny deserved better, even if Ray didn't.

Instead of deserting the situation, Nudger momentarily turned his back on Ray and got one of his business cards from his wallet. He always instinctively turned his back on Ray when he opened his wallet. Facing Ray again, he unclipped his ballpoint pen from his shirt pocket and scribbled on the back of the card.

"What are you doing, Nudge?" Ray asked.

Nudger handed him the card. "If you can somehow show her you really do have an injured back, Heidran might give you some more rope before you hang yourself."

Ray squinted at the card. "Dr. Fall? . . ."

"Dr. Fell," Nudger corrected. "That's his address. Don't bother to look up his number and call for an appointment; he doesn't make them. See him early tomorrow before you go in to Shag's. Maybe he'll give you a note confirming your back is sore."

Ray brightened and stood up straight. "Hey, that's a good idea, Nudge. Heidran shouldn't fire me if a doctor says I'm ailing. And if she fires me anyway, I might even be able to bring suit. I mean, Shag's will be depriving me of my livelihood."

"Maybe you can at least collect sick pay," Nudger said.

"No, I already checked on that."

"Then Dr. Fell might be able to buy you some time away from slaving over a hot grill or hoisting Three-eighths Pounders."

"I'll sure see him, Nudge. Lots of doctors have failed, but he might be the one who can help my back, finally give me some relief from the pain."

"He might even give you a real back brace," Nudger said. He turned away and walked toward where his car was parked.

"And some ointment," he called over his shoulder.

"Nudge! Wait a minute, damn it! You never did let me finish telling you why I was afraid to answer the door at first."

Nudger stopped walking and faced Ray, silhouetted in his apartment doorway.

"There was a big, creepy guy here about an hour ago looking for you."

"He leave his name?"

"Not hardly," the misshapen silhouette said. "He wasn't the type to leave a name."

"What did he look like? I mean, his face?"

"I don't know. Reason I said he was creepy, he stayed back in the shadows so I couldn't see his face. Not so far back, though, that I couldn't smell bourbon on his breath."

CHAPTER TWENTY-FOUR

Nudger switched on the window air conditioner in his apartment, removed his shoes, and padded in his socks to get a Busch beer from the refrigerator. He slid a footstool over so it was in front of the sofa, then sat back with his feet propped up and used the remote to turn on the television set.

He channel-surfed. There was a network special about violence in the streets. There was the Cubs game Ray was watching. There was another network special, about violence in the home. There was a rerun of the *Twilight Zone* Nudger had seen three times, the one where Agnes Moorehead, alone in an isolated cabin, battles miniature pesky space invaders who turn out to be from the planet Earth. There was yet another special about violence in the schools. There was *Strangers on a Train*, but Nudger had seen that oldy-but-goody at least three times. There was Pat Robertson, straining forward in his chair and smiling grimly about something. There was a CNN special about whether the media gave too much coverage to violence and were scaring people. Maybe that was why Pat Robertson was smiling. Nudger decided there was nothing special on, turned off the TV and sipped beer.

He became cooler and more comfortable. Then the beer can became empty.

Nudger didn't feel like getting up. And he knew he shouldn't fall asleep; it was too early and he'd wake up at 3:00 A.M. with his mind whirling like the out-of-control carousel in *Strangers on a Train*.

The phone was within reach so he put it in his lap and punched out Danny's home number. Now was a good time to tell him about the Ray and Heidran situation.

Danny didn't answer.

Nudger knew that if Danny wasn't home on a weekday evening, he was probably at the doughnut shop doing his baking for the next morning. During the summer especially, Danny often did his baking at night when it was cooler.

No answer at the doughnut shop, either.

Okay, maybe Danny was at the ball game. The Cardinals were in town, so it was possible. Danny had a friend who had a share of a season ticket for a terrace seat between home and third and sometimes let him use it.

While the phone was in his lap, Nudger decided to call his office answering machine and see if he had any messages.

The machine beeped and signaled that he had two. Nudger pressed the receiver to his ear and listened. He didn't bother with a pencil and paper; the machine would save his messages, and if they were important and he needed to remember anything, he could call back later and copy it down, or take care of it tomorrow in the office.

Beep.

"Nudger, this is Eileen. Did you get the letter Henry Mercato sent you? There's no use pretending you didn't. If you don't . . ."

Her voice faded as Nudger held the receiver well away from his ear. Sitting there in his apartment, there was no way he could fast-forward to the next message, so he waited patiently until Eileen's message ended.

Beep.

"Hello, friend. Did you ever wonder about why society is in a crisis state? Why our institutions are failing us? Why the very fabric of our once-great country is in disarray?"

Nudger knew. It was because of the media's undue emphasis on violence. It was scaring the bejibbers out of people.

"If you'll send ten dollars—or something more if you can afford it—to the American Patriotic Society of Psychic—"

"Nudge?"

Huh? Danny's voice. He must have picked up the phone in the office and cut into the answering machine's message.

"Nudge?"

There was something different about the voice. Something that made Nudger apprehensive.

"What's going on, Danny?"

"I'm hurt some. I could use your help over here. Can't quite get up all the way . . ."

"Don't try, Danny. I'll be right there. You bleeding? You need an ambulance? I can call nine-eleven."

"Not necessary, I don't think. Need help, though."

"I'm on my way."

As Nudger stood up and replaced the receiver in one motion, he heard the clatter of the phone in his office on the other end of the line, as if it had been dropped on the floor.

He ignored the red traffic light at Sutton and Manchester, and it took him less than five minutes to drive to his office and park directly in front of the doughnut shop. He could see faint light in the back of the shop. Apparently Danny had been baking earlier that evening. Nudger started to unlock the street door, then found that it was already unlocked. Of course! He wasn't thinking! Danny would have had to unlock it to go upstairs.

He dropped his keys back in his pocket, then opened the street door and charged up the narrow stairwell and in through the office door.

The desk lamp was glowing in the office. File cabinet and desk drawers were standing open, some of their contents scattered on the floor. Danny was sitting on the floor with his back against the front of Nudger's desk.

His face looked worse than Nudger's. Blood was streaming from a gash high on his forehead, and his already bulbous nose was even more crooked and unmistakably broken. Blood from his nose had colored the top of his white baker's apron black in the dim light.

He was conscious, gazing up at Nudger with dim and sad awareness. Then he smiled. It must have hurt him, because he stopped immediately and inhaled a sharp, rasping breath through his mouth.

As Nudger bent over him, he saw that not all the blood on Danny had flowed from the gashed forehead and broken nose. Danny's left ear was badly mangled.

"How'd this happen?" Nudger asked. His own breath was rasping. He was breathing hard, in fear and in rage.

"Heard somebody walking around up here, Nudge. So I left my baking and came on up. I surprised some big guy digging around in your files. When he saw me, he came at me right off. He was the size of a small house, only he moved faster than a house. I never had any chance even to run."

"Did you see his face?"

"Sure, but only for a moment. He had red hair and a bristly little red mustache. Mean eyes, but I couldn't tell you the color. 'Bout all I can recall about him."

"Did you smell liquor on his breath?"

"Yeah, that's right. Bourbon. How'd you know?"

"I met him once before." Nudger reached over on the desk and picked up the phone. "Stay put, Danny. Don't try to move or something might break."

"You trying to scare me, Nudge?"

"Only if it'll keep you from moving."

"Who you calling?"

"Nine-eleven. Ambulance. Don't argue." Nudger realized he sounded like Claudia.

But Danny didn't resist, as Nudger expected.

"The giant worked me over pretty bad, Nudge. Even while I was unconscious, I think. Hurts to breathe."

"That's his style," Nudger said.

Then the 911 operator answered.

Nudger's office was only blocks from the Maplewood Fire Department.

Things began to happen.

CHAPTER TWENTY-FIVE

Danny was resting in his apartment the next morning, and the doughnut shop had a TEMPORARILY CLOSED sign hanging on its door. Emergency at St. Mary's had treated him, kept him overnight for observation, then sent him home. His head was stitched, his broken nose set and packed with cotton and bandaged. He had been kicked in the chest while unconscious, like Nudger, only more gently and with less bruising, as if his attacker had thought perhaps his heart might stop more easily.

Nudger had driven him to his apartment an hour ago, made sure he was comfortable, then gone to his office.

The air conditioner still hadn't caught up with the heat by the time he'd gotten the place cleaned up and his files were more or less in order. Or at least close to their previous disorder.

He sat in his shirtsleeves at his desk and called Hammersmith, wondering if he really needed half the stuff he'd crammed back into his file cabinet drawers. Like that file with the photo of the attractive twin of a murder victim. Or the file on the case where the Pomeranian had bitten his hand three times. Not deeply, but three times.

"Danny was beaten up in my office last night," he said, when Hammersmith had answered the phone.

"He okay?" Hammersmith's voice was concerned. And angry, though only people who knew him would guess.

"Not okay," Nudger said, "but he wasn't seriously hurt other than a broken nose. He's healing at home."

"What was he doing in your office at night?"

"He was baking down in the shop and thought he heard someone walking around upstairs. He was right. When he went up to investigate, he found a guy rifling my files. I think it was the same goon who beat me up. Danny got a look at him."

"Second time someone's gone through your files," Hammersmith said. "Somebody must think you know something of interest."

"I wish I knew what it might be."

"Maplewood Police know about Danny?"

"I called them from the hospital and they sent an officer to take our statements. They want Danny to come by later and look at photographs and try for an ID."

"He should come by here, too. Our art collection is more extensive." Hammersmith's voice became muffled and indecipherable. He must have placed his hand over the receiver and said something to someone who'd entered the office. When he spoke clearly again, he said, "Why do you think this guy's interested in you, Nudge?"

"It's probably the Dupont case, but I can't rule out the possibility he was sent by Eileen and Henry Mercato to try to get financial information so they can squeeze more money from me."

"Mercato's a lawyer. You really think he'd hire a thug?"

"Sure. Hire him and then think of a way not to pay him. I know Mercato. Not as well as Eileen, who's sleeping with him, but I know him. He thinks being an attorney gives him a free pass when it comes to skirting the law."

"Aw, they all think that. And hiring somebody to commit assault and burglary is a bit more than skirting the law, Nudge. I think you'd better assume your giant thug's part of the Dupont case."

Nudger knew he was right. "That is my assumption, but if you knew Henry Mercato like I do—"

"You're bitter, Nudger. Your judgment is clouded when it comes to Eileen. Just because she's involved with the guy doesn't mean he's a criminal."

Hammersmith had always liked Eileen and still had a soft spot for her, which infuriated Nudger.

He was going to hang up on Hammersmith, but Hammersmith hung up first.

Almost as soon as Nudger had replaced the receiver, the phone rang.

Claudia.

"Do you feel any better?" she asked.

"Sure," Nudger said. "Every day in every way. Any luck with the St. Charles antique shops?"

"None," Claudia said. "And I covered about half of them. One woman, at a place called Old Tales, said the name was familiar but she couldn't place where she'd heard it. I'm beginning to think Vella Kling's supposed profession is a front for something illegal or immoral."

"Or both," Nudger said. "Something happened last night in my office." He told her about Danny being beaten by the giant with booze on his breath.

"Danny could have been killed," she said with a reproachful tone that suggested Nudger was in some way responsible. And maybe he was.

"I've warned him not to rush in when it comes to some of the lowlife that appear on the scene in my business," he said in a guilty voice that surprised him. "If my office walls could talk, they'd tell tales that would make the Mayflower Madam blush."

"After they asked to be painted," Claudia said.

"Yeah. I've told the landlord about that, too. He links a fresh coat of paint to my catching up on the rent."

"How unreasonable. You sound like Ray."

"Speaking of the devil, Ray could use a doctor's care and a note to prove he really does have a bad back. I sent him to Dr. Fell."

"Perfect," Claudia said.

"Time's running out on my client's client," Nudger said. "Can you help me out again today?"

"Can and will. Want me to cover some more of the St. Charles antique shops?"

"No," Nudger said, "I'll do that. What I need is for you to attend the trial today, let me know how it's going, tell me your impression of Roger Dupont as he continues to sink."

"What's been his reaction so far?"

"He seems only mildly concerned, as if he's facing a flu shot instead of dying at the hands of the state. It puzzles his lawyer more and more. I can read it between the lines of what he's saying whenever he takes time between words to inhale."

"What time does court convene?"

Nudger liked that; she was already talking like an attorney. "Ten o'clock."

"It's almost that now, and I just came back from breakfast."

"That's okay, they'll begin without you. It's impressions I want. Not just of the defendant, but of the jury. You're perceptive, even intuitive. See if you can get some idea as to which way the jurors are leaning."

"Which way to you think they're leaning?"

"I think they'd like to stone Dupont."

"If his guilt is such a foregone conclusion, what on earth was he doing walking around out on bail?"

"I think he was allowed bail so the police could keep an eye on him, hoping he'd lead them to more substantial clues, or maybe even to where his wife's body is buried."

"Apparently it didn't work."

"That's because anyone with the intelligence of a houseplant would suspect what was going on. Dupont's plenty smarter than that, despite the way he's behaving."

"Maybe he really is innocent and has a naive faith in the legal system."

"It's possible," Nudger said. "A houseplant would feel that way."

"Cynic. I'm going to feel guilty sitting in an air-conditioned courtroom while you're in St. Charles dragging your injured body from shop to shop in the hot sun."

"I told you, I feel much better. And the exercise will be good therapy."

"Does that awful-smelling gunk Dr. Fell prescribed really help your chest?"

"That depends on who rubs it in."

She laughed softly in a way he liked, then broke the connection.

He thought their conversation suggested possibilities for tonight. But this was morning, and there were other things to think about.

He thought about them all the way to St. Charles.

CHAPTER TWENTY-SIX

Nudger ignored the antique shops on 1st Street, already visited by Claudia. After the third shop, spelled "shoppe," he decided Claudia was right about his discomfort in dragging his aching body around in the hot sun. St. Charles lay on the west bank of the Missouri River, and the humidity in addition to the heat made the air seem like an extension of the river itself. Nudger occasionally wondered if he should walk or swim.

At the Calico Calliope—a name that made no sense to Nudger—an elderly man behind the counter squinted through wire-rimmed spectacles with interest when Nudger mentioned Vella Kling. He was small and stooped, maybe in his seventies, but his wrists were thick and his hands looked strong. He said his name was Barney Haupt. Something in the glint of his tiny dark eyes behind the thick, round lenses suggested he could be mean.

"Only met Vella Kling once," he said, "but I sure do remember her."

"She must have made an impression," Nudger said.

Barney walked along the counter to the glassed-in display section and pointed to an old Bulova wristwatch with a rectangular case and a brown leather band. "She sold me that watch. It's a collectible from the 1940s, still ticking with the original works. Antique and collectible watches are big business these days, so naturally there's lots of imitations flooding the market."

Nudger leaned close to the case and studied the watch. He didn't see why anyone would pay the two hundred–dollar asking price scrawled on the attached tag. But then he wasn't a collector. And he'd once seen a plate featuring a hand-painted portrait of Elvis sell for three hundred dollars. It hadn't even looked much like Elvis.

"The watch must be genuine, considering the price," Nudger said. "Or are you going to tell me the fakes are worth that much and the originals sell for even more?"

"Nope, the price is right in line. And it's an original, all right. Trouble is, I bought a dozen originals from Vella Kling for a hundred dollars each, all in excellent condition."

"Let me guess. The other eleven were imitations?"

"Not only that, their cases contained no works at all. Nothing but some wadded silver foil to give them weight. It didn't bother me that they didn't run, but they're not worth much without the original clockwork. They're worth even less if their cases are downright empty. Vella Kling used the valuable watch there in the counter for a sample, and like an idiot I trusted her and thought the others were as good as they looked."

"I'm surprised someone in your business would be so trusting," Nudger said.

Barney shot him an angry look. "I ain't so old that a woman can't still make a fool of me. She came in here all smiles and sweetness, and she's a pretty little thing to start with. She's got a smooth line of bull that'd fool men smarter'n I am. I admit it, I screwed up royally. Not the first time, but it ain't happened in a long while.

Last week I sold the other eleven watches to a collector for five dollars each. I was lucky to get that, considering they were nothing but shells of imitations."

"How long ago did you buy the watches?" Nudger asked, thinking that the sun had sapped his energy. He felt like one of Vella's eleven watches, a shell of an imitation.

"About two months, I'd guess."

"Do you have a dated bill of sale you could check to pin down the date?" Nudger asked.

"Nope, no bill of sale." There was something of a challenge in Barney's voice. A sly old man, ready to argue.

Nudger figured Vella had implied that the watches were stolen, and the bedazzled Barney had gone for the bait. Now he was mad at himself.

"Cash transaction, I suppose," Nudger said.

Barney nodded. "No receipt. She had the money, I had the watches, so I didn't figure there was any need for paperwork."

"When you found out the watches were empty fakes, did you tell the police?"

"Humph! No use telling the cops. The woman was long-gone by the time I realized she'd conned me."

"And there was no point in the police knowing it was a cash transaction, right?"

"Right as rain. There's lots of cash transactions in the antique business, son. Oh, we pay our taxes, but when the amount is based on cash changing hands, memory has to serve. Sometimes the IRS remembers it different, even though they weren't there at the time."

"Have you seen Vella since the sale?"

"Sure haven't." Barney's face got hard and his big gnarled hands knotted into fists. Veins thick as hoses stood out as if sculpted on his wrists. "And I been watching for her at all the auctions and estate sales, places like that."

Nudger laid one of his cards on the counter, directly above where the Bulova watch was displayed. "Will you give me a call if you do see Vella Kling again?"

"You can count on it," Barney said, examining the card at arms length, even wearing his fishbowl glasses. "You're a private cop, huh?"

"Yes," Nudger said, "a shamus."

"You seen too many movies and TV shows, son. Are the real cops looking for her too?"

"No," Nudger said, "so far it's only us unreal ones. But that could change in a hurry."

"I'm hoping it does," Barney said. "I shoulda looked closer at them watches."

"Or closer at Vella Kling."

"Oh, no," Barney said, "I was looking plenty close at her. That turned out to be the problem." He made a terrible face and a sound something like *Grrrrrr* and Nudger thought for a moment that he was actually going to break into a barrage of curses. Instead he simply growled, "Women! Can't live with 'em!"

Nudger thought he was going to exclaim how he couldn't live without 'em, either, but Barney let it go at that. At his age, maybe only half the maxim applied.

CHAPTER TWENTY-SEVEN

Sure I can't get you anything, Nudge? Coffee?"

Nudger shook his head, "Danny, you're supposed to be resting."

"Coffee's no trouble."

"Danny, stay put," said Nudger firmly. "I came by to find out if there was anything I could do for you."

"I'm fine." They were sitting in Danny's apartment, where he had spent the day, and he did not look fine. Part of it was the bandages, on his forehead and across the bridge of his nose. His eyes, in the crisscross of white tape, looked sadder than ever. As he eased back into his recliner chair, he winced. Nudger winced sympathetically; he knew what that blow on the chest felt like.

He'd run out of antique shops by late afternoon. He hadn't found out any more about Vella Kling. He didn't want to go to the courthouse and face Lawrence Fleck—who must be truly desperate by now—empty-handed. So he'd decided to check in on Danny instead.

"Well, there is one thing you could do for me, maybe." Danny hesitated. His hand went to the sash of his robe, as if he was looking for the gray towel he tucked there when he was in the shop. "But I hate to ask, Nudge. You look like you had a tough day."

"I feel useless, that's all. It's this case. Seems all I've accomplished is to get you beaten up."

Danny waved this off. "None of that, Nudge."

"Anything I can do, just name it."

"Well, okay. There is something that's bothering me. Won't let me rest."

"Where does it hurt?" Nudger asked. "I can call the doctor. He can call a prescription in to the pharmacy and I'll pick it up."

"Naw, it's nothing like that. It's Ray. I'm real worried about him. Could you go over and check on him for me?"

Nudger's stomach kicked rebelliously. Walked into that one, he thought; trapped in a box canyon of responsibility. "What's wrong with Ray now?"

Danny looked at him reproachfully. "I know what you think of Ray, Nudge, but he ain't faking. Not this time anyway. He's in real bad shape."

"That what he tells you?"

"Not him personally. I haven't heard a peep from him. He's not gonna trouble me when he knows I'm laid up myself."

"Well, he's always been considerate."

"Don't be sarcastic, Nudge. He's been to the doctor. Guy with an international reputation in musculoskeletal medicine, and he says Danny's back trouble is real bad. Ordered him to go right home, lie flat on his back in bed and not move a muscle, or the doc couldn't answer for the consequences."

Now Nudger remembered. He couldn't help grinning as he wondered how long it had taken Danny to memorize 'musculo-skel . . .' well, whatever.

Danny looked shocked. "It's nothing to smile about, Nudge. I know what you think about Ray's bad back, and to tell you the truth, there's times I thought he was maybe exaggerating a bit myself." Danny frowned and shook his head with remorse. "Right now I feel pretty bad about doubting him. Ray's in bad shape. We got the doctor's word on that."

"Danny—"

"Couldn't you please drop in on him? See if he needs anything? The poor guy, he must be miserable. Stuck in his apartment. Nothing he can do but lie in bed."

Ray must be in heaven, Nudger thought. "Danny, you didn't talk to this doctor yourself, did you?"

"No. That woman Hydrant, at Shag's, she called me. This doctor called her, to explain why Ray wasn't coming into work. She was plenty worried. And I've seen her when I ate at Shag's. She doesn't look like the type of woman to worry about nothing, would you say?"

Nudger shook his head. He could easily imagine Heidran on the bridge of her U boat, gazing pitilessly at survivors struggling in an icy sea. He said, "Dr. Fell must have done a good job to convince her."

"You know this doctor, Nudge?"

"Danny, he's not an internationally known musculo . . . Not a famous specialist. He's Dr. Fell, from the cash-in-advance clinic on Manchester Road. I told Ray to go to him, to get an excuse so he wouldn't have to go to work."

Danny stared at Nudger for a few seconds. "You mean, this doctor was sort of exaggerating Ray's problem when he talked to the German woman."

"More like inventing it."

Danny sighed. The gentle melancholy eyes inside the X of white tape regarded Nudger a moment in silence. "Oh. Well, I guess that oughta put my mind at rest. You—uh—you're absolutely sure Ray's okay?"

"Absolutely."

Danny's sad eyes were apologetic. "Nudge, I'm sorry about the way I ran on about Ray's back and all. I guess you figure you've done enough for him lately. Guess you don't want to go check on him."

"Danny, he's fine. He's been having a perfectly enjoyable day today, especially if there's a Cubs game on television."

"Sure, Nudge. Well, thanks for coming by." Danny swung his legs off the recliner. Wincing, he started to rise to his feet.

"You're not going over to Ray's yourself?"

"You know how I worry about the guy. No need for you to trouble yourself."

Box canyon, Nudger thought again. "Danny, you don't have to go right now, do you?"

"Better now than later, after it gets dark. I got some problems with my vision."

Nudger sighed. "Sit down, Danny. I'm on my way."

He expected the usual long wait for Ray to answer his door. But it opened to his first knock. Nudger found himself face-to-face with Heidran Kreb.

He almost didn't recognize her. She was out of uniform, for one thing. Her hair was covered by a bright kerchief, and she was wearing jeans and a blue work shirt. Even more unfamiliar and disconcerting was the smile of greeting she gave him. It was the first time he'd seen Heidran's teeth. They were large, white, and even. She'd probably flossed every day of her life.

"Oh, Ray," she called out. The dulcet voice was another novelty. "Your friend is here to see you."

"Who is it?" Ray called out from the bedroom.

"It's Mr. Nudger."

There was a pause, then Ray said, "Just the— Just who I want to see."

"Come in, Mr. Nudger," Heidran said. "Wipe your feet first."

Nudger looked down: There was a brand-new welcome mat, which actually said WELCOME. It had a motif of cardinals and bluejays. As he wiped his feet he asked Heidran what she was doing here.

"The moment I finished talking to Dr. Fell on the telephone I knew I had to come over," she said. "I couldn't bear to think of Ray alone here, helpless."

"Ah. Of course. Still, it's a wonder Shag's can get along without you."

"This is the first day I've missed in three and a half years," Heidran said. For a moment she looked misty-eyed over the loss of her perfect attendance record, but she snapped out of it.

Nudger stepped inside. He looked around, blinking. Ray's formerly sordid apartment now gleamed with cleanliness. The linoleum floor had the lustre of marble. The cobwebs were gone from the corners of the ceiling. There wasn't an old newspaper or empty beer can in sight. The horrible smell was gone, replaced by the tang of lemon and ammonia. The TV screen was blank. Nudger found he was placing his feet hesitantly, almost reverently, as he followed Heidran to the bedroom.

In this shining sea of cleanliness, Ray's bed was an island of squalor. There were still the same dingy sheets, with crumbs and even a few cellophane wrappers caught in their folds, and the same grimy coverlet.

Ray lay flat on his back in the middle of the bed, in striped pajamas. The shirt was unbuttoned, revealing the pallid, hairy skin of his midsection, crisscrossed with surgical tape. His eyes rolled toward Nudger. He did not smile."

"And here's your friend!" Heidran burbled. "Isn't this nice?"

Nice? Nudger gave her a sideways glance. Heidran certainly was different when she was with Ray in a domestic environment.

She was pulling up a chair for him, a little closer to Ray than Nudger would have preferred to be, but he sat down anyway.

"It's time to put the wash in the dryer," Heidran said. "Is there anything I can do for you before I go?"

"Yeah," Ray said. "I wonder if you could wheel the TV in here?"

"We've been over that, Raymond. You'd have to raise your head to watch the television, and Dr. Fell says you mustn't put even the slightest strain on your vertebrae. Besides, the excitement might be bad for you, if the Cubs are winning."

"I mean for Nudge. So he could watch."

"Mr. Nudger didn't come over here to watch television. Now you boys enjoy your talk."

Boys?

Ray waited until the screen door banged behind her, then said, "This is all your fault, Nudger."

"I've done my best for you, Ray. Dr. Fell—"

"That idiot! I thought when I saw him that he understood. But he didn't. He was supposed to tell her I could never work again, not say there was anything seriously wrong with me."

"Ah!" Nudger said, wondering if there might really be a few exotic diseases that fit Ray's needs.

"Know what she's doing down in the basement right now? There's five washing machines, and she's using all of them. She's washing everything I own. Even underwear I've worn only two or three times. I've got nothing left but this bed. Sooner or later I'll have to go to the bathroom, and then she'll change the sheets."

He nodded toward the night table, on which new white sheets, fresh from the store and still in their plastic wrap, waited.

"I think your place looks pretty good, Ray."

"You kidding? She's been pouring chemicals on everything. My home is a toxic waste dump. The fumes are shrivelling up the insides of my nostrils. My nose hairs are gonna fall out, and I'll have to move to Arizona. And just look around—everything's so shiny, the glare hurts your eyes. It's enough to give a person"—Ray paused for thought—"optic-nerve burnout."

"I'm truly sorry, Ray," Nudger said. "But I'm afraid there's nothing more I can do. I'm fresh out of ideas."

"Well, that's okay, cause I don't need you anymore," said Ray bitterly. "And I got an idea of my own. There's only one way to get rid of this woman. I'm gonna pretend I died."

"Of falling nose hairs, or optic-nerve burnout?"

"I'll leave that to Dr. Fell."

"Dr. Fell?"

"He convinced her I was sick, he can convince her I died. The guy owes me one."

Nudger felt relief and guilt at the same moment. Poor Dr. Fell. Probably the one way anyone ever got rid of Ray was to scrape him off on somebody else. Maybe Dr. Fell could send him to some sort of specialist.

"Well, I know you need your rest," Nudger said, getting to his feet. "Danny was worried about you, but I'll tell him you're okay."

"Tell him I'm dying," Ray said. "It ain't too soon to start the rumors."

Nudger didn't see Heidran as he left the building. Still down in the basement, no doubt, tending her five washers.

As he got into the Granada, he checked his watch: five on the dot. Quitting time. He could put off calling Fleck until tomorrow.

Coaxing the engine into life, he headed for Claudia's, to hear her report on her day in court.

"Thanks for asking me to attend that trial, Nudger. It was the most exciting thing I've ever seen. Much more dramatic than any movie or TV show."

Nudger didn't know what to say. When Claudia was this effusive, she usually meant to be ironic. But as she walked about her kitchen gathering ingredients for dinner, her movements were quick and her dark eyes glittered with excitement. Something really big must have happened in court today.

"Let me guess," he said, "Roger finally broke down and begged for mercy."

"No, no. It's Fleck I'm talking about."

"Did Judge MacMasters order him bound and gagged?"

"No, Nudger. You gave me entirely the wrong impression of Lawrence Fleck."

"I told you about the loud suits and the bad toupee."

"Yes, but you didn't mention that the man is a courtroom genius."

Nudger was stunned. "You sure you were in the right courtroom? *State of Missouri v. Dupont?*"

"Yes, and if I were betting, I'd put my money on Roger Dupont. Fleck turned the trial around today."

"Uh-huh. How did he do it?" Nudger was still skeptical; by her own admission, Claudia had never seen a real murder trial before.

She put the kettle under the faucet and left it to fill. She'd told him they were having linguine with clam sauce. Nudger didn't say anything, but he had reservations about clams. Their smell always made him think of the underside of a pier. Still, he was lucky she was cooking for him tonight. Moochers couldn't be choosers.

Placing a clove of garlic on the cutting board, she turned to address him. "For starters, Fleck made Alicia Van Moke look like a fool."

Nudger couldn't imagine anyone doing that, much less Fleck. "You're kidding. You *must* be kidding."

"No. Remember, Van Moke said she heard Karen screaming, 'No! Stop! Stop! No.'"

"Yes. Pretty damaging testimony, I thought. Pretty chilling."

"It was chilling, but it wasn't Karen. It was Fay Aldrich."

"Who?"

"Fay Aldrich, the movie star from the thirties who starred in *Revenge of the Gorilla*. First Fleck put the detective who'd searched the house on the stand to say that the Duponts had a copy of *Revenge of the Gorilla* in their video library. Then he set up a VCR and played a scene from the movie. And there was Fay Aldrich screaming 'No! Stop! Stop! No!' at the giant Gorilla who was about to drop her from the top of a tall building."

Claudia grinned over her shoulder at him as she turned off the water and moved the kettle to the stove. But Nudger was thoughtful. Fleck hadn't mentioned that he had this courtroom coup up his sleeve when they'd talked the day before. The obnoxious little defense lawyer had seemed on the verge of panic. When had he come up with this? How? The man must really know his movies.

Whack! Claudia smacked a garlic clove with the flat of her knife, peeled off the husk, and tossed it into the olive oil. Then she gave Nudger another smirk. She was rooting for Fleck, pleased he'd confounded Nudger's expectations.

"Well, that was great courtroom magic," Nudger conceded. "Jury must have eaten it up. But it doesn't exactly turn the case around. What about the evidence that Dupont disposed of Karen's body."

Claudia smiled and pointed at Nudger. She still had the knife in her hand, which made the gesture more dramatic. "He had a witness. Hannah Duskovic, from the Helping Hand domestic temp agency. She'd helped Karen with the housecleaning a couple of months before her disappearance."

"So?"

"Well, remember Dupont's claim that Karen used the furnace as an incinerator? This Duskovic woman confirmed it was true."

Nudger shifted in his chair. Dupont telling the truth? It was as unlikely, as unsettling, as Fleck mounting an able defense. "But the police found earrings in the furnace. And a pair of panties."

"Well, why not? Once your underwear turns grayish and starts rolling over at the waistband, you have to get rid of it some way. Right?"

"Sure," Nudger said uneasily.

"So why not burn it?"

Nudger wondered if there was a personal message here. *His* underwear was mostly gray and sagging. He got up and poured himself another glass of wine from the bottle of Gallo on the sideboard. Hannah Duskovic. The Helping Hand Agency. Must have been a lot of work to track her down. This wasn't Fleck's legal acumen, Nudger thought, it was Fleck's investigator making him look good. Problem was, that investigator wasn't Nudger.

Who had gotten this stuff for Fleck?

He leaned against the fridge next to Claudia. Close enough to smell the aroma of garlic and olive oil. "Okay, so there goes the evidence that he burned her body. But there's still the evidence that he buried her."

"You mean the muddy shovel?" She tossed her head. Her thick dark hair bounced and settled becomingly.

"Fleck explained that, too?" Nudger asked.

"He had another witness," Claudia said. "I can't remember the name, but he's a farmer from Sedalia. He was driving his tractor down the road when he passed Roger's Infiniti, and—"

"And Roger was digging the drive wheel out of the mud," finished Nudger. "Just like he said all along." He took a sip of his wine. "Well, all right. That still doesn't explain how one of Karen's hairs got stuck in the mud on the shovel, but I guess things are looking better."

Claudia shook dried basil, fresh parsley, and black pepper into the skillet. Then she took Nudger's glass from him and poured half the contents into the sauce. The skillet hissed and sent up an aromatic cloud of steam. If only she'd leave out the clams.

Draining what was left of his wine, Nudger wondered how that farmer from Sedalia had been tracked down. Fleck must have hired the entire Pinkerton Agency.

Claudia stirred her sauce. "There was one more witness. Amelia Barthelme."

"Who's she?"

"She runs the lost and found department at Chicago Public Transit."

Nudger took a not-so-wild guess. "Karen's suitcase?"

"Found in the waiting room of a North Shore train station, two weeks ago. Empty, kind of beat up, but with luggage tags that read Karen Dupont."

Putting down her spoon, Claudia picked up a can of clams and reached for the opener. "I'd say a reasonable doubt now exists, wouldn't you?"

Nudger nodded. He decided to put up with the clams.

Soon enough he'd be eating humble pie.

CHAPTER TWENTY-EIGHT

When Claudia turned on the television news after dinner, the announcer was saying that the jury was out in the Dupont case.

She and Nudger were sitting on the couch side by side, and Claudia turned her head to look at him.

"What?" Nudger asked.

"Shouldn't you be sharing the vigil with the defendant?"

Nudger sighed. She was getting carried away with this court-room drama business. "The defendant's locked away in a cell. I'd be sharing the vigil with Fleck."

"Nudger, really. You heard what the reporter said. The verdict's in doubt. It could go either way. I don't see how you can stay away."

Nudger did. He was tired and his bruised chest hurt. What bothered him most was that he wasn't sure what verdict he wanted the jury to return.

When Claudia went to do the dishes and the news gave way to a game show, Nudger got restless. His mind wouldn't let go of the case, so he decided Claudia was right; he might as well head over to the courthouse.

The office buildings of Clayton had emptied out and the streets were quiet. Nudger parked on Central Avenue, across from the County Government Center.

The day had been hot and oppressively still, but now the sky was overcast and the wind was picking up. A newspaper page sailed across Central Avenue, passing Nudger as he crossed the street. Stinging grit blew into his eyes. He blinked his way into the Courts Building.

There was no one in the lobby except the guard at the metal detector. The escalators thrummed in the silence. As Nudger rode up to the second floor, he popped an antacid tablet into his mouth. He expected the evening to be tough on his stomach.

The doors of the room where Dupont was being tried stood wide open. People paced, or sat on the benches and smoked. A videocam crew from one of the local stations was setting up a tripod. Nudger looked around, expecting to see Effie Prang or Joleen Witt. Instead he saw Lawrence Fleck.

The little lawyer was pacing stiffly across the corridor. One hand was plunged deep in his pants pocket, while the other ran distractedly and lightly over his hair, almost as if it were his own. Fleck practically vibrated with nervous tension. He spun around to pace the other way and spotted Nudger. His clenched features relaxed into a grin.

Nudger realized he represented an opportunity for Fleck to let off steam. His stomach muscles twitched in foreboding as he walked toward Fleck.

The lawyer folded his arms, tucking his hands into his armpits. He rocked back on his heels and lifted his chin. "Nudger! You here to tell me you've found Vella Kling? Well, my naive friend, you're a little late."

"No."

"No? You're not late?" Fleck retrieved his hands from where he'd stuck them and started waving them around. "The defense has rested! The case has gone to the jury! There's nothing more that even I can do."

"I meant no, I haven't found Vella."

"Wonderful! I'm glad you didn't spoil a perfect record right at the end. You've achieved nothing on this case, Nudger. Nothing! It's been a complete waste of time working with you. Any other lawyer, he had to work with you, know where he'd be? Finished! Kaput! Sunk! There'd be a trail of bubbles and nothing more. Fortunately I'm not *any* lawyer. A fool for a client, a complete fool for an investigator, and I may still manage to win this case. Know how?"

"I'd like to," said Nudger.

"Because I'm me! Lawrence—"

"No, really, Lawrence," Nudger said. "I'd like to know where you got that great stuff about the videotape and the farmer and the suitcase."

Fleck settled down. For once he looked reluctant to speak. Then he glanced over Nudger's shoulder and said, "Him."

Nudger turned. He recognized Walter Blaumveldt, the insurance investigator, idling with his back turned halfway down the corridor.

"Excuse me," Nudger said. He was halfway across the hall when he heard Fleck call out, "That's right, Nudger! Talk to a real investigator. Find out how it's done."

Blaumveldt heard—everyone in the corridor heard—and turned. He didn't appear to be gratified by Fleck's praise. In fact, his long, sagging face looked as gloomy as ever.

"Don't let the guy get to you, Nudger. He's a little tense."

"He's a little swine," Nudger said.

"True, but he's also wound up tight. The verdict's in doubt."

"It wouldn't be in any doubt at all if it weren't for you."

Blaumveldt shrugged his broad shoulders. "I haven't done all that well. I didn't find Karen Dupont."

"But you've done wonders for Roger Dupont." Nudger studied the other man in silence for a moment. "How come you gave Fleck what you'd found out? You didn't have to do that."

Blaumveldt looked puzzled. "C'mon, Nudger. I'm a working stiff. A guy who pays his bills and his premiums. You think I could sit on evidence when a man's on trial for his life? Besides, a lot of it came from Dupont himself, indirectly."."

Nudger stared. "From Dupont?"

"I interviewed him and he was able to point me in the right direction on a few things."

"When I talked to him, he didn't point me in any direction at all."

"I think once the trial got underway, it sort of concentrated his mind," Blaumveldt said. "He remembered a lot of stuff."

"If he'd remembered when the police were interrogating him, he might have saved himself a lot of trouble."

Blaumveldt made a weak attempt at a smile. "Sounds like you think he got himself put on trial for murder just to see what it was like."

Fleck walked up to them. Nudger braced himself for more abuse, but Fleck said only, "The jury's coming back."

Nudger looked around. People were snuffing out cigarettes,

tightening neckties, moving toward the open doors of the court-room.

"Know what the problem is?" Fleck went on, in a quieter tone than usual. "Rising expectations, that's what it is. You turn in a brilliant performance and people hold it against you. Yesterday I would have been a hero if I'd managed to get Dupont life in prison. Now, I'll be the goat if he doesn't walk out of here a free man."

"Maybe you'd better take your place at the defense table, Mr. Fleck," said Blaumveldt.

Fleck stayed put and made a face. "Naw, those jurors, they'll take forever to come back. Always do. Bailiffs have to round 'em up, herd 'em down the corridor like cattle. They trip over their feet going into the jury box. Fools. Saps. Total innocents. They don't know anything and we put our fate in their hands. Anyone know why?"

For once Fleck had asked a question and didn't supply the an-swer. Nudger wasn't going to, either. The little lawyer seemed re-luctant to go back into the courtroom. The three of them were now the only ones left in the corridor. For a moment Nudger wondered if he and Blaumveldt were going to have to lift Fleck by the elbows and carry him in.

But he was just gathering his courage. He spun on the heel of one of his clunky brown wing tip shoes and marched into the courtroom.

Nudger and Blaumveldt got almost the last seats in the specta-tor's section, way over to the side, about halfway back. The bailiff was bringing Roger Dupont in. His expression was somber, but otherwise he gave the impression of a man enjoying being the cen-ter of attention, smoothing his tie with one hand and shrugging his shoulders to make his jacket rest properly on his shoulders. Claudia had said the trial reminded her of a TV show, and Dupont re-minded Nudger of a TV actor—a bad one who couldn't do a con-vincing job of portraying mortal dread. Fleck, seated beside him, was doing a much better job.

A door opened at the back of the courtroom and the jurors filed into the box. Nudger had heard that if they were going to acquit, they looked at the defendant; if they were going to convict, they looked at the prosecutor. These jurors didn't look at anyone. They kept their eyes on the floor, as if they'd overheard Fleck and didn't want to trip over their own feet.

Finally the bailiff called upon all to rise and Judge MacMasters appeared. He looked as fresh and alert as if it were nine in the morning, not nine at night. He put the traditional questions to the foreman of the jury.

Dupont rose smoothly from his chair when called upon to do so. Fleck seemed hesitant to join him. The courtroom was quiet before, but now it was dead silent. Nudger noticed Joleen Witt, sitting at the other end of the bench. She was leaning forward, looking at her brother-in-law with hatred.

Suddenly she flinched as if she'd been struck. Nudger realized that the verdict had been announced: Not Guilty.

He looked back at Dupont. The man reacted like a tennis star who'd just won Wimbledon in straight sets. He turned, grinning— now Nudger saw Effie, behind him in the front row—and pumped with his fist.

There were gasps and applause. Judge MacMasters gave no clue as to what he thought of the verdict. He gavelled for order and quickly completed the formalities. Even as he left the bench, spectators were pushing into the aisles and up to the rail. Dupont turned and offered his hand to his lawyer. Fleck, his head bowed, his expression weary, slowly took it. Again Nudger was reminded of a tennis championship, of the winner graciously shaking hands with the loser. Odd.

Nudger and Blaumveldt stood up, then realized they wouldn't be going anywhere for a while. Roger Dupont was wasting no time getting out of the courtroom, and the main aisle was clogged with people wanting to shake his hand, pat him on the shoulder, or just get a close look at him. Nudger saw Joleen Witt shouting at him as he passed her. Her words were lost in the post-trial turmoil, but her features were contorted by fury. Effie Prang was following in her brother's wake. Both of them ignored Joleen.

The doors of the courtroom were open now, and through them Nudger could see the brilliant TV lights going on. He recognized the familiar blonde hairdo of a local reporter. No doubt she was one of many journalists waiting to do interviews.

The traditional place for the victorious lawyer was at his client's side, so Nudger was surprised to see Fleck still at the counsel table. He was shaking hands with a grim Seymour Wister.

Nudger turned to Blaumveldt. "What do you think? Was Justice done?"

The insurance investigator shrugged. "Sure. He didn't kill his wife."

"You still think she's alive?"

Blaumveldt gave an emphatic nod.

"And you still think this is all an insurance fraud?"

Blaumveldt turned and looked at Nudger with his cold, shrewd eyes. "You don't, I know. You gave me two reasons. The first was that Roger couldn't collect if he was convicted of murdering his wife. Well, that's taken care of."

Nudger conceded with a nod. "But my second reason still stands. There's no body, so he'll have to wait seven years to collect. What do you say to that?"

"It gives me seven years to find her." Blaumveldt gave his faint smile. "Would you care to bet on it?"

"Bet?"

"I have ten bucks says Karen turns up alive."

Nudger hesitated. It was unseemly, betting on a woman's life, especially since Nudger would be the one rooting for Karen to turn up dead. Still, Blaumveldt was smiling at him as if delighted with the idea, and there couldn't be much in life that delighted the dour insurance investigator. And it was only ten dollars."

"Okay."

For the first time, Blaumveldt offered Nudger his hand. They shook, sealing the wager. Then they rose and joined the milling throng in the aisle, which was slowly pushing toward the doors.

Looking to the side and sharply downward, Nudger was surprised to see Lawrence Fleck beside him. It would have been more in character for the pugnacious lawyer to push and shove his way through the crowd, but Fleck didn't appear to be in any hurry.

"Congratulations, Lawrence," Nudger said. "The press is waiting for you."

Fleck snorted. "Media people. Don't know asshole from elbow about the law. Tell them anything and they'll believe it."

"All the same, they're going to make you a hero."

"Hmph!" Fleck turned and looked up at Nudger. "You let me down, Nudger. I asked you to find the truth. Now we'll never know."

Nudger had no answer, and Fleck didn't seem to expect one. They were nearing the doors now. They could see Roger Dupont, his back to them, calmly facing the glare of the TV lights, the outthrust microphones, and the camera lenses. Fleck walked over to take his place beside his client. Dupont turned, and his eye caught Nudger's.

They exchanged a look lasting only half a second. Then Dupont turned back to the cameras and Nudger went on his way. But it had been a strange moment. Nudger had always found Dupont opaque, a perfect enigma, but now, for the first time, he was sure what the man was feeling. Dupont had looked at him with relief, pure and simple. Nudger was someone he wouldn't have to worry about any longer.

Which meant that at some point, Nudger must have had Dupont worried. When had it been?

Leaving the building, he found that the summer night had become cooler and the wind even stronger. He hunched his shoulders and slitted his eyes and hurried toward the Granada.

He tried to put away his frustration and bad feeling about the case. It was only the unusual case that you could wrap up in a neat package, place on your shelf, and look at with pride and understanding afterward. Most of them were messy and inconclusive, like this one. You forgot about them and moved on. The important thing was that Dupont and Fleck had won, which meant they wouldn't balk at paying Nudger's bill.

As Nudger started the Granada, he held that thought and tried to feel happy about having some money for a change. But he couldn't. At least, not as happy as Eileen and Henry Mercato were going to feel.

Nudger woke slowly, struggling upward from an unpleasant, confusing dream. When he finally broke surface, he glanced at the clock on the bedside table: 4:00 A.M.

Now he realized what had awakened him. It was raining. Pouring.

Before going to bed he'd switched off the air conditioner and thrown open the windows throughout the apartment to let in the breeze. A cool night was a rarity in a St. Louis summer, and he should have known it portended a storm. Now he could hear the sashes rattling in the window frames, the clatter of blowing venetian blinds, the patter of rain falling.

Inside the apartment.

He got up, a little dizzily, and rushed from room to room closing windows. He seemed to be standing in puddles as he did so: The violent and capricious winds had blown the rain in from every direction. Well, he'd get out the mop and rags tomorrow. It wasn't as if he had parquet floors and elegant window treatments. His shag carpeting and venetian blinds wouldn't be any the worse for the dowsing.

Nudger went back to bed. It was cool and comfortable even with the windows down. The downpour lost its force after a few minutes, steadied to a pleasant rainfall. Nudger drifted toward sleep, but he couldn't quite get there. He kept jerking himself back to consciousness, with the thought that there was some window he'd forgotten to close and the rain was still pouring in.

At last he fell asleep, the uneasy feeling still with him.

Shortly after dawn he sat bolt upright in bed, eyes open and heart pounding. He was sure that something bad—something monstrous—had happened while he slept. And it was something he should have been able to prevent.

Feeling foolish but unable to shake off the strange mood, he got up and walked around the apartment again. All the windows were shut; he had missed none of them.

The eastern sky was clear, and a hot red sun was coming up.

CHAPTER TWENTY-NINE
six months later

Christmas vacation starts tomorrow," Claudia said. "I can hardly wait."

Nudger nodded. For the last week she'd been monitoring final exams, grading papers, and talking about how much she looked forward to the last day of the term. He didn't think she'd stopped by his office just to tell him this again. It took something special to bring Claudia to his office, which she regarded as depressing and possibly indicative of Nudger's future.

To Nudger it seemed less depressing than usual simply because she was here. She was wearing a deep-red sweater, a long gray skirt, and high black leather boots. He especially liked the boots. Her lips were curved in a half-smile, and her big dark eyes held tenderness and humor. Nudger reminded himself that Claudia never looked lovelier than when she was about to give him bad news.

She crossed her legs and folded her hands over the top knee. "Something's come up," she said. "Something very . . . well, I guess I might as well just tell you."

His stomach roiled with foreboding.

"A group of the other teachers are flying to Colorado for some skiing. They asked me to come along. And I'm going."

"Uh-huh," he said. "So how long will you be gone?"

"Not long. A week. I'll be home for Christmas."

A week seemed very long to Nudger, but he said only, "I didn't know you skied."

"I don't. They teach you. They're happy to teach you so they can rent you equipment." She smiled wryly. "With what I spent on sweaters today, this vacation is going to cost the earth."

So she had doubts about this trip, Nudger could tell. Maybe, deep down, she even wanted to be talked out of it. If so, she'd come to the right place. He said, "I had plans for us. I was going to take tomorrow off."

"Really? What were these plans?"

In fact Nudger's plan was to get in bed with Claudia and stay there until noon. But he could see he was going to have to dress this up a bit.

"I was going to bring you breakfast in bed."

"Nudger! You'd actually bring me my orange juice and cereal in bed?"

She was laughing. He was going to have to up the ante.

"And coffee. And bacon and pancakes."

She stopped laughing. Her eyes widened. "Nudger! You're offering to cook for me?"

Nudger nodded gravely. It was a momentous step, and perhaps a mistake, but he really didn't want her to go to Colorado.

"Well, I'm flattered." She arched her eyebrows, smiling. "Also curious. But would my kitchen ever be the same?"

"I'm not much of a cook, true. But I can do bacon and pancakes pretty well."

"Really? This is a whole new facet of you, Nudger. How come you've kept it a secret?"

He shrugged noncommittally. The truth was, making pancakes depressed him. He'd learned how during the last desperate months of his marriage. He'd been trying to mollify Eileen by giving her a treat on Saturday mornings. It hadn't worked. He hoped that with Claudia the pancakes and the results would be better.

"Your plan sounds good so far," she said. "What comes next?"

"Sweet rolls from the St. Louis Bread Company." The Bread Company was a bakery that made delicious and expensive pastries. Expensive for Nudger, anyway. Maybe Danny would bake something and Nudger could pretend it was from the Bread Company. But he knew immediately that wouldn't work. What was he getting himself into?

"Sounds good, but I meant what comes after brunch? What do you plan for us to do for the rest of the day?"

"Oh." Again he sought inspiration. "I thought we'd take in a movie. Have dinner out."

Claudia was sighing and shaking her head. He must have lost her somewhere.

"See, Nudger, that's the problem. That's why I'm going skiing."

"Huh?"

"I feel the need to do more than sit around and eat, sit around and eat."

"But it's winter." He looked out the window at the gray sky. "Who wants to be outside in winter?"

"It's hard, I admit. All the more reason—"

"It's going against nature."

"Against *your* nature, Nudger."

"In winter all mammals become more sedentary, to conserve energy." Nudger the naturalist. "They eat more because extra fat serves as insulation."

"Next you'll be telling me you intend to hibernate."

It sounded pretty good, especially if he could share a den with Claudia.

"A friend of mine says the only way to stay happy and healthy through winter is to take up skiing and skating," she continued. "That way you no longer dread winter coming. He says life's too short to get depressed every fall. And he should know, he's from Wisconsin."

Nudger opened his mouth to debunk this absurd theory, then he remembered something.

Wasn't Biff Archway from Wisconsin?

In a flash it all came to him. Why hadn't he seen it before? This was just the sort of thing Archway would suggest. Nudger could just see him schussing down the slopes in form-fitting Lycra pants. Or sitting by the fire in the lodge, a cup of hot cocoa in his hand and Claudia by his side. Or maybe even vice versa. Nudger shivered.

"You catching cold, Nudger?" Claudia looked more smug than concerned. "You know, you don't get colds from being out in the fresh air. You get them from sitting around indoors, being breathed on by sick people."

"You said you're going with a party of teachers from the school?"

"That's right."

"How many?"

"Oh, at the moment I believe it's just four."

Two couples, then. Or, Archway and three women? Or Claudia and three men? Nudger's imagination was on a rampage. Suddenly he was angry. Enough of this tiptoeing around. He was going to ask her flat out if Archway was behind all this.

As he opened his mouth, the phone rang.

"Never mind, ignore it," Nudger growled.

"No, go ahead," Claudia said. "I know you've got business. I'll wait."

It was a lawyer he often worked for, asking him to look for a potential witness in a car accident case. A routine job, but it would pay. Nudger wrote down the information. The delay took the edge off his anger at Claudia. As he went on talking to the lawyer, he thought back over the years he had spent being jealous of Biff Archway. How many times had he suspiciously questioned Claudia about her feelings for that muscle-bound lunk, and where had it ever gotten him?

If he asked her if Archway was going on the ski trip, he knew what would happen. She'd get angry, accuse him of not trusting her, of refusing to respect her independence. She might even—the thought made his stomach loop and zoom—tell him she'd been back to see her shrink Dr. Oliver again, and he'd told her to validate her selfhood by seeing other men. That had happened before and it had driven Nudger to abject misery.

One thing she wouldn't do was answer Nudger's question. She would go off to Colorado, leaving him to stew in doubt and jealousy.

What would he do then? Follow her out to the resort to check on her? Nudger imagined himself skulking in hotel lobbies or shivering on snowy slopes, as he tried to keep an eye on his beloved and the treacherous bastard Archway. Wasn't love wonderful?

He finished with the lawyer and hung up the phone. Claudia was waiting, still with legs crossed and hands clasped around her knee.

Nudger's heart ached because she was going away from him. His stomach burned because she was going with another man. But this time for a change he was going to bring his brain into his relations with Claudia. Learn from his past mistakes and not press her and drive her further away with his jealousy.

"Well, I hope you have a good time," he said, as he came around the desk. "Give me a call when you get back."

Claudia looked surprised. Speechless, in fact.

He bent to kiss her on the forehead.

The look of surprise softened into something else. She caught his face in both her hands. Kissed him on the mouth.

"There'll be time for breakfast in bed before the plane," she said. "You want to come over tonight?"

Sly Nudger.

Reluctantly Nudger opened his eyes. The shades were down, but Claudia's bedroom was bright with morning light. He was alone in her bed. He sat up. He could hear noises from the other room: the mutter of a radio, and Claudia's footsteps. She was pacing. She said, quietly but vehemently, "Damn. *Damn!*"

Pulling on his robe, Nudger went to the doorway and peeked out.

Claudia's fists were propped on her hips, her face flushed with annoyance. She was walking an agitated circle around her open suitcase. It lay on the floor, spilling over with skiwear: stretch pants, gaudy parkas, hats and gloves, ski sweaters. She was going to look beautiful in Colorado.

"What's the matter?" Nudger asked. "Can't fit it all in?"

She flung out an arm, toward the window. "Look out there!"

Nudger walked over to the window. Looked outside. Smiled.

It must have snowed all night. Big soft flakes were still drifting down from a white sky. Cars parked along the street—including Nudger's and Claudia's—had become a row of rounded hillocks. An impeccable sheet of snow, so far unmarred by car, man, or dog, covered streets and lawns alike. Thick, downy cushions lined the higher branches of the tree in front of the building. They were on a level with Nudger's eyes, and he squinted, trying to measure the depth of snow. Eight or ten inches, he thought.

"We can't let a little thing like this keep us indoors," he said. "Let's put on our snowshoes and head for the airport."

Claudia gazed at him unamused.

"All right, I'll hitch up the dogs to the sled."

"It wouldn't do us any good to get to the airport, even if we could." Claudia indicated the radio. "They've shut down."

"Too bad," Nudger said.

"Too bad?" she returned. "It's unjust, unfair—we didn't get a single snow day last semester. No, it's got to hold off till the first day of vacation. It's got to ruin my trip."

"Yours and all the teachers who were going with you. I'll bet they're all so disappointed. It is unfair."

She looked at him for a moment. "You're delighted, you hypocrite."

"Delighted? Of course not. Just musing over the ironies of our modern age. That a snowfall should keep you from going skiing is—"

"Nudger, shut up and start making breakfast. I'm going back to bed."

He'd let his emotions get the better of him again, to crow over her like that. He'd forgotten that he was the New Nudger now. He followed her.

"Maybe you'd like to go out later on," he said. "If they get the streets plowed, we could go sledding on Art Hill."

She stopped and turned around. "Sledding, Nudger? I'll bet you can't remember the last time you went sledding."

"Sure I can. It was twenty-nine years ago."

"Well . . . it does sound like fun. You're sure you want to go?"

"Absolutely sure. I don't hate winter nearly as much as you seem to think."

Even saying the words, he was cold.

He remembered well enough how to make bacon and pancakes, but it took a very long time. The most frustrating part was that he had to search for every utensil and ingredient he needed. Over the years he must have sat in this kitchen and chatted with Claudia while she cooked hundreds of meals. Yet he'd never noticed where she kept things.

In the bedroom Claudia was talking on the phone. To Archway, no doubt. They were either putting the trip off until tomorrow, or cancelling it. He thought he had reason to hope for the latter. Her lovemaking had been unusually fervent last night. Yep, she was intrigued by the New Nudger.

She and the New Nudger both had breakfast in bed. Claudia proclaimed it delicious.

Nudger gloated. He'd finally found an arena in which he could beat Biff Archway. Archway might be a scholar-athlete, martial arts expert, sports car aficionado, and clotheshorse, but Nudger had never heard a word about his cooking.

Too bad this morning's meal exhausted Nudger's repertoire.

Later on they moved to the seat by the window with coffee. As they sipped, they looked out at the street scene. No snow plows had appeared yet, Nudger was pleased to see. The first heavy snowfall of the year usually took St. Louis by surprise. Schoolkids acted as if they'd never before seen snow, and drivers miraculously forgot they'd ever driven in it. Joy and fender-bender accidents abounded.

Claudia's South St. Louis neighbors, usually the most industrious of householders, seemed to have decided to sleep in this morning. Only a few appeared, and they merely searched in vain for newspapers and mail, or poked at the igloos in front of their houses to make sure their cars were still underneath. Then they went back inside.

So the street was given over to the children. They staggered through drifts up to their knees or even their waists, dragging sleds behind them, headed for the nearest hill. Right below Claudia's window armies were mustered, forts were built, and intensive snowball warfare broke out. The yells and laughter and crunching footfalls were the only noises in the snow-cushioned silence. It was as if nothing was going on in the city of St. Louis but this snowball fight.

But it was only a minute later when he heard an engine. A car was approaching. He stood to get a better view.

A Jeep was moving slowly toward the building. It wasn't one of those nifty and expensive Wagoneers, but a boxy old olive-drab Jeep with a canvas top. It looked like Army surplus. In fact, it looked as if it had been through the Battle of the Bulge.

The Jeep's horn honked. The children stopped and stared, and got out of the way reluctantly. A few threw snowballs at the Jeep. It didn't seem fair to them that their playground should turn back into a street so soon.

Right in front of Claudia's building the Jeep stopped. The driver didn't bother to park; no one else would be coming along. He opened the door and got out: a tall man, bareheaded and wearing a raincoat inadequate for the cold. He brushed his lank hair back from his forehead.

It was then that Nudger recognized Walter Blaumveldt, whom he hadn't thought of in months.

Claudia remembered him from the trial. "Blaumveldt," she said. "He's coming into this building. What do you think he wants?"

"I'm afraid he wants to see me."

She was still in her robe and pajamas. She shot Nudger an annoyed look and went into her bedroom, closing the door. Nudger went to the front door of the apartment.

He opened it as Blaumveldt came up the stairs. He was breathing hard, as Nudger usually was by the time he reached Claudia's floor.

Blaumveldt didn't say anything. He reached in his pocket and took out his wallet. Then he handed Nudger a ten-dollar bill.

Nudger swallowed hard. "They've found Karen Dupont's body?"

Blaumveldt nodded. "She was murdered."

CHAPTER THIRTY

Nudger knocked on the bedroom door and looked in. Claudia was back in bed, reading *The Little Sister*. For the last few months, she'd been rereading the works of Raymond Chandler, looking for the line he'd misquoted to her last summer. She was an English teacher; she did things like that.

"Find it yet?"

She shook her head. " 'She had a figure that could make a man kick a hole in the wall.' You're sure that's as near as you can remember?"

Nudger thought. "I think part of the joke was, the man was somebody important. A senator, maybe.

" 'She had a figure that could make a senator kick a hole in the wall?' I don't think you're getting any warmer. Is your friend still out there?"

Nudger nodded.

"How did he find you?"

"He went to the office. Danny told him if I wasn't at my apartment I'd be here."

Claudia put the book down in her lap. "Does Danny usually give my address to people who come looking for you?"

"No. Never. But this Blaumveldt guy doesn't take no for an answer. I'm going with him to talk to Roger Dupont."

Her brows drew together as she looked at him. "Why?"

Nudger could sense that all the points he'd made with Claudia last night and this morning were slipping away. "It won't take long. We'll still have time for a movie and dinner this evening."

"I'm not mad, Nudger. I'm just asking, why are you going out on a day like this to talk to Roger Dupont? His lawyer's not your client anymore."

Nudger nodded. It was a good question. "I guess I feel as if I never finished with that case. It's never stopped haunting me."

She went on looking at him for a moment. Then she went back to the book. "Okay."

"You understand?"

"Not exactly. But I'm used to you."

In other words, farewell to the New Nudger. Claudia must be thinking that he hadn't lasted very long. Must be planning to head out to Colorado as soon as the airport reopened. Nudger stepped back, quietly closing the door. Perhaps it was better this way. At least she'd never find out he couldn't make eggs Benedict.

He returned to the front room of the apartment, where Blaumveldt stood waiting for him. Nudger put on his coat. It was an old London Fog raincoat with a zip-in acrylic fur lining, much like Blaumveldt's, and equally inadequate to the cold. Blaumveldt at least had rubber galoshes. Nudger was going to get wet feet.

They went down the stairs and got in the Jeep. The kids sent them off with another volley of snowballs. It was very cold in the Jeep, and Nudger didn't hope for much relief from the heater. He could feel the wind whistling around his ankles. The Jeep had more rust holes than his Granada. "You get this used from General Patton, Walter?"

"I borrowed it from my next-door neighbor, soon as I got the call from the Illinois State Police. I knew I was going to need four-wheel drive to get to where they'd found the body."

"Where was that exactly?" Nudger hadn't pressed Blaumveldt for details the first time around. He wasn't particularly eager to hear them now. His stomach twitched.

"In the woods off Highway HH, seventeen miles south of Springfield." He wrestled with the wheel as they bounced through a rutted intersection. "They never would've found it if they hadn't had such a good description from their tipster."

"It was an anonymous phone call?"

Blaumveldt nodded.

"Do the cops have any idea—"

"Sounded like a man's voice. That's all. They traced the call to a pay phone in Springfield." That rueful twist of a smile came and went from Blaumveldt's face. "I don't think there's anything much to the tipster, personally. Just some guy who didn't want to get involved. The body wasn't buried very deep. And we've had a lot of rain this fall. So our guy is hunting or walking his dog in the woods and he sees Karen's hand sticking up through the ground."

Blaumveldt took his own hand from the wheel and held it up. "Just the bones."

Nudger's stomach quivered again.

"By the time I got there they'd put up a tent around the grave. If you can call it that. Otherwise the snow would have buried her again."

"How'd they make the ID?"

"Her purse was underneath the body. There wasn't much left of the leather, but her driver's license was in good shape. State of Missouri, Karen Witt Dupont."

"Anything else? Credit cards, money, papers?"

Blaumveldt shook his head.

Nudger put a hand over his stomach, hoping to calm it. Here came the tough question. "Were they able to make a positive ID?"

"There's not enough of her left. The maggots got to the soft tissues—face, breasts—and the entrails. They're very thorough."

Nudger took his hand away from his stomach. It wasn't helping. He reached into his pocket for his roll of antacids.

"But there's no doubt it's Karen," Blaumveldt said. "I just got off the phone with the State Police. They've matched the dental records. It's her all right."

"What about cause of death?"

"Skull fracture. Somebody beat her head in."

"Jesus," said Nudger.

Blaumveldt turned to him. His expression was weary and bitter. "Guess I've made a real ass of myself. I was so sure Karen was still alive."

"Have you been looking for her all this time?" Nudger asked.

"I've stapled HAVE YOU SEEN THIS WOMAN? posters to half the telephone poles in the Midwest. My contacts at the FBI and Interpol have been sending me reams of stuff every week, and I've gone through it all. Leads so thin anyone else would've laughed at 'em, I've checked out. If she was above ground I would have found her. So you'd think I'd know what to expect. But right up to the moment I got that phone call last night, I figured she was alive."

The insurance investigator sank into his gloomy thoughts. They came to an intersection and turned onto Grand Avenue. It was a main artery and traffic was moving intermittently. The center of the roadway had been churned into gray slush. They trundled north.

Has the Medical Examiner got an estimated time of death yet?" Nudger asked.

"No, and he's not going to. The body's too badly decomposed. Karen could have died as little as two months ago. Or she could have died at the time she disappeared, back in May."

"Then it could have been her husband who killed her," Nudger said, "And the cops have taken their shot at him and missed."

"Well, maybe that means something. Like that he didn't do it. The cops couldn't find enough evidence against him to convince a jury. And they investigated him thoroughly. They never really investigated anybody else. Been six months since the trial and they haven't developed another suspect."

"You think it's somebody else who killed her, then," Nudger said.

"I have my theories."

And apparently he meant to keep them to himself, because his wraithlike smile played about his lips and he kept silent.

"If you don't think Dupont did it, how come we're going to see him?"

Blaumveldt looked over at him. "Because he's the beneficiary. Remember, Nudger? You said there were two reasons Roger couldn't collect on his wife's policy. First was if he was convicted of her murder. Well, he got off. Second was, if the body wasn't found, he'd have to wait seven years for her to be declared legally dead. Well—"

"Yeah," Nudger said. "That's taken care of now too, isn't it?"

Blaumveldt nodded. "So, very soon my company's going to have to pay him half a million bucks. Unless some kind of foul play comes to light."

"But you think Roger's innocent."

"I don't think he murdered his wife," Blaumveldt replied. "But I would never say Roger is innocent."

By now they were on Highway 40, following the flashing lights of a salt truck through the swirling snow. Nudger was surprised when Blaumveldt took the Skinker Boulevard exit.

"Roger's moved," Blaumveldt said, in answer to his questioning look. "Sold the house in U. City. He's got an apartment now."

Roger Dupont had evidently decided on a major change of lifestyle, but he hadn't come down in the world. Skinker Boulevard, despite its name, was an elegant street, a St. Louis version of Central Park West. Forest Park stretched along one side, while the other was lined with fine old houses, churches, and apartment buildings.

Walter turned into the semicircular drive of the tallest of these apartment buildings. The doorman was surprised to see callers on a day like this. He put on his green uniform cap, hustled around his panelled console, and just managed to beat them to the door. Blaumveldt gave both their names. The doorman called up to Dupont's apartment, got his okay, and waved them to the elevator.

"I'm a little surprised he's willing to see me," Nudger said, as they ascended. "I had the feeling last summer that I sort of bugged Dupont."

"That's why I asked you to come along," Blaumveldt replied.

Dupont opened the door of his apartment and waved them in. He didn't greet them, because he was talking into a portable phone. The conversation was about P/E ratios and fundamentals: he must be talking to his broker. Nudger wasn't interested. He'd once dipped a toe into the stock market, and it had been bitten off. There were piranhas in there.

Dupont looked fit. His skin had a healthy glow. There was less gray and more brown in his hair—and in his bushy eyebrows. Nudger wondered fleetingly if people actually dyed their eyebrows.

He led them into the living room, padding across the glossy parquet floor in stocking feet. He was wearing a hand-knit sweater that was almost as attractive as one of Claudia's ski numbers, and jeans.

He waved them to seats, and Blaumveldt gingerly sat down in a contraption that, if Nudger remembered right, was called a Marcel Breuer chair. It was an intricate arrangement of steel bars and leather straps. Once Blaumveldt was suspended in it, he made Nudger think of an Easter egg about to be dipped.

Nudger remained standing, looking around the room. Like the Breuer chair, the other furniture was spare and expensive: a glass-and-steel coffee table, a low, sleek sofa, and a high, marble-topped chess table with stools on either side. By the mantle stood a vending machine—a glass bubble filled with jawbreakers—and on the wall was a large framed photograph of the Judds, mother and daughter, resplendent in clouds of hair. Nudger was struck by a sudden thought. This odd mixture of chic and tacky was strangely familiar. He'd seen decor like this before. Where?

Roger Dupont finished his call and sat down on the sofa. He hitched up his pants to do so, and Nudger noticed there were creases in them. Dupont was having his jeans ironed. Informality didn't come easily to him. Nudger perched on one of the stools by the chess table.

Blaumveldt began, "I expect the police have notified you—"

"Yes. Their call woke me up early this morning."

"Must have been a terrible shock."

Dupont dropped his eyes. "Yes. I'd given up all hope that I'd ever see Karen again. But still it was a shock to hear she was dead."

Nudger and Blaumveldt exchanged a look. In Dupont's voice

there was no expression, not even feigned expression. He was like a lazy, arrogant Broadway star who'd done a hit play too many times. He'd realized he could get away with simply parroting the lines, and he did so.

Nudger asked, "Do you have any idea what happened to Karen?"

Dupont turned and looked at him, as if noticing him for the first time. "Nudger. How nice to see you again. Check with your colleague here and you'll find he's been pestering me for the last six months, asking if I'd heard from Karen or of her, and the answer's always been no."

"But you were married to her for four years," Nudger said. "You must have been thinking about her. Must have some ideas about what might have happened to her."

"Well, she said she was going to Chicago, and her body being found near Springfield would certainly indicate that's what she did." Dupont paused for a moment. "She must have gotten involved with bad characters there. Chicago's a big, dangerous city, and Karen was impulsive."

Impulsive. The same word he had used to describe her last summer. Almost the only word. Either he was a lazy liar, or he hadn't known his wife at all. The questioning was getting them nowhere. Nudger glanced at Blaumveldt: your witness.

"I understand you've left the bank, Roger," Blaumveldt said.

"You certainly keep your ear to the ground, Walter," Dupont replied. Animation came into his face; he was interested now. "I quit my job. Got tired of reviewing other people's loan applications. Figured I was a lot smarter than any of them and I might as well start my own business."

"What sort of business is that?" Blaumveldt asked.

"I'm going to open an antique shop."

Nudger looked around the apartment. Now he remembered where he'd seen decor like this before: in Vella Kling's apartment. "Do you have a partner, Mr. Dupont?"

"Yes. Matter of fact I do."

"Would her name happen to be Vella Kling?"

Dupont smiled. "It would happen to be, yes."

"Last summer, you told me you didn't know Vella Kling."

Dupont nodded thoughtfully.

"Perhaps I've met her in the interval," he suggested.

Nudger sighed. There was no way to make a dent in this guy. He got up from his uncomfortable stool and walked to the window.

It was actually a sliding glass door, and beyond it was a snow-covered balcony. It had a splendid view. On a clear day you'd be able to see the downtown skyscrapers and the Gateway Arch. Just now the overcast obscured all that. The snow-covered hills and dales and the gaunt black trees of Forest Park seemed to go on forever. Directly below, on the edge of the park, a couple were striding along on cross-country skis. They looked tiny. Roger Dupont's apartment was on the top floor of the building. He seemed to enjoy looking down on people.

"Frankly, Roger, the timing of your decision to go into business on your own troubles me a bit," Blaumveldt was saying. Nudger listened without turning. "It's almost as if you expected to come into money. The payoff from Karen's life insurance policy, I mean."

Dupont didn't reply. The silence stretched on and on. Nudger turned.

He was in time to see Dupont rise to his feet. His face was flushed. "Just answer me one question, Walter." Dupont kept his voice low, but it was trembling with leashed-in anger. "Do you have something personal against me, or are you insurance people always tight-assed bastards about paying up?"

"Take it easy, Roger," Blaumveldt said.

"I won't put up with these damned insinuations. I've been cleared by a court of law. Isn't that enough for you people?"

Blaumveldt didn't seem rattled by the outburst. He looked as comfortable as anyone could look in that peculiar chair. He said mildly, "Just wondering where you got the money to start the business, Roger, that's all."

From the sale of my house in University City," Dupont replied. "One of the reasons I moved out of the neighborhood and quit my job was that I was tired of being notorious. Of being pointed at and whispered about. I'm an innocent man. And I'm damned if I'll put up with being investigated anymore. If your company doesn't send me a check soon, Walter, you'll be talking to my lawyer."

Then he turned to Nudger, who wondered if it was his turn to be threatened. But Dupont only looked at him. It was a long, appraising look that made Nudger feel queasy.

Dupont said, "I'll see you out."

As the elevator doors closed on them, Blaumveldt said, "Well? Still think he killed her?"

Nudger considered for a moment, frowning. "Two things. If he did it, he's a pretty inept murderer. Left incriminating evidence all over the place."

Blaumveldt nodded.

"Secondly, he'd have to be the bravest guy in the world. He was looking at the death penalty all through that trial, and he never blinked. No matter how badly things went for him, he wouldn't plea-bargain."

"True. So, what's it mean?"

Nudger slowly shook his head. "Means Dupont has me as baffled as ever. I'm glad it's not my case anymore. Are you going to keep on investigating?"

Blaumveldt nodded again.

"In spite of what he said?"

"Sure. Roger's right about one thing. We insurance guys are tight-ass bastards when it comes to paying off a claim."

CHAPTER THIRTY-ONE

It turned colder overnight, and in the morning Nudger's Granada wouldn't start. The battery was dead and would only make an odd sound like a chicken clucking. Nudger sat behind the wheel considering his options. He could call the service station on Manchester and ask them to send over the tow truck to give his battery a charge. Problem was, they'd charge Nudger, too.

The other alternative was Danny. He kept jumper cables in his trunk, and he had felt a certain responsibility toward the Granada ever since he'd persuaded Nudger to buy it. But Danny would be at the shop by now, and in the middle of his morning rush. He wouldn't be able to come over for a couple of hours.

Nudger leaned his forehead against the cold window of the car.

He knew what Claudia would say if she were here: Nudger, your office is less than a mile away. An easy walk. Move! Make your own heat. Lift your spirits. Don't succumb to winter.

So who cared what Claudia thought? Nudger reflected irritably. She'd sent him back to his own bed after last night's movie. She really hadn't liked his leaving her alone to go off with Walter Blaumveldt. For the rest of the day she'd been . . . well, not sulky, but a bit guarded. She hadn't let on to him whether she was still planning to go to Colorado.

Still, Nudger had files to work on and calls to make. If he went to the office, he might even find a new client waiting. It had happened.

And the cold vinyl of the car was freezing his backside.

He got out. Pulling down his hat and buttoning up his collar, he strode off down Sutton Avenue.

By the time he reached the corner of Manchester, he knew why his raincoat was called the London Fog and not the St. Louis Wind. He was shivering helplessly.

The Manchester Road merchants were doing their best to promote Christmas cheer, with banners stretching across the street and colorful displays in their windows. But this morning they hadn't yet arrived to salt and shovel their sidewalks, and that was bad news for Nudger. Manchester, being a main artery, had been plowed yesterday. All the snow that had been in the street was now on the sidewalks and was packed hard.

Gingerly Nudger set out over the slick, lumpy surface. He felt like a mountaineer crossing a glacier. He should be wearing crampons and leaning on an ice ax. Instead he was wearing loafers and grabbing desperately for parking meters.

Straightening up after a near-fall, reluctantly letting go of the parking meter, he chanced to look back. He was surprised to see another pedestrian in the block behind him. The man must have had better shoes than Nudger, because he was striding along slowly but steadily. His head was up. In fact he seemed to be staring right at Nudger.

Nudger felt that familiar prickling sensation in his stomach. But he couldn't be sure the man was staring at him, the distance was too great. He was an awfully large man. Perhaps that was the key. They always said a big, heavy car was best in the snow. Maybe the same went for people.

Nudger turned and went staggering and sliding on his way, but the thought of the other walker kept bothering him. At the corner he turned to look. The man was still there, no closer to Nudger, no farther away.

Nudger went on his way again, but the back of his neck was tingling now, and it had nothing to do with the cold.

When he reached Danny's door, he turned to look again. The man was nowhere in sight. Maybe he hadn't been following Nudger. Or maybe he was satisfied about where Nudger was going and had sought some warm place to wait while Nudger was in the office. Nudger shook off the unwelcome speculations and went in.

The doughnut shop was warm and smelled of fresh baked dough

and warm sugar. Half the stools at Danny's counter were filled. He nodded to Nudger and said, "You got somebody up there waiting for you. He just drove up in that."

Nudger turned and looked out the window. A big red Cadillac was parked at the curb, taking up two spaces. He didn't get many clients in Caddies. Better not keep his caller waiting any longer.

"Thanks, Danny. You still got those jumper cables?"

"Don't tell me the Granada wouldn't start, Nudge." His face fell. His shoulders sagged. Years ago he'd talked Nudger into buying the Granada, and now look what had happened. Guilt came so easily to Danny and departed not at all.

"It's basically a good car, Danny. Can we go over to my place in a couple of hours and start it?"

"Sure, sure. Least I can do. How 'bout a cup of coffee?"

Nudger accepted. When the shop was busy like this, the coffee didn't sit in the steel urn long enough to cook down to acidic sludge. It wouldn't do his tender stomach too much damage.

"And a Dunker Delite?"

Danny's hand was already reaching into the display case where the Delites resided. He picked one up. It left a distinct oval of grease on the white doily where it had rested.

Nudger backed toward the door.

"Thanks, anyway, Danny, but it wouldn't be polite to eat in front of the client."

"Then take two, Nudge."

But Nudger was already out the door. He let it close, pretending not to hear.

The stairwell, as usual in winter, felt colder than outdoors. He climbed it quickly and entered his office, where Lawrence Fleck was waiting.

Nudger hadn't seen or heard of the pugnacious little attorney in six months. He was speechless. Fleck was not.

"Jesus, Nudger, this an office or an igloo? It's freezing in here!"

That was true. But since Nudger's landlord didn't trust him with a thermostat, there was nothing he could do about it. "Heat'll be along in a minute," he said hopefully. For the present, though, he kept his London Fog on.

Waving Fleck to the client's chair, he sat down behind the desk. *Eeeeek!* went the chair. It always seemed to squeak louder in the winter. The cold got into its joints as it did into Nudger's. He put the plastic foam cup of coffee aside. He'd enjoy it after he got rid of Fleck.

Fleck remained standing. He made a show of surveying the office. "I see nothing's changed in *your* life."

This was Nudger's cue to admire Fleck's suit. Just in case he'd missed the Caddy at the curb. And it was a nice suit, a dark, pin-striped, vested job, which made the most of what height Fleck had. It almost made him look like a lawyer.

"I'm glad things are going well for you, Lawrence."

"Got an office in Clayton now. And a new secretary, prettier and permanent. May even have to hire a paralegal, just to keep up with the work. Know why I'm doing so well these days, Nudger?"

Nudger sighed. He had a pretty good idea why Fleck had come to see him, and he wasn't happy about it. "I expect a lot of clients have come your way since—"

"That's right, Nudger. Poor dumb innocents who've gotten in so deep, whose cases are so hopeless, they can see only one way out. Know what that way is?"

"Call in the man who got Roger Dupont off," said Nudger.

Under his immobile toupee, Fleck's forehead contracted and furrowed. He was trying to think of a reason to contradict Nudger's statement. Nothing came to him. "You're so smart, tell me why I'm here."

"You want to rehire me to investigate Dupont."

"Wrong!" brayed Fleck triumphantly.

Nudger was genuinely surprised. "Wrong?"

"How can I rehire you, when you never finished the job I hired you to do in the first place? Huh? Answer me that!"

"I—"

"You were supposed to find out the truth about Dupont, and you failed. I'm here to remind you that you're still working for me."

"Lawrence, the trial is over—"

"So what? You've still got to finish the job."

"The case is closed. You don't have a client anymore. You'd have to pay me out of your own pocket."

Maybe Fleck hadn't thought of that, or maybe he just hated the sound of it. He took a couple of turns about the little room in silence.

A racket began, a banging and clattering as if a knight in armor were falling down the stairs. Fleck spun around in alarm. "What the hell's that?"

"Good news," Nudger replied. "Heat's coming on."

He jerked his thumb at the radiator, which stood on the floor just below the air conditioner he always forgot to take out of the window every autumn. It was clanking and hissing. Nudger shrugged out of his raincoat. In five minutes the office would be comfortable. In ten it would be a steam bath and he'd have to crack the window.

Fleck came to sit in the chair across the desk from Nudger. He reached inside his jacket and brought out his checkbook. Nudger had never been so unhappy to see a checkbook.

"Lawrence, the case is over, you won, you've done well out of it. You should be grateful to Roger Dupont."

Fleck raised his eyes from the check he was writing. "That smooth son of a bitch used me. Made a fool of me. I have to know how he did it."

"You think he killed Karen? You think you got a guilty man off?"

"No. I've gotten plenty of guilty men off," said Fleck proudly.

"None of them acted the way Dupont did. Cool. Calm. Unworried. Let me tell you, Nudger, when a man's guilty and I'm defending him, he's plenty scared."

That would certainly be two strikes, Nudger thought. "So you think Dupont really is innocent?"

"No! Wrong again! I think he's not guilty of murdering Karen. That's how the jury found him, and that's as far as I'm willing to go. But he's mixed up in this somehow. I want you to find out how."

"You don't need me. Walter Blaumveldt is still investigating."

"He is? How do you know that?"

Nudger sighed. He didn't want to go into this. "It was Blaumveldt who told me the body'd been found. He took me along to see Dupont."

Fleck gave his sharklike grin. "See? You're already on the case. You can't resist. How come Blaumveldt took you along?"

"He says I bug Dupont."

"I've seen that too. That's why I want you on the case." Fleck was nodding to himself. He stopped and looked at Nudger narrowly. "Not scared of him, are you?"

Nudger decided to ignore the question. "Blaumveldt's investigating. So are the police."

"The cops! They've already blown this case once."

Nudger had no answer to that. He loosened his necktie. The temperature in the office was climbing steadily. Beads of sweat were trickling out from under Fleck's toupee.

"Know what I think happened?" Fleck went on. "Karen never got anywhere near Chicago. She was killed in St. Louis, at the time she disappeared. Maybe you should investigate the sister—what's her name? . . ."

"Effie Prang?" Nudger thought of the sweet Ladue lady with the overbite. "Why do you suspect she did it?"

"She put up her house to bail Roger out. That looks like a guilty conscience to me."

"Or it could be sisterly love."

"Maybe she loved him so much she killed Karen for him."

Nudger nodded slowly. It was an ingenious if sick theory, but there were big problems with it.

"If she killed Karen, she did it so ineptly she almost got her brother convicted of the crime."

"Who said you have to be competent to be a murderer? There's no qualification test. The bozos who come to me, you wouldn't believe the stupid mistakes they've made. If they were competent, they wouldn't need me. And they need me bad, lemme tell you. I'm their light at the end of the tunnel."

"Suppose she did kill Karen," Nudger said, resisting mentioning an oncoming train. "Ineptly, as you theorize. And Roger got the blame. Wouldn't she have come forward to save him?"

"And put her own neck in the noose? Jesus, Nudger! Weren't you listening? I said she was devoted, not suicidal."

"But if she loved him enough to—"

"Love shmove! There you go again, about to ask me a question and I'm paying you for answers. So get on with it! Finish the job you started." Fleck was tapping his checkbook on the desk impatiently. He said, "You are afraid of Dupont, aren't you?"

"I'm like you," Nudger said. "I can't figure him out."

"Know the reason I hired you last summer?" Fleck said. "First thing Gideon Schiller ever told me about you is you can't quit. Can't! You take a case, you see it through to the end."

Fleck held his eye for a moment, then looked down. He finished writing the check. Tore it off the pad and held it out to Nudger.

"I've got to know the truth about Dupont, Nudger. And you've got to find it out. Our compulsions coincide. We want the same thing. Take the check."

Nudger did.

CHAPTER THIRTY-TWO

Nudger wondered if he was going to find Effie Prang at home. Walking up her front path, he was making the first footprints in the snow. That didn't necessarily mean the house was unoccupied, though. In bad weather, people in Ladue didn't use their front doors. They went to their attached garages, got in their cars, and drove wherever they were going.

He rang the bell. While he waited his thoughts returned to the man who had been walking behind him, possibly following him, on Manchester that morning. He'd been thinking about this man a lot more than he wanted to. Was he Vella's oversized and jealous boyfriend, bruiser of chests with a punch like a freight train? If so, why was he bothering Nudger? He should be bruising Roger Dupont.

Nudger turned to look out at the street. The man hadn't followed him out here, anyway. He could be certain of that. This was exclusive Ladue, and there were no cars parked along the curb, and no pedestrians anywhere. Hearing the door open, he turned back.

He remembered Roger Dupont's younger sister as sweet and vulnerable, from their meeting last summer at poolside. His first impression this time was very different. Now, of course, she was dry and fully clothed. And he was entertaining the possibility that she'd murdered her sister-in-law.

At first glance she looked formidable. She had on an expensive steel-blue sweater—possibly cashmere—with a diamond-shaped monogram centered between her breasts, and tweed slacks. Her long hair was pulled back and knotted out of sight. The hairdo combined with her overbite emphasized her large eyes. She looked suspicious, if not downright hostile.

"Mrs. Prang, I'm—"

"Yes, I remember you, Mr. Nudger. And I have nothing to say to you."

She didn't shut the door, though, so Nudger said, "Your brother warned you not to speak to me?"

"Warned?" Effie Prang smiled, showing her prominent teeth. "He just said not to bother with you."

But still she lingered at the half-open door. Nudger couldn't see into the house, but a pleasant, citrus aroma wafted out to him, and he could hear soft music and the crackle of a fire. It was as if the house itself was welcoming him even if the owner wasn't.

"Maybe you should be the judge of that," he ventured.

"What?"

"Whether I'm a bother to you or not. Let me in. If you don't like my questions you can always throw me out."

She was still smiling. After a moment she stepped back, opening the door wide.

She led him into the living room. It was an inviting place on this dark, cold day. A well-nourished fire was roaring lustily in a brick hearth. There were deep sofas before a "home entertainment center" contained in fine wood shelves and cabinets. A half-completed jigsaw puzzle was scattered on a table. In a corner was a chess table with large, elaborately sculpted pieces all lined up and ready for the game. One wall was all bookshelves, bearing new hardcovers. When he saw a copy of *Architectural Digest* sitting on the coffee table, Nudger realized what the room reminded him of: the magazine's photo layouts in which the interiors always looked as if the happy, rich family and friends who usually filled the room had been shooed out for just a moment so the picture could be taken. It was odd to think Effie Prang lived here alone.

Nudger settled into the comfortable sofa. Effie sat across from him and picked up the piece of knitting she must have been working on when he rang the bell.

"You don't mind if I go on with this? I have to keep my hands busy."

Nudger realized there was no smell of stale tobacco in the house. Only of the log fire and a bowl of potpourri. "You've quit smoking."

"Yes. Aren't you the detective! Roger's been after me for years and I finally did it. Cider, Mr. Nudger?"

"No thanks. You've heard the news about Karen's body being found, of course."

Effie nodded. She kept her eyes on her stitching.

"What was your reaction?"

"Relief, I suppose."

"Relief?"

"That now she's definitely out of my brother's life for good. That she won't cause him anymore trouble."

The coldness of the comment took Nudger's breath away. After a moment he said, "You haven't given any thought to what might have happened to her?"

"No. Why should I?"

"She was your sister-in-law."

"Karen was always something of a mystery to me. I never met any of her people, except the sister, Joleen." Effie gave the name a mocking, hillbilly pronunciation. "Karen went to a public high school. Didn't go to college at all. She was living in a trailer park with her sister when Roger got involved with her."

Nudger had lived in a trailer park himself. His annoyance got the better of him. "So you're saying Karen was beneath you?"

Effie looked up from her knitting and shrugged. "No, just that I don't know much about people like her, so there's no point in asking me."

"I see. So your only feeling about Karen—ever—was that your brother would be better off without her."

Effie went back to her knitting. "Now you are starting to bother me, Mr. Nudger. Maybe you'd better leave."

There was nothing to lose, and Nudger might as well come out with it. "How badly did you want to get rid of your sister-in-law, Mrs. Prang?"

Effie's head jerked up. She stared at him, her eyes growing larger and larger. Then she got to her feet. The knitting, which she had dropped into her lap, now fell to the floor, but she was unaware of it. She backed up until she was behind the sofa. It was as if Nudger had placed a wild animal on the coffee table. Effie wanted to flee from it but was afraid to make any sudden moves.

"You think I killed Karen?" Effie asked, in a hushed voice.

Nudger said nothing.

"Oh my God! Do the police think that too? Are they going to be out here questioning me? The City Police?"

Effie, a Ladue-ite, was probably terrified of the city. There were people in Ladue who'd been to Bermuda more often than St. Louis. Nudger's belief in the possibility that Effie could be a murderer was fading fast. He shouldn't have let her snobbish comments about Karen mislead him. He'd known a lot of meek women who were ferocious snobs. It was as if they were so heavily put-upon by the people who were close to them that they couldn't spare even a smidgen of goodwill for the rest of humanity.

"Please sit down, Mrs. Prang," he said, "I don't really think you killed Karen."

She let out a long breath. She was relaxing slightly, but not enough to come out from behind the sofa. "Then that was a terrible thing to say. I really don't understand. Why would I have wanted to murder Karen?"

"When I was here before, you told me family was the most important thing for you. And Roger was all the family you had. You'd do anything for him. So I had to consider the possibility that you wanted to get him back from Karen."

Effie seemed to find his statement arresting. She stood still for a long moment, her gaze abstracted. Then tears began to track down her cheeks. She reached out to take a tissue from a box adorned with pink ceramic roses.

"You're right, Mr. Nudger. I guess I might as well admit that. I did hope to get Roger back. Not before Karen disappeared, though. After. It was during the investigation and trial that I was thinking he'd be acquitted and then he'd come live here with me."

She gave a sob as she dabbed at her eyes with the tissue.

"I'm sorry," Nudger said, "I didn't mean to upset you."

"It's all right. You just reminded me of my hopes. My disappointed hopes." Effie looked down at the tissue. It was now a wet ball. She absentmindedly stowed it in a pocket of the tweed slacks and reached for a fresh one.

"It seemed so natural, so sensible," she went on. "I mean, here's this lovely house, with no one in it but me. Roger's marriage had ended badly, just as mine had. Why shouldn't we live together? At least for a time? But Roger chose an apartment instead."

"Chose Vella," Nudger said.

She gave him a look. "I'm not supposed to talk about Vella. To you or anyone."

He nodded. "Your brother's orders?"

Effie hesitated. Then she gave an odd, bitter smile. "Yes. He can treat me . . . the way he's treated me, and still he can be perfectly sure that I'll do what he tells me."

"Why did you want him to live with you?"

She seemed to think about that. Then she nodded to herself. "Yes. I suppose I have to explain it to you. You probably think I have a pretty nice life. And I do. No children to burden me. No need to work. Plenty of friends, including a nice widower who doesn't want to disturb his estate plan by marrying me. I'm well-fixed. Life has left me high and dry. It's just that sometimes I get restless. I wish I could have an argument with someone. Wish I could go to bed tired. This house could even do with a little mess."

Nudger nodded. "And your brother?"

212

"What did I think he could do for me, you mean?" She leaned on the back of the sofa, dabbed her eyes again. "I thought he'd fill up my days. He did, once. When we were in high school, he was captain of every varsity team the school had. Never took a test he didn't ace. All the girls were crazy about him. He was my older brother and I idolized him. Maybe it was foolish to want him back, as if we were kids again, but . . ."

Her eyes flickered around the room. Her expression was rueful. Nudger took a guess.

"You bought the big-screen TV for Roger?"

She nodded. "He loves football. And the chess set too. I hate chess, actually. But I tried to make everything the way Roger wanted it. I even quit smoking. I wanted this to be the perfect home for him."

"Karen tried to make a perfect home for him too."

Effie frowned. "You don't believe she went away to Chicago."

"People have told me she would never have left her home."

"I can guess who told you that. It was the sister, Joleen, wasn't it?"

"Matter of fact, it wasn't."

"Well, I know how people portrayed Karen at the trial. As Roger's victim. The doormat. The meek little homemaker who idolized him and would put up with anything from him." Effie gave a sour smile. "That was me. That wasn't Karen."

"How do you mean?"

"She let him get away with a lot, that's true. But a change was coming over her, last spring. The last few times I saw her, she was different."

"How do you mean?"

"It's hard to explain. She wasn't defying Roger openly, exactly, but she had a gleam in her eye. Like she was planning something."

"An escape, you mean?"

"Yes, that's what I think. That she planned her getaway to Chicago, and when she was ready, she went."

She dropped her gaze to the floor and noticed her knitting lying on it. She hurried round the sofa to pick it up. She looked at Nudger without resuming her seat.

He understood that she wanted to be alone.

After thanking her for her time, he moved toward the front door.

She followed him. "Mr. Nudger, you ought to stay away from my brother."

"The police and others are going to carry on with the investigation, whether I'm involved or not."

"I don't expect you to believe me, but I'm telling you that for your own sake. There's something different about you. Something special. I can tell from the way Roger talks about you."

Nudger suddenly felt as if he'd swallowed a snowball. He could feel it, compact and cold, in the pit of his stomach. He waited, saying nothing.

"How can I explain?" Effie hesitated. "When I played chess with Roger, there'd be a moment when he would become very still. Then he'd relax, turn jolly. I came to know what that meant. I'd made some mistake, or I'd fallen into his trap. And there was no way out. He'd counted the moves it would take to checkmate me."

"I don't understand."

"He's playing a game now, with you. You have some moves left, but he knows he's going to beat you. He's going to enjoy it."

Her large, gentle eyes held his for a long moment. "It won't be so nice for you."

CHAPTER THIRTY-THREE

Nudger went to the drive-through window at Naugles and got a burger and chili-cheese fries. Then he returned to the office and ate at his desk. And in his coat, because the office was stone cold. It had been a long time since the last shot of intermittent heat.

He listened to his phone messages as he munched on french fries. There were the usual threats and insults from Eileen, who seemed to vent even more in the winter.

Then things improved. There was a call from Claudia, inviting him to come over for dinner. And a call from a lawyer named Rachel Gold. He didn't know her, but she had a nice voice, so he called her back right away.

"Law office of Rachel Gold," said a brusque male voice.

"This is Nudger, returning Ms. Gold's call."

"Rachel!" the man called out, "it's the *shmeggege*."

Nudger didn't know what a *shmeggege* was. Probably just as well.

Once Ms. Gold got on the line, he was glad he'd returned the call. She did sound nice, and she had a job for him, a surveillance that seemed likely to eat up hours and hours of billable time. They made an appointment for him to come to her Central West End office on Friday and talk about it.

In the background he could hear the man saying, "If you're really gonna hire this clown, at least have him bring some dough-nuts."

Nudger said he looked forward to meeting Ms. Gold. He wasn't so sure about the guy.

He hung up the phone and checked his watch. There was still time today to go to work on his other job, finding witnesses to the automobile accident. Two assignments in progress and a third pending: Nudger felt almost middle-class.

Problem was, Eileen could always tell when things were going relatively well for him. She seemed able to sniff it in the winds, or read it in cloud formations. But the result would be that she'd persecute him with renewed vigor. He was already in trouble: Her message had said that her lawyer/lover Henry Mercato was trying to get the judge to issue a "body attachment" for him. It made him shudder to think about the kinds of things Eileen would like to attach to his body.

He got up and looked around the office for his coat then realized he was still wearing it. The pipes were just beginning to clank with this afternoon's ration of hot water for the radiators as he went down the stairs.

The December dusk was drawing in when he got back. He parked on Manchester across from the office. In the cold and early darkness, the bright window of Danny's shop looked inviting. There was one customer sitting on a stool at the counter. He was a rotund man with a dignified bearing—head up, back ramrod straight—and Danny was listening to him with rapt attention. Maybe he was the Grand Doughnut Master, imparting to his eager pupil the secret of improved Dunker Delites. Nudger hoped so.

Spotting a gap in the rush-hour traffic, Nudger jogged across the street. Danny saw him and beckoned him into the shop.

"Hey, Nudge, say hello to an old friend."

The upright man did not turn his head, so Nudger had to come around beside him before he saw that it was Ray.

"Hello, Nudge," Ray said. He still held the rigid military bearing that had prevented Nudger from recognizing him in the first place. Only his eyes shifted to Nudger. They were even more aggrieved than usual, burning brightly with the consciousness of hurt and injustice. His skin was gray and glistened with sweat.

Nudger hadn't seen Ray since he'd moved down to Affton three months ago. Hadn't missed him, either. But for Danny's sake he nodded and asked, "How are you, Ray?"

"Can you put me in touch with a personal injury lawyer,

Nudge? A good one? 'Cause I got a cause of action here.''

"Against who?''

Being careful not to move the rest of his body, Ray raised one arm and pointed down Manchester. "Dr. Kripalkin.''

Nudger passed his office every day. "The chiropractor?''

"The man hurt me, Nudge. I'm injured for life. That bone-twisting bastard threw me around for fifteen minutes. He bent me in places where I ain't got joints.''

"Ray, why did you go to the chiropractor in the first place?''

"It was that woman made him do it, Nudge,'' Danny said. "Hydrant.''

"Heidran?'' repeated Nudger, astounded. "But I thought we'd given Heidran the slip.''

Ray managed a slight nod, a one-inch dip of his chin. "I thought so too, Nudge.''

On a blazing hot day in September, Danny had dragooned Nudger into helping Ray move. Dr. Fell, though not a scrupulous practitioner, had balked at assisting Ray in faking his own death. So moving was the only way for him to escape Heidran, who had continued to come over to clean house and morally instruct him. Nudger's arms and lower back ached at the memory of that day. Ray's television set and recliner chair were the heaviest pieces of furniture he'd ever picked up, and of course Ray's delicate condition limited him to a supervisory role. On the drive down to his new apartment in Affton they'd had to listen to his fretful complaints about the dangers of a change of address for someone in his position. He was sure to miss out on at least one disability check, thanks to the incompetence of government bureaucrats. Ray was a formidable combination: a welfare cheat who talked like a Republican.

They had made the move at an hour when they knew Heidran would be busy at Shag's. Affton was five miles away. Ray's new phone number was unlisted. Nudger assumed that his escape had been clean.

"How'd she find you?"

"I went to Shag's for a burger."

"You did *what*? Ray, of all the stupid—"

"Easy, Nudge," Danny said.

"No, it's okay," Ray said. "Let him rub it in if he wants to."

"Why did you go to Shag's?"

"I missed those Three-eighths pounders," Ray said, with a helpless shrug. He'd forgotten himself, and he winced and groaned. "I went on Tuesday evening, when I knew Heidran wasn't there. Made sure the girl at the counter was nobody I knew. Ordered from the drive-up and didn't get out of the car."

"So what went wrong?"

"The girl made me. Turned out Heidran had my picture taped to the cash register. I thought I got out of there fast, but when I pulled up in front of my building, Heidran pulled in right behind me."

Professionally speaking, Nudger was impressed. "How did—"

"Shh!" Danny interrupted. "Here she comes."

Nudger turned as the door opened. Heidran was wearing her brown Shag's uniform. No overcoat. She'd be one of those people who didn't feel the cold. She didn't say anything to Nudger, but she remembered him. The U boat–commander's eyes fastened on him, and he felt like a fat Allied tanker. He kept quiet.

"Hey, Heidran," Danny said tentatively, and was rewarded with a nod.

Then she turned to Ray and her face softened into a smile. She put her arms around his shoulders. He winced.

"Oh! Did Dr. Kripalkin hurt you?"

"It was agony. Fifteen minutes seemed like a year."

"My poor Raymond. But you'll feel better tomorrow morning, you'll see. Let's go home, get you into bed where you'll be comfortable."

Slowly, and to the accompaniment of heartrending groans, she maneuvered him into a standing position. With his arm draped over her shoulders, they headed slowly toward the door.

"I won't feel better," Ray was saying. "He hurt me permanently. Every move I make I can feel my bones grinding against each other."

"Is it worse than it was before?"

"Worse than it's ever been."

"Even worse than when you were at the steel plant? I am sorry, Raymond. You never have to go back to him again. But we'll keep searching until we find the doctor who can help you."

Nudger held the door as they went out. Ray was leaning all his considerable weight on Heidran, but her firm stride didn't waver.

As Nudger closed the door, Danny said, "Poor guy. We gotta think of another way to help him shake her, Nudge."

Nudger smiled and shook his head. "Can't you see it, Danny? They're a couple."

"I don't get you."

"She thinks she knows what Ray needs. She's going to get him fit. Put him to work. Teach him self-reliance."

"That ain't what Ray needs."

"No, but as long as she thinks it is, she'll keep listening to his complaints. And that's what he needs. They have a misunderstanding of each other to hold them together. They're a couple."

Peering out the window, he could see them moving slowly down the sidewalk. It put him in a romantic mood, seeing two people whose compulsions coincided.

Claudia laughed delightedly and gave him a kiss when he presented her with the half-dozen white roses he'd brought her.

"They're beautiful, Nudger." She held them up to smell them. Then she looked at him and her dark eyes became mournful. "You'll have to take them with you."

"What?"

"I'm not going to have a chance to enjoy them. I'm leaving tonight."

Nudger sighed. Now he noticed what he hadn't seen before: her suitcase, standing by the door.

Biff Archway. Delayed but not defeated in his scheme to get Claudia away to Colorado.

She smiled and gave his arm a consoling squeeze. "Come have a seat. Dinner's ready. And there's plenty of time. My plane's not till nine."

Nudger wished he'd decided on chocolates. At least he could have eaten them.

Claudia said, "Nudger?"

"Hmm?"

"Biff isn't going on this trip."

"What?"

"I'm going with the Schwartzes—Jane and Bob—and Ravindra Malabandar from the Chemistry department. Biff never had anything to do with this trip. He's scuba diving in Cozumel."

Nudger felt relief, and he felt like a fool. He'd never actually asked her if Archway was going to Colorado. He'd simply assumed.

He started to say he was sorry, but he merely stammered.

"It's okay, Nudger. Really."

"I'll drive you to the airport," he said.

"I'm not driving, I'm taking Metrolink. But you can go with me and help with my luggage."

Metrolink was the light rail line, of which St. Louis was very proud. It had only been in operation for a couple of years.

All aboard, Nudger thought.

CHAPTER THIRTY-FOUR

After riding out to the airport and seeing Claudia off, Nudger boarded Metrolink again for the return trip. Claudia's fellow teachers had been waiting for her at the ticket counter. They were all excited, looking forward to their trip. Nudger decided he would much rather be flying off to Colorado than taking the train back to St. Louis. The snow was always whiter . . .

His fellow passengers seemed to feel the same way. They were a lugubrious bunch. There were businessmen with suit bags and laptop computers, hairless young soldiers in green uniforms, and a young couple in shorts and straw hats, whom the cold weather seemed to have put into a state of shock.

The car livened up when a party of middle-aged vacationers pushed on board. They'd obviously made the most of the in-flight liquor. Nudger figured they were gamblers heading for the riverboats at the other end of the Metrolink line.

The train pulled out of the station. On a high trestle it crossed the river of flowing lights that was Highway 70. Nudger thought about Effie Prang. About Heidran and Claudia. Effie Prang thought Roger Dupont needed a happy home. Heidran thought Ray needed a job and self-respect. Claudia thought Nudger needed shaping up in myriad ways. If a woman loved a man, why couldn't she simply leave him as he was?

What had Karen Dupont thought her husband Roger needed?

Or had she ever really loved him?

The party of aging drunken louts, whom Nudger had pegged as casino-goers, got off at the University of Missouri stop. The car became quiet again. Nudger's thoughts drifted back to the case.

He believed Effie Prang had been honest with him today, up to a point. She would never tell him anything against her brother's interest, so Nudger wasn't sure yet what to make of her description of

Karen. Karen had changed somehow, Effie said. She'd acted like a woman with secret plans. Nudger wondered what could have happened to change her. And what had been her plans? Was it possible that Karen had some sort of secret life going? Had she vanished into it, only to meet her death?

Nudger mused, posing questions for which he had no answers, as he looked out the window. The train was pulling out of Delmar station. They were back in the city now, just a few stops from Union Station and his waiting car. He turned away from the window.

His view was abruptly blocked by a vast expanse of tan parka. He raised his eyes and saw a wide, jowly face with a bristly red moustache. Nudger didn't recognize the face, but the smell on the breath was familiar: the reek of cheap bourbon. His stomach tried to leap into his throat.

Vella's boyfriend said, "We're getting off here."

The train was beginning to slow down for Forest Park Station. Nudger looked around the car. There were still a dozen or so people on it, mostly tired businessmen, reading their newspapers or talking to each other or looking out the windows. No one seemed to have noticed what was going on at his end of the car yet.

"Get up," the big man said. "Vella wants to talk to you."

A huge right fist—the one that had almost pulverized Nudger's sternum—was on a level with his eyes. God, this guy was tall. And broad. And mean. Nudger wasn't about to get up and go out in the dark with him. He said, "I'm not getting off."

"But Vella's waiting." Now there was an odd plaintive note in the rumbling voice.

"You'll have to give her my regrets."

The train was slowing, pulling into the station.

"I promised Vella to bring you," the big man said. "So you get off, or I'm gonna put your head through the window."

Nudger looked around. But the big man had spoken softly, and no one had noticed.

"This car's full of people," Nudger pointed out. "There'll be an armed guard at the station."

"None of them's gonna stop your head from going through the window."

"You couldn't possibly get away afterward."

"That ain't gonna help you either."

The right fist opened into a U shape. The big man was forming a clamp for Nudger's neck. He was going to lift Nudger out of his seat and slam his head through the window, all right. The train was coming to a stop at the platform. It was going to happen in about five seconds.

The train stopped. The doors opened. The giant in the tan parka shifted his weight, prepared to strike.

"Let's go," Nudger said.

The big man backed off, just enough to allow him to get to his feet. Nudger crossed the car and went down the steps to the platform.

Vella's huge pet was right behind him.

"Up the stairs."

Nudger obeyed, clutching his coat to him against the cold. It occurred to him that this was the closest Metrolink station to Roger Dupont's apartment. Very convenient for Vella. The big man must have been following him around all day, and he'd chosen his moment with care.

Halfway up the steps, the giant hand clamped around his bicep. It hurt considerably.

"Wait a minute," the giant growled.

Nudger stopped and half-turned. With his free hand Vella's boyfriend took a roll of tablets out of his pocket and thumbed one into his mouth. Nudger thought at first they were antacids. Did his assailant have a delicate stomach too? Would he share his tablets with Nudger?

Then the man bit down, and a strong scent of mint escaped into the cold air.

"Vella don't like the smell of liquor."

"Oh," said Nudger.

"Move."

At the top of the steps a shining black Infinti sedan was waiting. Its engine thrummed softly. The big man opened the passenger-side door.

"Hello, Nudger," said the woman behind the wheel. "I'm Vella. Hop in."

Vella Kling was a petite, lovely young woman with coal-black hair and bright blue eyes. She was wearing blue jeans and a brown leather bomber jacket.

Nudger got in. The big man shut the door behind him. It was very warm in the car, and there was a pleasant smell of perfume and expensive leather. The giant climbed in the back. The car's springs settled under his weight.

Vella shifted in her seat to face him. Her thick dark hair was cut off in a straight line at chin-level. It formed a curtain that swung with her every movement. Her eyes probed at him.

"Don't look so worried. We don't mean you any harm."

"That's nice to hear. Five minutes ago your boyfriend was talking about putting my head through a window."

Vella's eyes got big and then she laughed. "You thought Rolf was my boyfriend? Well, I'm sorry, Nudger, but I'm not that kinky. One boyfriend at a time is usually enough for me." She laughed again. "Rolf's my big brother."

"Big is right," Nudger said.

Vella beamed a brilliant smile into the backseat. Nudger looked over his shoulder at Rolf. He smiled back at her, exhaling a rush of mint-scented breath.

"That explains a lot," Nudger said. "But not why he was going to put my head through the train window."

She stopped smiling. "I just don't understand why you're still going around asking questions and pestering people about Karen

Dupont. The case is over. You and that funny little lawyer you work for, you won and you got paid. Now why can't you leave well enough alone?"

"Maybe because we don't really feel it's over. Maybe we think Roger used us. Got the better of us."

"Of course he did!" Vella laughed again. "Roger gets the better of everyone."

"Including you?"

She shook her head, setting her curtains of hair to swaying. "No, I'm different. I'm not everyone. Roger and I are full partners, in love and in business. I'm going to handle the antiques and he's going to handle the finances, and we're going to make a fortune." Her blue eyes glinted at him.

"But I don't see what you have to be upset about," she went on. "So what if he used you? He didn't do you any harm."

"Why did Roger lie to us about you, Vella?"

She didn't answer right away. She sighed and looked at her brother. "I can see I'm going to have to tell him everything, Rolf."

"No," Rolf said.

"But he's so stubborn. He won't stop if I don't."

"Don't worry about him, Vella. He ain't worth spit. Let me take care of him."

The car shifted on its springs again. Rolf was leaning forward. Nudger's stomach revolved. He was sure they were playing out this little scene in order to scare him. Thought he was sure, anyway. He was scared.

"No, Rolf," Vella said, "my mind's made up. I don't want anymore trouble." She turned back to Nudger. "You're right. Roger did lie. The truth is, he and I were what you might call an item well before Karen disappeared. And we kept our relationship secret for the obvious reason. Because it would have looked bad for Roger."

Nudger nodded.

"And because we decided to keep it secret, Roger couldn't tell all he knew about Karen's disappearance." Vella took a deep breath, then let it out with a little sigh. "The truth is, the real reason Karen left is that she found out about us."

Nudger nodded again. It seemed appropriate.

She leaned back in her seat and smiled at him. "Now are you satisfied? Will you go back and tell that to Mr. Fleck, and will the two of you leave us alone?"

He shook his head. "Roger had had affairs before, and Karen tolerated them. Why should it have been different this time?"

Vella's lips compressed. Her pretty blue eyes turned hard and cold.

Like a good watchdog, Rolf responded instantly to his mistress's change of mood. Nudger felt the car shift on its springs again but before he could react Rolf's arm swung around and lodged beneath his chin, pinning him to the headrest. He could feel the pressure on his Adam's apple. Rolf only had to squeeze to cut off his breathing.

"Asshole. You fucking *asshole!* I'm trying to do you a favor, and you ask me a question like that." Vella's voice was entirely different now, harsh and angry. She was so mad she was trembling. As she glared at him Nudger's stomach was doing somersaults. It was no act this time. She was about to give Rolf a nod, and that was all it would take.

"You want me to convince Fleck, don't you?" Nudger croaked. "So I have to ask."

Vella looked away. To have that angry glare removed from him was a relief in itself. It felt almost as if Rolf had let up on the pressure. She sank back in her seat, closed her eyes, and took a deep breath.

Rolf and Nudger waited a long moment.

When she opened her eyes, she was the other Vella, smiling.

"I have a really terrible temper," she told Nudger. "Rolf, let him go."

Slowly, reluctantly, the big man complied. Nudger took a breath and raised a hand to massage his Adam's apple.

"It's true what you say," Vella went on. "Roger'd always played around, Karen had always looked the other way. I guess she knew those other girls were no threat to her. But I was different. She knew it right away."

"How could you tell?"

"She caught us together at the house one time. We weren't in bed or anything. Just sitting in her living room talking and she walked in and . . . well, she went ballistic."

Did she know already that you and Roger were . . ." Nudger's voice trailed off. He felt the need to phrase questions delicately.

"I don't think so," Vella said. "But as soon as she saw us she knew." There was no sign of Vella's violent temper now. She was leaning back against the door, with one elbow on the steering wheel and the other arm draped along the seatback. She was enjoying telling this story. "Roger and I have this aura when we're together, this glow of sexuality. Everyone notices it. People turn and look at us in the street. When we go out with other couples, even old married couples, just being with us turns them on. They're eager to get home and to bed."

"Uh-huh," Nudger said, wondering if this could be true. "And how did Karen react?"

"Went crazy, like I said. Screaming and yelling, pulling things down off the shelves and smashing them. She even tore down the drapes from one of the windows. She probably would have wrecked the place if Roger hadn't grabbed her and held on. I don't know how he calmed her down. We figured it would be better if I left."

"When did this happen?"

"About a month before she disappeared. But she was never the same after that day, Roger told me. She was very cool and distant, he said. Avoided him in the house. They hardly spoke, unless there were other people around and they had to keep up appearances. I tried to warn Roger." Vella gave a slow smile and dropped her eyes. "I know about these things. I know how women react when I take away their men. Karen was getting ready. She had a plan.''

Nudger remembered what Effie had said about the change that had come over Karen. "What was the plan?" he asked.

"It was for revenge on us, of course.''

"Revenge?''

"That's why she went off to Chicago without telling anyone. She knew exactly what would happen. That awful sister of hers, Joleen, would jump to the conclusion that Roger had murdered her.''

Nudger was trying to absorb all this. "You're saying it was Karen who planted the evidence of her own murder? To frame Roger?"

Vella nodded.

"What happened to Karen, then? How did she die?"

"I know nothing about that, and neither does Roger. But it's easy to get into all kinds of trouble in Chicago. I know. I've been in trouble there myself.''

Vella laughed. Then she leaned forward, studying him intently.

"Do you believe me?'' she asked.

The answer was no. But Nudger was not about to give it, not with Rolf sitting behind him. He swallowed hard and nodded his head.

"Good!'' said Vella delightedly. "And you'll go back to Mr. Fleck and explain, won't you?"

"Sure," Nudger said.

"And that'll be the end of it. You won't go around asking questions anymore?"

"No. There'll be no reason for anymore questions."

"Well, then. Everything's fine.'' Vella straightened up in her seat and reached for the shoulder belt. "Good night, Nudger. There should be a train along any minute.''

Rolf got out of the back seat and opened Nudger's door. Nudger climbed out of the car and stood up. His eyes were on a level with Rolf's shirt collar.

"Don't forget what you promised Vella,'' Rolf said to him. "I'm gonna keep an eye on you, make sure you remember.''

It was time for him to take another breath mint. The bourbon smell was coming through again.

Rolf stepped past him and got in the car. It's lights came on and it swung out onto DeBaliviere and turned left, heading for Forest Park and Roger Dupont's apartment.

Aside from a couple of people huddled in a nearby bus shelter, Nudger was alone. He turned and went down the steps to the station platform. He needed another ticket to get back to Union Station and his car.

His hands were shaking and it took him a long time to fumble a dollar bill out of his wallet.

Fear was such a motivator.

And such a squelcher of motivation.

CHAPTER THIRTY-FIVE

Next morning, Nudger was awakened by an acute attack of indigestion. It felt as if a small animal with sharp claws—a weasel, perhaps—was trying to dig its way out of his stomach.

Clutching his gut, he staggered into the bathroom. The budget-size jar of antacids he'd bought on sale at Walgreen's was sitting on top of the toilet tank because it was too big to fit in the medicine chest. Right now he felt like emptying the jar. Restraining himself, he popped two tablets into his mouth and trudged back into the bedroom. He sat on the bed and waited to feel better. He told himself that Claudia had used too much spicy Italian sausage in last night's lasagna.

It wasn't lasagna, of course. It was fear.

After a long ten minutes, he felt well enough to take a shower and get dressed. Then well enough to think about planning his day.

One option was to go to Lawrence Fleck's office and pass on what Vella Kling had told him. Fleck wanted to know how Roger Dupont had fooled them, and here was an answer. Not a true or complete answer, but one Fleck would have to be satisfied with, because Nudger was taking himself off the case. So Nudger could say.

The other alternative was to continue going around and asking questions. Every second he would be looking over his shoulder for Rolf and fearing another beating. Or worse. He had no doubt that last night's warning was the last he'd get.

He was still undecided as he left the apartment. It was another cold day. He looked up at the gray sky. It wasn't going to snow today, he judged. Wasn't going to clear either. Something like his mood.

He paused and looked around. From where the Granada was parked behind his building, unrelentingly charmless vistas opened out on every side: the backs of other apartment buildings, garbage Dumpsters, chain-link fences, telephone poles, patches of snow stained with car exhaust and dog urine. Then there was his Granada, mottled with gray salt-spray and almost audibly rusting.

As he got into the car, he decided to try altering his mood.

Gently urging the engine to life, he drove up to the St. Louis Bread Company on Delmar and got himself a breathtakingly expensive apple Danish and a cup of hazelnut coffee. There was a gas station with a car wash on the next corner, and on impulse he decided to give the Granada a treat, too. He topped off its tank and ran it through the car wash.

He parked half a block from his office and slipped surreptitiously into the stairwell door. He didn't want Danny to see him carrying the Bread Company bag.

The pipes were clanking noisily. Nudger was arriving just as the heat was coming on. His mood improved even more. He hurried up the steps.

Walter Blaumveldt was sitting in his client's chair. As usual, he looked as if he'd just come from burying his dog. His suit was blue, his tie black, his expression saturnine. He had a plastic foam cup of Danny's acidic black sludge in hand.

"Bread Company, Nudger?" he said, as Nudger placed the bag on his desk. "Somebody must be paying you well."

Nudger took off his coat. Already the office was so warm that he could do that. "Know something, Walter? You ought to do something nice for yourself once in a while. Give yourself a treat."

One corner of Blaumveldt's mouth twitched. "I'm just a working stiff with two daughters in college. I got no money for treats."

Had Blaumveldt come by to speak for Nudger's Puritan conscience? Sitting down behind the desk, Nudger said, "What brings you here, Walter?"

"I'm on my way to see Joleen Witt. I was hoping you'd drive me. If she sees my car Joleen won't open her door. She's not speaking to me these days."

Nudger hesitated. He wasn't sure he wanted to get back on the Dupont case. At least, not until he'd had his Danish.

He opened the bag and carefully lifted it out. Rotated it until he found a place where he could get some of the apple filling on his first bite.

He took a sip of hazelnut coffee and looked back at Blaumveldt. The dour insurance investigator couldn't have looked more censorious if Nudger had been disporting himself with a naked harlot.

"One thing, Walter. If we take my car, there's a possibility we'll be followed by someone you don't want to meet."

Blaumveldt smiled thinly. "You and I are making a lot of friends, huh, Nudger? Who might this one be?"

"Rolf."

"Who is?"

"Vella Kling's brother."

"Vella? Roger's flame? You found her?"

"She found me."

He went on to describe last night's encounter, pausing frequently for bites of Danish and sips of coffee.

Blaumveldt listened in attentive silence. When Nudger was finished, he said, "So what do you think?"

"I think it's a mixed bag, partly true and partly false."

Blaumveldt nodded. "How about the most important part? You think Karen contrived her disappearance so as to frame her husband for her murder?"

"No."

Blaumveldt nodded again. "So what part do you think is true?"

"That scene Vella described, when Karen found them together in the living room. I think that happened."

"It just sounded right to you?"

"More than that. I was in the house last summer. The drapes on one of the front windows had been pulled down, like Vella said."

"You were in the house, huh. The cops let you in?"

"Not exactly."

Blaumveldt managed another faint smile.

"Also, Effie Prang told me a change came over Karen shortly before she disappeared. She acted as if she had some kind of secret plan, Effie thought. I think the change came after she found out about Vella."

"You think she was planning to disappear?"

Nudger took a sip of coffee. "I'm not sure."

"I am," Blaumveldt said. "She didn't disappear. You and I are divorced guys, Nudger. We know wives don't disappear. They hire lawyers, and they make you pay for years. They do that even to guys like you and me, honest working stiffs. So just think what a wife would do to a two-timer like Roger."

Nudger didn't want to give the Blaumveldt view of the world too much thought. He'd only get depressed again. He said, "You say Karen didn't disappear. You mean, you think she was killed way back in May?"

Blaumveldt nodded but said nothing.

"What do you want to see Joleen Witt about?"

"Come along and you'll find out." Walter being Walter, holding his cards close to his vest.

Nudger took the last delicious bite of his Danish and washed it down with the last of his coffee. "All right, Walter," he said. "I'll drive if you'll watch my back."

Nudger wasn't kidding. All the way out to southwest county on Highway 44, he had Blaumveldt looking out the back window while he drove slowly in the right-hand lane. As they exited the highway, Blaumveldt turned around to face front.

"I've never seen anybody so skittish. Nobody's following us."

"You sure? This guy Rolf is good in addition to being mountainous. He was on me all day yesterday and I didn't know it until it was too late."

"He's not there now. Maybe he's not worried about you anymore. Figures he scared you away last night."

"He wouldn't be far wrong."

Nudger pulled into Cherokee Estates and bounced over the rutted road toward Joleen's trailer. The well-kept lawn and garden he remembered from his summer visit were buried under dirty snow. The awning that had been above her door was gone. But she'd found time to put a fresh coat of blue paint on her old Pontiac. It looked almost as good as Nudger's shining Granada.

As Nudger parked, Blaumveldt ducked down in his seat. Nudger said, "What did you do to get Joleen so mad at you?"

"I caught on to her," Blaumveldt said. "Go knock on the door."

Nudger crunched across the snowy yard and rapped on the door of the trailer.

"Who is it?" Joleen called out.

"Nudger. We talked last summer, during the trial."

"I'm busy."

"Ms. Witt, I'm continuing to investigate your sister's murder—"

"What for?" she yelled through the door. "Roger killed her. He got off. It's over."

"There's been a new development. I wish you'd give me a minute."

The door swung open. At first glance Joleen was as he remembered her, a tall, big-boned woman with unruly red hair. Her summertime tan had faded, though, and that made a change in her. Her healthy, outdoorsy look was gone. She looked somehow drained and tense. She was wearing olive drab cargo pants with the cuffs tucked into lace-up boots and a waffle-knit long underwear top.

Behind him he heard the squeak of rusty hinges as Blaumveldt opened the Granada's door. Joleen looked beyond Nudger at him, hooding her eyes and setting her mouth. She flicked a disgusted look at Nudger, which made him feel a little ashamed of the subterfuge.

Joleen got tough. "I told you before, Blaumveldt, I'm through talking to you. Take your pal and go away."

Nudger felt the need to speak up for himself. "It's not just a trick, Joleen. We really do have something to tell you."

She gave him a longer look. "Now I remember you. You seemed a decent enough person. Not like your friend here. He's been harassing me ever since the trial."

"I haven't been harassing—" Blaumveldt began, but she overrode him.

"Coming by or calling. Always with just a few more questions. And when I wouldn't talk to him anymore, he took to following me around. I think he even bugged my phone—"

"That would be illegal," Blaumveldt said.

"Just leave me alone, you fucking pest."

Blaumveldt stood very straight, his arms hanging at his sides, his face expressionless. His tone was mild. "It's nothing personal on my side, Joleen. I work for the insurance company, so I had to consider the possibility your sister was alive and attempting to per-

234

petrate a fraud. I had to keep checking whether she'd gotten in contact with you.''

All this time Joleen had been standing in the doorway, blocking their entry. Now she leaned against the door frame, hanging her head. She seemed very weary. She shot another glance at Nudger. ''I don't really care about the harassment. The thing I can't forgive this jerk for is he almost got me hoping again. I knew last summer that Karen was dead and Roger killed her. But Mr. General Mutual Insurance here kept coming around and coming around, and I started thinking, maybe he's right. Maybe Karen's alive. I knew deep down it wasn't true, but God, I wanted it to be true so bad. I couldn't stamp out the hope. Every time I picked up the phone, every time I went for the mail . . .''

She covered her face with her hands, so they wouldn't see her tears. She swallowed hard, then in a steadier tone she went on, ''And then they found the body. I've had to go through my sister's death twice. Now leave me alone, please!''

Nudger took a step back from the door. He felt sorry for Joleen and regretted the trick he'd played on her.

But Blaumveldt stood his ground. In the same neutral tone, he said, ''It's no good, Joleen. I've found out what you've been hiding all these months. Now, you want to talk to us about it, or do I take it to the police?''

Nudger looked from Blaumveldt to Joleen. What was going on here?

Whatever it was, it worked. Joleen stared at both of them for a long moment, then shrugged and stepped aside.

They entered the trailer. The quarters were cramped and utilitarian; they suited Joleen's military style. Nudger looked around for a place to sit but didn't see one. No chair faced another. All the chairs faced machines: the television set, the computer, the microwave. Joleen's home was a series of workstations. Nudger thought she must lead a lonely life. Her sister must have meant a lot to her.

She sat on a stool at the counter that divided living room from kitchen. Nudger and Blaumveldt remained standing.

"All right, Blaumveldt," she said. "What have you found that you think's so important?"

Blaumveldt smiled sourly and shook his head. He wasn't going to be hurried. In half a year, Nudger thought, these two had had plenty of time to build a poisonous relationship.

"You already know," Blaumveldt said. "It's what you were afraid I'd find out. But let's start at the beginning. Nudger, go ahead. Tell her what you learned last night."

Joleen's eyes shifted to Nudger. He said, "You told me last summer you thought Roger fooled around. You thought he had a girlfriend at the time your sister disappeared. You were right."

"Oh? What's her name?"

Joleen was staring straight at him. The wide green eyes, the aquiline nose, made him think of a wild creature both furtive and dangerous. He didn't know if he was afraid for her or for Vella, but he knew he'd better not tell her Vella's name.

"That's not important right now," he said. "What matters is that Karen found out about her." He went on to narrate the scene in the Dupont's living room. Joleen rested one elbow on the counter behind her and looked at the floor as she listened.

When he'd finished talking, she didn't look up. "I knew about that," she said. "Karen told me. Funny how different it sounds when the slut tells it to Nudger. What's that she said about an aura?"

"She said she and Roger have an aura of sexuality. Everybody who's around them gets turned on."

Joleen laughed. "Well, I'm glad she's enjoying the sex, because with Roger, sex is all you get. He's not a man, he's a dildo."

Turning away from them she reached across the counter to pick up a glass. She filled it with water from the kitchen tap and turned back to them.

She took a sip of water and said, "There was nothing special about this girl, whatever she thinks. The reason Karen got so upset was that Roger had brought her to the house. That was something he hadn't done before.''

Joleen looked at Nudger. "Their home was important to both of them. By that time, it was about all their marriage came down to. For Roger to bring his latest girl into their home—that was telling Karen he had no respect at all for her anymore. That he wasn't going to leave her with anything.''

"So Karen came and told you this," Blaumveldt said. "What did you decide to do about it?''

Karen returned her gaze to the floor. She suddenly seemed deeply bored. "Fuck off, Blaumveldt.''

Blaumveldt sighed and reached into his shirt pocket. "Okay, I'll tell you what you did. You decided to make Roger pay for his sins. Literally. You started selling his possessions.''

He unfolded a piece of notebook paper. "You sold only things he wouldn't miss, and you were pretty cagy about it. Took me a long time to dig this up. Most of Karen's jewelry went to a jeweler downtown. You got thirty thousand for it. Or was it closer to forty?''

Joleen said nothing.

"Then there was the silver service. That brought about fifteen thousand. The painting you sold through a gallery in New York netted you over twenty thousand.''

"It was an abstract by a contemporary artist," Joleen said. "Roger didn't like it and made Karen keep it in her dressing room. He never missed it.''

Blaumveldt folded his list and put it away. "What else did you sell, Joleen? How much money did you raise?''

She continued her stubborn silence, staring at the floor.

"Where's the money now?" Blaumveldt asked.

Nudger didn't expect Joleen to answer. But after a long moment she said, "Karen spent most of it.''

Blaumveldt raised his eyebrows, which for him was an extreme expression of surprise. "On what?"

"I'm not sure, exactly." She met Blaumveldt's skeptical look and her own eyes hardened. "She was my sister and all I wanted was to help her. I didn't press her for answers she didn't want to give. But she used to talk about a house of her own. A little cabin in the country. It was kind of her dream. A place she could get away to, that was hers and not Roger's. She didn't want him to know about it. Didn't want anybody to know about it, not even me."

"So you don't know where this cabin is?" Blaumveldt sounded skeptical. But Nudger thought Joleen might be telling the truth, considering how Roger had apparently treated his wife.

"I don't buy it, Joleen," Blaumveldt said. "I think Karen kept the money in cash—or maybe a secret account. I think that was her slush fund, in case she decided to run away from Roger."

Joleen shook her head vehemently. "No, no! Don't start that again. Karen wouldn't run away to Chicago. She didn't know anyone there. She didn't like big cities. She—"

"I don't think she ran away either," Blaumveldt said. "She just wanted to know the money was there if she needed it. Problem was, you knew about the money, too. And it tempted you, seduced you the way I've seen money seduce people before. You killed your sister for it, Joleen."

Her eyes widened. Otherwise she was perfectly still. In the silence Nudger could hear her shallow, choppy breathing. It was as if a small pump were working, filling the room up with anger. The air seemed to thicken and darken. Nudger's stomach, perceptive as always, reacted to the change. He would have popped an antacid tablet, but he found that he couldn't move.

Joleen could. She hurled her drinking glass at Blaumveldt. It was no mere gesture. She had a shortstop's arm and the glass would have hit Blaumveldt in the face if he hadn't ducked. It shattered against the wall behind him.

"Get out!"

To Nudger's amazement, Blaumveldt persisted. "Sure you've got nothing to say? You know I'm taking this right to the police."

"Get out!" Joleen said again, this time with the sort of menace that made Nudger wonder if there might be a gun in the trailer.

Joleen had turned her back on them.

Nudger grasped Blaumveldt's sleeve and pulled him toward the door.

He knew when a party was over even if Blaumveldt didn't.

CHAPTER THIRTY-SIX

Back in the car, Nudger popped his antacid and started the motor. Blaumveldt kept silent until they reached the exit from Cherokee Estates onto Indian Lane. Then he said, "This is the only way out of the trailer park. I've checked. Let's park where we can watch it."

Nudger had been mulling over the same idea. He turned left and drove to the crest of the hill. There was no cross-street here, only a widening of the gravel shoulder. He turned the car around, parking it in front of a copse of trees that would break its silhouette and make it less noticeable.

"You figure Joleen's going someplace?"

"I figure she's going wherever she's got the money hidden," Blaumveldt said. "She's got to run before the police can get to her."

Nudger looked sideways at Blaumveldt. His eyes were cold and alert, his complexion as ashen as usual. Nudger's own face felt hot and flushed. He'd left the police department because he'd realized he would never acquire the hardness cops had to have, the ability to push people to extremes of anger or fear without being affected by the emotions himself. Blaumveldt had that hardness. He'd just proven it.

"You really think she killed her sister?"

Blaumveldt shook his head with rueful amusement. "I still remember the first time we talked, Nudger. You told me the way you work. You go around and get a feeling for the people, and then you know what happened."

"Right."

"So now your feeling is Joleen didn't kill Karen?"

"I'm not sure. You have no proof she did."

"Nudger, this woman works on an assembly line. Lives in a trailer. And here's this fortune that only she and her sister know about. She did it, then she tried to put the blame on Roger. Remember, she was the one who reported Karen missing in the first place. Then she kept after the cops until they arrested Roger."

"All right," Nudger said. "One of us should stay here and keep an eye on Joleen. But the other should check out the cabin."

"Karen's little place in the country, you mean? It doesn't exist. Joleen made that up on the spot."

"Maybe. But we have to check it out."

Blaumveldt thought it over, then gave a curt nod. "You're right," he admitted. "So who goes and who stays?"

The two men exchanged smiles of professional amusement. There were times when it seemed to Nudger he'd spent half his life sitting in cars waiting for something to happen, and the other half on the phone, trying to wheedle information out of people. Doubtless it was the same for Blaumveldt.

There was no shortcut available for finding out if Karen Dupont had recently purchased a house in the country. It would be a matter of calling land title companies and realtors in the countless little towns surrounding St. Louis. There would be suspicious people who would say nothing, and gossipy people who would waste time and generate false leads. The search might take scores of calls.

On the other hand, it was better to be sitting in a warm office than a cold car.

"I'd prefer to make the calls," Nudger said.

"So would I." Blaumveldt reached in his pocket and brought out a quarter. "Want to flip for it?"

Nudger looked at the quarter. The sight of money clarified his thoughts. This search was going to generate a whopping long-distance phone bill. He'd have to pay it and hope for reimbursement from Fleck, which might not be forthcoming. Better to let Blaumveldt's insurance company foot the bill.

"I'll stay here," he said.

"Suit yourself." Blaumveldt shrugged, but he looked relieved. "I'll walk up to that gas station on the corner and call a cab."

"Want me to drive you?"

Blaumveldt looked down the hill at the entrance to the trailer park and shook his head. "Better not. She could come barreling out of there any minute. Or maybe she'll sit and stew for hours before she makes up her mind."

"Or maybe she won't come out at all."

Blaumveldt shook his head. "She did it, Nudger. That money's sitting in a bank account or safe-deposit box, or a suitcase buried in the woods. And Joleen will be going for it."

Buttoning up his raincoat, Blaumveldt got out of the car. Nudger got out too, but only to go to the trunk for his stakeout kit—a box containing a packet of stale Oreo cookies, a six-pack of diet Pepsi, and a wide-necked jar. This last was for what the police called "personal relief."

Blaumveldt looked on with approval. "I bet you sit a good stakeout, Nudger."

Nudger gave a nod of acknowledgment. That was no doubt one of the highest compliments this dour man had at his disposal.

They parted without further words. Nudger got back in the car while Blaumveldt trudged down the road.

Nudger turned up his coat collar and pulled his hat down over his ears, not so much for disguise as for warmth. He fixed his gaze on the entrance to Cherokee Estates. Trailers and a stand of pine trees blocked his view of the approach road to the entrance, which meant he wouldn't see Joleen's old Pontiac until it was about to turn onto Indian Lane. If she turned left, he couldn't miss her; she'd go right by him. He'd have to duck and hope she didn't remember what his car looked like. But if she turned right, she'd be over the next hill in a matter of seconds. He could easily miss her, especially if passing traffic got in the way.

For the first few hours, Nudger did well. He didn't allow daydreams or musings to distract him. He reduced his consciousness to something like a dial tone. He kept his eyes fixed on the entrance to the trailer park while he nibbled and sipped, and even while he availed himself of the wide-neck jar. He didn't glance at his watch. Time had nothing to do with this job. He'd stay here until Joleen appeared, then follow her wherever she was going.

At some point in the afternoon, inevitably, boredom got the better of him. His thoughts began to wander. It was less than a week to Christmas, and he hadn't done any shopping yet. He'd been waiting for a free evening to go to Big Lots, a vast barn of a store on Manchester, and rummage through the bins of bargain merchandise. But now he had two jobs going and a third soon to begin. He was flush, so he could—

Nudger leaned forward, blinking. There was the Pontiac! Joleen was turning right onto Indian Lane. He'd almost missed her. Now he'd have to move fast to catch up with her.

He twisted the ignition key. The starter ground and ground as he watched the Pontiac recede in the distance.

Finally the engine caught. There was a break in traffic and Nudger swung out onto the road. With a clunk, his current can of soda fell over and began spilling its contents on the floor mat.

The Pontiac disappeared over the top of the hill. Nudger stomped on the gas pedal, but the Granada's engine was still cold and balky. He chugged slowly up the hill. A battered black pickup truck waiting at a driveway entrance saw its chance and pulled out in front of him. It accelerated even more slowly than he did and he had to let off on the gas. His stomach clenched. He pulled the roll of antacids from his pocket and thumbed one into his mouth.

When he reached the top of the hill, he saw a red traffic light about a quarter mile ahead. Scanning the waiting cars as he coasted toward them, he was relieved to spot the Pontiac in the left-turn lane.

Nudger switched to that lane and eased to a stop. There were four cars between him and Joleen.

The green arrow appeared on the signal. Joleen, first in line, got moving at once. Nudger held his breath, hoping the arrow would be long enough for him to get through. The next three cars followed the Pontiac, curving through the intersection. But the driver in front of Nudger seemed to be asleep. Nudger couldn't honk for fear of drawing Joleen's attention. He banged his fist on the wheel and yelled "Come on!" into the cold windshield.

At last the car got moving. Nudger followed, a foot from its rear bumper. The green arrow disappeared while he was in the intersection, but no one honked at him.

They were out on Tesson Ferry Road, a broad, busy street. Nudger glanced at his watch. Four-thirty. A reasonable time for Joleen to be heading for her job on the night shift. But she was going in the wrong direction, and she was going very fast. Nudger had a hard time keeping up as she wove through traffic and jumped yellow lights.

When a signal up ahead turned red, Nudger was afraid for a moment that she was going to blast right through it. Then the Pontiac's taillights flared, and he stepped on his own brakes. The car behind Joleen turned off, into the entrance to a shopping center. The next car in line followed suit. Suddenly there was no one between Joleen and Nudger. She was stopped at the white line, and there was nothing he could do but coast slowly up behind her and hope the light would change.

It was no good. She made him. He saw her green eyes in the rearview mirror. She swung round in her seat to get a better look at him.

The next instant she faced front. Her arms flew as she cut the wheel sharply. Then the engine roared and the tires squealed and the big car cut across traffic. There were more squeals as other cars stopped short to avoid hitting her.

The Pontiac ploughed on across the road, bounced and lurched over the concrete divider, then swept into a turn going the other way. Oncoming cars honked, skidded, plunged to a stop. A mini-van missed her rear bumper by inches.

By the time Nudger was through wincing, Joleen had disappeared.

If this were a movie, he'd cut the wheel, stomp on the gas, and go screaming after her.

It wasn't a movie, though. It was real life, complete with large, heavy cars driven by confused, scared, vulnerable people.

He decided high-speed chases were for the cops.

Leaving the snarled traffic to sort itself out, he turned right into the shopping center. There was a public phone next to a McDonald's.

He called Hammersmith at the Third District, then went inside to catch up on breakfast and lunch.

CHAPTER THIRTY-SEVEN

The rush-hour traffic was heavier than usual, and it was dark by the time Nudger got back to Maplewood. A block away from the office, he ran into yet another jam. After five minutes of stop-and-go, he reached the cause of the backup. It was a St. Louis police car, double parked in front of his building. A tall young cop was standing in the doorway of the doughnut shop, talking to Danny. Had someone actually died from eating a Dunker Delite?

Double-parking in back of the police car, Nudger got out and walked over to the sidewalk. Danny pointed the cop toward him.

The cop looked very stern, very fit. Fresh out of the Academy and ready to take on the world. He bobbed his head at Nudger but didn't smile. "Mr. Nudger?"

"That's right."

"Would you come with me, please, sir? You're wanted at Third District."

"Lieutenant Hammersmith send you?" This was strange; ordinarily Hammersmith would just leave a message on Nudger's machine."

"No, sir. Captain Springer."

Bad news. Springer was an old enemy. He'd probably told the cop to mace Nudger if he hesitated. "Sure," Nudger said. "Any idea what it's about?"

"There's a meeting scheduled for six o'clock and the Captain wants you to be present. That's all the information I have." He went over to his car and opened the back door. He was going by the book: He intended to put Nudger in the backseat, behind the cage, where the door handles didn't work. "If you'll just step into the vee-hicle, sir."

"You mind if I follow you?"

"You mean, in your own vee-hicle?" The young cop's face went blank for a moment as he tried to figure out whether the Captain would mind this modification of his orders. "Well, I guess that's okay."

In convoy they headed east on Manchester. The young cop wasn't using his roof lights; he probably figured they could make it to Third District comfortably before six.

They were on a dark and lightly traveled section of Manchester when the cruiser's roof lights began to shine and ripple. It slowed and pulled over to the side of the road. The young cop got out and trotted back to Nudger's car. Confused, Nudger rolled down his window.

"Sir, I just got a radio call. We're not going to Third District. If you'll follow me, I'm going up Kingshighway to Highway Forty."

"What's happened?"

"There's been a homicide reported. Captain Springer is now at the scene, and he wants you there."

"A homicide? Who was killed?"

The young cop went blank again. It took him a moment to come up with the name. "Victim's a male. Blaumveldt. Walter Blaumveldt."

The cop led Nudger into a multilevel parking structure across the street from the General Mutual Building. They drove up three levels and came to the crime scene.

As Nudger got out of his car he could see only a cluster of haphazardly parked vehicles: patrol units, unmarked cars, an EMS van, and a forensics van. A few curious office workers, with briefcases in one hand and keys in the other, were hanging around trying to see what was going on.

Nudger didn't really want to see what was going on. He walked slowly toward the crime scene, accompanied by the young cop.

Hammersmith emerged from behind a van and glided toward him. He was wearing a camel's hair overcoat out of a thirties gangster movie. It reached almost to his ankles. He looked a lot warmer than Nudger felt.

"Hello, Nudge," Hammersmith said. He dismissed the young cop with a nod.

"What happened?"

"I was hoping you could fill me in some more." Hammersmith turned and fell in beside Nudger, walking him back toward the vehicles. Toward the body. "You said on the phone it was Blaumveldt who was suspicious of Joleen Witt. So I called him at his office, asked him to come over to the station. He said fine, he had a lot of information for me, he'd be right over. I waited, but he didn't show. Instead we got the call about this."

They skirted the ambulance and came up to Blaumveldt's car. The driver's side door stood open and the interior light was on. That was going to run the battery down, Nudger thought inanely.

The body lay facedown on the cement floor next to the car. The keys were still in Blaumveldt's outstretched hand. Blood stained the light-colored raincoat. Nudger was relieved that he couldn't see Walter's face.

"Tummy okay?" Hammersmith asked.

"Sure," Nudger lied.

"A secretary from a law firm across the street called it in," Hammersmith explained. "She was on the way to her car when she saw the body. It must have just happened. The killer was either really stupid or really cool. Took a helluva chance of being seen. Apparently waited by the car, then came up behind Blaumveldt and shot him in the back of the head. It was a light caliber weapon, probably a twenty-two handgun. Didn't make much noise, but it did the job."

Hammersmith's fleshy features sagged. "It's too bad. Walter was a gloomy old cuss, but he was an honest man."

Nudger couldn't improve on that. He nodded.

Hammersmith sighed and went on. "His wallet's gone. Probably that's just to throw us off, make us think it was a mugging."

Nudger deliberately took his eyes away from the body. Looked at Hammersmith. "I'm not sure about that. Was there anything in his pockets? I mean, did it look like the killer searched him?"

"We haven't found any papers that'd indicate what he wanted to talk to us about, if that's what you mean. You think the killer took them?"

"Nudger!"

He knew the voice, and it was not one he wanted to hear. He turned to see the pale, pinched face of Captain Leo Springer. Springer bore down upon him, arms swinging and fists clenched.

"I want to talk to you. Come over here."

He stalked away with that slinky walk of his. Nudger thought he resembled an angry ferret.

Nudger shot a glance at Hammersmith, who avoided his eye. Then they followed the short, wiry figure of the Captain around the ambulance.

"I didn't know you were on this case," Nudger said.

"I'm trying to deal with a very delicate liaison situation with the Illinois State Police," Springer replied. "And you are not helping. Now tell me about Joleen Witt."

"Have you put out an APB on her?" Nudger asked.

"Yes. We can do our job without the benefit of advice from you, Nudger. Now answer my question. What the hell was going on between Blaumveldt and Joleen Witt?"

So Nudger explained the events of the day. Springer folded his arms as he listened and rocked back on his heels. When Nudger got to the scene in Joleen's trailer, he began shaking his head and rolled his eyes.

Hammersmith listened impassively. He took out one of his big green cigars and lit it. For once, Nudger welcomed the resulting cloud of noxious smoke. He knew Springer disliked the smell even more than he did. Maybe this little confab would be cut short in the interest of lung health.

248

Nudger hadn't quite reached the end of the story when Springer ran out of patience.

"What the hell is with you two?" He pointed a stiff finger at Nudger. "You should have gotten out of this case when Roger Dupont's trial ended. Blaumveldt should have gotten out of it when Karen Dupont's body was found. Instead the two of you keep on poking around, interfering with an open homicide investigation. And today you engineer this lunatic confrontation with Joleen Witt. Trying to throw a scare into her, I guess. I hope you're satisfied with the results."

Nudger's insides squirmed. His face felt hot. Springer was demonstrating his usual talent for probing the sorest spot.

"Didn't it occur to you that once she lost you, Joleen might go after Blaumveldt?" Springer stormed at him.

"No," Nudger said. "Maybe it should have, but the fact is, it didn't occur to me."

Springer stared at him.

Hammersmith said, "Why not, Nudge?"

"I don't think Joleen has the money. I don't think she killed her sister. Which means she had no reason to kill Blaumveldt."

"So who do you think did kill him?" Hammersmith asked. He looked at Nudger and went on, "You're thinking about our old buddy Dupont, aren't you?"

Nudger nodded.

"This is ridiculous," Springer said. "This reject doesn't know anything."

"Just a sec, Captain," Hammersmith said. He blew some smoke Springer's way and turned to Nudger. "A minute ago you wanted to know if the body had been searched, Nudge. What did you think had been taken from it?"

"When Walter called to say he had some new information for you, it's possible he wasn't just talking about Joleen. He might have located the cabin."

"What cabin?" asked Springer.

Hammersmith had picked up on it. "The cabin. The place in the country that Joleen thought Karen had bought for herself."

Springer screwed up his face even more tightly. "But you said Blaumveldt didn't believe that story. He thought Joleen made it up."

"I thought it was worth checking out. And Walter agreed." Nudger turned back to Hammersmith. "I'd check his desk and his computer. Also get hold of his phone records."

It annoyed Springer that Nudger was talking past him. He stepped directly in front of him. "I told you before, we don't need your advice. I think Blaumveldt was right. There is no cabin in the country. Joleen made that up. Even if there is a cabin and Blaumveldt found it, so what? It corroborates Joleen's story, but why should Dupont care?"

Nudger said, "It's possible that this cabin's where Karen went when she disappeared. If that's true, it may hold the answers to what happened to her, to who killed her."

Springer rocked back on his heels and looked up at the low concrete ceiling. "What makes you think she was at this cabin after her disappearance?"

"No one's ever been able to find any convincing proof that she was anywhere else."

"That's brilliant, Nudger. What a mind you have. Know what I think?" Springer dropped his eyes to Nudger's. "I think you just want to believe somebody other than Joleen killed Blaumveldt. It's easier on your conscience that way."

Nudger winced. Score another low blow for the Captain. He remained silent.

"Take it easy, Captain," said Hammersmith mildly.

Springer swung around to face Hammersmith. His nose wrinkled up. He chopped at the air with one arm, clearing away the smoke cloud.

"Listen, Jack, I think your pal is spinning fantasies here. Right now, I don't give a shit about Karen Dupont's country house and whether it exists or not. We know Joleen Witt hated Walter Blaumveldt's guts. We know they had a violent argument this morning. So when Blaumveldt turns up dead, my first priority is to get hold of Joleen Witt. You see the case any different?''

Hammersmith exhaled smoke. He said, "No, sir."

"All right then. Maybe you want to walk your friend back to his car, Jack. And while you're doing it, maybe you want to impress upon him that he'd better quit interfering in an open homicide investigation."

Hammersmith rolled his cigar between his fingers. He examined the length of the ash and flicked it away. "Yes, sir," he said.

Gripping Nudger's arm, he turned him around and headed him back to the car.

He didn't speak until they got there. Then he said quietly, "We'll search Blaumveldt's office, Nudge. We'll keep our eyes open for an address. But you keep out of it from now on."

Nudger nodded unhappily. "Yeah, Jack. I got Springer's message."

"That's not the only reason." Hammersmith nodded his head toward the corpse. "You think you're that much tougher than Blaumveldt?"

Without waiting for an answer, he turned away and walked back toward the murder scene.

They both knew the answer anyway.

CHAPTER THIRTY-EIGHT

Nudger snapped awake. Opened his eyes. He'd fallen asleep with the TV on. On the screen was a *Star Trek: The Next Generation* rerun. Captain Picard and his officers were sitting around their conference table under the stars. Everyone looked thoughtful. Data suggested running a level-three diagnostic. Captain Picard approved.

Nudger ran a diagnostic of his own. He was sitting in the recliner chair in his living room, fully clothed except for his shoes. An empty can of beer was grasped in his hand. He checked his watch: three o'clock in the morning. He knew he should go to bed, but he'd apparently slept his fill. He felt wide awake now.

He rose stiffly and went into the kitchen, where he threw away the beer can and put on some coffee. While the machine gurgled, he went back into the living room, switched off the TV and sat down next to the phone.

He'd missed a call from Claudia early in the evening. He'd called back right away, but she'd gone out again. Now it was too late to try again; he'd wake her up. For a moment he considered calling anyway and pretending the time zone differential had confused him. Then he realized that was selfish and rejected the idea.

When the coffee was ready, he poured a cup, sat at the kitchen table, and thought about the murder of Walter Blaumveldt. There had been no call from Hammersmith; the phone would have awakened him. Which meant either that the search of Blaumveldt's office hadn't turned up the whereabouts of Karen's cabin, or that Captain Springer hadn't bothered to order the search yet.

Nudger thought about Joleen Witt. He thought about Vella's ominous big brother Rolf. If Blaumveldt really had located the cabin, and if that represented any threat to Dupont and Vella, Rolf would have been the one to pull the trigger. Nudger felt certain that was what happened, even though he couldn't prove it. The police were chasing the wrong person.

The situation wouldn't have surprised Blaumveldt. He'd always seemed to feel that people got away with too much in this world. He would have thought it typical that someone was getting away with murdering him. Nudger wondered if there might be some sort of karma working here.

It was funny how Blaumveldt took such pride in being an exception, a rock in the fast-flowing stream of the world's heedlessness and injustice. He'd had a highly developed sense of obligation. Nudger smiled to think of him showing up at Claudia's apartment with the ten-dollar-bill in his hand so soon after Karen's body was found, as quick to pay off a debt as other men were to collect one.

Suddenly Nudger sat up straight. Suppose Walter'd been just as punctilious this time? What would he have done, if he *had* found a lead to the location of the cabin?

He'd have called Nudger.

The moment the idea popped into his head, Nudger was sure he was right. The answer he sought was on the answering machine at the office.

He called to use the remote to retrieve his messages, but the phone rang and continued to ring. Which meant the machine was turned off.

Nudger never switched it off.

He gulped down the rest of his coffee, then went into the living room, stepped into his loafers, and grabbed his raincoat.

He passed only two other cars on Manchester, and for once he was able to park right in front of his building. As he stepped out into the cold, he smelled a warm and delicious aroma. Danny was in his shop already, making donuts for his morning customers.

Nudger went in the stairway. It was bitter cold. The landlord didn't waste heating fuel at night. The office radiator wouldn't start clinking and clanking with heat until well after sunrise. He ran up the steps, opened his office door and flicked on the light.

His chair was occupied. A woman was leaning far back in it with her feet up on Nudger's desk. She was bundled in a parka, with a knit cap pulled down to her eyebrows. It was the fact that her red hair was concealed that deceived Nudger.

Only when she opened her eyes did he recognize Joleen Witt.

"What are you doing here?" Nudger asked in a stunned voice.

Joleen put her feet on the floor. The chair *eeeked* for her just as it did for Nudger. Her broad face had looked peaceful and unguarded in the instant before the light had awakened her. Now she blinked a couple of times and became the wary, scornful woman he'd come to know.

He took a step toward her. Her hand went into her coat pocket and came out holding a gun. She pointed it at Nudger. He froze with the proper respect. It was a small target pistol, a .22 caliber. Like the gun that had killed Blaumveldt.

Or maybe it *was* the gun that had killed Blaumveldt. Nudger's thinking had been all wrong. Joleen was the murderer.

Nudger stared helplessly at the gun muzzle and waited for the bang and flash. His mind went blank, except for a forlorn wish that he'd called Claudia when he'd had the chance.

But the gun didn't go off. Instead, Joleen started talking, in her usual irascible tone. "What am I doing here? Where else am I going to go? I'm a fugitive, thanks to you. I've got a police scanner in my car. I found out I was wanted for murder as I was driving to work. Try *that* some morning and see how it ruins your mood. I knew I had to dump the car, right away. I rode the bus here."

In his mind Nudger took a step back from the abyss. Joleen wasn't going to shoot him, at least not immediately. She was talking like an innocent woman. He wanted very much to believe in her innocence.

"How'd you know where my office was?" he asked.

"You gave me your card last summer, remember? I didn't even have to break in. You left the door open."

"Oh," said Nudger. He'd have to reconsider that policy. Better to lose a client than what he might yet lose tonight.

"I didn't kill my sister," Joleen said. "I didn't kill Blaumveldt. His charges were so ridiculous they made me angry, that's all. Certainly not angry enough to kill."

"In that case the safest thing for you to do is surrender to the police," Nudger said. "I know a lawyer who can help arrange it. Want me to call him?"

He took a step toward the desk.

Joleen raised the gun and shook her head.

Nudger stopped in his tracks. He said, "That's an unfortunate choice of gun. Blaumveldt was killed with a twenty-two handgun."

"Not this one. I use it for shooting at tin cans. You're the first person I've ever aimed it at."

Not an honor Nudger would have chosen. He noticed now that the office had been searched. The file drawers were open and there were piles of paper on the floor and desk. He said, "What were you looking for?"

"You and Blaumveldt claimed to be detectives. I wondered if you'd done any work on the lead I gave you this morning. About my sister's place in the country." Joleen glanced ruefully about the office. "It took hours, and I didn't find anything. God, your files are a mess. And then I thought to check that."

She lifted her free hand and pointed at the answering machine on the edge of the desk.

So Nudger's hunch had been right: Blaumveldt had called. He said, "What did you find out?"

"That your ex-wife hates you, for one thing. Are you really that bad?"

"No, I'm not. As a matter of fact, Joleen, if you'd put down that gun and let me talk for a minute, you might find out I'm on your side."

"You'd better be," said Joleen dryly.

"No, really. I think you're innocent. I think Blaumveldt was killed by Roger Dupont, or at his orders. Because Blaumveldt located Karen's cabin. I came here to check the machine, to see if he'd called me."

Joleen's face seemed to soften a bit, though he couldn't be sure of that. But she did lower her gunhand. Nudger could no longer see the hole in the muzzle and he felt a lot better.

"Maybe you're not so dumb after all," she said. She switched on the machine. "Listen to it yourself. It's the last message. Don't rewind too far or you'll get your ex-wife."

Nudger stepped over to the machine and pressed the button. The tape whirred and gabbled. He pressed Stop then Play.

"Looks like you win, Nudger," said the dead man's voice. "I just got off the phone with the Goshen Land Title Company, over in Illinois. Karen bought a place on Chatwin Bottom Road outside town last May. I think we ought to take this to the cops. What do you think? Call me at the office."

With a click the phone went down. Nudger stopped the tape. "This is evidence," he told Joleen. "It corroborates your story. If we take it to the authorities—"

She was shaking her head. She propped her elbow on the desk and aimed the gun at Nudger's sternum. He could see down the barrel again. The small black hole down which his life would vanish if Joleen tightened her finger.

"I'll tell you, Nudger. I'm kind of fed up with the authorities. I've known for seven months that Karen was dead and Roger Dupont killed her. And for seven months the so-called authorities have been botching the case. Now I'm taking matters into my own hands."

Nudger swallowed hard. He didn't want to ask the next question. Didn't need to. Joleen went on.

"We're going to the cabin. Now."

"Why?"

"Because Roger doesn't want us to. He was willing to kill to prevent anyone from finding that cabin. If we go there we'll find the truth. I'm sure of it."

"If that's your plan, what do you need me for?"

"You have a car the cops aren't looking for."

"I'll give you the keys."

She shook her head. "I can't very well leave you here. Anyway, you might come in handy searching the cabin. You're supposed to be a detective, aren't you?"

Nudger tore his eyes away from the gun muzzle. But he found himself looking into Joleen's wide-set green eyes, and that was hardly reassuring. She'd been put through months of frustration. Now she was on an adrenaline high, thrilling to the release of action, and the risks. She was flying. If the cabin didn't supply the answers she was counting on, she would crash. Might explode. Nudger didn't want to be around if that happened.

He decided to stall.

"Let's wait until daylight. It'll be easier to find the place."

But she was already getting to her feet. As she backed up, she straightened her arm, bringing the gun muzzle level with his eyes. For a person who said she'd never pointed a gun at a human being before, Joleen certainly wasn't squeamish.

"Turn around."

He turned to face the open door. He could hear her coming around the desk. "Down the stairs, slowly," she said.

Nudger descended. The wooden steps creaked behind him as Joleen followed. Fear was scraping and burning his stomach. He wondered if he could take the roll of antacid tablets out of his pocket without getting shot.

"Stop!" Joleen called out, when he reached the bottom of the stairs.

He stood staring at the peeling gray paintwork of the door as she came down behind him. The gun barrel with its hard blade sight nestled intimately into his backbone.

"Out."

Nudger opened the door and stepped out on the sidewalk. Joleen stayed right with him. There didn't happen to be a police car passing at that moment. There was no one on the street at all.

When they reached the car she said, "You drive." She stationed herself by the passenger door as he walked around the car. He fumbled his keys out of his pocket with cold, stiff fingers and unlocked the door. When he got behind the wheel, he could see the gun, aimed through the window at him. He leaned reluctantly toward it to unlock her door. She got in.

"Let's move!"

Nudger twisted the ignition key. For the first time in weeks, the Granada's engine started on the first try.

As he pulled away from the curb, he noticed a movement out of the corner of his eye. He turned his head slightly. Through the doughnut shop window he could see Danny coming out of the back, behind the counter. He was looking down, wiping his hands on a towel.

Look up, Danny! Nudger silently begged.

But in a second Danny was lost to his sight as the car accelerated away. Nudger didn't think he'd looked up. He checked the rearview mirror, hoping to see Danny step out onto the sidewalk and look after him. But it didn't happen.

"Those doughnuts sure smelled good," Joleen remarked beside him.

CHAPTER THIRTY-NINE

They got on the highway and drove through the sleeping city and across the Mississippi. Soon they left the lights of the suburbs behind them. Every few minutes a big tractor trailer rig would appear in the rearview mirror, gain fast, and *whoosh* by them. Otherwise there was hardly any traffic.

Joleen relaxed somewhat. She even put the gun down in her lap to unfold Nudger's well-worn road map of Illinois and look for the town of Goshen. She eventually located it, some fifty miles to the east.

"Is Chatwin Bottoms Road on the map?" he asked.

"No. But the Chatwin River is. It should be near there."

"Well, we can always knock on doors and ask directions," Nudger said. "Of course, Walter didn't give us a house number."

"Shut up!" Joleen said. "I'm right where I want to be—in a car the police aren't looking for, getting farther and farther away from St. Louis. I like your car. As for you . . . well, if we can't find Karen's cabin, you're no use to me. So think positive, Nudger."

She was looking sideways at him across the dark interior of the car. Nudger tasted bile and swallowed. "I'm going to have to take something out of my coat pocket, okay?"

"What?"

"Antacid tablets."

Joleen sighed. "They don't make tough private detectives like they used to."

Nudger got one of the chalky white disks from his pocket and chewed. Another semi thundered past them, buffeting the Granada. He gripped the wheel tighter and glanced in the rearview mirror. Then looked again.

There was a pair of headlights far behind him. Too low to the ground for a truck, they had to belong to a car. Nudger might have been imagining things, but he thought he'd noticed this car before. Noticed it keeping a fixed distance behind him. It would disappear from view as a truck pulled between it and Nudger, then reappear when the truck passed him. Was it possible that Danny had seen the car pulling away from in front of the doughnut shop, that he'd grown suspicious and called the police?

Possible, but unlikely.

"Maybe it'd help if you told me your story." Nudger said, swallowing the jagged fragments of the antacid tablet.

Joleen remained silent.

Not Nudger. "You said this morning that Karen came to see you after she'd caught Roger and Vella together at the house."

"She didn't *catch* them," Joleen corrected. "Roger set up the whole thing. He wanted to hurt Karen. And it worked. She was devastated."

Joleen put the map aside and turned sideways to face him. The pistol was still her lap. He was relieved that she didn't pick it up.

"You have to understand how much home meant to Karen. She was the complete opposite of me. I used to tease her because she was always comparing fabric swatches and reading up on window treatments. It wasn't a status thing with her; she just liked to make herself and other people comfortable."

Nudger was thinking of Effie Prang's house in Ladue. "Roger likes to be made comfortable."

"Oh, yes. We're simple people, Nudger. Not sophisticated Ladue types like the Duponts. And he made the most of that. Over dinner at the country club, when his friends' wives got to talking about their careers or their charity projects, he liked to say that Karen's big concern in life was keeping the coffee hot and fresh flowers on the table, and that was what he wanted in a wife."

"Ouch."

"Yeah. And after he got tired of sleeping with her, when her body wasn't a novelty anymore, he made it clear to her that home-making was all she was good for. He was getting his excitement with other women, and he didn't think she had any right to complain. He'd bought her the house she wanted, and he was paying the bills. What he did outside the house was none of her business."

Nudger nodded. "So when she saw Vella in her house . . ."

"That was Roger's way of letting her know she didn't count for anything anymore. That he had no respect at all for her. And she got the message. When she came to my place that night, she was ready to fall apart."

"Did you suggest they get a divorce?"

"Oh, Roger didn't want a divorce. He didn't want to lose Karen, not when he had her where he wanted her. Roger likes to rub it in. If I was going to describe him in one sentence, that'd be it. He's a guy who likes to rub it in."

Nudger remembered that the same description had once occurred to him as he observed Dupont. "But Karen must have wanted a divorce."

"She wasn't ready yet. She didn't think she could earn a living on her own. He'd completely destroyed her confidence. 'Codependency,' the psychiatrists call it. Whatever it's called, Karen was a victim of it and was psychologically incapable of leaving her oppressor."

"So you decided the way to start rebuilding her confidence was to make her financially independent of Roger."

"That's right. She had to put away a little money of her own." Joleen was smiling. "We enjoyed selling things behind Roger's back. Karen had devoted herself to furnishing the house, and he didn't care anymore, so it seemed like poetic justice. And I'm pleased to say it wasn't just the silver, the jewelry, and the painting. We sold a lot of other stuff Blaumveldt didn't manage to trace."

"And you helped Karen build up this slush fund without ever asking her what she was going to do with it?"

Joleen shrugged. "Just having it made her feel stronger, and that was good enough for me."

"When did you begin to think she'd bought a place in the country?"

"Not until later. When she disappeared, and I didn't hear from her, I figured right away that Roger had killed her. But after he was acquitted, and Blaumveldt kept coming around, telling me he was sure Karen was still alive . . . well, like I said, my hopes got the better of me."

"But you still didn't believe Roger's story that she'd gone off to Chicago."

Joleen gave a quick, decisive headshake.

"Why not?"

"It was just wrong for Karen. She wouldn't want to lose herself in a big city. She wouldn't simply run away. She'd have prepared some kind of refuge she could run to."

"A home of her own," Nudger said, nodding. "One Roger couldn't bring one of his girlfriends into."

"One he wouldn't even know about."

A big semi roared past on the left. The Granada shook in the wind of its passage. As the behemoth went on its way, Nudger checked his mirror.

The headlights he'd noticed before were still there, the same distance behind him. It could be another car that happened to be traveling at exactly the same speed, or it could be the police. Or—

Joleen's voice broke into his thoughts. "Take the next exit."

He nodded. "What exactly are you expecting to find at the cabin," he asked?

"I've told you. Answers. I'm sure this is where Karen was between the time she disappeared and the time she died. The answers will be here. Between us, we'll be able to figure out the whole story.

He nodded, hoping again Joleen wouldn't be disappointed, in the cabin or in Nudger. The exit ramp was before him. He signaled and tapped the brakes. At the bottom of the ramp, Joleen told him to turn right.

As they drove away into the darkness, he glanced in the mirror and saw another pair of headlights descending the ramp.

Joleen spread the map over her knees and held a flashlight on it. She gave terse directions, which he followed. They didn't see the town of Goshen at all, but took a road that led downhill through the woods. He kept checking the mirror, hoping to see headlights flickering through the trees. But whoever was following them had switched off their lights.

Or there was no one following them except in Nudger's imagination.

Joleen instructed him to make a right. As he turned, his lights swept over the street sign. They were now on Chatwin Bottom Road. She told him to go slowly so she could get a good look at the houses they passed.

It was an unnecessary instruction. The road hadn't been plowed, and it was only by staying in the ruts other cars and tractors had made in the snow that he was able to keep going at all. The Granada lurched and bounced along at a walking pace.

Joleen was leaning forward eagerly, peering out the window, but there were no houses to see, only fields and fences half-buried in snow.

Then they heard the barking of a dog. Over the next rise they came upon a house and barn. The space between them was brilliantly illuminated by a spotlight, and in it stood the dog, a big German shepherd. It barked furiously at them as they went by. Nudger looked for lights to come on in the house, but it stayed dark.

He could hear the dog barking for a long time after they'd passed the house. Then they went down another hill and all was quiet again. The going was even slower now. Nudger was struggling to keep the Granada's wheels in a set of distinct herringbone-patterned tracks. Only one vehicle—obviously a tractor—had passed this way before them.

After another mile or so, the tracks turned off. Nudger looked down the drive and saw in the distance another house and barn. This farm didn't have a dog, apparently, but it did have pigs. Their pungent reek came to him across several hundred yards of snowy field and through the closed windows of the car. It was a warm intimate smell; it almost made him envy the pigs, who were in no imminent danger of being shot.

No one had been any farther down this road since the snow had fallen. The Granada would get no more help from the ruts left by other traffic. Nudger shifted into low. They wallowed on for as long as the downhill lasted, but the next rise, slight as it was, turned out to be too much for the car. It stopped, its rear wheels whirring. He took his foot off the gas.

"We're not stopping," Joleen said. "Her house must be farther down the road."

"You should have kidnapped somebody who had a four-wheel drive," Nudger said.

"Get out. I'll drive. You push."

Some determined woman, Nudger thought. He opened the door and stepped into the snow. By the time he reached the back of the car his shoes were full of it. He thought of running, but there was nowhere to go. So he planted his feet and placed his hands on the trunk.

"Now!" Joleen called.

He pushed. The rear wheels spat snow at him, and the car lurched forward. Joleen took it to the top of the rise and stopped. She got out and leveled the gun at him, beckoning to him with her free hand. There was gratitude for you. He trudged toward her. Just before he reached the car, he heard the dog at the first farm they'd passed, barking again.

Another car? Nudger wondered. Danny? But he didn't really think so. He no longer believed Danny had seen them drive away or that the police were following them. He and Joleen were going to be left to play this out to the end.

They resumed their places and drove on. After ten minutes the Granada stopped again. Nudger got out and found that they'd blundered into a drift. The snow was up to the bumper. He leaned down to Joleen. "That's it," he said. "It won't take us any farther."

She got out. After seeing that Nudger was right, she peered down the road. It went into a wood just ahead of them. The trees looked black, the snow light-blue. Glancing up, he noticed that the overcast had broken into fleecy, drifting clouds. Black sky and bright stars showed through the rifts. Behind one cloud was a smudge of brightness: the moon.

Joleen turned to him. "It's not far now."

"How do you know that?"

"The river's up ahead. Karen's place will be near the river."

"How do you know?"

"Never mind that. Let's go. I want you in front of me."

Nudger started walking. He fastened every button his London Fog raincoat had, but the cold still found a way in. His thin shoes and socks soaked through in no time, and he felt as if he were wading through an icy stream. His teeth began to chatter. He bit down to stop them. There wasn't a sound, except for the crunch of their footfalls.

As they followed the road into the woods, the moon came out. The change was almost as marked as if it were day. Nudger hadn't been in the country for a long time, and he'd forgotten how strong moonlight could be. The snow turned from washed-out blue to silver-gray. The long, tangled shadows of the trees became black and distinct. Joleen gave a gasp and stopped.

A cabin—Karen's cabin?—stood directly before them. It was a foursquare, agreeable little place in gray clapboard, with brightly painted shutters; in the moonlight he couldn't tell if they were red or blue. It had a stout chimney and a big front porch. The river must not be far away. He couldn't see it but he could hear the faint rush of water.

"I knew it would be like this," Joleen said breathlessly. "Karen's refuge. It must have made her feel so much better, just to know she had this place."

"How can you be positive this is it?" Nudger asked.

"I knew Karen. I can be positive."

Before Nudger could say anything more, Joleen was off, running laboriously through the snow toward the house. She must have put the gun in her pocket. It didn't occur to her that Nudger would try to escape now. It didn't occur to Nudger either. Held by curiosity, he followed her toward the house.

When he reached her she was at the front door, scrabbling at the knob. The door was of course locked. She threw her shoulder against it, but it was a heavy piece of wood hung on strong hinges. It didn't budge. She went over to the nearest window to examine the shutter. It was barred and padlocked. She turned to Nudger.

"Don't just stand there. Get us in."

So here was his first piece of detective work under the gun. He hoped he wouldn't let Joleen down. Karen's cabin or not, this was breaking and entering in the eyes of the law. Not proper professional behavior. Except for the gun.

Taking off his gloves and flexing his cold fingers, he stepped up to the door. From his wallet he drew his well-honed Visa card. He uttered a silent prayer that the door wouldn't have a dead bolt lock. Then he grasped the cold knob in his bare hand and slipped the card into the crack.

After a few seconds' struggle, the door opened. He was amazed. Usually he tried the card, failed, and had to kick doors open.

"All right!" Joleen said. Nudger had never been happier to please a client.

She pushed past him, shining her flashlight around the dark interior. The place smelled musty and felt colder than outside. Joleen's light settled on a camping lantern, resting on the floor. She got it burning and lifted it up.

Nudger's first impression was of a beautifully furnished room, a sofa and chairs with plump, inviting cushions, a cheery and delicately patterned wallpaper, elaborate window treatments. Here was the same fine taste he'd noticed in the house in University City. It was what he expected of Karen's refuge.

But as Joleen turned the flame up and held the lamp higher, he saw something else.

The place had been trashed. It didn't look as if there had been a sudden outburst of destructive fury. Rather, it was as if someone who didn't care about the house had been living in it. There were cigarette burns in the Persian rug, food stains on the arms of the sofa. The marks of muddy boots disfigured the ottoman.

Nudger walked on, into the dining area. There were more cigarette burns and scratches in the handsome, oval mahogany dining table. A breakfront cabinet in one corner stood open, and the shelves were bare. The tall plastic wastebasket from the kitchen had been moved next to the table. He looked into it. Broken and food-stained Wedgewood plates and cups filled it to overflowing. Someone had been using and discarding the fine china as if it were paper plates.

"Bastards," Joleen hissed behind him. "What do you think—people from around here noticed the place was empty and broke in?"

"I don't know," Nudger headed for the kitchen. "Bring the lantern in here, would you?"

She followed and held the light up. She gasped. There were greasy bags and containers from various fast food outlets heaped up on the tables and counters. They were studded with the corpses of flies.

"All this food!" she said. "There must have been an army of them."

"Or one man, who was here for a long time." Nudger was beginning to suspect what had happened here. His stomach was churning.

He walked on to the back door. An open cardboard box rested

on the floor. It was full of trash, including several empty bottles. Their labels said COLONEL'S HERITAGE. It was a cheap bourbon. He bent over and sniffed. He'd smelled that sickly sweet odor before, on Rolf Kling's breath.

Turning to the counter, he began to open drawers. The third he tried held what he expected to find—bottles of pills, mostly tranquilizers, and syringes and ampules. They would be powerful sedatives.

So this was what Roger Dupont had done. It was a simple trick, but not one a normal human being would be likely to guess. To think of it you had to be more than clever and cruel. You had to be inhuman.

"Nudger," Joleen whispered. "What is it? Your face looks . . ."

He took the lantern from her and went into the living room. He crossed it and followed a short hallway down to the bedroom. He had to make his way around what had been the bedroom furniture, a disassembled bed, a broken chair. Rolf had cleared out the room when he turned it into a prison cell.

Nudger opened the bedroom door. The window had been boarded up. There was nothing in the room but a cot. The bedding was gone, revealing that the thin mattress was foully stained. A radiator pipe ran up the wall beside the cot. Nudger knelt and peered. Around the pipe's base was one ring of a handcuff. The other ring was open.

He hadn't heard Joleen come in behind him. "Oh, my God," she whispered. "Oh, no!"

"Seen more than you bargained for?" asked Rolf Kling.

CHAPTER FORTY

Nudger swung around. The big man was standing in the front doorway. The floorboards creaked under his weight as he walked toward them. The sound of his labored breathing seemed to fill the house. He'd made the same strenuous walk they had. He'd been behind them all along.

Joleen turned to Nudger. "Who is—?"

"He's Vella's brother."

Joleen's features set into a fierce mask. Her right hand flew to her jacket pocket.

Rolf's arm came up, leveling a small automatic pistol at her face. "Don't," he said mildly.

She let her arm fall to her side.

He gestured with his free hand. "Come on out here. I don't like this room."

He lowered the gun but kept it pointed at them. They followed as he backed into the living room. He said, "Now put the lantern on the floor and stand back."

Joleen obeyed. In the lamplight, Rolf's face with its coarse-pored skin, drooping moustache, and doughy features looked weary. More than that, Nudger thought, he looked ill. The legs of his pants were soaked through to the knee, and he was wearing the same sort of inadequate raincoat as Nudger. He had no hat, and his ears were red with cold. Even confronted with the evidence of what he'd done for Dupont, Nudger could find something pathetic about Rolf.

Still breathing hard, Rolf sank down in the easy chair and put his feet up on the ottoman. His heels dug into the mudstains he'd made last summer.

Joleen said, "You held my sister prisoner here, didn't you?"

Nudger had to give her credit. She wasn't frightened by Rolf's gun. In fact, he seemed to be the one who was intimidated.

"How long did you keep her locked up here?" Joleen asked.

Rolf didn't answer.

"From the time she disappeared back in May, she was here," Nudger said. "Rolf kidnapped her. And he held her here until Roger Dupont was acquitted of her murder. Until it was safe to kill her."

Joleen gasped. She covered her mouth with her hand and shut her eyes tight. After a long moment she opened them and looked at Rolf. "Oh, you bastard," she breathed. "You fucking creep. You kept her here for weeks."

"It wasn't so tough on her," Rolf said. He seemed to find it easier to point his gun at Joleen than to look her in the eye. "See, the plan was, if Roger was found guilty, then I'd leave here and make an anonymous call to the police. They'd find Karen alive, and she'd tell them she'd been kidnapped."

"You made her think she was being held for ransom," Nudger said.

Rolf nodded, still catching his breath. "Yeah, right. She didn't know me, and I made sure she didn't get a good look at my face. I convinced her I was some guy from around here, I'd spotted her as a rich woman from St. Louis, and I was going to get big money from her husband to give her back."

Joleen was shaking her head. "Karen would never fall for a story like that."

"Sure, she believed it. It gave her hope. A person'll believe anything that gives 'em hope. And anyway, she wasn't thinking too clearly, because of the . . . you know, the drugs I had to give her to keep her calm."

"Fucking creep," Joleen said again.

"I had to do it. For Vella." Rolf looked appealingly to Nudger. "You've met Vella. You understand. She's so pretty, so nice. She's always cheerful. Going out of her way to make you smile. She's like a TV star. She's not like people in real life, is she?"

Nudger nodded. He figured Vella wasn't like the sort of people Rolf had met in his life.

"You can't blame Vella for wanting a guy like Roger. Real smooth, real handsome. When they're walking down the street together people turn and look. They're thinking, yeah, those two are perfect together. And they're going to make big money with that antique shop. Vella really knows antiques and all that shit. All she's ever needed was a backer. Now she won't have to pull those cheap con tricks anymore. That kinda stuff was never right for her."

"Was it Vella who wanted my sister dead?"

Rolf shook his head. "No way, lady. It was Roger. He followed Karen down here one time, found out about this cabin, and right away he started planning to kill her. He didn't give Vella and me no choice. You want the truth, I was kind of hoping he'd lose that trial. That I'd get to let Karen go. Then she'd be found alive and they'd have to turn Roger loose and reverse his conviction."

"But Roger didn't lose," Nudger said.

"Nope. Never does."

Not at tennis, not at murder, Nudger thought. "What happened that night?"

Rolf didn't answer. His breathing had settled down but was still stertorous. Despite the cold there was sweat on his brow. He unbuttoned his raincoat. "I'm not gonna talk about that," he said. "Christ, it's bad enough I should have to come here again, let alone—"

"Tell us what happened, damn you!" Joleen interrupted.

Rolf looked at her uneasily. His gunhand rested on his knee. With his free hand he fumbled in his coat pocket and brought out a flat bottle of Colonel's Heritage. He unscrewed the cap with his left thumb and took a swig.

Joleen took a step toward him. He raised the gun and took the bottle away from his mouth so quickly that bourbon splashed all over the front of his shirt.

"You killed my sister, didn't you?"

"No!" Rolf shouted. "It was Roger. Vella called that evening to say Roger'd been acquitted. So I knew right then Karen was a goner. It was weird having to be here with her. I started feeling kind of bad. But Roger made me wait all night. Didn't get here till dawn. He said the media people wouldn't let him alone after the verdict and he had to make sure he wasn't followed."

"And then he killed her," Joleen murmured.

"Not right away." Rolf looked into the darkness of the room beyond. "He went in there. Tore off her blindfold. He wanted her to see him and know what was going to happen. He told her he'd just been acquitted of her murder. The double jeopardy law meant he couldn't be tried again for the same crime, and after a little time had passed and her body'd decomposed enough, there'd be no way for the police to prove she hadn't been killed *before* his trial. She didn't like hearing any of that. She knew Roger'd won again. She screamed and cried and begged till I couldn't take it listening to her. Had to get out of there. When I came back she was lying on the floor with her head beaten in with a hammer Roger brought."

He looked up at Joleen, meeting her eye for the first time. "I had to do what I did," he said in a voice that begged for absolution. "For Vella."

Joleen's features were set in a mask of cold hatred. Rolf went on looking at her. He seemed to know what was going to happen next. So did Nudger. There was nothing anyone could do to stop it, not even Joleen.

Her hand flew to her coat pocket.

The muzzle of the target pistol hadn't cleared the pocket when Rolf fired. The noise was a light, hollow pop. Joleen's head snapped back. Her cap fell off. She crumpled to the floor.

Rolf swung the pistol to cover Nudger. When Nudger made no move, he smiled sadly and said, "Not gonna make it easy for me, are you?"

Nudger said nothing. He looked down at Joleen. She lay still. Now that her cap was gone the loosely piled up locks of her red hair were coming undone, sliding down to cover her face.

The room reeked of cordite. It was a smell that always made Nudger sick. His stomach was heaving from the odor and from fear.

Rolf sighed heavily and stood up. He bent and took the gun from Joleen's hand, glanced at it before putting it in his pocket. "A twenty-two target pistol," he said, "like mine."

Nudger said nothing.

"A lot of guys, they use those big-caliber guns. There's no call for that. They just want to blow a hole in a person's face. Blow the back of his head off and splash his brains all over the wall. With my kinda gun you get just the one small hole, the entry wound. And the bullet bounces around inside the skull, fucks up the brain good, kills a person plenty dead. But without making a mess."

He looked at Nudger, as if he genuinely wanted to hear his comment.

Nudger said, "You killed Blaumveldt."

Rolf nodded. "Had to. It's this fucking cabin again. Can't afford to let anybody see it."

He kept his eyes on Nudger's as he picked up the Colonel's Heritage from the sofa, took another swig, and held out the bottle to Nudger. Nudger shook his head.

"You sure? You understand what I gotta do now. This is gonna make it easier for me. Might make it easier for you, too."

Nudger tried to swallow his fear. It came back up and tried to choke off his voice. He said, "All this so your sister can have Roger Dupont."

"It's what she wants. She looks after me and I look after her. Keep her safe. That's why I'm gonna get rid of this goddamn cabin right now. There's enough evidence here to hang both of us."

"Why didn't you take care of that months ago?"

Rolf shook his head with annoyance. "Roger couldn't make up his mind. He wouldn't let me burn it, said that'd only call attention to it. He said what we had to do was clean it out, get rid of the furniture, paint the walls, scrub the floors. Get rid of all the evidence. But he kept stalling. He said it didn't matter, nobody was ever gonna find the place anyway. Nobody'd even be looking."

Nudger thought about Blaumveldt. "He was wrong."

Rolf looked around the cabin grimly. "Well, enough of that. I'm gonna burn the place right now. Before the sky gets light. Maybe nobody'll notice the smoke. But even if they do, they won't get here till it's too late."

"It won't work, Rolf. They'll find bones in the ashes. Teeth."

"No. You and her are going in the river." With his free hand Rolf pointed to Joleen. "Drag her outside."

Nudger bent and grasped Joleen's wrists. Her skin was still as warm as if she were alive. He dragged her out onto the porch. Rolf stood in the doorway watching. He pointed again, and Nudger went down the step, pulling Joleen to the snowy ground.

"Now come back here."

There was a can of gasoline standing on the porch just outside the door. Rolf had come prepared. "Splash it around good," he said.

Rolf stood leaning wearily against the doorjamb with the gun in one hand and the bourbon bottle in the other, watching as Nudger walked around the room, pouring gas on the carpets, furniture, and drapes. The fumes filled the little house, overpowering the cordite smell.

When the can was empty he stood in the middle of the floor, near the pool of Joleen's blood, and looked at Rolf.

Rolf was fumbling the bottle back into his raincoat pocket. He took a book of matches from his pants pocket. He was moving slowly and clumsily and his face was seamed with concentration. He was uncertain about where to put Nudger where he could keep an eye on him while he set fire to the house. Possibly the bourbon was getting to him a little, too.

Nudger was instantly alert. Maybe Rolf was vulnerable. Maybe

Nudger was going to get out of this alive. With an effort he kept the hope from showing in his face.

Rolf stepped out onto the porch and said, "Come out here."

Nudger walked slowly toward the gun that was pointed at his midsection. Rolf ordered him to halt when he was one step outside the door. Then he moved cautiously around him into the doorway.

For the first time he had allowed Nudger to get within arm's reach of him. But the gun was still pointed at Nudger's stomach, and the eyes didn't leave him for an instant.

How could he light a match one-handed? Nudger wondered. Perhaps he'd hand the matches to Nudger, order him to set the fire.

But he'd forgotten about Rolf's dexterity. The big man thumbed the matchbook cover up, curled out one match, slid the cover closed behind it with his forefinger. He was keeping his eyes on Nudger. With his thumb he scratched the match across the striking surface. No result. He hadn't done it fast enough.

Annoyance flitted over Rolf's face but he didn't look down. He curled out another match and scraped it. This match caught fire.

And ignited the first match.

Instantly the flame leapt to Rolf's shirtfront, where he'd spilled bourbon a few minutes before.

The blue flame licked upward toward his face. Rolf stared horror-stricken at it. He dropped the matches and began beating at the flame with his hand.

Nudger crouched and drove his shoulder into him. Rolf staggered into the room. The matches he'd dropped ignited the gas-soaked rug. It went up with a *whoosh* as Nudger grabbed the knob and pulled the door closed.

Over the rush and crackle of the spreading fire Rolf roared at him from the other side of the door. There were no words, only his rage and terror. Nudger was still holding onto the doorknob with both hands. It turned under his fingers. Nudger braced himself. Rolf pulled. Nudger hung on. The pressure steadily increased.

Nudger dug in his heels and leaned backward. What was he doing? Did he really think he could win this macabre tug-of-war? The big man was much stronger than he was. But if he let go and ran for it, Rolf would shoot him in the back before he'd taken five steps.

There was nothing to do but hang on. Nudger felt the heels of his shoes sliding. A gap opened between the edge of the door and the doorjamb. Smoke curled through the gap and Nudger smelled burning cloth and wood. It must be hell in there, but Rolf was winning. Nudger put his left foot up against the side of the house and heaved with all his might. The strain was almost unbearable. He thought his arms were going to pull out of their sockets. But the gap slowly closed. Rolf was breathing in smoke, weakening.

The moment after the door met the jamb, the pressure ceased. Rolf had stopped pulling. Nudger didn't let himself relax. He expected a sudden yank at the doorknob.

When he heard the pop, he thought it came from the fire. Then he saw the small hole in the wood of the door. A few inches to the right and the bullet would have hit him in the face. At that instant another hole appeared as Rolf shot again.

Nudger sidestepped to his left. While still holding on to the doorknob, he leaned against the side of the house, hoping it would protect him. He didn't think Rolf's little .22 could shoot through walls.

It didn't matter. Rolf went on shooting through the door. Wisps of smoke curled from each small hole. Nudger was sweating and the doorknob felt hot against his skin. Tongues of flame were licking through the shutters on the window on the other side of the door.

Suddenly the doorknob seemed to come alive. It twisted in his sweaty grip and nearly sprang from his hand. Rolf had given a tremendous heave from his side. Nudger braced his shoulder against the wall and hung on. He heard Rolf scream. It sounded shrill and small in the tumult of the fire. But the pressure increased steadily. The door opened a little, and Nudger could hear Rolf coughing. More smoke poured out. The gap increased, slowly, steadily. Nudger was coughing. He could feel the heat from inside the cabin; it was like opening the door of an oven. He didn't know how Rolf could still be alive.

He couldn't pull as strongly from his protected position at the side. He'd have to take the chance on Rolf shooting again.

He swung away from the wall and put his foot up against it, and leaned all his weight back. He looked at the gap between door and jamb, hoping to see it narrow.

Out of the smoke and darkness Rolf's face loomed up. The moustache and eyebrows were gone, the skin was red and puckered. Rolf's eyes were shut and his mouth open. A terrible sound came from his throat as he tried to suck in air.

Nudger's stomach turned over in horror. He couldn't do this anymore!

Letting go of the doorknob, he turned and started to run, praying Rolf's gun was empty.

Before he could get off the porch he felt a sudden rush of heat from above. He looked up. The porch roof above his head was on fire. Before he could move, a flaming beam let go and swung down toward him.

He ducked and ran but he was too late. The beam hit him in the back as he jumped from the porch. He fell heavily on his hands and knees. There was a searing pain at his back—his clothes had caught fire!

He dropped and rolled in the snow. There was a hiss as the flames went out. The chill and wetness felt wonderful to Nudger. It was hard to believe that an hour ago, in what seemed another life, he had felt cold.

He got to his feet to look for Rolf. But the big man hadn't gotten out. He wasn't going to, for at that moment the porch roof collapsed. A shower of red sparks shot into the snow. The fire was roaring now, devouring the little house. And the body of Rolf Kling.

Bending low, holding his arm over his face against the intense heat, Nudger moved close enough to the house to take hold of Joleen's body. He dragged it away to a safe distance.

Then there was nothing to do but stand and watch the fire. It was now so hot it melted the snow on the nearby evergreen trees. Water poured from their boughs. The snow on the ground was lit by a soft glow and flickering shadows played over it. The yellow flames were crawling over the roof, feeding more black roiling smoke into the column that ascended far up into the sky, which was just beginning to lighten with the approach of dawn.

Nudger leaned against a tree trunk and waited for someone to notice and come out to investigate.

CHAPTER FORTY-ONE

Nudger lay on a cot in a corner of the Emergency Room at Central Illinois Regional Hospital. He was lying on his side because of the minor but quite painful burn on his back. He didn't think it had hurt this much before the doctors bandaged it.

He was supposed to be under observation, but no one had observed him in quite a while. They'd surrounded his cot with those rolling screens and forgotten about him, or so it seemed to Nudger. A television monitor on a nearby wall was playing a tape of medical advice. He'd heard it all the way through twice. There were tips on diet, rest, and exercise, but not a word about how Nudger, who had no medical insurance, was supposed to pay for all this. He reflected irritably that Dr. Fell of the Cash-in-Advance Clinic on Manchester would have had him patched and on his way by now.

One of the screens rolled back and Hammersmith came over to him. "How you doing, Nudge?"

Hammersmith was resplendent in his camel's hair overcoat, dark suit, and tie. Nudger felt sillier than ever in the backless, thigh-length smock they'd given him. He sat upright. "I'm okay, Jack. Still breathing. It was in doubt for a while."

"You get any sleep?"

He shook his head. "I'm not looking forward to sleep. I think I'm going to see Rolf Kling's face. God, what a death!"

Hammersmith's face hardened. "You want, Nudge, I'll show you Kling's yellow sheet. It's a yard long, full of ugly, vicious stuff. You had to do what you did. He'd have killed you, then gone on hurting people for years."

Nudger nodded. You could always count on Hammersmith for the hard-nosed point of view. Still, Nudger was sure that Rolf's scorched, hairless face was going to haunt his dreams.

"Listen, Nudge, let me fill you in. I gotta go soon."

Hammersmith was always in a hurry when he was in a building where he couldn't smoke. He was probably aching to go down to the loading dock and light up one of his noxious cigars. Nudger said, "I can guess what you're going to tell me. You guys plan to hang all three murders on Rolf Kling."

"It's more the Illinois State Police than us, but yeah. You remember how it goes, Nudge. A cop wants to clear cases and close files. Anyway, Kling did kill Joleen and Blaumveldt."

"He didn't kill Karen. Roger Dupont made the plan and struck the blows. And I'm sure Vella Kling knew all about it."

"We got no case against either one of 'em. Go after Dupont and we'll really look stupid. He's safe as he can be. Even though we recovered Karen's body, there's no way by now to determine anywhere near an exact enough time of death. The state would have to prove Karen was alive during Roger's trial, and that's impossible.

So technically we'd be trying him twice for the same crime."

"Technically," Nudger said.

"Technically walks, Nudge." Hammersmith paused, shaking his head. "It's really something, isn't it? He gets himself acquitted of the crime so he's safe, then he commits it. The guy is fucking James Bond, double-oh-seven. He tricked the court into giving him a license to kill. It was some plan."

"Dupont's some guy."

Hammersmith cocked his head to the side and studied Nudger. "I don't like that look on your face. You're not going to do anything rash, are you?"

"No. I'm just going to talk to Dupont one last time."

"He won't talk to you."

"Sure he will. He's expecting me. I've known all along that Roger had something in mind for me. I thought he meant to harm me, but that wasn't it."

"You better be sure about that before you go see him."

"I'm no threat to him. Never was."

"So why's he going to see you? What is it you say he's got in mind for you?"

"He wants to explain his whole plan to me. He wants me to sit there and admit to him that he outsmarted me and I can't touch him. You have to understand what kind of guy Dupont is, Jack. He really likes to rub it in."

Hammersmith slid his hands into his pants pockets and frowned. "I'd skip the whole scene, if I were you."

Nudger shook his head. "I have something to say, too."

"To Dupont?"

"More to Vella. I want to give her something to think about. I don't want them to live happily ever after."

It was Saturday morning. A few days until Christmas. Mere hours until Claudia returned from Colorado. A thaw was underway.

Nudger had the window down and his elbow out as he drove up

Skinker Boulevard along the park. The sky was cloudless. Sunlight glittered in the drops of meltwater that showered from the trees at every breeze. On the park's golf course, large patches of grass were showing through the snow. By afternoon there would be manic golfers out there attempting to play a round.

The path was already busy. A narrow band of pavement that snaked all the way around the park, it was immensely popular with the fitness crowd. Walkers strode and joggers puffed, while Rollerbladers and bicyclists wove among them. Some recreation, Nudger thought. It would be like being in rush-hour traffic without a car.

He turned into the semicircular drive of Dupont's high-rise apartment building. The doorman was standing outside, under the awning. Nudger gave his name.

As he expected, Dupont was willing to see him.

Indeed, Dupont was smiling as he opened his front door. Apparently he was just getting ready to join the exercisers in the park. He was wearing black tights and a form-fitting red jersey, with pads strapped to his knees and elbows and sweatbands around his head and wrists. Give him a cape and he could be a superhero out of the comics, Nudger thought. Captain Malicious.

"Come in, Nudger," he said.

The living room was decorated for the holiday. A green, bushy tree festooned with ornaments and tinsel filled one corner of the room. Gaily wrapped presents were heaped on the floor around it; Santa must have come early to the Dupont household. More greenery lined the mantelpiece, and two stockings were suspended from it. A fire was burning in the hearth. Nudger looked away. It would be a while before he'd feel comfortable near a fire.

The day was so mild that the sliding glass door stood open. Vella was on the balcony, leaning on the railing and looking at the view. It stretched all the way to the Arch, a glittering band of silver against the blue sky. She too was outfitted for exercise, in black tights and a thong leotard splashed with colors. She looked as bright and enticing as the presents under the tree, though her wrappings didn't do as good a job of disguising what was underneath.

"Vella, we have company," Dupont announced in a smarmy voice that might have been reserved for visiting in-laws.

She responded like a good child, turning and putting on her company smile. It fell apart when she saw Nudger.

"Roger, what . . . what's he doing here?"

"I'm sorry about your brother," Nudger said. "I had no choice."

He barely got the last word out before she launched herself at him. Nudger saw long red talons flying at his face. He backed up, putting up an arm to protect himself.

Vella fell upon him, spitting curses, pounding on his chest with her fists. He kept backing away, and finally the fusillade ceased.

He lowered the arm that had been protecting his eyes. Roger had Vella in a bear hug. She was still struggling and kicking, trying to get at Nudger. He suddenly remembered the scene Vella herself had described to him, when Karen had found her and Roger together in the house. Roger had had to restrain Karen, as he was now restraining Vella. He did seem to enjoy setting up scenes and creating effects. In fact, he was smiling now.

"You bastard!" Vella was screaming. She'd stopped struggling but her face was flushed and she was crying. "You killed my brother, you vicious bastard."

"Vella darling, that won't help," said Dupont in soothing tones. "Rolf's gone. Nothing will bring him back. I know you miss him, but you still have me to look out for you."

He kissed her wet cheek. Vella's rage seemed to pass as quickly as it had come on. When he let her go she didn't even look at Nudger, but ran across the room and disappeared down a corridor.

Dupont looked after her thoughtfully. Then he caught Nudger's eye and said, "I had no idea that would happen. But perhaps I should have suspected. Vella has a horrendous temper. Well, sit down, Nudger."

Nudger did so, on the sleek, uncomfortable sofa he remembered from his last visit. He was careful not to lean back. The burn was still bothering him. Dupont remained standing. He probed for pockets to put his hands in, remembered he had none, and rested his hands on his hips.

"I expect you have questions. I'm willing to answer them, because I'm impressed with you, Nudger. I don't know how you managed to defeat Rolf, for one thing, but I was impressed with you before that. When you found out about Vella during the trial. You gave me my one moment of uneasiness." What a good sport he was—provided he was winning.

Nudger was relieved that he wasn't expected to shake hands. He said, "How could you be sure the body would eventually be discovered."

"Right after I killed Karen, Rolf and I put her body in the car and drove to the woods outside Springfield. We buried it. Then we waited for it to decay to the point where a medical examiner couldn't establish the time of death. When I was ready, I sent Rolf out to partially uncover the remains then make an anonymous phone call to the police. It was easy enough for them to identify the moldering corpse as Karen. I placed her purse with her plastic-coated identification beneath her. And of course I was careful not to damage her teeth."

Nudger nodded. "If the remains weren't found, you'd have had to wait seven years to cash in her insurance policy."

"Oh, everyone who's ever seen *Perry Mason* knows that," Dupont said.

There was the sound of a door opening and shutting and Vella returned. She had a pair of Rollerblades draped over her shoulder by the laces. "I'm going to the park to work out," she said, without looking at them. She headed for the front door.

"Don't go yet, lover," Roger called after her. "I want to go with you."

Pretending not to hear, she opened the door.

"Vella," Dupont said, softly but firmly.

She swung around. "I can't stand to be in the same room with him, Roger. I want to go."

"This won't take a moment. And I want to go with you."

"But you don't even have 'blades."

"I'm going to, though, aren't I?" He smiled and nodded toward the tree. "I've guessed what that biggest box is, you see. I know my darling Vella would give me just what I wanted. In fact, I don't think I can wait."

Vella looked somewhat mollified. She was still standing in the doorway, but she was smiling slyly at him. "You mean you can't wait for Christmas, Rog?"

"I've never been able to. My mother used to say she'd never seen a child so eager for Christmas. If I didn't get one present early, I'd be impossible. And I haven't changed. Come on, let me have that big box."

She shut the door and walked across the room. Setting her own skates down, she picked up the big box. It was red with a silver ribbon. She held it out to Roger, who beamed as he took it.

In all the excitement Nudger seemed to be forgotten. But as Roger sat down in the Breuer chair and started noisily demolishing the wrappings, he said, "What else do you want to know, Nudger?"

"Why did you hire Lawrence Fleck?"

The question gratified Dupont. He smiled at Nudger as if he were an apt student. "Hire a famous, high-priced defense lawyer, and people assume you're guilty. You need tricks to get off. Hire Lawrence Fleck, and people feel sorry for you. They assume you're innocent—not just of the crime you're accused of, but of any knowledge of the world. And that was the role I wanted to play."

Dupont opened the box. He made an astonished face. "Why, it's a pair of Rollerblades! Exactly what I wanted. Thank you."

Vella seemed to find this very witty. She bent down so he could kiss her. Then he began to put on the Rollerblades.

284

"How about a little lesson here and now, Vella? Before I go out in the park with these whizbangs."

"Sure," she said. She was smiling fondly down at him. She'd recovered her good humor and seemed determined to pretend Nudger wasn't in the room.

"Anyway," Dupont said, as he laced up a skate, "I didn't need a smart lawyer, since I was handling the defense myself. In fact, I handled the prosecution, too. I set up each piece of evidence against myself and arranged for each one to self-destruct at the right moment. It was delicate work."

Dupont finished tying his laces and stood up. He rolled a few feet on his skates and laughed. As he came to a stop he began to teeter. He threw out his arms to steady himself. "Whoa! This is wild, Vella. No wonder you love it so much."

He coasted sedately over to her. She smiled and put her arm around his waist. He strapped his around her shoulders. They beamed at one another.

"Anymore questions, Nudger? I'd like to wrap this up."

"Just one," Nudger said. "Why'd you do it? It wasn't just for the insurance money."

Dupont was less prompt with an answer this time. He turned back to Vella. "I want to try my wings, darling. What's the secret?"

"Keep your knees bent and your arms out." Vella hovered watchfully as he trundled over the hardwood floor. He put out his hands and caught himself against the wall. Then he started back. He was grinning, having a high old time.

Nudger thought he wasn't going to get an answer. Then Dupont straightened up and came to a stop in front of him. "I don't know why you discount the insurance. Half a million is a lot of money."

Nudger waited.

"The fact is," Dupont said, "I was in love with Vella and not in love with Karen. A divorce settlement would have cost me a fortune. Karen was a large potential liability. Dead, she became an asset."

Dupont was playing the banker from hell. His sly smile invited Nudger to express shock or outrage. Dupont would have enjoyed that.

Nudger said, "That's not the whole story, is it?"

Dupont slowly shook his head. "No, I suppose not. In a way it was Karen's own fault. I began to suspect she was up to something because I'd call and get the answering machine. Come home and find the house empty. And even when she was there, her attitude toward me was different. So one day I followed her, and she led me right to that cabin."

Dupont's face hardened with old anger. "I figured out the rest. How she and that sister of hers had robbed me to pay for the place, how she'd kept it secret from me. I didn't know what her plan was, whether she intended to leave me, or whether she wanted to have a place to meet a lover. I didn't really care. Because I saw the opening she was giving me. So Karen had a secret place. She liked to think she could disappear. Very well then. I'd make it permanent."

Nudger glanced at Vella. She'd become very still and attentive. He said, "One last question."

"I don't know if I can allow that," said Dupont, sparring with him. "I thought the previous one was the last."

"Sorry. But why didn't you destroy Karen's cabin last summer?"

Dupont had his eyes on his feet as he rolled along. "Hmm. I told Rolf to do that. I guess he forgot. It didn't seem urgent."

"No. I don't think that's the answer." Nudger turned to address Vella, across the room. "You believe that, Vella? Rolf always looked after you so carefully. You think he would have forgotten? That house was filled with evidence of your crime."

Dupont caught himself against the coffee table. He straightened up and looked at Vella, and what he saw in her face worried him. "Darling, Rolf and I just didn't think the house was important, that's all. We didn't think anyone would find it."

"That's not exactly true, is it Vella?" Nudger asked. "The house wasn't important to Roger. He was safe, he couldn't be tried for the same crime again. But you and Rolf weren't safe."

"That's enough, Nudger," Dupont snapped. "Time for you to leave."

"Roger," Vella said slowly, "if you'd thought to destroy that house, Rolf wouldn't have died. Would he?" Her large blue eyes looked pained and confused.

"Vella, I'm sorry. I—I guess I made a mistake." It cost Dupont something to say this. "No plan can be perfect, darling. But don't you see, we're safe now. Everything we dreamed about is going to be ours."

"It was no mistake," Nudger said.

He got up and crossed the room toward Vella. Dupont moved to cut him off. But he forgot he had the skates on. He stumbled and threw out his arms to catch himself.

Vella was paying no attention to him now. She was gazing steadily, almost fearfully, at Nudger as he drew near her.

"Roger left the house intact because he wanted someone to find it," Nudger told her.

"Don't listen to him!" Dupont shouted, as he struggled to stand upright.

"His plan wasn't a complete success until someone found it out. His victory wasn't complete. It wasn't enough for him to kill his wife and get away with it. Lots of men do that. No, people had to know what he was getting away with, and be helpless to stop him."

"That's crazy, Vella! Don't listen!" Dupont was standing upright now, but teetering.

"What do you think I'm doing here today?" Nudger said to Vella. "Why did he let me in? It's because he had to explain it all to someone. Had to lay out every detail of his crime to me and watch me sit there, helpless. Beaten. Unable to touch him. You saw how much he enjoyed it, didn't you, Vella? Of course your brother had to die to make it possible, but it was worth it."

"Darling, don't listen to him," Roger said. "He's just trying to make trouble between us."

Vella's lips were compressed so tightly they were almost white. She shifted her gaze from Nudger to Dupont. Her blue eyes had seemed clouded with puzzlement, but now they cleared. They were unblinking and hard, with pinpoints of light like the bright tinsel on the tree.

Dupont took a step and almost stumbled again. "Damn these things!" he exclaimed. "Come to me, darling. Come to me."

He held out his arms.

Vella stood very still for a long moment. Then she began walking toward him, slowly at first, but as she drew nearer she hastened her steps. Suddenly Nudger realized she wasn't running to Dupont. She was running *at* him.

She threw her arms straight out and slammed both palms into Dupont's chest. He rolled backward across the room. He looked at Nudger with wide startled eyes, his arms windmilling wildly. But Vella hadn't taught him how to stop yet.

He flew over the glossy hardwood floor, through the open door, and out onto the balcony. He came to rest with his back against the railing, supporting him.

He seemed relieved only for a moment.

Vella wasn't finished. She raced past Nudger and out onto the balcony, driving both fists into Roger's chest. It had all happened too fast for him to react. He shot backward, his Rollerbladed feet flying into the air as he toppled over the railing.

He screamed, but not for long. It actually only took a few seconds to fall twenty stories. It wasn't like in the movies, it was real death.

Afterward, Nudger wondered if he might have had time to grab Vella and stop it from happening.

Wondered if he'd deliberately let it happen.

He was standing under the canopy with Hammersmith when they brought Vella down. Her hands were cuffed behind her. She kept her head bowed as she walked past them. A crowd of curious tenants and passersby watched as she was put in the back of the police car. The ambulance had taken away Dupont's remains some time ago, and traffic was flowing normally on Skinker.

Hammersmith said, "Well, Nudge, you said you were gonna give her something to think about."

Nudger nodded. "She thought fast."

CHAPTER FORTY-TWO

Nudger! Pick up the phone. This is Lawrence Fleck. You can't fool me, I know you're there. Who'd go out on Christmas morning?"

Who'd take a call from Fleck on Christmas morning? Nudger wondered. He was sitting up in bed, with a cup of coffee and an apple-cheese Danish from the St. Louis Bread Company at his elbow. He was browsing through Claudia's copy of The Long Goodbye. She was almost out of Raymond Chandler novels and she still hadn't found Nudger's quote. He kept groping for it. "She had a figure that could make a lawyer kick the jury box?" No. "She had a figure that could make a doctor break a window in his examining room?" No.

Claudia was in the bathroom, and the hiss of the shower kept Nudger from hearing what Fleck was saying over the answering machine very well. Which was fine with him.

"Well, okay. Maybe you're really not there. Reason I called is, you probably heard I've been asked to represent Vella Kling."

Nudger sat upright so abruptly he almost spilled the coffee. He rose and went over to the answering machine.

"Think you're gonna be the prosecution's star witness, don't you, Nudger? The guy who saw Vella push Roger out the window. And you really think a thing like that matters in a court of law? Not so! Poor dumb innocent.''

Nudger was standing by the phone listening, but he decided not to pick up. Fleck didn't really need answers to his questions—he supplied his own. The machine was listening patiently. They were getting along fine and Nudger would only be in the way.

''So now you're thinking about what it'll be like to be cross-examined by Lawrence Fleck, eh, Nudger? You're sure I'm going to destroy you. Aren't you? *Aren't you?* Well, you're wrong! Know why? Think it's 'cause I'm a nice guy? We're friends, so I wouldn't unload on you in court? Right? *Wrong!* Only a naive lamb would think that. You know why it is I won't destroy you? Because I refused to take the case! I turned her down flat. Even though the fee was—''

Fleck broke off with a gulp, like a man who couldn't bear to say the name of a loved one who had died. ''Anyway, I turned her down. Want to know why, Nudger? You probably figure I'm afraid I'd lose. How wrong you *are!* I could get her off and the judge'd give her a ride home. Maybe you think I'm afraid the case'll make me look like a gullible idiot. Wrong again! The reason—''

Click! The connection was broken. Nudger's answering machine was, like everything else he owned, old, cheap, and unreliable. The tape had probably run out.

Or maybe the machine had just gotten fed up with Fleck.

''What was all that, Nudger?'' Claudia called through the bathroom door.

''Fleck called to wish me a merry Christmas. Don't give him another thought. Did I say how much I like my present?''

''Several times. I'm glad, Nudger.''

He'd felt some anxiety on the subject of Claudia's present to him. She'd returned from Colorado glowing with the effects of high-altitude sun, exercise, and fresh air. Now she was even more of a winter sports fiend. She'd already been ice skating at Steinberg rink, and there had even been ugly rumors about early morning jogging. Nudger had shuddered to think what her gift to him might be. A pair of skates? Or running shoes with cleats, and an orange reflective vest so cars wouldn't run him over when he was out jogging in the predawn gloom?

He had let slip some of his anxieties to Claudia, and she'd laughed. She didn't demand that he share her enthusiasms, she said. Her gift was something he could use indoors.

Nudger feared a NordicTrack.

But when he'd opened the box this morning, he found a robe.

It was a luxuriously thick blue flannel with natty red piping. By far the nicest robe he'd ever had.

He needn't have worried. Claudia understood him.

"Come back to bed," he called.

"Just give me a minute," she replied.

And a minute later she came into the bedroom wearing his gift to her that he'd bought during a courageous journey through Victoria's Secret.

As she unwound the towel from her head and her dark hair cascaded about her shoulders, the camisole seemed to turn a deeper and richer shade of green. She assumed a *contraposto* pose, with her head turned and hands behind her. The fine satin flowed, clung, and puckered bewitchingly. Nudger gave a sigh of abject lust.

He said, "A bishop!"

"What?" Claudia asked, confused. Was this chess?

It took Nudger himself a second to realize why he'd blurted out the words. "The Chandler quote. It's something about a woman built so well she might make a bishop kick in a stained glass window. Seeing you in that outfit must have jogged my memory."

"That's it!" Claudia exclaimed. "Or at least it's close." She ran her fingers along the smooth silk of the camisole and smiled at Nudger.

She was immensely pleased, which pleased him immensely.

Literary Nudger.